THE TRAVELING CAT

ANTONOV DOWN

JP ROSSELLE

The EC Publishing LLC books may be ordered
through booksellers or by contacting:

EC Publishing LLC
116 South Magnolia Ave.
Suite 3, Unit F
Ocala, FL 34471, USA
Direct Line: +1 (352) 644-6538
Fax: +1 (800) 483-1813
http://www.ecpublishingllc.com/

Ordering Information:
Quantity sales. Special discounts are available on quantity purchases by corporations, associations, and others. For
details, contact the publisher at the address above.

Printed in the United States of America

TABLE OF CONTENTS

BOOK IV

❦

CHAPTER I

LEFT FOR DEAD

When I arrived home from Nassau, My wife Mare was there ready with the Donzi in the water; she was sitting behind the boat's steering wheel. I took the igloo that was full of fresh crawfish and conch into Betty, put on my speedo, and met Mare out on the boat. Using the lights that Mare had purchased that day, we skied until 9:30 p.m. Even with the lights, I didn't feel comfortable with us skiing in the dark. We agreed that we wouldn't repeat the same again. By the time we got in from putting the boat back on the trailer, Betty had fresh Crawfish fitters ready. The Crawfish were appetizers to a great dinner.

The Government had given our fabrication shop the order to build three of the modified Sonar Spheres. The plans were marked TOP SECRET; since making these spheres at my Dad's shop wouldn't be very secret, I leased a double warehouse in Hialeah near the New Container Terminal. The warehouse had two sections; we would build each sphere on a device that was on wheels that would also permit the globe to be rotated while on the same machine. This would allow us to build the base part of the sphere in one section of the warehouse and once we got to a certain stage, move the sphere to the connecting warehouse. The second stage of work would be performed only by Joe and myself. Joe and I would be performing this work, four nights a week, until, one by one, we finished the spheres. Mare wasn't too happy about this, but I would still keep my word of us going places together every other weekend. One weekend we could go out in the sailboat with Joe, Karen, and anyone else that showed, then the following weekend, it would be Mare and me by ourselves. Mare and I had already gone one weekend for a concert by James Taylor, New York's Studio 54, and three days in Jamaica and the Caymans. The extra days in the Caymans enabled me to do some banking. Mare never once asked me about money. Of course she was never short of money either.

Back in Nassau, Cat had begun investigating Rusty's little Martha's adopted family. Both Tim and Mary seemed to check out. Tim was offered a job by our Peter. I told Peter he was to push Tim just a little harder into some kind of leadership role. I would decide how we were going to assist Tim and Mary even though Mary didn't want any help.

Mare and I had been married three months when Bob called and wanted to meet without the wives urgently. My friend Carson had been a no-show at our wedding. We hadn't seen Carson for quite some time. Bob's news involved Carson. Bob informed me that Carson served two masters, the FBI and CIA. This had crossed my mind before, and I wasn't surprised. The U.S. President had authorized the CIA covertly to do whatever they could to disrupt the advances of the Cubans in Angola. The Vietnam War had just ended, and Congress didn't go along with the President's thinking. Congress cut all funding and their CIA personal should have been moved out of there. Bob said that Carson had been down in the Angola area giving the 30,000 plus Cubans hell. The additional bad news was that apparently Carson and two others were captured and were being held by the Cubans in Angola. As of two days prior to Bob and my meeting, the captured men were confirmed to be still alive. Bob said his contact said freeing the men by force would be almost impossible. Bob said his man down there would try to negotiate some kind of payment for their release; Bob said this needed to be done before they were sent to Cuba for interrogation. Bob said he had attempted to contact the new CIA director but without reply. Bob said our window of time was closing every minute. I asked Bob what he needed and Bob replied that we might be able to get into Zaire, the MFP would need to take charge of the prisoners and then sell or ransom them to us, them buying the prisoners from the Cubans. I asked if a $1,000,000.00 would do it, and Bob said he thought yes. Bob would go to Zaire the next morning while I would start working on the money. The same night I called Big Ted and said that it had been a while but that I would need every man from his group that didn't have children. Ted knew what that meant. He asked about the price and I confirmed the daily rate. In this case half in advance. I needed someone that spoke fluent Portuguese and Spanish. My next call was to my old friend Ralph, he hated Castro. Ralph said he was going. Next, I called Benny and said I would need his leer jet and the five men that had worked with me before in Nassau and Haiti. I told him the mission was going to be rough. I also asked about someone who may speak Portuguese. Benny didn't ask when; he knew it was for yesterday. He indicated that the package would be at the Opa Locka airport by no later than 8:00 p.m. Ted called and said he had seven, including him; Steve wouldn't be going because he was a new father just 60 days ago. I had Karen get me some cash to give Ted and had her telex my Cayman bank with my requirements; I would be picking up the money tomorrow morning when the Cayman bank opens. Ralph was at my office with an older Cuban man that wanted to go and could speak Portuguese. There were 15 of us, Bob had called in leaving a message where I should meet him with the money in Zaire. Bob had no idea that I was coming with friends. Ted had stopped by our training center and picked up enough gear for the entire group. Our gear was top of the line; the best money could buy. I had gone by the house and packed a small bag telling Mare that I would be gone a few days; she wasn't happy. I called Joe and Roy informing them that I was going off on one of my fishing trips.

The leer jet and men were there at the airport before 8:00 p.m. Once the Leer was loaded and refueled, we all met, I told the men where we were headed, saying we intended to buy Carson's and the other men's freedom, but if not, we would do whatever it took to free them.

I told the men I would understand if they changed their minds once they had heard the mission. All confirmed that they were ready. We took off at 9:20 p.m. Our first stop would be the Caymans. I hadn't had the chance to speak with Ralph in years. We sat next to each other on the first leg of the trip, talking about old boy scout times. It's funny, the last time Ralph and I had talked was over a beer down at the sailing club, and the conversation was about us going to Cuba one day to over-though Castro. As we recalled it had been about six or seven years ago, we were just kids then.

When we landed in The Caymans it was in the wee hours of the morning. At 9:00 a.m. I was at the bank waiting. By 10:00 a.m. we were off to our next stop. From Cayman we would have to return to New York and refuel for the trip to the Azores. During our short stop in New York I received a package that was delivered by one of Benny's men, it was kind of an exchange.

The Azores is where the Cubans were also refueling their airplanes on the way too and back from Angola. The U.S. had a good size air and navy base there but in different locations. We would be using the same airport as the Cubans. Once there we refueled, we moved the leer to a holding area. Up in the cockpit I explained to the pilots what was going on, we were waiting for another Jet. The men were getting restless and I told them to take the time to get some extra rest. An hour passed, and the pilot announced that there was a military jeep approaching. Then he said it was an U.S. Air Force jeep. The jeep stopped and a Colonel jumped out, I opened the door and walked down the steps to meet him. The Colonel introduced himself and said that they were informed that our Jet was parked out here and the tower had called to ask if we were with them. May I ask your cargo he asked? Peaches I said. I don't know how that came out of my mouth but that is what I said. The Colonel asked to see the peaches, he walked up the leer's stairs way and looked in. When he stepped down, he said that he didn't know that New York had peaches that looked like such.

The Colonel asked if this possibly had something to do with our captured men in Angola? I told him that we were a privet group and that we were going to bring those men back. The Colonel said that the CIA had left an unmarked C-130 in a hanger here at this same airport. He also mentioned that the pilots and a few CIA men were still here grounded. We talked a while about what he could and couldn't do. He left in the jeep saying he would return.

An hour later the jet that I was waiting for landed. It too was refueled. Once refueled, it moved closer to our jet. A man exited that jet and walked over. I again walked down the steps, as the man got close by he stopped and saluted. He said, Colonel Baker reporting for duty Sir. How many men do you have with you I asked? Twenty counting myself he answered. I had charted the jet and sent it to Haiti. Pilar, the young President's mother, was lending me twenty of her top men.

I wasn't sure about waiting for the American Colonel, but soon we saw his jeep again approaching. This time there was a bus following him. The jeep and bus stopped at a nearby hanger, several men got out and went into the hanger. I few moments passed and some of the same men came out and started opening the hanger doors. The jeep then approached us and the Colonel exited again. Jim he said can you possibly pay cash to fill her up with fuel? As we spoke, the large plane now out of the hanger, I heard the engines of the large plane start. I confirmed about the fuel payment, and as we spoke, the plane's engines were shut down, and a fuel tanker pulled alongside.

The Colonel said that he had brought with him, the crew of five, six men that belonged to the CIA group plus 12 volunteers from his group. All were fully armed and all without uniforms or ID. In total, besides our crews, we had 53 men. The Colonel made it clear that he would be Court-martialed if we lost the airplane and or if any of his men were killed or captured.

I picked four men to stay behind, this would include the older Cuban friend of Ralph's that spoke Portuguese. Both Ralph and the older gentleman were upset, this until they heard what I was asking the four being left behind to accomplish while we were gone. Our group of 49 now started boarding the C-130. Before the bus retired the back doors were opened, and several boxes were unloaded from the bus into the C-130.

We were all aboard, the pilot informed me that we would need to refuel in Niger, Niger it is I said. We landed in Niger and had no problem being refueled. Looked like our Uncle Sam would get the bill. Our next stop would be Zaire. We had no idea what to expect when we got there, the CIA pilots had gone this route several times, they seemed to think that the Zaire airport tower would just think things had started up again. This time while in the air there would be no talking; the damn motors made a terrible racket. After many hours in the air, the Zaire tower radioed asking about the plane and its intentions. The Pilots just gave their old information as they had before. It worked, at least for now. The CIA Pilots knew right where to go, we parked in front of a large hanger, and the Pilots called for refueling. If we needed to take off in a hurry it would be useless without the fuel. I had changed my clothes to look somewhat of a diplomat. I had my nice black suit with body armor on under my shirt. A side and leg arm, all my pants legs were made with extra room by the ankles.

Hopefully Bob would be nearby. Bob was a trading partner with the Mobutu family. President Mobutu had been in power in Zaire for some time. Bob traded with everyone and anyone. Everything looked quiet, a Zaire military jeep pulled up, and the CIA pilot speaking through the cockpit window, told the Zaire Captain that we needed a tow truck to move our C-130 into the hanger. The Zaire Captain held out his hand, and the CIA pilot asked me to grease the Captain's hand with a $100.00-dollar bill. I had pockets of $100.00 dollar bills for the greasing process. The CIA man said as long as we had grease, the wheels turned without much squeaking. It was strange to hear French being use here in Africa. This CIA man spoke good French as well as Portuguese and Spanish. His name was Harden; Harden had been working in Africa for almost 18 months. Harden said that since the Vietnam War had ended, Langley had seemed to have forgotten them. Everything had been put on hold. Langley knew that the Cubans had three of ours but didn't seem concerned. Once we were fueled the small tow truck came and backed us into the hanger, the doors were closed and it looked like no one was home.

We sat tight for another two hours. My men had rations that they shared with the others. Food wasn't one of the priorities at the moment.

Soon a taxi showed up at the door, it was Bob. Bob said the news wasn't so good. He said that he had located the place where our men were being held but that he couldn't make contact as yet. Bob said that two of the men were seriously wounded, he didn't know who or how bad. Bob opened the taxi trunk and pointed out that he had brought food with him. We looked inside the trunk and laughed. What did you think I asked? Did you think the lord was going to break the bread? Bob didn't get the joke but he laughed anyway. My meaning was that without Jesus breaking the bread, there was only food for three or four, Bob didn't know, but there were 49 of us.

Ok Bob what's the plan I asked? Bob said that he wanted to give his people a few more hours. The place where our men were being held was just over the border, about 5 miles away. How many men I asked Bob? Bob said he should know when his man got back. Bob asked how I had come across the C-130, and I told him we borrowed it and needed to get it back before it turned into a pumpkin. Bob never asked how many men I had and I didn't tell him. Another hour passed, it was about 2:00 a.m. when a small truck approached. It was Bob's man. The man said that he had spoken to the Cuban in charge and the man wanted to see the money. Bob's man said the Cuban radioed to somewhere, and they told him to make the exchange, but if the money wasn't right, to leave all the bodies on the tarmac. Bob's man said the Cubans would be right behind him.

Bob said he had already cleared the way for the exchange with Mobutu. For years Mobutu had received CIA aid money for his cooperation. Bob said he couldn't stay but said his man would lead the Cubans to the hanger. Please, Jim, Bob said, give them the money, get Carson, and be on your way. I told Bob I was looking forward to a walk in the park. As Bob left we got ready.

The lights inside the hanger were off with just one outside light on over the hanger door. Three jeeps and a covered truck were heading our way, all with white flags waving in the air. They all stopped about 100 yards out and then the lead jeep approached. Ralph was standing at my side. It was just the two of us and my special case of the money. The jeep pulled within 10 feet of us and stopped. Gringo you have my money, a man in military clothes tasked in Spanish? You have our friends Ralph asked back in Spanish? Ah, the man in the jeep said, a Cubano, speaking to Ralph. Apparently Ralph said something like, yes you piece of S—t and if you want to see how a real Cuban fights just step on over here, and we can talk about it. Gringo the man in the Jeep said. I think I'm going to kill you both and take the money. Just about then one of the vehicles that were parked at the 100-yard mark blinked its lights. I nodded my head and a 50 caliber started making scrap out of the jeep's front tires that was in front of us. My orders were not to shoot the occupants but just the jeep's front tires so as not to permit it to move. Once the firing stopped Ralph and I were at the jeep, Ralph pulling his newly made Cuban friend out onto the tarmac We had taken them by surprise. The Haitians had come out of the Dark Side and taken over their other three vehicles without firing a shot. The Cuban on the ground starting yelling that they were under a flag of truce. At about that time Ted showed up driving the truck with our people; Carson was one of the wounded and unconscious. I asked Ralph to ask that SOB if they had a medic with them, the Cuban said no. I told Ted to get them all aboard, including the four Cubans. The other Cubans were disarmed and their vehicles cleared from our path and then disabled with a single grenade under each hood. The shot up jeep was pushed out of the way too, it didn't roll too easily, but it was moved. We opened the hanger doors and with all aboard, and not waiting for the tow truck, we taxied out on the runway. Once there on the runway, we asked the tower for permission to take off, but they refused. The Pilot thanked him and we began our take off. The tower called on us to stop several times but we kept going. Once in the air my attention was on the wounded. Carson's wounds consisted of a compound fracture of his right leg and some kind of a large cut in the right part of his chest. The other wounded man had a shoulder wound and looked like he was stable. We had lots of first aid equipment and I cleaned and bandaged Carson's wound. Still, he didn't look good. After cleaning and re-bandaging the second man's shoulder, he tried to tell us what had happened to them. We just couldn't hear over the engine noise. Niger was a U.S. friendly country and we needed to get Carson to a hospital. If Carson were still alive when we landed in Niger, we would leave Carson and two CIA men that had joined us in the Azores. The two men of the CIA volunteered to stay with Carson to insure he was well taken care of. I would have to leave him in their hands as our mission wasn't finished. When we landed in Niger, they had an ambulance and medical staff there at the airport to take care of Carson, but they wouldn't take the four Cubans. I left $50,000.00 in cash with the men staying with Carson. We refueled, and we were gone, so far, the Colonel that had helped us should be pleased. Landing in the Azores, we saw two older Soviet troop carrier Antonov An-22s on the tarmac. Looked as if we might get some kind of welcome.

By now the 4 Cubans that we had aboard didn't look so good. Ralph had taken a special likening to the big mouth Captain. I noticed their hands were all swollen and purple. I couldn't imagine that their hands would ever be the same. We landed and taxied over to the hanger where our two leer jets were parked. The American Colonel was standing there with two Cuban officers. First off of our C-130 were the 20 Haitians who were still looking for some additional action. We asked the Colonel's men to stay out of sight until the Cubans were gone. Our Cubans prisoners were blind folded the entire flight. Ralph cut them loose and took off their blind folds as they kind of walked down the C-130 ramp. The Cuban captain required some assistance as the extra care that Ralph had given him on the trip had taken a toll. There were two extra U.S. jeeps there to transport the Cubans to one of their planes that would take them back to Angola or Cuba, whichever. Through Ralph's interpretations, he told the Cuban officers that received our four prisoners, that we had no connection with the U.S. government and we had stolen the C-130, which we used to secure the release of our friends. Ralph also told them that I had arranged to pay a ransom but that their Captain had said he would kill us all and keep the money. Ralph said it hadn't worked out the way the Cuban captain planned and that he should consider himself lucky to be alive. I handed the Cuban officer the case with the money. There's one million dollars in the case I said. I live up to my agreements. The Cuban officer put the briefcase on the hood of the jeep, opened it and looked at the money then looked back at the Cuban Captain, who was now sitting in one of the jeeps. The Cuban officer apologized for his comrade's behavior and said he would be sent back to Cuba.

Standing at the hanger was the old Cuban man that we had left behind. I looked back at him, he had this big smile on his face and gave me a thumbs up. The Cubans left but the American Colonel stayed. I asked if there was any way that our people could get some food, he had already thought of that. He radioed and a chuck wagon appeared. The American Colonel thanked me for bringing his men and the equipment back. I thanked him for the use of the 50 caliber which had come in handy. He looked at the Haitians eating and asked how that happened? I told him that I had picked up some friends along the way. I asked the Colonel to please make arrangements to get Carson to a U.S. hospital just as soon as possible. The Colonel promised he would. I asked the Colonel to stick around until we got off, he agreed. Ralph and I went and spoke with the men we had left behind. Well I asked? The old Cuban said they couldn't find the amount of sugar that I told them to use. However, they did locate a 55- gallon drum of molasses. The two Cuban planes now should have about 20 gallons or so each in their fuel. With a smile, I asked if we should let the Cubans know; Ralph said hell no.

I gave each of the 20 Haitians a big hug and $2,000.00 in cash. Please, my gratitude to the Haitian people. I also thanked all involved and told the CIA Pilots that whenever they were free to come talk about a job. I thanked the CIA men and all the volunteers. I left them a bag with close to $20,000 in cash to split up. We boarded our leer and the Haitians theirs. We took off, not knowing how Carson was doing but hoped we would have heard something by the time we reached New York. Once we landed in New York the New York gang got off here, I thanked and paid each man. Each and every man said they were ready to go whenever I called. They had invited Ted and me up to go hunting with them during the Holidays. The jet had refueled and once again us, Miamians, were on the way home.

When we arrived in Miami I noticed Ted unloading three of the boxes that had come from the back of the Air Force bus. Ted said these would add a little up-grade to our arms collection. One box had in it 25 grenades, and in the other two, a shoulder launch Redeye missile in each. Ted said we had to have some souvenirs from the trip. I paid and thanked the jets crew; they also said they were happy to serve and looked forward to the next adventure. We were all glad to get home but still I hadn't heard anything about Carson. Ralph and the old Cuban man seemed proud that they had contributed so much. They both said it was hopeful that both plane's motors had failed somewhere over open water. If only one of the planes were lost and had a full troop load, that alone could even the score for their Bay of Pigs invasion.

CHAPTER II

LAS VEGAS

Mare was glad to see me but wasn't too happy about the whole thing. She said she had visited the office and Karen had told her that as far as she knew I was fishing. Ha she said, no tan and no fish. Mare said that at least I decided to show up for Thanksgiving.

It would be almost two weeks before my office received a welcomed call. It was Carson calling to let me know that he'd be home from his trip in a week or so. Bob also called that day and wanted to meet for lunch; he told Karen he had some news about Carson. I told Karen to call him back and ask him to come by the warehouse after 6:00 PM tonight. Joe and I had almost finished the second stage of the second sphere. This weekend Mare and I would be skiing and the next flying out to Las Vegas; it would be like a payback thing as Mare knew I didn't want to go to Las Vegas; it would also be Christmas.

Business was doing great, seamed that the Feds had finally stopped bothering me, and CTI was having a hard time sending equipment to Florida Containers. Our service and pricing was much better than any of our competition. Our new Terminal was at full speed now being open 24 hours a day. It seemed our computer guy Tim had something new every week. The customers loved the speed and accuracy in which they received their information, the format was also how they wanted it.

Bob showed up that evening, it was the first time he had seen the new sphere design. The first new generation sphere had been lowered overboard just the week before and was sending data. Bob told me that Carson should be discharged from the Hospital within the week. Apart from almost dying, Carson's leg had lots of work, and Carson would take some time getting it back to where he needed it to continue working and or flying again. Bob said that Carson didn't want anyone to see him just yet. I told Bob that this and the next weekend were Mare's but that if Carson wasn't back when I returned, I would go south and get him. Bob said there were lots of rumors that someone had sabotaged the two Cuban troop carriers on the tarmac in the Azores that night. Both Cuban planes had engine troubles, one made it safely back to the Azores, and the other had also turned around but crashed into rough seas just miles short of the airport. Bob said there was loss of life, but he didn't have any up-to-date information. Bob said he hopped that the new news wouldn't ruin what everyone was calling a successful mission. Bob said before they heard of the Cuban plane crash, it looked like Langley was going to take credit for the safe return of their men. Bob said, you could have given me some heads up about the number of personal you had with you and the sabotage. Well, if it was sabotage, I said, it must have been someone else as my people couldn't have gotten anywhere close to those planes, nor did we have the time. Yes Bob said, and fish can't fly.

Bob brought along with him a new set of drawings. These he carried in two large tubular containers made out of Aluminum. Take these he said looks like they want to keep you busy. They probably figure if they keep you working, maybe you won't cause so much trouble. And the last thing, Bob said, the commander of the U.S. base in the Azores asked to ensure his missing redeyes didn't end up in the wrong hands.

Bob started walking and then turned and said, not too many people have a friend stupid enough to risk his life and pay a million-dollar ransom for them to get back home safe. I consider it lucky to be a friend of such a person, he said. You secured that friendship long ago I said. Bob Laughed and said yes, it cost me $1,000.00 and my best girl.

When Bob left I walked into our small drafting room. We had purchased two large drafting boards where we would lay out design plans. Joe and I had our people beef up the security on the second part of the warehouse and our drafting room. If someone wanted in they were going to work hard for it. We also had security cameras and alarms that would call me and the police when we had trespassers.

I cleared off one of the tables and opened Bob's new drawings. The drawings marked Secret were of lots of beams, channels, base plates, diamond plate walkways and much more. It seemed that someone was building quite a lot of buildings. Once the material was made ready it was all to be galvanized. If it wasn't galvanized, then the material used was Stainless Steel type 316. The material list was page after page, 26 pages in the first tube. It seemed that I had opened the second tube first. I rolled it all up and put it all back in the tube. Joe was calling me to get me back to work but I just had to see more. The next tube, which was the first tube showed a location, I was surprised to see that all of this was going to Andros on some kind of Naval Base. Here in this tube were another 31 pages of material. Now I understood what Bob had said about keeping me busy. There had to be at least a year's worth of work here and millions of dollars involved. I walked out to the shop and saw Joe with a mig welding handle in his hand. He was finishing up installing the attachment of one of the sonar boxes.

Joe stopped and saw me watching him, what he asked? I just looked at him and wondered if he really knew what he was in for. I walked back in and rolled up the drawings, and put the roll back in the tube. We didn't have a safe at the warehouse, but I now figured we needed one. Tomorrow I would have Karen call Miami safe. It was now getting late, and Joe was wrapping up. We didn't do much tonight, but we'll give it hell tomorrow night, he said; Joe said the same thing every night.

Mare and I would go the Las Vegas on a Friday night. Mare was so impressed with the big hotels and all the lights. It was late for me on Friday night when we got there, but that didn't stop Mare. We stayed out until 4:00 AM, went for a champagne breakfast, and then took a small nap. Three hours later we were into our bathing suits and headed for the pool. Mare had big plans for Saturday night; she had us going to two different shows at two other Hotels. Mare said she would gamble with $5,000.00. Between shows, Mare changed clothes. The second dress was the most beautiful I had ever seen. When Mare told me what it cost I was surprised. Not because of how little it cost but because any dress could cost so much. The dress was a long black evening dress with what looked like thousands of diamonds that were attached to the dress. Mare had short blond hair and of course big emerald green eyes. Her dress included this head band that was also filled with dark red rubies and sparkling white diamonds. As we were being led to our reserved table, we heard a call, Captain Jim! We looked, and it was Benny and Jena. Benny had met Mare at our wedding; Benny came over and kissed Mare, took her by the hand, and led her over to introduce her to Jena. Jena was being her usual jerk and didn't even get up. Benny apologized but still asked us to sit with them, I was explaining to Benny that it was our night out, but Mare stepped in and said she would be happy to sit with them. It was now a table for 4. Right off the bat, Jena said Mare's dress must have cost a fortune. Before Mare could answer, Jena kept right on talking. Benny asked Jena to stop talking so much, but she kept right on talking. Thank God the show started and we got a break. At the first curtain call, Benny said he appreciated how generous I was with his people from the trip. Jena looked at Mare and asked, you didn't know? Know what Mare asked? Please I said, let's not talk shop. Shop hell Jena said; your new little wife here doesn't know you were in a war zone shooting a 50 caliber machine gun at the Cubans. I stood up and said alright that's enough, we need to be going. Mare didn't move, Mare said she wanted to hear the story. Benny looked at me and said he was sorry. Mare asked me to sit back down. Jena said that my friend Malcolm had got himself into trouble down in Africa and I went down and paid over a $1,000,000.00 in ransom. We heard, Jena said, that Jim's team killed over 135 Cubans. Mare looked at me and asked if that was true? I said a small part, number one I hadn't fired a single shot, nor was I shot at, the money wasn't mine, and there were no deaths on either side. Everyone ended up happy I said. Jena wasn't there and probably only heard rumors. Jena looked at me and asked? Did you tell her about Haiti? And don't tell her I wasn't there because I was. We were in this huge gun battle and Jim just walked toward the men that were shooting at us, and some men died that night too. I could see Mare was upset, she stood and told Benny good night, and we left. As we walked away, I could hear Benny saying that he was sorry. Mare was walking out with me right behind; she stopped and turned, then put both arms around me and said she was sorry for getting upset. She took my hand and pulled me into one of the many bars. We sat there for several hours just talking about sailing and how she wanted us to look for another sailboat and go sailing and leave all this behind. I asked for four more years. She countered with two. There was no set date, but then her mood changed, and Mare, the one I had fallen in love with, came shining through. Vas Vegas wasn't necessary anymore; now, the rest of our short trip was about us.

—◦◦◦✦◦◦◦—

CHAPTER III

CARSON'S SAFE

Monday morning came so fast, I received a call that I waited too long for, it was Carson. Carson said he had arrived on Christmas day, he had called the house, but there was no answer. I told him that Betty had gone to Nassau for the holidays and that Mare and I had gone to Las Vegas. Carson didn't thank me, he said he wanted me to see something at his house. I told him that I would love to come but that I couldn't leave Joe working by himself at night. Ok, he said I understand; how about dropping by this afternoon? It will just take an hour or so. I said I'd be there at 3:00 PM. The day, as always zoomed by. It was 3:00 PM as I drove into Carson's yard. He was sitting on his porch waiting. He stood; I wouldn't have recognized him on the street. He was skinny as a rail, pale white, and using a cane. I walked up and he hugged me, saying he was sorry that he didn't know what a good friend he had. I finished saying and still have. Carson said yes. Carson was anxious to get inside but whispered that there still could be some listening device in the house. We walked in and passed a 24-year old bottle of whiskey, he said that the first night we have the chance, he would bring it to the sailing club. We walked into what he called his war room. The room was still full of photos on the wall. It looked about how I remembered it. Carson said that they had been here. They I asked, who's they? Just they Carson said. Carson said every photo had been removed and replaced just as before he had gone to Africa. The difference is that now even his prints had been wiped off. Carson said that even his safe had been opened, but nothing was missing. Nothing was missing because they weren't looking for money, they wanted to know where I was in my investigation. I want to tell you I'm sorry, I lied to you, he said. I did have more than what I shared. Don't be sorry. I said I knew there was more. Carson asked how I knew? Well I said for starters when you first showed me the photos you had removed a few, you're not such a good house keeper I said. There were at least three photos missing. I could tell from the dust and the small pin holes that were left there. All the photos had dust, the dust covered the wall except from where you removed those three photos. There was also some kind of book on your desk that was missing the day I came. I figured it was your log. Right you are, Carson said, right you are, you should have been a detective instead of a fisherman, and he laughed. He held his index finger to his month and walked into his garage. He opened the door of and old Mercedes car that looked thirty years old. He sat in it and pulled off the steering wheel, and started up the engine. He then got out of the car with the steering wheel. Carson was all smiles. Carson turned on an exhaust fan switch, then walked on over to his work bench, he got an attachment that fit to the steering wheel's shaft then walked on over to a floor drain and inserted the shaft into a small hole in the drain. Then he started turning the wheel clock wise. No one would have ever found this I thought. As Carson turned the wheel, the concrete rose. The concrete was 6 inches thick, and once up about 10 inches, there was a box; Carson reached in and took the box out. As he opened the box it was just like a movie, the first thing was a loaded 45 Gold Cup. Then there was a log and under that more photos. There were two plastic bags of photos. He took out the first three photos and whispered that these were the missing photos on the wall. One was an old photo of four men. The photo was worth much more that any $1,000,000.00 that I had spent. It was a photo that could rock the world. Take it Carson said it's yours, Carson tried to put it in my hand but I wouldn't take it. In the photo was Oswald, DeManschildt, Ruby, and another man whom, at first, I didn't recognize. Carson said that when I sat and looked at the other photos it would be easy to put the whole thing together. Carson said the photo of the fourth man was none other than the same man that left him in Angola. The other two photos were my old neighbor the ex-President of Cuba with DeManschildt and Hunt with the another CIA man that I knew. Carson had all seven names of the photo of seven, Papa Doc whom died of a heart attack, John Rosselli whom had just two months ago had been found stuffed in a steel drum, George DeManschildt, The ex-Cuban President, Howard Hunt, Charles Nicoletti and James Ciles. All seven men in one photo. As we looked at the photos, Carson hugged me again and thanked me for coming for him. One of the CIA men that stayed with him in Niger told Carson that when I had met with the original group in Miami, I had explained that we would attempt to buy his freedom, but we were going to do whatever we must to bring them back. Carson said he was grateful. Then he asked what had happened to the two Cuban airplanes? I told him I had no idea but to me it all had a sweet ending. Carson said he didn't have a lot of money saved up but that all of it was right there in that box. I told him to save it for a rainy day. Everything that came out of that box went right back in. As Carson secured the box back in its spot, he looked up at me and mentioned that it was also fireproof. He re-wound the cement block back down, took out the steering wheel, then walked back to the workbench, grabbing a tube of some caulking. He re-caulked the cement edges then dusted a power on top. Carson said the power would harden the top part of the caulking. He then took the extension off of the steering wheel shaft and then carefully replaced the steering wheel in its place. He turned off the car, then shut the car door and said now you know. Ok I said, we know who did it, and we certainly have a motive. But to pull all that off, we are missing quite a bit of the puzzle. I told Carson that this Assignation thing still wasn't on my priority list. I mentioned that I had tapes upon tapes from Michelle's apartment. If Carson wanted I would hand them over to him. The only interest I had for the tapes were Michelle's two derringers. I wanted to know how Mr. Thompson got the one and maybe even both guns. I told Carson that I believed there was still an unsolved murder that was tied to Thompson's son's death. It could have been Mr. or Mrs. Thompson, their daughter Anny or even Michelle. If it wasn't Michelle, then we still have someone out there that is capable of murder.

Carson said that he would be off from work for another 30 days and that he love to check out the tapes. I told him to meet me at the apartment on Friday at 4:00 PM for the tapes. And if he was up to it he could go to the 1800 club and this time really invite one of the girls on a trip to Nassau. I would make sure we had a room and time for him to take out the Hatteras. Carson said he'd see me at the apartment at 4:00 PM. He turned off the fan and then we went back inside. Inside I said my goodbyes and left for the Warehouse. Carson did come and get the tapes but didn't feel up to the 1800 club.

— ❧ ❧ ❧ —

CHAPTER IV

THE RETURN TO NASSAU

The weekend passed by, and I found myself working that much harder now, finishing up the second sphere plus starting the newest project that Bob had given us. Bob was right about keeping us out of trouble. The project had a completion date that would call for a second shift at work to include Saturdays. Still, I kept my promise to Mare. Now, Mare knowing that when we got home she would hardly see me during the coming week would almost ruin the trips mood. It was heavy on her mind.

Mare made a friend while taking classes, her new friend Andrea was also studying to be an attorney. Andrea and her husband were competition water skiers and belonged to the Miami Ski Club. Mare wanted us to join too. Andrea's husband was Doug; he worked for the US Customs and was stationed at none other than the Chalks Sea Port. Doug said he had seen me pass through customs several times. Mare and I stopped our weekend trips to ski with Andrea and Doug. On my first trip to the ski club Doug showed me how to jump the ramp. Looked easy enough. It was my turn to try as Mare said, I wasn't afraid of anything. Well as you come up to the ramp at 32 miles per hour, it looks like you're running into a cement wall. The skies were thicker than normal, I hit the ramp and went over on my side. The entire boat laughed and laughed. It took me five times to finally land on my feet. For months we skied every weekend, still Mare wasn't satisfied.

Joe and I finished the last sphere, we decided to keep the warehouse and start doing fabrication work there too. We ordered two large Cincinnati Machines, a big shear and a break press. With these machines we also started making our own container panels, corner post, cross members and more. We also got into the parts business, we were now selling parts to other shops.

It had been some time since I had been to Nassau and it was about due. I called well in advance but the Hatteras was booked solid. Yes, months in advance. Cat was booked too. Cat would get free Sunday morning, returning at about 10:00 AM from the Saturday night trip. I would come in Sunday morning and stay until Monday afternoon. Cat looked different than I had ever see her. She was more confident and also put on some weight in the right places. It was great to see her; I didn't realize how much I had missed her. It was good to see everyone. Cat had moved little Martha's family into town. Deanna's first house was vacant so she placed them there. Tim, the only father little Martha knew of now, worked with Peter. Peter and Cat said Tim was a good worker. Mary was still teaching and we had hired a woman to work in their house and help take care of the children. Mary still didn't trust us 100%, it was getting better every week. Angee was always taking them food from the restaurant. Little Martha had grown quite a lot since the first time I saw her on the beach. Cat had made arrangements for all the children except the baby to get swimming lessons. I still hadn't seen or heard from Joel. I asked Cat to track him down so I could meet with him on one of his days off. Cat said the people that worked the Cruise Ships didn't get many, if any days off. She laughed and said it was like working for Captain Jim. She asked if I had met Captain Jim, and she laughed. It was awkward not taking Cat's hand and swatting her butt. I was hoping for a good kiss. It looked like the shower that I was so much looking for was a pipe dream. Cat said we were having dinner with Deanna and Jacob, I said I preferred it be just the two of us but she said she wanted me to see how well Deanna looked. By now I even was wandering where I was going to sleep. Cat finally walked me over to the apartment and said I should go up and change into my bathing suit. She said she had her's on. We caught a taxi and went to my old favorite beach spot. She told the taxi to wait. We walked over the buff and there it was, that glorious spot. Cat dropped her shorts and shirt and ran in. If I didn't get a hug and kiss here and now, it wasn't going to happen. I went in and she swam away, I swam closer and she swam further. I stopped chasing her and she went under. I could see her coming at me from under the clear water. She swam right up to me coming up face to face. She latched right on to my neck hugging me with both arms. She then asked if I still loved her. I said, yes I always have.

We went by taxi to Willy's, man it was great to see him. It hadn't been that long but it seemed like years. He came around the bar and gave me a hug. You're just in time he said pointing to the wharf. It was our first boat arriving back from pulling our crawfish traps. Come on Cat I said as I walked out the door. Cat yelled I'm staying to speak with Willy. Peter had gotten off the Hatteras at the same time as Cat this morning and he had retired for the day. Everything and body looked good. Otis was now the Captain of the "Johnny" with a crew of two. Mark was there with a new captain that Mark was training. Three boats made it in while I was there. It was all so pretty that I had tears rolling down my eyes. I could imagine Johnny, Michelle, Deanna and Rusty, all with their big smiles. It was funny; I never had not even one argument with my old group. I thought about it, at this moment this is where I wanted to be. Yet I lived so far away in another world. I turned and looked back at the bar and started walking. The closer I got I could see that Cat was no longer there. As I walked in Willy had a Polly Girl on the bar. Sit a while Willy said. I sat down and Willy started talking. Janie had been here over the summer, she came with her boyfriend and his Family. The family was impressed with Nassau and especially their Hatteras trip. Cat had taken them over to Harbor Island. I noticed, Willy said that they weren't impressed with the color of Mr. Johnson's skin. I bet that boy got an ear full when his Papa got him by himself, Willy said. More than likely Janie didn't tell the boyfriend her father was a brown man. The boyfriend's father, Willy said, called me boy. Sorry, Willy said, but there's going to be some hurt feelings sooner or later. Another visit we had here was Jena and her boyfriend, Willy added. I don't understand how you got hooked up with that one, he said? She was in here scaring Cat telling her that you probably wouldn't live much longer. Jena told the whole bar that you were over in Angola fighting the Cubans. Jena told a story where she was with you in Haiti and saw you taking and returning fire while you were standing, walking right at them with no cover and no fear. Willy said I sure hope all that aint true, it ain't true, is it he asked? Hell no I said I'm not looking to get killed, you all would miss me too much. I will have to curb that girl's big mouth, though. Sorry about Janie's in-laws, I sure hope that doesn't ruin her thing there. What you going to do with Cat Willy asked? You haven't seen her in months, and you come back into her life just like that. Cat said she tried not to let it happen but she said she couldn't help it. Why don't you just drop what you have back on the mainland and come live over here with us, you belong here. By the way, Deanna is about four months pregnant, she looks good and she too still loves you. That one is out of your reach but Cat's right here and ready. All three of those Johnson girls come in here and cry in their beer. Now Willy asked, did you bring me over my catch of the day or do I have to wait for Otis? A big smile came over Willy's face, and he said there's always going to be lots of time for the women folk when you get older. Take your time and don't forget to come visit your old Friend Willy.

When I got to the apartment Cat was asleep. Her clothes were dropped on the floor alongside of the bed. She had a long day as she didn't get much sleep the night before. We were to eat at the beach house at about 8:00 PM. I figured I'd get a quick shower and then also catch a small nap. As I got in the shower, Cat was right by my side.

Cat and I didn't dress up for dinner, Cat wore pants and I just a light jacket. Cat drove the pick-up, and we arrived at the beach house on time. Jacob came to the door, he looked good and gave us both a hug. Deanna came out of the bedroom holding Wendy Michelle's hand. Deanna looked great, she had regained all her weight back and if she was pregnant I couldn't tell by looking. I looked at her with a smile and asked, hey, where's the baby? Deanna didn't say a word. Little Wendy Michelle was getting big. Cat received a hug and a kiss but I only got a hug. There wasn't much chit chat, and we sat right down to dinner. The food was better than the company. Not much talking,

Deanna talked about little Wendy, and that she could now swim like a fish, Deanna also said business at the tourist shop was good. Deanna asked about Rusty's Martha and what I had planned to do about it all. I said I would support her as she grew up and would be sure she had whatever she needed, including US Citizenship. I asked what they had heard of Janie and if she was still going to the University? Jacob spoke up, saying that Janie had moved and was now going to a college close by where her boyfriend was living. The Boyfriend had graduated and was living at home. I said that if she would have asked, I would have advised against that move as now the boy could see her at his convenience. I mentioned that Janie has light skin but possibly having a black in-law might not fit into the boy's parents plans. What about your parents Jim, Deanna asked, what would they say? I probably made a mistake by not marring Cat, I said. But if I would have married her both my parents would have received her with open arms. What about Anny I asked, anyone hear from Anny or know if she's still at FSU? Jacob said that her tuition was paid for by the trust this year but that he hadn't spoke to her since summer. Jacob said that she had actually worked in Tallahassee during the summer with the State Attorney's office. Oh God, I said, not another attorney, and we laughed. How is Marilyn, asked Deanna? Any children as yet. Nop, no plans for children. I'm not doing so well as a married man; Marilyn says I'm not home enough. I work four nights a week, I leave from the house at 6:00 AM and return at 11:30 PM. When do you see her Deanna asked? We spend weekends together I said. Then Cat spoke up adding when he's not off on some adventure. Yes Jim Jacob said, tell us about this Angola thing we heard about. I've never been to Angola in my life I stated, please don't believe the stories you hear. Does that mean your adventure days are over, Deanna asked? Well, I think my adventure days have switched more to working adventures. I plan to work until I'm 30 then sail the world, or at least get to know every nook and cranny of the Islands. I'd like to also look for and find the perfect spot to call home. Have you found that perfect woman as yet Deanna asked? Well if you're asking about Marilyn I'm not sure she'll put up with too much more of the waiting. Why not bring her here with you, Deanna asked? Nassau is off bounds for Marilyn; before we married, I told her that I wouldn't give up Cat, not for anyone. Cat asked then why not marry me? Because you belong here I said, not sitting around in Miami waiting for me to come home. With that Cat got up from the table and walked out. We soon heard her truck start and it pulling off with the tires spinning. Jacob would you please call me a taxi I asked? Why asked Jacob you don't think she'll be back for you? Please call the Taxi I asked again. Before I knew it Deanna had got their car and was pulling up at the front door. The horn beeped and I got in. Where do you think she'll go, Deanna asked? Well we can pass by Willy's first but if she not there maybe that bar where she used to work. When Cat was in Miami the only reason she came here was because I was sick Deanna said. No, she came because she was bored; she stayed because you were sick. I screwed it up again, Deanna said. No, mam, you didn't; I shouldn't have left you for those six months. I could have made some arrangements but I didn't. I could have stayed home that night but I didn't Deanna said.

Once at Willy's, I said, her trucks not here go on to where she used to work. It was another short drive; there, there's her truck, I said. Please drop me here. Do you want me to wait Deanna asked? No you've done enough. I leaned over to kiss her cheek but she turned into me, kissing me. I know it's too late for us but I wanted you to know I still think about us every day she said. You and Cat still have a chance; she also loves you too. I got out and told her to go straight home, don't wait or stop. I shut the door. I stood and saw Deanna turn her car around and pull away. I then walked into the bar.

Cat was there at the bar talking to the bartender and two men, one sitting on each side of her. I caught Cat's eye and she turned her head away. I wasn't known in this part of town anymore, and trouble was here almost every night. Right at the very spot where she was sitting is where her ex-boyfriend if you wanted to call him that, had his throat cut. I didn't know exactly what to do. I looked around and saw and empty table so I went and sat facing Cat's back. I saw her look again and noticed that I was no longer standing where I was. She then turned to her right and back around to her left. She spotted me and then turned back to the bar. By now a bar maid was at my table asking what

I would have to drink. I said whisky on the rocks, make it a double. I hadn't looked up, not taking my eyes off of Cat's back. When I did look up it was just another kid, she couldn't have been more than 14. This somehow got me started. I stood up and called to Cat, "Cat let's go now". As she turned I felt pain coming from the top of my head and my right shoulder. I hit the table and rolled to the left onto the floor. I was yanked over from right to left seeing someone take my gun from my shoulder hoister. I rolled from right to left under the table but was dragged out by my right foot. With my blood blocking my right side vision, I could only see with my left. The man with my gun yelled that I was the one that had shot his friend three times. While I was still on my back, Cat came running at him full force knocking him back but not down. With his left arm he pushed her to his right. While that was happening, with my damaged right arm, I pulled up my left pants leg enough so that my left hand got a hold of my browning 9mm that was in an ankle holster. The shots just rang out, BAM BAM BAM. I rolled to my right and pushed myself up with my now gun hand. Things were still blurry but I was on my feet. The man that took two of the three shouts was yelling in pain. I took a 360 look around, everyone was backing off. Cat picked up my other gun and came to give me assistance from my right. We were backing out toward the door when Deanna's father busted in; Cat handed her father my gun. I shot two more rounds in the air. All stopped, we backed out and Deanna's car was there waiting outside the door. As I went out the door I yelled "the first one out the door gets popped". I told Cat I'd watch the door while she and her father got her pick-up. Once her truck was moving I got in with Deanna and we followed. Deanna was hysterical about all my blood. The pain that was coming from my right shoulder was something that I had not experienced thus far in my life. No matter how I moved, there was pain and lots of it. Deanna asked if I was shot? I said I didn't think so. With my gun still in my left hand I felt the large cut on the top of my head. We went straight to the hospital. I would need several stitches in my head. I still had blurry vision but I didn't mention it. Mr. Johnson asked how bad I thought the man I shot was? I said that my first shot had missed, I was aiming at his right shoulder.

The other two hit his knees. Cat confirmed that the man was shot once in each knee. Cat, you were wonderful! I said. We were at the hospital only 5 minutes when the other man was brought in. The Doctors were just about to put my shoulder back into place. I think it was my yell for joy, but his was for the pain. My pain was over just as soon as my shoulder was back in its place. His was just getting started. Believe it or not, at the same time, my shoulder got put back in its socket; I started seeing straight for the first time since that chair hit me. That SOB had used a chair on my head and right shoulder. The hospital wanted to keep me over night. No way was that going to happen. The Doctors had just given the other guy something for the pain. I walked up to him, bent over close and whispered something in his ear. I then stood straight up and asked if he understood. He nodded his head. Deanna then drove Cat and myself home. Deanna's father was going to follow Deanna home in Cat's pick-up. Deanna's father was about to leave and I stopped him to ask if he would need the gun? If you take it I suggest you remove the safety and put a bullet in the chamber, it works better that way. I then said that if he checked back, the prints on the gun that I had turned in a year or so ago would patch the man's that I had shot tonight. Cat and I got upstairs and into the apartment. Cat said she was so sorry, I said, so much for a quite evening. I went to the safe and got out my Smith & Wesson 32-20 and reloaded my Browning.

The next morning, the top of my head with its stitches, some of my face, and my right shoulder were black and blue. We got up and in the shower Cat washed off lots of my dried blood. I ask Cat to call someone to go to Deanna house and clean out the blood in her car, I was sure it didn't get cleaned last night. We dressed and went to get something to eat. As we walked cat holding my left arm, she asked, did you really mean it when you said you should have married me instead of Marilyn? Let me see I said, was that before or after my shoulder was out of its socket? She jumped out in front of me and said she was serious! I said so was I and kissed her. We ate and returned to dress for church. I wanted to see little Martha singing in the choir. At church the whole gang was there, Mary and her family, Deanna, Jacob and Wendy Michelle and Mr. & Mrs. Johnson. As we walked in to get seated Mr.

Johnson whispered that he wanted me to leave the Browning here in Nassau, just in case the man in the hospital wanted to press charges. I whispered back I'd make a trade with him. And then I said not to worry he wouldn't.

Martha sang beautifully, I couldn't help but stand and applaud. It was church, I was the only one that did. Apparently, one didn't applaud in church.

After church Cat and I went back to the apartment. I had in my small bag a copy of a tape that Carson had made for me. I gave it to Cat and asked her to walk it over to her father's and retrieve my Beretta. Tell him to make sure there's not a bullet in the chamber and it has the safety on. Tell him to look at the tape in private.

The tape showed one of Mr. Johnson's visits with Michelle in her apartment. In this clip Michelle was asleep when Mr. Johnson opened a drawer in her nightstand and put something in, probably money. Something caught his attention, and he pulled out a box. He opened the box and took out a small derringer. While the derringer was still in his hand he walked to Michelle's purse, opened it and stuck his hand in. When taking out his hand it was holding a second derringer. He then placed both guns back into the box and left with the box in hand.

Mr. Johnson didn't know that I was in possession of one of the guns, but he did know where the other one was. Mr. Thompson had been called down to the police station once before about the Juan Carlos death, but now this tape showed that Mr. Thompson had had the gun that killed Juan Carlos in his possession before the shooting.

Cat returned with my Beretta and stated that her father said that wasn't the trade he thought you were talking about.

Cat said her father had asked her what was on the tape? She said, I told him that I didn't know. I took the Beretta and checked the chamber and returned the clip in and put the safety on.

Cat, I said, I can't stop you from doing or going anywhere, but I beg you not to go back to that bar or that area of town again. Cat again said she was sorry and promised never to go back there, never. Cat then asked if she could come live in the apartment in Miami. She said that way she could see me more. I told her I was going on a trip to Chicago and that I would stop by and see Janie while I was there. I would attempt to get Janie to attend the University of Miami. I promise to be back in two weeks and if not Cat was to come to Miami. Two weeks, can you wait two weeks I asked? Cat smiled and said yes.

I returned the 32-20 to the safe, while in the safe I asked where the extra cash had come from? Cat said it was her tip money. There was stacks of it. When you visit Miami, who will take your place on the Hatteras, I asked? I don't know, but I think it's nice to have a woman's touch, Cat said. I agree I said, why not be on the lookout, in fact find a nice local girl. There should be a few girls that would enjoy the job. There's not too many girls in Nassau that know their way around a fishing boat, Cat said. Yes, and only one that can tackle like a linebacker, I said. Of the whole thing last night, I can't get over your charging that man. He could have shot you. My father said that is why you keep that gun the way you do, with the safety on and the chamber empty. My father said it gave you that extra few seconds in case someone took your gun as they did. Well, I said we were both lucky last night.

What will you tell Marilyn about your injuries Cat asked? Oh I don't know. I'll think of something before I get off the plane. Speaking of planes, it's time we get going. Please get me Janie's phone and address. Sorry to say, Cat said, but we'll have to get that from her mom. Janie and I don't do much communicating. Ok we'll stop by on the way to the seaport but you should have the number and give her a call sometime. Janie's one of those few girls that you were talking about that could make her way around a boat. It would be nice one day if the three of you could work together. Cat said, that would be fine I guess as long as they're both married.

We stopped by and got Janie's information, Mrs. Johnson asked me to bring Janie home. I said I would try to get her to Miami. We were off to the seaport. My seaplane was there waiting. It wasn't a sad good-by; it was cheerful and happy, I was glad that Cat and I were good, and she was pleased that she would see me in two weeks. If I don't get back in two weeks and you don't come to Miami, then it will be on you I said. Don't worry Cat said; you better figure out how you will keep me busy in Miami. I kissed her good-by and I was off.

I slept the entire flight home. As I went through customs, I heard a familiar voice. Hey Jim can we talk outside. It was Doug, Mare's new friend's husband. Sure I said, I finished up inside and there he was in the parking lot. As I walked up, he asked what had happened to my head? It's nothing I said; I was coming up from diving and did a foolish thing; I ran into one of the propellers. What's up I asked; you guys go skiing over the weekend? No man, Adrian and your Marilyn went out Sunday night. Adrian didn't get home this morning until 4:00 AM. She's been acting funny lately; we seem to be drifting apart since she met your wife. The two of them are always going out to bars and discos. Doug said he had asked his wife not to go out last night, but she went anyway. So I asked, you blaming me or Marilyn or both? Doug said he was giving me a heads up as Marilyn was offered a job at the law firm where his wife was working, and he had heard something like Marilyn was apartment hunting. Well I'm sorry about you and Adrian. I'll talk to Mare about it. Doug said thanks and that he was also sorry if it wasn't going to work out for Mare and me.

I drove home and was greeted by Betty, boy you sure can pick-um she said. That woman done got herself an apartment and left you a Dear John letter. The letter is on your bed; I told you you should have married one of those Johnson girls. Hey, Betty asked, what happened to your head? Someone trying to knock some sense into you? I was on the way to read the letter. "Dear Jimmy, sorry for leaving like his but I just couldn't face you to tell you. I've gotten a job and an apartment. I used our credit cards to buy what I needed, I'll pay you back if you want. The cards are in your top draw. I just couldn't wait around anymore. If you ever buy that big sailboat and want someone to sail the world with you look me up. Love always, Mare". Betty I called, yes sir she answered, pack up we're moving back to the apartment. Anything that's Mare's put it in boxes. Yes sir, I sees that your Dear John letter got you upset, she said. Any messages I asked? Nop the only one that's been a calling was Marilyn's mother. She said for you to call her as soon as you walked in.

I went in the bath room and took off the head bandage. I looked in the mirror using another mirror. The stitches were right on what looked to be the beginning of a small bald spot.

My brother Bob had started going bald when he was 28. I was now 25, oh well I thought, now I can say it's a scare and not a bald spot. I left the bandage off and called Joe, he was most likely just getting off work. I dressed and headed out for the 1800 club. I wasn't sure if it was to bury my sorrows or celebrate.

Once at the club the girls noted that they hadn't seen me in there for quite some time. With the bar not being too well lit, no one noticed my bruises or stitches. At about 7:00 PM I called Joe's house again and a girl answered the phone. Good evening young lady I said, by any chance is Joe at home? The girl said that Joe was in the shower. Could you tell him Jim's at the club. I'll let him know she said. When I hung up I thought that Joe's showers must be boring. Then I thought about Cat. Man, was she going to be surprised.

Joe hadn't showed up at the club but Karen did. The first thing she asked was if Joe was going to show, then asked me how I got out of the house? I don't know if Joe is coming and when I got home Mare wasn't there so here I am. Karen said that Joe was sporting a new girlfriend he met while buying some clothes at Burdines. Imagine, he just showed up with her at the boat and expected me to go too. I don't get it she said. Well for one thing Karen, everywhere you go everyone stares at your beauty, you also are a flirt. I don't flirt with you Karen said. Yes, you do, I just ignore it; she then gave me the finger.

Well, Mare had made it easy for me, the following day, I asked Karen to call Janie and tell her that I would be there in Chicago this week, and I wanted to take her and Lee to dinner. Tell her I won't take no for an answer. Set the day and then make reservations at a nice Italian restaurant. Call Benny's secretary and have her give you the restaurant's name. Then get me a flight and hotel. While you're at it, get me the name of Lee's father's construction company and who the partners are, if any. Karen asked, you going up there to stir up trouble? Nop, I had enough of that over the weekend.

I called Joe and asked him to meet me at the club after work. Karen over heard the conversation. Karen didn't know as yet I was single.

During the day Karen found me and said the Benny had called and asked me to call him. I stopped at a pay phone and called. Benny wanted to know what I was going to be doing in Chicago? He wanted me to know that his influence was limited in the windy city. I asked for a name and he gave it. Benny asked Business or personal; I said both.

I met Joe at the club and said I wanted him to be the first to know about Mare and I. Joe said he knew it wouldn't last, but he was sorry because she was so much fun and a good sport. Joe said business was busier than ever and that backlog for container repairs was now two months, but the available stock was good, and all the customers were happy. The Fab shop was on schedule us, having made three Andros shipments so far this year. The first shipment had arrived on site, and Joe had flown over to see that it met with their approval. The contractor's superintendent over the island project said it was the best work he had ever seen.

CHAPTER V

CHICAGO

As coincidences go the name of Lee's father's partner in Chicago was the same as the construction company working on Andros, Gianetti Construction Inc. Benny sent me a name, it was also Gianetti. It seemed this Gianetti person was a busy guy.

Janie picked me up at the Chicago airport, she said she knew I didn't have any business there but was coming to visit her. Janie was happy to see me but asked me please not to interfere. We stopped at a coffee shop, and Janie said that Lee's parents said it would be one thing to have a black in-law, but a black grandchild was for them out of the question. I could hardly hold my tong. I asked her if she loved this man Lee, she said she did. I asked if he loved her, and she said he did. So what's the problem? I said, who cares what the parents think! Lee's not like you, he doesn't have a lot of money. He has a good job and the possibility of owning the business one day. Lee's father owns the business, I asked? Yes Janie said. Is he picking you up for dinner, I asked? Janie said no that we would meet him there. I asked how her studies were doing? She said passing. She dropped me at the hotel, and I said I would meet them at the restaurant.

I checked in and left my bag at the desk. It was 10:00 AM; I had an appointment with Gianetti at 11:00 AM. I was at his office early and waited. His secretary said he was being held up at court. He was held up alright, I didn't know at the time, but he was arrested while in court. The secretary said that Mr. Gianetti had something urgent come up and would have to postpone until next week. I returned to the hotel and called Benny to see what was happening. Benny said he hadn't heard anything and would get back to me ASAP. It turned out that Gianetti's construction company was being investigated for bribes, and Gianetti himself was arrested for tampering with a witness of the Grand Jury.

I called for Bob, and his office said he was out of town. I asked for Rodger, I asked Rodger if he could find Bob and he said that Bob was in a Cuban jail. Rodger said it was just a misunderstanding and he'd be back with-in a few days. I asked Rodger whom I could talk with about the Andros Project. Rodger said he didn't know what I was talking about. I called Carson; Carson was back at work but not yet in the field. I had walked to a pay phone, called a number and waited for a return call. I stood in that the chilly wind for almost two hours. The pay phone rang; it was Carson, I told him what I wanted, and he said he understood. I told him where I was staying and if I wasn't there to leave the correct message. I called Benny from the same pay phone and Benny confirmed the news on Gianetti. I went back to the hotel and waited. It was time for me to leave the hotel for our dinner, with no answers as yet from Carson. I caught a cab and was at the restaurant within minutes. Lee and Janie were waiting in the bar. I had only met Lee once before some years back. He was a big good looking young man. Hello Sir he said giving me has hand. Lee paid their tab from the bar and said our table was waiting. Lee seemed to know his way around. We were seated and Lee asked what I was drinking? Chivas Regal rocks I said. We said our nice things and ordered the food. I interrupted Lee and said I wanted to get right to the point. Lee you love this young lady? He said, well yes of course I do. Well then why is she living an hour's drive from you and doesn't see you but twice a week? Well Lee said I don't see where that any of your business. Ah a strong answer, I like that in a young man. Yes, well, hears my answer. I said, next week, I will have someone move Janie back to Miami. Hey both said at once, "you can't do that". Oh, but I can, and I will. You both may stop me, but then again, Lee, you will have to start supporting her room, board, and school. Sorry Janie, but if his intentions are good, Lee will do the right thing. I'll help you Lee by getting you a good job in Miami making enough money to support a family. Our salads were brought to the table and I asked what they were thinking. Janie I said, the second room in my apartment is empty and both of you are welcome. Lee asked what kind of job? I said that's my boy; what do you know how to do I asked? Now I'm the foreman on the job site, Lee replied. Could you run the job, I mean everything, I asked? Yes, but that won't be happening for a while yet. Why because your dad doesn't think you can or you can't. I've been working the job ever since I can remember, Lee said. We're just waiting for the right time. If the time was today could you do the job yes or no? Lee without even hesitating said yes. And what would your parents say if you took a job down south? My dad would say I was blowing a great opportunity. What would he say about Janie I asked? My dad would most likely say that I'd had to love her to give up what I always wanted. And your mom I asked? Well, we'd hoped that over time she would accept the facts, Lee said. But this is all just talk, right Lee asked? I'm afraid not, I said as I cut my steak. Janie's going back with-in the week. Janie said I won't go! Oh yes, you will; it's my way of pushing things right along, I answered. Then the waiter came saying that there was a phone call at the desk for me. I excused myself and went to take the call. When I returned I said we had a change of plans, Lee are you an officer of the construction company? Lee said no, do you sign on any of the accounts? He said no. You do know that your father's partner was arrested today? Yes, but my father said that he was being framed and that it would all go away with-in a few days. Go call your house see if there's any news, I said. Lee got up and went to the phone. He came back and said his dad had also been arrested. I need to go he said my mother will need me. Please sit for one more minute I asked. First, don't talk to anyone and try not to get your photo taken even from a distance. Tomorrow most likely, the government job site will be shut down. Your dad will most likely bail out tomorrow afternoon. Tell him I've offered you a good job until this blows over. Catch a plane to Miami by Thursday afternoon. Janie will come with me tomorrow, give Lee the Miami address and phone numbers. Lee if your car or credit card is from the company don't use them again to include tonight. Lee please cover your face when you go home. I handed Lee my card, there was no name on the card, just the emblem that had been on the "PRINCESS'S" sail, a cat walking with a nap sack placed over his shoulder. On the reverse side, there were two phone numbers. Lee stood, kissed Janie and walked away. What is happening Jim, Janie asked? To tell you the truth I'm not sure, but it looks like Lee's father could be facing hard times. Has Lee ever mentioned the mob to you before? No way, Janie said; he doesn't even own a gun. I laughed and said, I carry a gun, and I'm not in the mob. Janie said lots of people say you are. But I'm not I said. I believe that the mob owns Lee's father's construction company. I finished my meal and told Janie also not to talk to anyone. I would have her a ticket for my same flight out tomorrow at 8:40 AM and be there at least an hour early. I told her to leave her car keys on her kitchen sink. What about school she asked. We'll figure that out in Miami, I said. We left the restaurant; it was almost 11:00 PM.

That same night I called Jacob and told him to open a construction company with Cat as president, Janie as vice president and Deanna secretary. I needed the company to at least be two years old and have the Bahamian Government listed as a reference. What's the name of this company Jacob asked? Blue Ocean LTD I said, and if that's not available something with the word ocean in the name. As soon as you get the company set up, open an account at the Nassau bank and send Karen a telex with the banking information. Start depositing the daily boat receipts in that account. Set up Cat, Deanna and Janie as the signers on the account requiring a minimum of two signatures. Jacob asked if there was anything else and I said that's all for now. I could hear Deanna in the back ground and her asking about my head wound. Tell her I'm fine I said.

I then called Karen and asked her to get a ticket on my same return flight for Janie; it's a must, I said. Ok boss she said as she yawned. I then called Betty, when she answered the phone she said, yes Sir Boss, what is it that you need. Have you moved as yet I asked? No, sir, I haven't. She said I'm only one person. The movers will be here in the morning. Ok I said there's been a change. Oh lord she said, Marilyn's coming back! Nop I said. Janie and I will be there tomorrow afternoon. We'll pick you up and go furniture shopping. We's a staying here in this house Betty asked? Nop we're moving I said. We just might use that house for Lee and Janie. Whose Lee Betty asked? That Ms. Janie's boyfriend I said. What we gona move? Nothing but yours and my clothes I said. We's really going to go shopping? Betty asked? Janie will stay at the house with us until we have the apartment ready. Ok Betty said I'll be a ready when you get here.

There were two calls from Carson. I returned his call at about 1:00 AM. Carson had checked on Bob's situation. Carson knew not to say much over his phone but just let me know that Bob was on house arrest and in good spirits. Jim, Bob said not to send the calvary. You got that message loud and clear right? Yes Sir, loud and clear. Carson said he was still waiting on the rest of the information that I had requested. Seems some people don't work through the night he said. Thanks Carson, I owe you one. Carson said yes, will I see you at the range? Not this week but maybe a drink at the club tonight at 7:00 PM, see you there he said. Carson had turned out to be a good friend but he was getting up there in age, and I thought it only a matter of time before they would retire him. Me I was 26 going on 40 but still full of adventure. My thoughts were on the construction on Andros. Maybe just maybe we could have the government switch that contract from Gianetti to us having Lee run the job. Of course I would keep the same engineers on the job. It was a long shot, but that's where I was aiming. That side of Andros was only an hour and a half boat ride from Nassau, and Andros we knew was just full of fish. Not too many, if any tourist but the Fish, conch, and Crawfish were for the taking.

I laid in my bed and once my head was on the pillow it was spinning with the thought of the adventure. I needed to call Cat and tell her the news about Mare and me before she heard it from someone else. I turned and picked up the phone and had the overseas operator call her. Cat answered on the first ring. I asked if she had found another man as yet? She said no! I asked if she still loved me? She said always. I told her to get someone to cover for her starting this Friday and to come on over. I said she be staying with me. She asked about Marilyn and I told her she was no longer in the picture. Cat said she'd be there.

The next morning, I was at the airport early and was a little concerned about whether Janie would show. Janie's ticket was at the check-in counter. Janie showed up and we boarded. To get seats together, Karen had to put us in first class. Now days I would check in my side arm with the Captain leaving me with my ankle gun. I didn't like sitting in first class because up there I couldn't see what was going on. In the past there had been some Hijackings that I didn't want any part of.

Once in Miami I stopped by the office and then we picked up Betty to go shopping. We first went to Levitz's; I wanted the exact bedroom furniture I now had. From there I caught a taxi and the girls would be on their own. Betty had the credit cards.

As I walked into the office Karen came and gave me a hug and said welcome back to the single life. I stopped in to see Joe, the office manager, and asked for a meeting with him, Tim, the computer guy, Manny, the transport manager, and my partner Joe for 4:00 PM. I wanted updates on the status of all four of our main businesses and to hear what changes and updates Tim had made to the system.

The Meeting took place and all were in attendance to include Karen.

The container repair and storage business was steady with a two months back log. The container growth was coming from the BBS side. We were moving large amounts of full and empty containers by rail. The BBS facility in which our main office was located was almost like a mini inland terminal with 24/7 operations. BBS was already asking if we could duplicate the terminals in Savanna and Norfolk. The transport business was also booming. We were also getting calls every day to move loads that weren't shipping with BBS. BBS expressed their concerns that if we took on new customers we could hurt their availability to our trucks. BBS wanted a designated amount of trucks but didn't want to pay for any downtime; I wasn't concerned about the downtime at the moment but about the possibility of BBs having any slow down. BBS said they were readying one of their accounting people to be full time in our office. I conditioned that, to them paying his full salary and expenses. I told Manny the transport manger to set aside 5 trucks and see what business he could drum up. Those five trucks could be used moving BBS when they were free. And last but not least the fabrication shops. The shop at my Dad's business was steady, we had 6 men working. Joe said with the sphere's finished, he had moved part of the Andros project into the second warehouse. Joe said that even with the additional space, we were working two shifts to keep up. We were half way into the second of three parts. We had just received a Fed Express package in which some changes were made and additional requirements for more material for that same Andros project.

Our total monthly sales were toping $2,600,000.00, looked like we would surpass the $30,000,000.00 mark before years end. We were still making quarterly tax deposits but needed to increase those amounts not to owe a staggering some at year's end. Our tax reserve at present was just under $3,000,000.00.

The meeting finished at about 6:00 PM. I asked my partner Joe to hang around after the rest had left. I told Joe my thought of taking over the construction part of the Andros project. I knew he had a lot on his plate but us having that job on Andros could open a whole new world for us. Joe asked when we would get the time to spend some of this money. Good question I said. You need a break I asked, maybe a trip somewhere? No Joe said I like to hire two more good men to start training. They will have to be high pay men that don't mind spending all their time or most of it at work. You know any one like that I asked? Joe said no, but I'm looking. I told Joe I was going to meet Carson down at the 1800 Club, Joe said he wasn't going by the club as he had his new girl staying at his house, and they didn't want to run into Karen.

My visit with Carson was interesting, Carson said the FBI was involved in Gianetti's case and the case reached all the way to New York and Miami. Carson said he had also heard Benny's name mentioned. Gianetti's big problem was that he had bribed and threatened a Grand Jury witness. Gianetti hadn't done the bribe himself, but his people had. The person they threatened went to the police and then they set Gianetti up. The state has a solid case as the Grand Jury had also voted to indict Gianetti and his partners. This even without the testimony of the person that Gianetti had attempted to bribe. Gianetti made bail for the tampering of the witness and was rearrested that same day on the other charges. Carson said that he didn't know what was to happen with the Andros project but that it too was included within the case. Gianetti's group seemed to have made payoffs to get many of his contracts.

Carson said that what he had gotten on Bob's problem was that the Castro brothers wanted a bigger piece of the pie. Bob was being stubborn and said he'd sit there until Castro missed the money he was receiving. Carson said he would keep me informed on both situations. I told Carson that Mare had left, He said he wasn't surprised. Carson, still using a cane said his therapy was slowly getting him back in shape. He'd be up to that Nassau trip soon.

Janie and Betty had purchased all but the kitchen sink. Deliveries would start today and the apartment would be ready by Friday late afternoon. I hadn't heard anything yet from Lee and wondered what was going on. I couldn't call, so I would have to wait for his call. Today Karen and Janie would contact the University of Miami to see how we could get Janie enrolled there ASAP.

Friday came and I was looking forward to seeing Cat. I picked her up at 5:00 P.M. from the seaport and we headed on over to the apartment. Betty and Janie were there setting up the new furniture. I had filled Cat in on what was going on to include the Andros project. Cat was happy to see both Janie and Betty. Cat hadn't told me but she told Janie that she was planning on two weeks here and two weeks in Nassau. It was now 7:00 P.M. and we decided to go eat at the 1800 club. Right after we left Betty had received a call from Lee, he was at Miami International. Betty told him we had just left for the club and to stay right by the pay phone. As we walked into the club Jane handed me the message. I gave Janie the number, she called and would go pick Lee up. I told her she could drop his bags and come back here, or they could use the car, and Cat and I could catch a taxi.

It was great to be at the club with Cat. Most of the girls that worked there remembered her. Janie and Lee would come back, we would eat dinner and then go dancing until almost 3:00 AM. Betty cooked me a good breakfast, it was cold for Miami, at work Joe and I decided to take out the Chris Craft instead of the Morgan. It was a good choice. We left a note on the Morgan that said if anyone wanted to bare the weather, we would be going from the Miami Marina at 3:00 P.M.

Down at the marina it was even colder, it was the wind. It was a sweat shirt kind of day. Cat didn't have one so she used one of mine, she wore a bikini with my sweat shirt. Joe's new girl wasn't near as pretty as Karen but Joe seemed to be content with her. Only the six of us left, I guessed it was too cold for the others. We motored on down to Elliot's Key having cocktails all the way down. We started our grand barbecue early as it would be dark and even colder later. The food and the trip was great. All got along just fine.

Sunday night Lee and I got to know one another better with him telling me what his Father had told him. Lee's father agreed that it was good for him to get away until this all blew over. The Feds had talked to his father about testifying against Mr. Gianetti. Lee's father said he would have none of that as he knew where that would get him. I mentioned the possibility of getting Lee work on Andros. Janie might study at the UM, and if not, there was a university in Nassau that she could attend. Lee and Janie could see each other on the weekends in Nassau. Lee didn't seem too excited about the Andros thing, but it was a wait-and-see thing

Cat stayed her two weeks and was on her way. Both Janie and Lee went with her. Janie couldn't start the UM until late August and besides Jacob had opened both the new company's and needed the girls to sign the corporate documents as well as the bank accounts. I had a great time with Cat and Janie but again I was working every week night. I wanted Cat to go and sign the paperwork in Nassau and come right back, but I didn't tell her so.

Bob had spent Christmas in Cuba, it turned out the Castro brothers had loaded the ship on their own. The ship arrived in Freeport only to be denied entrance to the Harbor. Bob was freed and that was that, business as usual.

Cat came back to Miami and stayed two weeks, Janie and Lee had stayed in Nassau. Cat said that Janie was helping Deanna in the store as Deanna was having a bad time with her pregnancy. Lee was going out with one of our crawfish boats. Cat said both seemed very happy together.

CHAPTER VI

SHOOT TO KILL

During one of Cat trips back to Nassau Carson had decided to open that 24-year-old bottle of whiskey. Joe and I had taken the night off. Having the night off, I met Carson at the sailing club at about 8:00 P.M. Carson started pouring to whoever wanted a drink. Paul was also participating, and the three of us closed the bar at 3:00 AM. As I was exiting the club I noticed a car that was parked on the Park side of the street. The park closed at midnight and when I turned right onto Biscayne boulevard, that car's lights came on. Usually, I would have traveled due east right to my apartment, but that road had poor lighting, so I turned left onto 27th ave heading north. I wasn't going fast, and that same car also turned behind me. I reached US ONE with the light turning Red. I slowed and looked both ways and ran the light with a bit of gas. Boom the car behind had also run the Light and was coming fast. I was in the left lane closest to the median, they were coming up on my right. By now I had my Beretta in my hand, got a bullet in the chamber and clicked off the safety. As the chasing car pulled alongside, I remembered getting off several shots and then nothing.

When I next opened my eyes, there was a heavy smell of gasoline; my car's motor was sitting to my right. I unbuckled my seat belt and tried to open my door. It wouldn't open, blood covered most of my view, but I knew from experience that my right shoulder was out of joint. I broke out the rest of the already broken left window with my left elbow and managed to get out the window. Falling from my window to the street, I once again pulled up my left pants leg and somehow got my Browning out with my left hand. I stood up to see that my car was totaled and there was a large concrete light post down in the street. I was still stunned but realized what had happened. I went over to the other side of the car to find my Beretta of which I had in hand at the time of impact. It had three shots missing. I replaced my angle gun and leaned up against the car. My forehead had blood gushing out of a gash just inches over my eyes. I managed to get out my handkerchief and apply pressure to the wound. One could see that a bullet hole had shot out the front passenger's side window. My Beretta in my left hand, I used it to break out the rest of the window. By now I could hear the sirens and people were coming out of their homes. One woman walked up and helped me hold the soaked handkerchief to my head. The women said you're ok now you can put the gun down. I said, sorry, mam as I tucked my Beretta between my pants and left side under my coat. The woman said she had heard two crashes, one being up the street a way. Then squealing of tires as the other car sped off. The police were pulling up and I asked her to please not talk to the police. She didn't confirm one way or the other. The first policeman asked if I was ok and what had happened. I didn't answer, he asked me for my driver's license. Another police car and the ambulance got there and the ambulance personnel asked if I could walk to the ambulance? Before I went into the ambulance I mentioned to the police that there was a gun in the glove compartment and a shotgun in the trunk. He again asked what had happened and I said I must have fallen asleep. When I said that, that same woman stepped forward and said she had seen the whole thing. The woman said that a car had run the stop sign and I had swerved to miss them and hit the pole. The police said they couldn't move the car with the arms and asked if there was somewhere, they could drop them off. I gave them my Dad's address. I also asked if they could contact Big Ted with Metro as these were city cops. I was helped up into the ambulance and as they laid me in on the stretcher bed I reached for my Beretta and held it out handle first calling the policeman. Might as well add this to the collection I said. The policeman smelled the gun and looked at me, and raised his eyebrows. That same policeman looked down at my left leg and said it's good you gave me this because the hospital doesn't allow guns. I said thanks. The ambulance attendant was closed in with me and we were off to Mercy Hospital. Once at the Hospital ER, I told the Doctor that I didn't want to be put to sleep and needed them to put my shoulder back into place. I also asked them to call Dr. John Turner to stitch up my head. The Doctor on call said he wouldn't put my shoulder back unless he put me to sleep, but the head nurse got one of the other nurses, told me to stand, and wham. My shoulder was back into its place. My tears were from joy, I said as I thanked her. She then walked back with two sticks of chewing gum and said this is for your breath. The nurse then said that Dr. Turner said to let you know he be here within 30 minutes or less. He said to take good care of you because you were special. Doctor Turner was a well-known surgeon and a good friend of the family. The good Doctor had visited our house on 160 on several occasions to sew up one or the other of us kids.

When Doctor Turner looked at my wound he asked how it happened. I told him I was in a car accident and the broken windshield had cut my head. Not stopping, he asked if that was what I wanted the report to state? I said yes. He then said that the bullet had only grazed my forehead and that I was a fortunate young man. Doctor Turner was about 70 years old; his hand with the needle shook right up to the time he put the stitch in. When the needle got close to my head his hand steadied for the stitch. As he was finishing up, the same police showed up, letting me know that they had dropped off my guns at my Dad's house. Doctor Turner then asked, took a trip over to 160 did you? The policeman answered yes Sir. Well, Doctor Turner said, we'll be seeing Paul at any minute then. It wasn't three minutes before my Dad showed up. Doctor Turner told my Dad good morning and assured him I was fine. Doctor Turner told my Dad that a piece of glass had put a good size cut horizontally across my forehead just an inch above my eyes. The police gave me a ticket for careless driving and returned my license. Big Ted had showed up as the Doctor was putting in the last stitch. When I saw Ted, I asked if he could give me a ride home? My Dad said he would take me, but I insisted that Ted take me. I thanked everyone especially

Doctor Turner and the head Nurse. I told my Dad that someone from my office would be by in a few hours for the guns. Ted said he could help out with the ticket but I told him not to bother. When I got in the car with Ted, I told him what had happened and asked him to take me back to the accident scene. I informed Ted that a woman that had been at scene said there were two crashes. When we arrived it was still dark, I got out and walked north on the east side of the street. At about 75 yards I could see what looked to be tire marks indicating some breaking then the braking stopped. At another 50 yards I found where the car had hit a bus bench and then on into a tree. At the crash site there was a large amount of blood just where the driver's door could have been opened. Then the car had been put into reverse, rolling through the blood and returning onto the street again, heading north. Ted looking at the amount of blood and what he said looked like brain matter, said it could have been a headshot, possibly killing the driver. Ted was off duty, so he said he would drop me off at my apartment and start a quiet investigation. Ted asked what kind of car it could have been? I told him it was big and fast, maybe black, maybe a Lincoln. Ted asked? Whom lately was pissed at me enough to send two hit men? I said it could be the Cubans, Gainetti, or even Oscar from Florida Container. Well Ted said just as soon as you get home you need to call Carson and let him know. If they followed you to the club, then they also saw Carson.

As I walked in my apartment, Betty was in the kitchen fixing coffee. That you Captain Jim she asked? Yes Betty, I answered. You shouldn't be a staying out all night. What would Miss Catherine say? I went right to the phone and called Carson. Carson answered and I told him what had happened without all the details. He said he'd be right over. Betty walked into my bedroom and said here's your coffee, even if you don't deserve any. Lord have mercy she cried what happened to you she asked? I had a car wreck Betty; I'll pass on the coffee for now as I want to get some rest. Wake me when Carson gets hear. I went to the safe and opened it and got out another handgun, putting it on the nightstand next to my bed, then passed out fast asleep.

It wasn't much of a nap as Carson was there within 45 minutes. I was getting really sore by now with my hips and left shoulder now heavily bruised. Carson came into my room, we closed the door and I explained all that happened. I told Carson that I had forgotten to say to Big Ted to see if he could get to my car and retrieve the three shells. Carson said he get right on it, and then started checking hospitals and the morgue. Carson said if it were the mob, then we most likely wouldn't find the body, but the wrecked car with all that blood shouldn't be too hard to locate unless they had dropped it off at one of the junk car spots on the river.

I called Joe and also told him about what had happened and for him to be extra careful. Betty didn't tell me but she called Cat for her to come back to Miami.

It was the first day of work that I could remember that I missed. My Dad had put the guns in his trunk, and Joe would pick them up from my Dad's shop and bring them to me after work. It seemed I would have several visitors. Cat arrived just after 5:00 PM, then we had an unexpected visit from Mare. It wasn't Cat's and Mare's first meeting. It was the first time I had talked to or seen Mare since she had left me. Even though Mare had just come from work, she looked like a million. Cat was in jeans and an old sweat shirt. While Cat was standing there, Mare, looking at Cat, asked what I was doing out so late? Mare didn't stay long and said that if I needed anything that to call her. Mare left her new numbers with Betty. Mare looked at Cat and said she should keep me on a tighter leash. As Mare left, Joe arrived with my guns and rifles wrapped in towels. Joe said his hello's to Mare and vice versa. Joe asked Cat to leave the room but she refused. I said she could stay. Joe didn't normally carry a gun but tonight, I noticed one under his shirt. While Joe was still there, Big Ted came by with Steve. Ted said they had decided that I would get a body guard until we got to the bottom of this. Ted said there was no sign of anyone with unexplained wounds at any hospital. There were two Lincoln rentals that were still unaccounted for. One was rented by man whom checked out, the other by two men from Chicago. The police were running the name of the renter. They were also checking with the airlines that had come in from Chicago the day of the rental. Ted said he was sure they would at least have the names of the two men by tomorrow. Steve would stay the night in Janie's room.

I asked Joe to pick me up a rental. Joe said that Karen had already got one and would be dropping it off tonight. Joe said he was leaving early because he didn't want to run into Karen. Joe asked Cat to keep me out of trouble; Joe kissed Cat and said he was glad she was here. Karen showed up with her sister. Yes, the flirty married one. Cat liked Karen but said she got bad vibes from the sister. Karen had rented a Black Lincoln. Karen also noted that I had gotten several calls in the late afternoon, one was from the Secretary of the Navy, someone from the State Department and Bob which I was to have lunch with tomorrow at Joe's. Karen brought with her the names and phone numbers of whom she indicated that I would return their calls at 9:00 AM. I didn't say, but I thought I knew why they were all calling. At least I hoped it was. If it was, the timing of my morning's problem meant that Gianetti may have already received the news. After all the visitors had gone, I went into the bathroom and removed the bandages. Wow I thought, what a nice scar this is going to be. I took off my clothes and looked in the mirror at the rest of my bruises; as I looked, Cat appeared alongside me. Cat said I looked terrible but she still loved me. The shower wasn't as frisky as usual, but I enjoyed it. It took getting shot to get you in the shower with me tonight, I told Cat.

Cat said that Mare was even more beautiful than she had remembered. I said beauty was in the eyes of the beholder and that I'd be holding her. Cat asked if I missed Mare and I said that I would miss her as a friend. If I hadn't married her, we'd still be best friends.

The next morning, we were up and at them early, Betty cooked a great breakfast and the three of us were off to the office. At 9:00 AM I made the first call, it was to the Secretary of the Navy. His secretary said he was expecting my call and she put me through. Ah James, the Secretary said, yes Sir I said. I'm calling with reference to our Andros Construction Project. You come highly recommended. Not to mention the Inspector General of the Air Force and two Directors of the CIA. On my side he said, the work that you've sent from your Miami plant has been exceptional. We trust you will keep up that same quality and of course stay within the original budget. We've reviewed your offer and decided to award you the contract if you still want it. Yes Sir, we sure do. Yes Sir, I said again. Ok he said we'll send the contracts via Fed Express next day; once you've looked it over, please re-contact my secretary to set up a date for the signing. All moneys are being withheld to the present contractor until you go to the sight and agree with our people down there on what has been completed. We are looking forward to you restarting down there ASAP. Welcome aboard James see you soon. When we hung up, I then had Karen make the next phone call. The State Department was asking for all the paperwork regarding insurance and some kind of bond. I said I would contact our attorney to contact them today to get them all the documents they required. I then called Karen into my office. Karen asked well? Well, what I asked, did you have any doubts? Karen smiled. I called in Cat and with both Cat and Karen there I said that first I needed them to call Jacob and Roy about getting everything document-wise for the State Department. The contract should be here within two days and must be looked over by Roy and Jacob together. Cat you get Deanna, Jacob, Janie and Lee here today if at all possible. Cat reminded me that Deanna wouldn't be going anywhere in her condition. Karen, you're in charge of transport and clothing. I told Karen that the girls were to wear a nice business dresses and buy an evening dress too. Karen and Joe are also to go to the signing and must dress the part. Joe, Lee, Cat, and I will fly on over to the job site just as soon as I meet with Bob. Karen held out her hand for the credit card.

I asked Karen to get me, Benny, on the line if possible or if he wasn't available to set up a time after 4:00 PM. Tell Benny's secretary it's a privet matter. It was getting close to my meeting with Bob. Before I left, Karen said Benny's secretary had called and said she would call back with the call time. Better yet, I said to call her back and ask if we could meet for dinner tomorrow night in the city. Call the Chevy Dealer and buy me a Black Manual Corvette, red leather seats, and T-tops. Can I buy one for me too Karen asked? No, I answered.

I hadn't seen Bob since he had come back from his stay in Cuba. When I walked into Joe's he was sitting at the Bar. Robert I said, James is it now he said. How are you, Bob, I asked? Good Jim how about you. I hear you had a rough night of it the day before. Nothing a few stitches didn't take care of, I said. And you, how does it feel to be a free man, I asked? It feels like it wasn't a coincidence that my ship was denied entrance into Free Port; how much did that cost you, he asked? Well, Carson told me not to send the Calvary for you, and I figured that the Castros wouldn't let your ship sit in the Havana harbor doing nothing. Bob said I should have seen Raul's face when he came to tell me the news. Bob said he also heard that they had cleared my new construction company for the Andros Contract. I hope you're ready, Bob said; that will be a never-ending project. Have you talked to Gianetti as yet, Bob asked? No I will go and visit with Benny first. Benny will come up with something. Well, as long as you know you're playing with fire, Bob said. Bob then asked if the Navy had paid up on the spheres as yet. No but the Admiral said there would be two checks for me to take with me. I suppose one is for the spheres and the other for the first two loads of material that we shipped. Have you heard any more about the spheres I asked? Well, Bob replied, all that I have heard was good. Seems the Cubans or the Russians sunk the steel one. Your design of the Aluminum one doesn't send out information 24 hours a day like the steel one had. Now the information is being sent via satellite and is almost impossible to track, Bob said. Bob said they already have your next project ready seems the Russians have temporarily lost contact with what the Navy thinks could be one of their listening devices. The Navy wants you to make some adjustments so they can return it back into their service. Of course, they want the work done at the Andros facility. When can you get over there Bob asked? I told Bob that after my visit with Benny we would fly over and meet with the workers. It would be a busy couple of weeks but once caught up, I'd look at what they had found. Bob said that he used his money to pay the workers so that they wouldn't leave the island. Since Bob was doing all the shipping, I asked how much construction sand he was sending to the island. Bob said to his knowledge that the job site was using the sand from the island. That doesn't seem right I said that sand surely has too much salt. Please do me a favor and send over eight 40-foot open-top containers with as much good sand as they will hold.

I then asked Bob, how if everyone knew about his ship's ins and outs of Cuba does our Government allow this to continue? Bob said it's all about the money. The Castro's get 50%, my group acquires 25%, and the other 25% gets deposited in a Swiss account. Where the Swiss money goes, I don't know and don't care, Bob said. You getting that multimillion-dollar Andros contract, you don't think all that money will be yours, do you, Bob asked? Well I said if they need any money it would have to come from some kind of over-budget thing. I'm not doing any kickbacks. Bob said they'll find a way. Bob said, why do you think every Government job runs over budget.

Bob said while in Cuba he had met a Cuban girl that he would like to bring to Nassau. Bob noted that way he would visit Nassau more often. If I do, Bob said, please don't try to adopt her; one daddy will be enough. Does she have green eyes I asked? Bob said no, but that neither did Michelle. You have a point there, I said.

While sitting with Bob, the waiter brought the phone to the table and said there was a call that I was expecting. The call was from Ted. Ted said that two men had come in from Chicago and only one had left. The one that had left was Charles Nicoletti. Both were mob enforcers, Martinelli being Nicoletti's driver. The other man Guido Martinelli had rented a black Lincoln and two days later reported it stolen. Mr. Martinelli never showed up in person to make the report, nor had he reported the theft to the local police. Ted said that Nicoletti had gotten off the plane in Chicago with his right arm in a sling. Ted said that the Lincoln likely wound up in a chop shop and wouldn't be seen again. If Martinelli was dead, then he too wouldn't be found. Ted said that the surprise was that I had most likely hit them both. Ted said for it to have been an approved action that, Benny should have known in advance. I mentioned to Ted that I was familiar with the Name Nicoletti and that I would be seeing Benny tomorrow. Ted said to be careful. While I had the phone, I called the office. Karen was out but Carson had called leaving the message that three tickets that I was looking for were in hand. I took this as meaning that he had my three spent shells in hand. Bob and I had a good productive lunch and I was on my way back to the office.

I had one of the other girls, Lourdes, call for Captain Mike. The Captain had gotten bored sitting around and quit his job with us for some other adventure. I was thinking of maybe sending the Chris Craft over to Andros; this way, Janie could live in Nassau or Miami. Lee would be living on Andros and could easily travel to and from Nassau in the Chris Craft, plus the Chris Craft could be moving fish and Crawfish to Nassau. Anyway, I would need Captain Mike to do this.

I wouldn't see Karen or Cat for the rest of the day. I went from work to the 1800 club. Joe would meet me there to discuss plans for Andros. Joe said we were going to be short handed and for us not to think that Lee was capable to just walk in there and taking over. I had called two friends of my Dad and both said they would be interested in giving us a hand. One of the friends, Mr. Makey said that he would send two men over to Andros with us on our first trip to access the completed work and see just what the next step was.

Cat had called home and Betty said I must be at the club so that's where Cat and Karen came. The girls came in with big smiles, I asked Karen if I was broke yet? Karen said to give her a few more days. Cat said they had been by the Chevy Dealer, and my Corvette should be here within two days. I informed Cat that she and I would go to New York tomorrow and that she would need some of the clothes that she purchased today; Cat looked thrilled. Karen started to ask and I said no. Cat said that Jacob was likely already in Miami and would be staying at his grandmother's old house. Janie and Lee would be here either in the morning or at the latest tomorrow afternoon. Karen was happy to see Joe by himself and they arranged to buy a new suit for Joe. I mentioned that not to make any plans for the weekend as Joe would be on Andros with me. I looked at Karen and again said no before she could ask. My new driver helped the girls transfer some of the shopping boxes into the Lincoln. Cat and I left Joe and Karen sitting at the bar. Once we got home Cat said how much she enjoyed Karen. I warned Cat not to pick up any of Karen's bad habits. Cat was also happy with the clothes they had picked out. I told her we would stop by the jewelry store tomorrow before our trip. Cat asked if we were picking out wedding rings? I didn't bother to answer. I called Carson and asked if he could meet me at Denny's for breakfast. Carson said he'd be there.

The next morning, I left early without Cat. She was up and I said we would pick her up after my meeting with Carson.

Carson looked bad, he was losing weight when I thought he should be putting it on. Carson said he just didn't have any apatite. Looking at him I thought about how Michelle looked before her death. I got up and went to the phone and had Karen call Dr. Tuner. I wanted Dr. Tuner to see Carson and check him out. I went back and told Carson that in my case, it was Nicoletti that was the shooter and that it was quite possible that he had caught a bullet in his right shoulder. Carson said that could explain why the bullet only grazed my forehead. Cason said it was no coincidence that Nicoletti worked for Gianette. It will be interesting to hear what Benny says Carson said. The pay phone was ringing and it was for me. Karen said that I should take Carson to Dr. Turners and Dr. Turner would see him at once. I told Carson and he didn't want to go. We stopped by Carson's house to pick up all his medicine, most of which was given to him while in Nigeria. I went with Carson and informed Dr. Turner, what I thought was a possibility that maybe Carson was being poisoned. Dr. Turner had met Carson before at my Uncle Bob's house when he lived in the grove. Dr. Turned took blood and took all Carson's medicine away. Dr. Turner said one container didn't quite smell as it should. Dr. Turner had me drop Carson over at Mercy Hospital so he could run a few test. Dr. Turner said most likely Carson would spend the night. Carson wasn't too happy about it but did what we asked of him.

I went back to the apartment and called Karen, she said that Benny wanted me at his house at about 8:00 p.m. for dinner. Karen told him there would be two for dinner. Cat had only been home a few minutes from the hair salon and was in the shower. I had already had my morning shower but couldn't pass up the chance. When I jumped in the shower, it was odd to see Cat with a bag over her hair. I had the urge to pull it off but I didn't.

Cat and I were cutting it close as our flight would board at 3:00 p.m. and there was still a stop that I wanted to make. Now knowing that we were going to Benny's home the stop was more important than ever. We stopped at the Miami Diamond Exchange. Cat and I went in and I told Cat to pick something out. Cat went right over to the engagement and weddings. A beautiful ¾ carat caught her eyes and she asked to see it. The engagement ring, of course, came with a matching wedding ring. Cat tried on the ring and said this is what I want the most. I asked the jeweler to fit the ring. The jeweler asked if it was just the engagement ring or both? Cat replied both. I asked if there was anything else that she wanted and she quickly said no. While they were doing the fit, I told the jeweler that I wanted a matching one-carat diamond earring set with a matching neckless and bracelet. I told him that they needed to be one of a kind. While he was doing that, a pair of gold sea shell earrings caught my eyes. The jeweler came back with I thought were quite stunning ear rings, neckless and bracelet. Yes, we'll take those and these pair of sea shells. Cat wasn't paying too much attention to what I was buying. She was all about the rings. Once the jeweler fitted the rings, Cat looked at me with them on her finger and asked if she could wear them both? I asked if that was what she wanted and she replied "more than anything in the world and that she would never take them off." I said there yours to keep. Cat reached to me with both arms and said she loved me and was the happiest girl in the world. As she hugged me, I thought, yes, she'll stay that way as long as Jena wasn't at her Dad's house tonight. Maybe we'll be in luck and Jena will be in Miami at the UM.

We were off to the airport. We would be traveling alone, at least that's what I thought. While on the plane I noticed a familiar face from our Africa trip. It was one of Big Ted's men. He nodded as I walked by his seat.

Cat and I didn't check baggage, we would only be in New York for the night and we would return early the next morning. Our plane landed, and Benny had one of his limos pick up Cat and me. The driver would be assigned to us the entire visit.

Cat's hair looked good but I liked it much better when she didn't do anything to it. At the hotel, I changed into a fresher shirt and suit while Cat, well, she had an operation going on. I watched as she stepped into her dress and pulled it up. Oh my lord I said. It had been some time since I had seen Cat in something like this, but it was the first time she looked so good. She turned and said that if I didn't like it she had brought along another. I told Cat with that dress on her; it would be hard for anyone to concentrate on business. When I looked at her, I just wanted to take it off. Cat was pleased with my answer. I gave her the other jewelry I had purchased; when Cat saw the sea shells, that was it. I want to wear these she said. It was true; Cat wearing those sea shells made her look way more beautiful than the diamonds would have. Just the sea shells it is, I said.

The limo was waiting, the driver wanted me to know that Jack, Ted's man had come and talked with him. On the way down in the elevator, I mentioned to Cat that there was the possibility that Jena could be there at the house. Cat told me not to worry that she could handle anything Jena could dish out.

We got a warm welcome at Benny's house. Benny said that Jena was upstairs changing as she had flown in when she heard we were coming to dinner. Benny said that Jena still had that crush on me. Benny thought he had met Cat before but he had not. Benny said that it was hard to keep up. Cat said she was going to change that. Benny just smiled. Well, Benny asked, business before or after dinner. I said whatever was better for him. Benny said he would wait and introduce the girls, but Cat said she already knew Jena. Ok, Benny said if you don't mind, you could sit right here until Jena comes down. Cat said that would be fine.

Benny led me to the study and poured some of his best whisky. He sat behind that big desk of his and said that he guessed that I already had the news. Benny said that even though it looked bad, Gianetti said that Chucky had acted on his own. Benny said that Gianetti said that he would get to the bottom of it all. Benny said Gianetti wasn't too upset about the Andros thing just as long as he got his cut. I asked what he thought his cut was and Benny said 5%. I asked 5% of what? Benny said sales. That's $50,000.00 on each $1,000,000.00, Benny said. Well I said, I'll be going down there within the next few days with some engineers. We will meet with the Navy personnel to decide where the work is and to check the quality of the work that has been completed.

If everything is good, I agree to pay you 6%. How you get the money to Gianetti is up to you I said. Any discrepancy's we find down there will be deducted from those amounts. Agreed I asked? Well, Benny said as long as the Navy brings up the discrepancies, he said and not your people. If it's just your people that think any completed work a problem and not the Navy, then it's on you, he said. Ok I said I agree. Ok then it's settled then. Ok I said, what about Nicoletti, I asked? Benny said I told you Gianetti said he look into it. I said No, that's not good enough. Was this approved or not I asked? Benny said no. Then according to you I have my rights I said. He's not going to be allowed to come with the intent of killing me and walk away from this and I don't care who he is. Benny said to give it a week and then he would send word. That's just another week he has to finish the job, I said. Benny said that Chucky was under surveillance and if he made any move, Benny said he would know. Now Benny asked, can we eat?

We walked out and found the two girls chatting. We didn't see any blood which was a good sign. Jena would definitely lose that battle.

Dinner was also very civil, seamed whatever happened between the girls before Benny, and I came out from our meeting set the stage for the night. It was almost 11:00 p.m. when we got into the limo. Jena said she enjoyed the evening and looked forward to going out in the Donzi with Cat. When we started off Cat said that she and Jena had started badly but that Cat had asked if Jena needed a friend? Jena said yes. So Cat said I may have my first friend in Miami. I leaned over and whispered to watch her back. Once back at the hotel I was more than happy to assist Cat with the removal of that beautiful dress. The only things that stayed were her rings and those earrings.

The next morning, we were back to Miami. Once at the apartment I called Dr. Turner. Dr. Turner said that Carson would be fine. The Doctor had sent the medicine off to be analyzed but said he was sure something wasn't correct. Dr. Turner said that Carson had gone through kidney dialyses not because his kidneys were failing but to help cleans Carson's blood. Carson's blood counts were all messed up but that they were working on that and should be normal within the next couple of days. I would stop by and see Carson before leaving for Andros. Carson said he was feeling much better and if the medicine came back anything but normal, he would know where to look.

It was now Saturday and there were ten of us that would travel to Andros. Big Ted and one of his men were included in the ten. Andros had a small airport that wasn't used very much. We had chartered a flight due to there not being scheduled daily flights. There were two Gianetti pick-ups awaiting at the airport. We were told by the drivers that the Navy didn't work on weekends. The Bahamian driver said that the job superintendent would meet us at the construction site. About 5 miles down the road the fence started. As we drove on it was apparent that the Navy had lots of wide open space. We came to a gate that appeared to be manned by our Navy's military police along with what looked like some British Troops. I counted a total of five men. We then drove to where there was a small portable aluminum office. Outside the office more than twenty men were waiting for us. We went inside and met the two men in charge. The office was clean and neat, with drafting boards taking up most of the space. We all gave our own introductions. The two engineers that Mr. Makey had sent were asking most of the questions. Gianetti's men seemed quite sincere. I asked about the sand with which they were mixing the cement. Gianetti's men said they had raised that issue, but Gianetti said the sand that they had on the island was good enough. Mr. Makey's men asked what percent of salt the sand had in it? Gianetti's men said they didn't know. We asked to what point they were at in the construction and Gianetti's men showed us each point on the plans that were partially complete or completed. It was getting late and we agreed to start fresh on Monday morning. Of course Joe, Lee, Mr. Makey's men and I will be looking over the site tomorrow. We walked out of the office, many of the workers were still there, and they wanted to know what was going on. I first asked if they had been paid for the week? The men answered all at once, yes Sir. Ok I said that money came from our group. I introduced the seven of us, letting them know that we would be in charge of the work from here on. The men were asking about the pay? I told them that we hadn't even seen their payroll yet, but I was sure it would be fair. I asked how many were Bahamian? All but four raised their hands. I informed them that the new owners were Bahamians, and most workers showed their approval. I said that if the foremen could work tomorrow showing us around it would be appreciated. Two men raised their hands, we agreed on 7:00 a.m. Ok men, we'll see you then. The drivers then would show us to our quarters. This was a surprise as it looked like they were expecting us to stay in some barracks-looking rooms. I asked the drivers if there were any hotels close by and they said about a mile up on the beach. I said let's go. We had to exit the facility to get there but we were on our way. The small hotel was right on the beach. Not all the rooms had air-conditioning but the view and beach were great. Each room had that same type of netting over the beds that Johnny's house had used years ago. This I took as the bugs would be bad.

There was no pool but a small restaurant that looked to have bar service to the beach. We asked the driver about night life and they said there was a local bar down on the beach within walking distance, the man said you don't need a flash light, but you could trip over a turtle laying eggs. We all checked in, leaving their small hotel full. I asked the men to leave one of the trucks with us and if they both could work tomorrow, that would be great. I said they could come early to have breakfast with us.

It was almost dark but Cat and I quickly changed into our bathing suits. The water was great, with hardly any waves. We had brought with us bug repellent and it was needed when getting out of the water. As we got out there was a young girl named Lucy waiting with our welcome to the island Rum punch. Wow, it was good. Lucy said that not many used the beach because most feared LUSCA, is a sea monster she said. I asked if she had ever seen this sea monster? Lucy said she had not, but there were many stories from the fishermen. Cat and I returned to our tiny room to get that shower I was looking forward to. The water was cool and salty. Cat said that Janie had asked her about the rings. I told her that we were married, Cat said. You didn't, I said. Yes, I did, she said. You were joking, I said. I was serious she said. You wouldn't want to make me into a liar to my sister would you? Someone that can tackle like a linebacker she said. It didn't take me long to answer that one. No, I said.

Dinner was, you guessed it, fish. Not crawfish but a fish, the entire fish. It was tasty, but it wasn't going to attack many tourists. Desert, however, was the most delicious apple pie. The apples, Lucy's mother, said, were from a can. The hotel was owned and run by one family; everyone pulled their load. Cat ended up sitting with Lucy's mom and listening to complaints about the Navy personnel drinking too much and turning several of the younger girls into prostitutes. This really upset Cat. I was sitting under a ceiling fan; Cat came on over to voice her displeasure. I said that it was something to be expected with Navy men that didn't have much else to do. I said maybe she could talk to the local government and could keep the military on the base if she could convince them. I mentioned that this island unlike Nassau only had a small population with very little if any tourist. The Navy is most likely their most significant source of income. I said she could also talk to the base commander about under age stuff. I was sure that they don't want any bad publicity. Cat said she would make this a priority.

Morning came and we checked out what had been built. Mr. Makey's men said that anything that had been built using the local sand wouldn't hold up to the test of time and or weather. The work that was done labor wise was good. We didn't need to bring but two or three men from the main land. Lee spent most of his time with Mr. Makey's men. Gianetti's engineers didn't bother to show up Sunday, this even though they knew we would be here today. We were told that the Navy picked this location because of three things, a large blue water hole that looked as deep as the ocean itself, the many underground caves, and one of the world's deepest and largest channels, the TOTO.

The locals said that there were caves in the blue hole that they believed reached the reef outside edge. This they said because they sometimes saw large sharks in the blue hole and even crocodiles swimming along the reef. The sink hole's water was brackish, partly fresh and partly salt. The locals said they didn't swim in these blue holes. Lucy's mom had told Cat that Lusca would come up and swallow up the swimmers and sometimes whole boats of men. I noted it was most likely large sharks that had come in from the reef. Our driver said

No, it was a monster because there wasn't any blood from the bodies, they just were swallowed whole and never seen again.

The base also had a nice beach, all it needed was a bar that served drinks at the waterside. The Navy had built several docks that kept two medium size ships. The dock looked to be 25 years old and in need of repair. Mr. Makey's men said most of the older docks and buildings were built using top quality materials. Sunday went by fast and again we stayed close to the small hotel. The next morning, Cat and I had a short meeting with the base commander. When Cat attempted to speak about the girls and prostitution on the Island, the Commander said, "mam this is a Navy base". Our people spent Monday with the Gianetti engineers. That afternoon, just before dark our chartered flight returned us back to Miami.

Once we arrived in Miami Jacob was told to get back to Nassau, as it looked liken Deanna was about to go into labor. Jacob called home, Deanna was in the hospital but wasn't having the Baby just yet. Jacob would be on the following morning's flight back to Nassau.

It was Monday night, Lee and Janie stayed in Sunday night with me speaking with Lee about the job. Lee wasn't too happy about the accommodations and said that he would get bored there alone. Begrudgingly it was agreed that just as soon as the contract was signed, he would move to the island.

The next morning, I met with Roy. Roy said that the Andros contract looked like it had been written by the contractor and not the Navy. Everything was in the contractor's favor. There were to be no changes.

Before we had left for Washington, Joe and I had discussed a new office for Andros and we mentioned it again in front of Lee. Joe would take three 40-foot reefer containers and build an office and living quarters that would be put together over on the island. Joe said that Lee would be happy with both.

Karen had found Captain Mike and once he was back with our group, we would buy what he needed to move the Chris Craft to Andros. We had received permission to use the Navy dock for 90 days while we built our own dock. That meant that yes we were also going to buy a piece of property on the beach and build something, I wasn't sure what, but something to include a good size dock close by the Navy facility. It looked like we were off on another adventure.

❦

CHAPTER VII

THE ANDROS PROJECT

I called the Admiral's secretary and said we were ready for the signing. The secretary called back and asked if we could be there by tomorrow at 2:00 p.m? Karen said we'd be there. Karen got the reservations and we would all be going to Washington DC the next morning. I called Cat and asked if she wanted to leave early to visit some of the DC sights. Cat said yes and a few moments later she called back saying they all wanted to go today. Karen changed the flights except for her and Joe which would go the next morning. We got to DC and saw the sights. Cat was most impressed with the Lincoln memorial. She didn't like the part that he was assassinated. I then told her that when I was only 11 years old our then President Kennedy was also assassinated.

That night in bed Cat said that she was worried about something happening to me and wanted us to have a child. I said no children until after we retire. Cat again asked when that would be. I said three more years. Well Cat said I'll wait the three years but after that I'm having your child like it or not. Those were the last words said before morning.

We all met at the hotel, the girls looked out standing! Us guys well, we didn't look so bad either. We had eaten breakfast but wouldn't be eating lunch until after the signing.

The meeting with the Admiral went good. He was certainly impressed with the women. He wanted a photo of the signing with all the girls in it. The Admiral didn't give us men the time of day. The

Admiral did give me three envelopes and said to make sure I opened the one marked secret before I left the building.

As we left the Admirals office I opened the envelope that he mentioned. The letter said I was invited to a top secret briefing the next day at 9:00 a.m. At Langley. I then opened the other two envelopes. Both were checks, the first for $1,345,003.00 for the sphere work, and the next was a check for the first two loads of material received on Andros. That check was for another $848,772.00 bringing the total of just over $2,193,000.00. I handed the checks to Karen as we walked, she looked at the checks and said, "I think I just got a raise". I said that should help cover what she had spent shopping. I then stopped and looked at our group. Then looked around us, everyone was looking at us, everyone.

The hotel had furnished us with a limo, which we filled. We asked the driver to take us to the best restaurant in town. We ordered two bottles of their best champagne and I toasted. To the three most beautiful women in the world. While sitting next to Cat I told her that I needed to go to Langley and that if she wanted she could go but she might have a long wait. Cat said she was going.

The gang all except Cat and I went from the hotel to the airport. I told Karen that Cat and I would most likely be back by tomorrow afternoon and that Joe, Lee, Cat and I would be flying over to Andros Friday afternoon; Janie could go if she wanted. All but Lee wouldn't be returning Sunday afternoon.

The next morning Cat and I traveled to Langley via helicopter. Cat enjoyed the trip. Once in the building Cat was escorted to the waiting room. There were lots of people there. The subject was Cuba and Russia; the Navy had picked up what they thought was a listening device. They thought that because there was nothing being transmitted that it was maybe somehow been damaged. They showed photos of something that was almost round but had outside tits that appeared to have once been sharp but now was worn down to almost round. Bob had mentioned the object but the photo didn't match what was in my head. The lights were still out when the man at the podium asked me what I thought. It doesn't look Russian I said. A person then asked what a Russian device should look like? The comment was full of sarcasm. If not Russian, then who's the podium asked? I said it almost looked like it came from outer space. Then a laugh came from that same front row of seats. I then stood and shared my Boy Scout experience of years ago. I told them that high up in the mountains, something had been watching us. The airborne machine that was watching us was not of this world, I said. This time the man in front stood and turned to me and said that I was a quack and asked whom had invited me? A voice came from the dark and said I did. The lights went on and the man that said that he had invited me walked to the podium and excused all but me. The man looked at me and asked, do you always give your opinion so freely. I responded well unless I'm warned in advance. The man introduced himself as the head of the sonar project that I had been working on. He said that the design that we had furnished and built was working very well. He said the new devices had picked up movements that he also didn't believe were the Russians. The movements were deep in the channels just off Andros. Our sonar device led one of our unmanned subs to what you just saw the photo of. We don't want to bring this thing to the mainland as we don't know what it is. Hell he said it could be some bomb for all we know. The man looked at me and asked if I'd take a look at it on Monday. I told the man that I had planned to visit the island Friday and would stay through Monday. I asked if I could take along my partner and some tools. The man agreed. He then walked over and shook my hand. Sure you won't reconsider he asked? Reconsider what I asked? Joining our club, he said. No thanks I said I saw how you treated the three men left in Angola. The man said we planned to get them out, and we did. You don't think that Colonel lent you that C-130 and those men without permission do you? Your money will be returned soon he said. I didn't quite understand what was going on but I wouldn't hold my breath on getting my money back. The man then said he had one last question? What had brought that Russian plane down? I said it was one Cuban's pay back to another. Kind of a sweet revenge I said, and I said no more. The man said there would be two security badges awaiting me in the visitor's room. One for me and one for my friend, these would get us into see the object that was on Andros.

When I entered the waiting room to retrieve Cat it was none other than the Director of the CIA talking with her. Jim he said it's good of you bring by your beautiful wife, I understand she has just signed up with the Navy, now if we could just barrow your husband a little more often. Cat said no way, stood up and said, we'll be going now. The Director said strong headed woman you got there Jim, I said yes, Sir, the linebacker class.

The Director followed us out where our helicopter was waiting. He was still standing there when we took off. We were dropped off at the nearest airport where we got a flight home.

Once again at home we would be getting ready to travel to Andros. This time only seven of us would be traveling. Big Ted sent Steve as my security. I spoke with Joe as what to bring to attempt to open the device. Lee was going with us and would be staying. Mr. Makey was sending one of the engineers back on Monday to start testing the concrete that was poured using island sand. Cat would travel with us to look for beach front property nearby.

We arrived Friday night and stayed at the same small hotel. In fact, Cat and I had the same room. After check in, Joe, Lee, Matt, Janie and Steve had decided to walk on down the beach to the local bar that we had missed the week before. Joe was an ex-marine, and Lee that star football player. Well, you know boys will be boys. At the bar, the Navy crew saw Janie as fresh meat and had mouthed off just a little too much. Janie had come running back to the hotel for help. By the time I got there the MPs had arrived and Joe, Lee, Matt, and Steve were having a cold beer. I said you four look terrible, Joe said I should have seen the other guys. By now the girls had also arrived, they couldn't run as fast as I did. We all walked back to the hotel and patched up the boys the best we could. Mostly band-aids, Lee had one cut that could have had a stitch or two, but a butterfly band-aid would have to do. I said that would be one of his character scars. Janie said she didn't think I was very funny. Joe said his injuries only hurt when he laughed. Steve also didn't complain.

Morning came as it always does when you're still living. There was a military jeep parked just outside the hotel. They wanted to know if there was anyone that was involved in the fight that needed a Doctor's care. Seemed that the Navy had three in the hospital and four in the brig. I told them our guys had already gone for a run on the beach. Cat overheard me and laughed. Cat and I didn't see much of Joe, Matt, and Lee Saturday. The girls and I looked for someone that knew about the properly around here. We did find the right person and we did find two possible properties. Cat took lots of photos, looking down the beach from one of the properties we could see the Navy's docks. Neither Ship was in port. If we built here we could use the same channel to get past the reef. My idea was again we could build a small house with 3 or 4 reefer containers and have a good sturdy house for us to stay in while here and or while we built something. The dock would be the first thing I wanted.

Sunday was beach day. Cat and I had walked to the south for at least 3 miles counting only two small houses that were made of wood with thatched roofs. The message here was there just weren't too many people living here.

Monday came fast and Joe and I found ourselves standing in front of the object that the Navy had found in that deep channel. We stuck out as odd as there were four others with us. The four others were dressed in white suits like some kind of Doctors ready to perform surgery.

The first thing we found was that it looked rusty but it wasn't at all magnetic. We couldn't find any type of weld and or seam where it could come apart, this maybe because it looked like it had been down there forever or perhaps even longer. There were twelve outside pins that looked like at one time were pointed but had been worn down by heat or even from being tumbled on the ocean's floor. Maybe it was heat from it coming into our atmosphere? We got brave or stupid and started using an electric powered stainless steel wire brush. Once we had it cleaned up it looked more like something that could have been from earth instead of Mars. We found several seams and four sets of 3/16-inch double matching holes. Now it reminded me of something my Dad could have built. When my Dad would build something that he didn't want someone to open, he would first put in a key shaped hole that meant nothing. This for whomever was trying to open it, would try to open it using the key hole when actually the key hole had nothing to do with getting it open.

We weighed the object and estimated that its shell was most likely 3/8 of an inch thick. We noticed that there were four pins that didn't have the twin holes on the opposite sides. We arranged the object to be sitting on those four pins. Now for some reason the object looked different. We thought this out as if I were my Dad. One hole could open the lock and the other used to re-lock it. We pushed in on one hole using a 1/8 diameter stainless steel rod, it didn't move inward. We then used the same rod on its twin hole and bingo we felt and heard some movement. I looked over to the four other men and they now had head gear and a small tank of oxygen connected. I walked on over to them and asked what was going on with the masks. The one that spoke said something about contamination. I looked at Joe and him back at me. I then looked back at the suited man that had answered and asked if they had two more suits? The man pointed to the side room. Joe and I suited up and returned. Joe tapped one of the two corresponding pins with our ball pin hammer and it was now loose. Joe then pushed both pins at the same time and a door popped open. As it opened a very bad-smelling liquid came oozing out. Inside was what looked like some transmitter. Before I could touch it or investigate further, I was tapped on the shoulder and asked to back away. As we backed up, three of the white suited men moved to the object. The last man standing back asked us if the other three sections should open up in the same way. I said yes, and he then replied that they would take it from here. Joe and I walked back into the small room where we put on the suits and watch though a small window. Joe looked at me and said let's go; all they wanted us to do was to open it for them. We disrobed, there was some kind of special shower there but we didn't use it. We left in the same manner that we came.

Lee had spent the morning with the Gianetti's engineers while Mr. Makey's men tested poured concrete. Lee would be the only one staying with me informing Gianetti's men that for now all employees would be moved to our payroll and that Lee was their Boss on the island. I asked if anyone had questions, there were none.

On the flight back Mr. Makey's man said that the newly poured concrete had already started to deteriorate and would continue to do so. In his opinion all the concrete poured by Gianetti's group should be replaced, this due to them using island sand that had a high salt content. Other than that the work was good. Mr. Makey's man also said he didn't see any reason that Lee couldn't finish the job.

CHAPTER VIII

ELIMINATED ONE BY ONE

We arrived back in Miami early Monday night, once back at the apartment Betty said that Carson had called for me to call him just as soon as I got back. I called and Carson, who was now at home. Carson said that last Friday the body of Mr. De Mohrenshildt had been found in his Miami house. Carson said the newspaper said it was an apparent suicide. Leaving no suicide note, Mr. De Mohrenshildt was killed by discharging a 20 gage shotgun in his mouth. Carson noted that for him, De Mohrenshildt's death wasn't a suicide but a way to stop him from talking. Carson said that according to the newspaper, De Mohenshildt's daughter had gone to get them both lunch and she had been the one to find him dead. Carson said that De Mohrenshildt would have known that his daughter would have been the one that found him. No Carson said, this man didn't kill himself.

Carson said he would look further as he had just been released from the hospital at 2:00 PM.

The next morning at work I received a call from Benny, "Did you hear who got knocked off last Friday?" Yes I did, do you have anything on what happen? I asked? Benny said he had been shot three times in the back of the head. Wait a minute I asked, whom are we talking about? Chucky, Benny said, Nicoletti, who else did you think I was talking about? Wait a minute, Nicoletti got knocked off last Friday I asked? Yes Benny said, it happened in Chicago. I then told him about the De Mohenshildt's death that happened on the same day. Benny didn't know about the photo of seven, it was impossible that two of the seven met their death on the same day, Impossible. Ok Benny I said I'll call you later this week. Benny must have been surprised how I took the word of Nicoletti, but my mind was elsewhere. I immediately called Carson, Carson agreed that the two of them dying on the same day was highly unlikely unless connected. Of the seven in Michelle's infamous photo four had now died. Papa Doc in 1971 of an apparent heart attack, Johnny Roselli last year found in a 55-gallon drum in the Miami bay, Charle Nicoletti shot in the head tree times last Friday in Chicago and George De Mohenschildt who was also found dead last Friday in his Miami home. This left only The ex-president of Cuba, Hunt, and Files. I was aware that Hunt was serving jail time at the Eglin Air Force Base. I didn't know where Files was, but Prio, Prio, was still living here on Miami beach. I had Karen call the ex-president's house, but his housemaid said he was in Puerto Rico on business. Karen said she had asked for a contact number but she said they couldn't give it out. Karen whom didn't speak Spanish said the person answering the phone didn't speak very good English. I figured that The ex-President would get the news of his friend De Mohenschildt and understand he could be in danger too. I was sure The ex-President would lay low at least for a while.

I then called Doctor Turner and asked about Carson and the pills that he was taking. Dr. Turner said the results were inconclusive but that even if the pills were real taking all three at the same time would deprive him from sleep, leave him without an appetite and make him paranoid. Of the pills none were to help fight off infection. Carson didn't have an infection but not because of the pills he was given. Doctor Turner said that Carson should now have a full recovery.

It was now April the fourth, the year 1977; my friend, the ex-President, returned my call and asked me to visit him at his Miami Beach home. "Jimmy, he said come over tomorrow and we'll talk over a Cuban coffee." I asked him if he had heard about De Mohenschildt? He said yes.

On the morning of April 5th, I dove my new Corvette to my friend, the ex-President's house, finding two police cars and an ambulance parked out front. As I slowly passed by they were loading a body with a covered white sheet into the ambulance, I was a day to late; I knew it was him.

I also noticed a car parked across the street with two men in the car. The car was parked pointing in the opposite direction as mine, and when I turned my head to get their plate number, they pulled away. Only one week after Nico an De Mohenschildt, they now had also killed my friend. Now there were only two left of the seven.

I drove back to the office and called Carson and then Bob. Carson said he wasn't surprised while Bob was shaken by the news. Bob had seen the news of De Mohenschildt and had also reached out to his other partner the ex-president. De Mohenschildt and the ex-presjdent were both partners with Bob in the shipping venture. Bob was sure neither had money problems. Bob had said, De Mohenschildt had just got re-acquainted with his daughter and things were going good with them. Bob now said that the ex-President was still full of that Latin macho man stuff having a young girlfriend down in Puerto Rico. Bob said he'd like to meet with me during first part of the week.

The next morning Herald also claimed that the Ex-Cuban President had committed suicide just as De Mohenschildt had. Of course neither had left any letter or notes to their family. The Herald did however mention De Mohenschildt and Prio were scheduled to testify in Washington during the up comings weeks to the Senate Committee on Assignations to include JFK and others. The Herald had not reported Nicoletti's death nor that he too was on that same list to appear at that senate committee. I was sure someone or a group had silenced the three.

CHAPTER IX

SAVANNAH

Cat was looking for some time alone with me before she headed back to Nassau. She said she'd like to see Key West. We drove down Saturday afternoon seeing the sites to include meeting some family members and visiting the house where my Dad had been born. This house they said had been built initially on Harbor Island, taken apart, and shipped to Key West.

Saturday night, we went bar hopping, and on Sunday morning, we attended Church services at the Old Stone Methodist Church. This was the same church that my grandparents had met at and gotten married in.

Janie had left for Nassau on the morning before. I dropped off Cat at the seaport for her return Sunday afternoon to catch the 3:30 PM flight to Nassau. I told Cat that I'd do my best to see her on the dock Sunday morning as she was returning from her Saturday night fishing trip. Cat said for me not to forget that I had a wife. I would have been fine with her staying but Cat now had that salt water running through her veins.

It had been several weeks since we started depositing the daily fishing receipts in the Blue Ocean account. Cat would change that order on Monday. I had asked Deanna to set up some credit with the Nassau

Bank so Blue Ocean and the girls could start their credit lines. Bob was buying and sending most of the supplies to Andros from Miami. Blue Ocean only needed payroll and a few things the islanders supplied, such as food and lodging. Mike would have the Chris Craft in Nassau this week and start his first run back with Lee Friday night after work. Mark and his crew made two weekly trips to Andros's west coast. Cat would give him the message to scout the east coast near the Navy base. If it looked good, I had no reason to think it wouldn't. We would drop traps just on the inside of the reef and pull them early Fridays and then again on Mondays. This would be coordinated with the delivery of payroll and Lee's trips to and from Nassau. If the crawfish part worked, this could add another $6,000.00 a month to our profits. This also meant that we could use Nassau as the travel hub to Andros for two scheduled weekly trips, Thursdays and Sundays nights.

On the way home from dropping Cat off, I stopped at the 1800 club. It would only be Betty and I at home. Mare's friend's husband Doug was there and gave me the news that he too was about to be single. It seemed that our two ex-wives would be sharing an apartment. I felt terrible for Doug as he didn't have the same kind of friends I did. I invited Doug over to Nassau whenever he was ready to start having fun again. The girls at the bar had heard Doug talking and said he didn't have to go to Nassau to have fun; they could take care of that right here in Miami. He thought they were joking, but I knew better.

The week went fast, and the weekend in Nassau even faster. Bob had called to thank Joe and me for opening the Navy's "object" or whatever it was. I asked if they discovered its origin and Bob said no but its technology was way ahead of ours, ours being the USA. Bob mentioned that his partner the ex-President had a last will and testimony, but it was read at a family-only meeting. Bob said he would wait and see whom came knocking at his door for their share of the shipping money. Bob said that on the other hand De Mohenschildt had not left a will. Here again, Bob mentioned that De Mohenschildt, if committing suicide was on his mind, would have wanted his daughter to receive his shares of the Oil money. The three of them had never drawn up any ownership papers, just how to split up the money each month. Bob asked if I wanted to buy in, I told him I didn't want to complicate my life, Bob laughed and laughed.

If I wasn't working, Cat and I didn't miss a weekend. She eventually trained a new girl for the nightly tourist boat trips; we were together more often than not. Andros was moving right along, Janie would start the UM and she traveled to Nassau on Friday afternoons, and Lee would usually get to Nassau Fridays before 9:00 PM, those same nights. Lee also learned how to operate the Chris Craft. Lee didn't hear much from his parents; his father's case was still pending.

The newest news was that Janie was three months pregnant. This meant that Janie most likely wouldn't finish the year at school and or if she did wouldn't be traveling as much.

Betty said she wouldn't be taking care of no little ones; I was a hand full, she stated. It was decided that Janie would finish years end then take a break from school. The only thing here was that Cat said she wanted one too. I said we'd stick to our agreement of no children for now.

Rusty's little Martha was getting big. At 10 she was skin diving and fishing with Cat and I. I purchased a 12 foot Boston Whaler with a 40 horse power electric start motor. The boat was given to little Martha as her own. Her Mother wasn't too happy but then she understood that Martha had become quite attached to myself and the sea. Nassau had grown quite a bit, more and more boats were coming and anchoring in the Harbor. During the summer months there just wasn't enough space at the docks. Little Martha's whaler was used to ferry the tourist to and from their boats. The whaler had its own ship to shore radio and would come on call or appointment.

Cat and I purchased that property on Andros and had started building our dock. It was strange to see jetties and docks going up without a house.

Deanna had given birth to a boy and had named him John Paul, they said she was calling him Johnny. Deanna and I had promised Ms. Angee our first boy would be named after her son. Rumor had it that Deanna was again sick. I sent Betty to help her. Cat too moved into the house with Deanna to help. I hadn't been to see her but would stop in to see Deanna and the kids on my next trip.

Everything seemed to be going good. Carson was going to have a retirement party at his house. He was forcibly retired. Carson said it wasn't too bad, he would be receiving two pensions plus social security. Carson said he wanted to visit Andros and see what we were doing over there. The party was for Friday night as Carson knew that I would be going to Nassau on Saturday morning. The pre-party started Thursday night at the sailing club. Even my uncle Bob had driven up from Tavernier. By the time Friday night came around Carson and my uncle were drunk before the party started. I should say they were still drunk from the night before. There were at least 100 or more people at Carson's house. All looked like they were armed; I couldn't tell a good guy from, well, a bad guy. I left when both my uncle and Carson started shooting at the stars from Carson's back yard.

Cat picked me up the next morning at the Paradise Island seaport. Cat said that Deanna wasn't doing so well and Cat was back at the apartment. Janie had told Jacob and Jacob told Deanna that Cat and I had gotten married. Cat said things went downhill from there. How about poor Jacob I asked? Cat said that he and Deanna fought because Deanna wanted to name their newborn James. Jacob said he wouldn't have it. Well, I can certainly understand what I said. Well I guess I should go back to Miami I said. No Cat said you need to tell her that she needs to move on. Even I know you wouldn't ever take her back with two children that weren't yours. Wait just a moment, I said. Who is talking about Deanna and me? That's been over for quite some time now. Its Deanna Cat said, she has even told Jacob that she's going to leave him for you, that you will come for her. Cat stop the truck I said. Cat stopped the truck, and I got out, walking to the side of the road. Cat also got out and came to me. Cat I said, I'm in love with you. Just you; I love it when you're with me and miss you when you're not. I know I don't tell you all the time, but I also don't want to smother you. If I go over there to see Deanna that's what I will tell her. Now, what about getting that Lady Doctor from Miami to see her, I asked? It was almost 9:00 AM; Cat and I went back to the apartment and put on our suits and went to our old beach on the east end of Paradise Island. We had decided to catch the Saturday afternoon flight and return to the mainland. On our return to the Nassau apartment we found Deanna waiting on the steps. Cat walked right by her on her way up the stairs. Deanna didn't stand, it might have been because she couldn't. Deanna didn't seem herself. Deanna said she would leave Jacob and wanted us to get back together. I told her that we had tried that with just one child and that it didn't work. I said it didn't work then and certainly wouldn't work now. Besides all that, I was now with Cat, and we had a good chance of completing our dreams. Deanna said that she just knew that I didn't love Cat and that I still wanted her. Deanna said she just knew it, she just did. I told Deanna that she was mistaken and that I did love Cat and wouldn't be leaving her. Not for her or anyone. Deanna slowly stood and walked to her car, got in, and drove off.

When I turned to climb the stairs Cat was there, and I was sure she had heard most, if not all, of the conversation. I met her half way up the stairs. Cat was crying and could barely speak. I said that we needed to go up and change. We had one of those remarkable showers but without a word being spoken.

When our shower was finished Cat asked if we could stay. She said we were leaving to not confront Deanna but that was now over for the moment. Please, she said, I want to stay and see the boats come in, visit with Willy and go to church in the morning. Cat said we would likely run into and could talk to Captain Mike before they left for Andros early tomorrow morning. Captain Mike had the Chris Craft at the city docks. Will you do this for me she asked? Yes of course I answered.

We got our Nassau clothes on and walked to the city bar. The bar was busy but Willy cleared two bar seats for us to sit with him. Good to see you both Willy said. What will it be he asked? With that, Willy noticed Cat's rings and asked her if that was what he thought they were? Yes, Cat said yes. Well Willy said this calls for champagne! Cat asked to hold off on the champagne until maybe tomorrow. Just a beer she said. Make it two I said. Willy put two Polly Girls on the bar. Willy said, the thought of us being together made him happy. Willy had heard the news about Deanna having a boy and naming him Johnny;

Willy thought that was great. He hadn't heard that Janie was with child, wow, he said, I guess we'll soon have more little ones running all over the docks. Willy was referring to little Martha. Little Martha was everywhere with that whaler. Tim had two or three younger brothers, and one of them, the one that was 16, was operating the whaler, with Martha being the captain. Willy said it wouldn't be long before they needed a bigger boat. Cat said speaking of boats here comes our first one. She grabbed her beer and this time I stayed to speak with Willy. I asked Willy what was new, and Willy said that Odis himself had a girlfriend. You don't say I said. Yep Willy said but you might not like her too much. Why who is it I asked? It's the youngest Thompson girl Willy said. Oh my word, I said she must be only 14 or 15. Nop Willy said she's a school mate of Otis, 16 I believe Willy said. You do remember when you were 16 Willy asked? Oh my I said, what's her dad say about all that? He don't like it Willy said. The man looks at Otis, and I'm sure he sees you. Mr. Thompson still don't like you much, no, not much at all. How's Otis behaving I asked? Otis is a gentleman just like you were before you changed. What do you mean changed I asked? Well Willy said the thing with the King Fish, before that you still called me Mr. Brown. That's what Otis calls me Willy said. Look at what we got now Willy, who'd have thought we'd have Rusty's daughter running around on our docks every day. Willy said I had changed the subject. Yes I said, but I still have all the respect for you Willy and if you want I'll start calling you Mr. Brown again too. Willy laughed and said it was too late for that. I just hope you don't shoot up my bar one day, Willy said with a laugh. Like I always said Willy just keep the trash out. I asked Willy how he and Captain Mike were getting along. Good Willy said. Mike drinks a few every night and then goes to sleep early. With that, I could see the second boat coming in; well, I said, let me go over there and see the men. Willy said to please bring him a few crawfish when I came back.

By the time I walked to the wharf the third boat was pulling up to the dock. I knew they did this everyday however they worked like they enjoyed every moment. Cat was giving and receiving high five with the men. I could see she was the leader. As I got closer, the men that knew me stopped and came to say hello and shake my hand. Of course Otis and Mark came too. Otis proudly said he had his first girlfriend. Oh yes I said and when do we get to meet this girl I asked? Tomorrow at church, Otis said. I'll be sitting with her tomorrow at church. Ok I said, then I said, must be a special girl for you to miss work tomorrow. Otis said it would be the first Sunday he missed work since Christmas. That special I said. Otis smiled. Ms. Angee knows the girl I asked? Yes Otis said, but, she said that you won't approve because of her father. Otis don't you worry about how I feel, if she's the right girl it will work out. I opened my arms, and we hugged. Cat was watching the whole thing and came and joined in on the hug. Otis looked at me and said I was lucky to have found Cat. You must be the luckiest man in the world Otis said. Otis said he wished he could have seen Cat tackle that man in the bar when she saved my life. Everyone talks about the story Otis said. Yes I said, she is a fearless linebacker, she attached that man even though he had my gun in his hand. Wow Otis said it's really true he said. Yes, Otis it's true. Otis said in that case maybe Cat should be the one to talk to Mr. Thompson about Maggie and me. Oh no, said Cat, that's on you. We all smiled. Mr. Johnson had come over saying that he also had heard the good news. It's about damn time one of my nieces got you hooked, he said. Now he said its official with a healthy hug, welcome to the family. I felt like saying that I had only brought her a wedding ban but, it was much too late for that.

Mr. Johnson always thinking about business said that he had seen Mike leaving out to Andros with a load of traps on Thursday Night. Yes, that would have been his first trip, I said. Mark too said he had dropped off traps just south of the Navy docks. Mr. Johnson said he never though the day would come that they wouldn't have enough fish heads for all those traps. Sorry Captain Jim, Mark said, I was planning to tell Cat this week but she was busy at the beach house. What do you suggest, Mark, I asked? Well Sir we'd have to look for a spot where we could fish that side of Andros, there are lots of fish but nowhere we can anchor to catch them. What about sharks I asked? I bet the locals could catch as many sharks as we needed. Hell I said just putting a few big sharks on Mikes dock and cutting them up would bring more sharks.

Mark said he was sure that would work but it would be nice to find a way to catch fish that we could sell. Besides Mark said, he wasn't so sure that crawfish would be attracted to shark meat. Well, I said, we're using the larger traps, and if we have to use five crawfish heads to catch 20 others, I'm good with that too. Mark said that sounded much better than the shark thing. Mark said that Ms. Angee would be selling a lot more crawfish fritters. Not only Ms. Angee I said, surly the hotels would buy just the tails. Mark said that was what they would do. I looked at Cat and said you good with that Cat, she smiled and said yes. I looked at Mr. Johnson and asked if he could be able to market another 300 live crawfish each week, Mr. Johnson said yes. Mr. Johnson congratulated us once again and said he'd be buying the beer at the bar in about an hour if any of us were all interested.

We all visited Willy and took Mr. Johnson up on his beer offer. Otis dropped two nice crawfish for Willy and was on his way. Otis said he would see us at church tomorrow morning. Cat and I stayed about an hour or so and then walked up the street and ate dinner at my favorite Bahamian restaurant. The Hatteras had pulled out on time with its tourist aboard. Cat and I decided to take out one of the Bertram's and anchor somewhere to watch the stars. At anchor and while watching the stars Cat said she dreamed of the day that we were free. Free to go and do whatever we wanted. Cat was also worried about Deanna and asked what would happen to her?

The next morning, we pulled up anchor and went back to the wharf. Mark was there with one of the other Captains getting ready to shove off to pull traps. Cat and I would stop by the Chris Craft and invite Captain Mike for breakfast. Captain Mike said that the crossing to Andros only took three hours, he'd be leaving today at about 4:00 p.m. Captain Mike said that we now had 16 traps out on the east side of Andros. He had 8 more aboard for today's trip. Next week we should have 32 of the large traps ready to start pulling. Mike said that Lee seemed like a fine young man but was lonely alone on the Island during the week. Mike said that the jetty for the new dock was almost finished. Once that was done he said the pilings should only take a few days. Mike said he figured in about another month we'd have our dock. I mentioned that once the dock was ready we move a small generator there for electricity. Fuel and that fresh water would be the biggest problem.

At church, Jacob was there with Wendy Michelle, Jacob said that Deanna was doing poorly. He said that he didn't think that Deanna had eaten in days. Jacob also would be sitting with the Thompson's. Jacob was on one end with Otis sitting on the other. In between were Wendy Michelle, Mrs. Thompson, Mr. Thompson, and Maggie. Otis was already seated before we got there. It irked me that one of my favorite people was sitting with the Thompson's. I hadn't spoken to Mr. Thompson in years. I looked but didn't see Angee, but knew she was there. I could see little Martha sitting in with the choir and Mary, Tim, and the kids sitting in the front row. When Church was over Cat and I waited just outside the doors. Angee appeared and waited with us. As their group came out I stuck out my hand to Mr. Thompson. He hesitated but did take my hand. Hello Jim, he said; from all the stories we hear, it's obvious you're still quite the cowboy. I could have jabbed back but for Otis's sake I held my tong. Mr. Thompson turned and introduced Maggie to me. Maggie, Mr. Thompson said, this is the famous Captain Jim. Maggie said, it's a real pleasure to meet you, Sir. This is my wife, Cat I said. It was the first time I had ever introduced Cat as such but it just seemed that it would help Otis's cause. Mrs. Thompson was quick to interrupt and congratulate Cat and myself. Maggie said she had heard so much about the both of us. Otis was all smiles as it seemed to be going good for him. Mrs. Thompson looked at Otis and asked, Otis you are coming to dinner at the house? Otis said yes Mam, thank you. Mr. Thompson gave that same look that I got from Deanna's dad many years ago. That look meant that the Mrs. didn't give him any warning before she asked. Mr. Thompson was taking this much better than I thought he would. We continued to wait at the church's door until Martha and Tim came out. Little Martha had come down from the choir stands and was with her family. When she saw Cat she came to give her a hug. Little Martha said hello to me almost hiding behind Cat. Cat assured little Martha that her uncle Jim didn't bite. Cat invited little Martha to go to the Royal Inn pool for lunch, this so she could show us how well she could swim. Little

Martha looked at her mom for permission and her mom said yes. Yes, little Martha said. Cat and I would take little Martha to the pool and lunch. It was true little Martha could swim like a fish. Little Martha reassured me that even though she was a good swimmer she always wore a life jacket while out in the whaler.

Cat and I caught the 3:30 seaplane to the mainland. That night I called the same Doctor that had seen Deanna with her last bout of depression. Hellen said she was quite busy but agreed to go just as long as she flew out of Miami Airport on Friday nights and stayed at the Club Royal with an Ocean view, with a return ticket Sunday afternoon. She would see Deanna for two hours a week. Seemed a little much but at least Deanna knew Hellen. Therapy would start this coming Saturday morning.

On Tuesday morning Karen, Cat, Joe and I caught the red eye to Atlanta then transferring Jets to arrive in Savannah Georgia at 8:00 AM. We would be met there by Mr. Collins of BBS. BBS wanted us to purchase a depot there that wasn't doing so well financially nor were the customers happy with the service. Two of those unhappy customers being BBS and CTI. This time BBS wanted us to include as partners their stevedore company Harrison and Company. What BBS wanted was 33 and a third % for them, 33 and a third % for Harrison and 33 and a third % for us. BBS would put up all the cash and we would manage the business. Our management fee would be 2% of sales. Management would include anyone that wasn't on the payroll at the moment. So our people from Miami that would come and manage wouldn't be paid by the group. The 2% of sales should cover those people. I added in the travel and lodging to be covered by the group and they agreed. Boom it was as easy as that.

We had two weeks to start the change of management. Again CTI wasn't too happy with the arrangement because they would lose more control over BBS. Sea Containers were also customers of the Savannah Depot and, like others, were thrilled with the change of ownership and new management.

Savannah was a special place with a special history. Cat's father's family could have very well come from the slave trade. The Savannah water front was full of night life; I really should just say bars. The five of us had a great time. Mr. Collins noted that he would have to spend more time with us as he said we really knew how to have a god time. While visiting, Mr. Collins again said that their Idea was for us to also open in Norfork Virginia. I told him, we'd see how this went with our new partner and how long it would take to make the turn around here in Savannah. Collins agreed.

The next day we spent on site asking questions and getting to know the workers and office personnel.

We were back in Miami on Thursday morning with still another new project. One of the first people we needed up there would be Tim the computer man. Tim ordered another IBM 34 to be delivered to Savannah at once. If the group didn't want to pay for the computer, that would be fine with me as the programming we had spent so much time and money on would stay ours.

Friday came and Hellen was on her way to Nassau, that same night we were celebrating our new depot in Savannah. Things seemed to be going good.

Saturday, while I was at work, Cat received an alarming phone call from Hellen. Hellen had called an ambulance to come take Deanna to the hospital. Hellen told Cat that Deanna was in and out of consciousness and, when conscious, talked, not making a word of sense. Hellen was quite upset at Betty and Jacob to find Deanna in such a state. Jacob had left with Deanna in the ambulance so Cat spoke to Betty. Betty said that Deanna hadn't eaten or even drank anything for days! Betty said she was with the kids and would call when she heard anything.

When Cat called she was crying but I did get the message. Cat and I would catch the afternoon seaplane. We were there at the Nassau hospital by 6:00 PM. Hellen was there waiting with Jacob. The Doctors where giving Deanna fluid directly into the veins. Jacob said that Deanna refused to go to the hospital and seemed ok the night before. By 10:00 p.m. the Doctor came and said that Deanna should be alright in a few days. He asked why she didn't eat and Jacob said she just didn't have the will to live anymore. The Doctor said that we only had a small window to change her thinking because the nourishment was receiving now would most likely bring her back but that the same thing or worse would happen if she didn't start eating. Jacob and Cat would stay the night in Deanna's room, Hellen said she would check back tomorrow before going back to Miami. Me I would go get a nap and come back early in the morning.

I came back at about 5:30 a.m. Jacob had just left, Cat said that Deanna had come too and talked with her. Cat said that Deanna had apologized to her for the weeks before and knew it wasn't her fault. Deanna took all the blame. Deanna said that I had told her that I loved Cat, Cat said Deanna told her she should hold on to me just as close as she could. Cat said that Deanna said she had wished it could have been her that had saved my life in that bar that night. It just wasn't to be Deanna said. Cat said as Deanna went back to sleep she asked Cat to please take care of the children. Cat said that was the last thing Deanna had said. I told Cat to go get some rest and that I would stay with Deanna until Jacob returned. Cat kissed me and said she loved me with all her heart.

About two hours later Deanna opened her eyes, she asked if it was really me? I said yes of course it was. She tried to lift her hand but could not. I took her hand, and she told me she had talked with Cat. Please Jim Deanna said, take care of her she loves you as much as I do. Deanna said she was going to visit the angles soon. I'm happy to go she said. We need you here, I said, the children need you, I said. They will be fine Deanna said. Do you remember those first days Deanna asked, those three years were the happiest days of my life. Even if we did lose Wendy she said. She said she remembered that first shower and every shower after. We were so happy together she said. Please don't ever forget those days she said, those days belonged to you and I, oh yes she said and sometimes Michelle. I knew you loved her too Deanna said. I'll be seeing Michelle soon she said, we'll be watching you she said, Michelle, Wendy and I will be watching. With all that said Deanna fell back to sleep.

One by one the group started to return to Deanna's bedside. Hellen said that unless we could get Deanna to want to live she would not.

On the first Doctors visit he said that Deanna was in a coma, Cat and I both said that was impossible because we had talked with her. The Doctor asked if during the conversation if Deanna had responded to anything that we had said. Both Cat and myself thought about it and said no. Cat said that Deanna had asked her to take care of the children. The doctor said that it was possible that Deanna could have been aware of whom was at her side but that she hadn't been conscious. The only thing we can do for her right now is to keep feeding her through her veins and prayer. Janie had also arrived and Cat and Janie said they would take turns by Deanna's side.

Cat said to me when we were alone minutes before I left that she had a bad feeling that Deanna wouldn't make it back. I felt the same but didn't tell Cat.

Before Hellen left, I asked if it would help to move Deanna to Miami. Hellen said no. Hellen said in order to address Deanna's mental health, Deanna first had to get her health back and want to get better. Hellen had told me in privet that she had seen such cases that the will to not to live was stronger that all the help one could give. Hellen and the Doctor said the next 48 hours could pave the way for either direction this could go.

Cat would stay while I would return to Miami. With the apartment being empty I called Carson and would meet him at the 1800 club. I was worried about Deanna but I was more worried about Cat.

Carson said his retirement had brought him several opportunities and that he had gotten placed on a few lists of work that the company would job out, big things like delivering foreign correspondents. Carson laughed and said that it was a boring job but it paid well. I didn't stay long as I was to catch the red eye again for Savannah at 2:00 AM. In Savannah, Karen and Tim would set up the computer systems while I would take a better look at their inspections and repairs. After a days work in Savannah the three of us hit the Charter House for dinner. I went back to my room while Karen and Tim went down to the riverside. I called Nassau, first calling the apartment, with no answer I called the hospital. Cat answered the room phone. She didn't have any news; all was the same. Deanna hadn't come around nor spoken again. Cat said the Doctors now looked more concerned than on Sunday.

Tuesday Karen and I few back to Miami leaving Tim there to train the Savannah personal on the new equipment. When I arrived back to the office I had more bad news about Deanna, the Doctors had now put Deanna into a drug induced Coma. Deanna was now on life support. Cat said the Doctors said they would keep her there for about two weeks and then attempt to bring her back. Cat said that she was now spending time with Wendy Michelle and Johnny as was Mrs. Thompson. Betty had her hands full. Cat also noted that Jacob looked bad.

CHAPTER X

THE FBI WATERFRONT STING

It was just past 11:00 PM when the apartment phone rang, when I picked it up I was expecting bad news. It was Big Ted that called, a friend of Ted's that worked at the Herald had just called him with a tip. The FBI was in full swing of arresting more than 50 people that were involved with the water front. Ted's friend said that the Herald was holding the press and would print the story by midnight tonight. Ted said he would be at the Herald waiting for the first print and meet me at the 1800 club with it. The Herald building was located just two blocks from the 1800 Club. I got dressed and headed for the club.

It was about 1:30 AM when Ted walked into the club with the News Paper, the head lined read "FBI Sting Nets 54". There on the front page was Oscar of Florida Container being led out of his house in handcuffs. There were about 15 other photos mostly snap shots of others that I knew. My new Savannah partner was one of the many arrested for various reasons. The article was all about the water front being organized by two New York Mob Families. The article indicated that those same Families had total control of the ILA. The ILA president and officers were of the ones with the longest list of Charges. George Baron, the Miami ILA president had a long list of prior convictions of which he had been sentenced several times. I was surprised and happy that Benny's name wasn't on the list. The most astonishing thing of the article was that every one of my competitors were on the list. Each of their companies was mentioned as being involved in the wrongdoings.

I read the article over and over again. I could just see my Dad sending his dog Chief out to get his morning newspaper. My phone would be ringing off the hook all day. As for the Savannah Company, Harrison didn't appear on any of the corporate paperwork and it was BBS that had proposed his involvement. CTI couldn't complain either. Before I knew it, the club was closing down. It was 2:30 a.m.

When I got home I called Joe and said that I would meet him at the Dunking Donut on 103rd street at 6:30 a.m. Joe, still asleep asked, it's not Saturday already is it? Saturday morning Joe and I would meet there if I were in town.

Joe wasn't surprised at the news; he didn't like most of those people anyway. Joe asked how I thought the news would affect our business? I said that now it was our time to shine. Joe said now you'll really need that full-time bodyguard.

That week, clients that were using multiple facilities were sending all their equipment to us. Each of our facilities received record inbounds of equipment. The BBS terminal was the only facility that didn't swell. Mr. Collins had called and assured us that Mr. Harrison would be cleared of any wrong doing. Mr. Collins apologized for any inconvenience it may cause.

The Miami Herald had called several times wanting to speak with me, they even showed up with camera crews at our gates.

I went by and visited my Dad at his shop and assured him that I had no involvement in any of what he read. My Dad took me to his office and told me that even before this, some of his longtime friends had mentioned that I was big time with the Mob. Look at you, son he said. You wear fancy close, drive a fancy sports car, carry a gun and live in a fancy place. What are people supposed to think he asked? They're supposed to think the same as you should; I earned it. I turned and walked out.

One of our clients had moved more than 100 chassis from one of our competitors yards. There were so many we were parking them outside on the road. I say road because our largest depot was located on a dirt road just about a half mile off of SW 8th street. That same night we were hit by thieves that stole more than 35 tires from the chassis parked on the street. The yard manager called me the next morning, and I said to buy new ones and to make sure they were installed today! I was pissed to say the least. 35 tires wasn't a lot of money but what would the clients think if they heard such a thing.

The very next morning at 1:00 AM the thieves came back! It was the same company that we were buying our tires from. The thieves came back with a big tire truck and had removed about 16 tires. Yes, I was sitting on top of a stack of three high 40 foot containers. I was waiting for them, I had my 306 with a scope and my AR15 with three clips, two of 40 rounds each and one of 20. My first shots were at the front tires of their truck with the AR15, about two bursts of ten rounds each. Then I changed rifles and emptied my 306 at the trucks engine. I lost sight of the three men and wanted to do a little more shooting so I finished my other 20 rounds of the AR15 in the dirt along the dirt road. I climbed down from the top of the containers, got in my vet, and pulled off toward 8th street. Our facility had some older Cuban man working as guard. I don't think he even saw me come or go. I would drop off the rifles at the Morgan and spend the rest of the night on board.

The next morning the yard called the police to report the truck sitting there. Karen called the truck's owner and said that someone had left their service truck parked out on the street. At noon the owner called Karen and said that someone had stolen their truck the night before. We didn't pay them for the 35 new tires and never heard from them again.

That weekend I did go back to Nassau, there had been no change and the plan was that the following week they would bring Deanna out of the coma.

I asked Jacob if Deanna had written a will? Jacob said she had used Michelle's ex-attorney. It was Saturday but I knew where the attorney lived. Me at his door, he said he wasn't surprised to see me. He said that the will was a privet matter but said that Jacob had been left out of the will. When I saw he wouldn't add anything else, I thanked him and moved on. I had long ago moved any of the jewelry and cash that Deanna and I had in safety deposit boxes. There was nothing in the banks that I had in joint names with Deanna. The only thing that

Deanna owned 100% of was her small house that Mary and Tim were living in plus one of the two boarding houses. I would stay in Nassau until Monday afternoon so I could do some banking before I caught the afternoon flight back. I knew that Blue Ocean's account should be almost depleted as the Navy hadn't even received any of our invoices as yet. I would take Cat and show her where my safety deposit boxes were and what was in them. These boxes would be in my will for her. My keys to these boxes were in our apartment's safe of which Cat could get into.

Cat didn't look good and mentioned that she was worried about the children, she again said that Deanna had asked her to take care of them. The thought went through my mind; Deanna might have had a plan. If I can't have him no one will. Deanna knew that Cat having those kids wouldn't go over well with me and my relation with Cat. Where would Jacob fit into this? Even if Deanna came out of this, who would care for the children? Betty had made it clear she didn't even want to be in the same house with Jacob and didn't like taking care of the kids either. I took Cat to the apartment and we talked about it. I made it clear that I wasn't going to lose her over this. Cat asked, ok, then what's the plan? Who would take care of the children? I didn't have the answer. We said we didn't want to separate them but what there was the good possibility that the Thompson's could request custody of Wendy Michelle if Deanna died. With Mr. Thompson's clout with the Judges, this was a good possibility. I didn't mention it to Cat, but I could stop him if needed.

Jacob of course would get custody of John Paul. What about my father Cat asked? Surely they would take Wendy Michelle. Ok let's stop by later and speak with them both.

With nothing solved we would check on the store and eat lunch with Angee. Angee was sad about what was going on with Deanna but content with Otis having his first girlfriend. Angee said that the Thompson's had so far been nice to Otis. Angee was a bit worried that young people didn't have much to entertain themselves with. I asked her what we had when we were young. Angee said that's just the point. Look at the things you were doing back then. Well mostly, I was working, I said. Yeah and playing around a lot too Angee said. Angee said that

I was terrible with the young ladies and that Michelle, Angee said my how she cased the Captain around. I don't know how your sister put up with that women? I just don't know. Cat said that I had changed quite a bit lately and was staying home more. Angee said she was glad to hear that, and happy that we had gotten married. You keep a tight line on him you hear. Yes mam, Cat said.

It was time for Peter to come in with the Hatteras from their night trip. Cat and I walked on down the city dock to meet the boat. Aboard was Peter, Tim, the new girl, and someone that Peter was also training. The three tourist were as pleased as could be. What a trip they said, we caught fish all night one said. You should have seen the shark I hooked the man said, it must have been ten feet long. I got photos that my friends would never believe he said. I asked if the trip was worth the money they had paid? The man looked at me and asked, you thinking about going out? Peter said that's the owner and laughed. The man said that it was the best fishing trip they had ever had. Peter told us some of your stories the man said. I'd sure like to sit and buy you a beer someday and hear that story about the 14-foot hammerhead that Peter told us about. Peter said that if we caught that shark we'd have to just cut him loose because he was a friend of yours. Well I said, let's just say we respect each other. Well, the man said we sure had fun. Please tell your friends and come back I said. Oh he said you don't have to worry about that.

Cat and I would spend the rest of the day at the beach, we would swim and walk, swim and walk until 3:30 p.m. when we went back to the wharf to receive our crawfish boats. That night we visited Willy and ate at our usual restaurant. Sunday was church and Monday Cat and I visited the Banks. I would fly out that afternoon and I will be back when the Doctors would remove Deanna from the life support and try to bring her back. Cat didn't want me to go but things were really cooking in Miami.

CHAPTER XI

A SENSELESS DEATH

It was Thursday when Cat called and said I should return. The next morning the Doctors removed the life support and Deanna had no reaction. The Doctors declared her dead that Friday at 2:00 p.m.

The funeral would be Saturday, Bob and Carson flew in that morning. The church inside had standing room only and people lined up outside all the way into the park across the street. Deanna was only 27 years old. Her casket was closed as if you knew her you wouldn't have recognized her 80-pound body. When it was my turn to talk it was hard to even get one word out, but once I started I couldn't stop. "At a young age Deanna worked day and night right along side myself and a woman we all knew as The Queen of Nassau, we formed the largest fishing company in the Bahamas. We fished and dove the sea bottom. The three of us shared a sunken treasure that Deanna and Michelle used their part to help the poor, Deanna had built a school, more than 50 homes and a clinic. Her social programs have helped many young girls stay off drugs and the street. Drugs had played a role in her sister's death at a young age. Deanna herself was drugged and raped at the age of 18, a rape that she never fully recovered from. She didn't have a selfish bone in her body, the only thing she ever did to hurt us was to leave this earth to go to a place where she could finally find peace, I'm sure she and Michelle are up there in haven hugging and laughing as they use to do, we will all miss you Deanna, but we will never forget you". Deanna was buried in the Methodist cemetery behind the church. Willy's bar had been closed during the funeral as were most of the businesses in Nassau. After the procession was over, all of our group met at Willy's bar. As was the church, the bar had over flowed onto the docks. It was an open bar that Willy had iced up extra beer for. Peter and his group were the only bunch that would work that night. The tourist business would go right on. By 11:00 p.m. many of us still being at the bar, Willy had run out of liquor.

The next day after church Mr. Thompson made his approach, he came to me and demanded we hand over Wendy to his wife and himself. He said that he took offense at me saying that Deanna had been raped at 18 and that had contributed to her death. I stepped right up to his face and said that if he or anyone lifted one finger to get custody of Wendy Michelle that I would do everything to see to it that he would be arrested for the murder of Juan Carlos. I told him that I had a tape showing him taking both derringers from Michelle's room while she slept. You placed one in Juan Carlos's hand after you shot him, where is the other gun I asked? Don't bother to look I said, we have both guns in good keeping, both having your prints. Mr. Thompson turned white as a sheet and then red with rage. I either had stepped back or was it Cat pulling on me. I looked at Cat and she said we should go.

Bob and Carson had caught the morning flight back home; I would follow in the afternoon. Cat said she would stay until the children were settled where ever that would be. Mr. & Mrs. Johnson, Deanna's mother and father agreed to take Wendy Michelle. Jacob said he would be moving back into his father's house and take care of John Paul. I assured Jacob that monies would be provided for both him and Johnny.

For some reason it really didn't hit me that Deanna was gone until I was on my flight back to Miami. The people at the sea port had also mentioned that they had heard about Deanna's passing. As I sat there aboard, I remembered the many times that I had got on this flight smelling like fish or fresh crawfish as that big Bahamian woman had said. Closing my eyes, I could see Deanna in that bathing suit or scuba top or even her first evening gown. I envisioned Deanna, Michelle and myself out there together working the treasure site or just fishing the reef at night. It was hard to believe that our journey had started almost 12 years ago. Deanna had once said that I was like a cat with nine lives. I thought about and remembered that it was then that I had my cards made up with the image of the traveling cat and those phone numbers. I reached and pulled one out, it too made my memory bank come into play. Rusty where was Rusty I thought? I had heard that he and Iris were having some problems but I hadn't been by to see him. That first sailboat, the Princess was now at my Dad shop upside down on wooden blocks. My Mom and Dad had been devoiced now for some time. My three brothers were now all married, Bill had moved to Gainesville because Miami had gotten so rough that he didn't want to raise his children there. I was sure that Rusty didn't even know that Deanna had died and his daughter Martha well he hadn't even seen or visited her. Martha was now 12 years old and quite the fisherman. Rusty would like that. Yes, I would find Rusty and somehow get him to Nassau. I also knew that it was important to get Cat back by my side just as soon as I could. Cat was the last one of the group and had more sprit than Deanna.

Cat called me the next day and said that Deanna's attorney had called to notify us all that Deanna's will would be read on this coming Wednesday. I said that I wouldn't be there and that she would most likely get a copy at the reading. Cat paused and then asked me to come. I didn't want to go but I did.

It was 11:00 a.m. Wednesday morning, Deanna had requested the reading to be done at the beach house. There were five sealed letters, one for Janie, Cat, Jacob, her parents and myself. The attorney said Deanna asked not to read them until her will had been read and that when reading the letters, it be in privet and standing on the beach.

The will it's self was short and read without any emotion. Janie would receive the bulk of things. Including Deanna's half of the Law office, the one Boarding house that Deanna received as a wedding gift, and all stocks and all personal items such as jewelry. Deanna asked that the Bahamian Fishing and Tourist LTD business be somehow divided so that Janie would receive her shares of the Tourist shop and property. Cat was to receive the fishing and boating part of her Bahamian Fishing & Tourist LTD shares. Jacob was left the first house that she had purchased just before having Wendy Michelle and whatever cash they had saved. There was one strange part, Cat was left the children to watch over and carry on as the care taker of Michelle's monies that were to be used to help the poor. I was not mentioned in the will.

Cat and I then took our letters and walked out to the beach. Mine read. "My dearest Jim, I wanted you from that first moment we saw each other in the straw market. I soon after fell in love with you and never stopped. Please don't think badly of me but I just couldn't go through life with or without you. I couldn't get you out of my head. Please somehow take care of my children, Wendy Michelle and Johnny. I know there not yours but they should have been. I know by asking Cat to take care of them may force Cat to make that ultimo choice, it's for her to make. I feel you will never stop looking for the next adventure or as you might believe your last one. You will one day break Cat's heart; better she loses you now than later in life. Sorry if I've made a mess of things but I need that piece that we always dreamed of. Love Deanna".

I crumbled her letter and passed it into the ocean. I didn't cry as I thought I would but was somehow angered. I looked for Cat but she was still reading. When she finished Cat came to me sobbing. She asked if I wanted to read the letter but I declined. I said I'd be going back to Miami on the 3:30 flight and ask Cat to go with me. Cat said she'd be staying to see what would be decided about the kids. I said it was simple, Wendy Michelle should go live with Deanna's parents and Johnny should stay with Jacob. Cat then said that Deanna wanted the children to stay together. Don't you see I said that Deanna is using this to separate us? What about us adopting them both Cat asked? When we have children I want them to be ours and not shared with the Thompson's and Jacob I said. Cat said she was staying and that she'd come to Miami a week from this coming Friday. I took her hand and we would go by the apartment and then she would drop me off at the seaport. Neither of us were happy about the situation.

As I was seated on the seaplane I thought about the ways this could go. I couldn't see one way that we all could be happy with. Rusty was the last one left from the old days. I'd have to somehow get him to Nassau. I would call him tonight to get together and talk about old times and maybe plan a sailing trip back to Nassau. I again thought about the sailboat that Rusty and I had made the crossing in. The "Princess" was upside down on blocks at my Dad's shop. I'm afraid she had made her last trip. Before I knew it we were landing in the channel in Miami.

Time would fly by, I did the red eye Monday morning at 2:00 A.m., seemed it would be almost a weekly thing. Once back in Miami, CTI had called me in to a meeting upset that I was sending offers to their customers asking them not to use Florida Container any more due to their problems with the law. I asked to see any of these letters and CTI retracted their statement. Florida Container had passed CTI some bad information. My word is my bond I told CTI. There are no letters and I've made no such calls nor visits to Florida Containers customers for their business. It was stupid, the customers didn't need to be asked to leave Florida Container.

With the Chris Craft now being in the Bahamas, the Morgan would be used almost every week. Joe would be here this weekend so we would be going out Friday Night instead of Saturday afternoon. Joe's traveling had put a damper on his relation with his new girl and she wasn't going this weekend. This made Karen a happy girl. We started out at the 1800 Club and being Friday we had lots of customers at the bar, when we left at about 11:00 p.m. we asked if there was anyone that wanted to come along. One girl said she wanted to go along but would have to stop by her house and get changed. Karen said there were clothes on the boat that would fit her. Her name was Nancy; she was a good looking Jamaican girl of about 19 or 20 years old.

It wasn't odd to have single girls on the boat, this particular night there was Karen and Joe, my child hood friend Carlos, two girls from our office, Nancy and myself. The odd part was the sleeping arrangements. The cabin had the master up front, plus two doubles and a single in the main cabin. Karen and Joe were to sleep upfront; Carlos got a single, the two office girls got one double, and Nancy the other. Not to share a bed with Nancy, I would need to sleep out in the cockpit. The cockpit was comfortable and I had slept out there many times. We had sailed until about 2:30 a.m. Karen had given Nancy a pair of lose shorts and a bikini top of a swim suit. Karen had also joked a lot with Nancy that the new girl which was Nancy would have to share a bed with me. We put out the anchor for the night and everyone was getting into their beds. I took a boat cushion and headed for the cockpit. As I did, Nancy came out and laid down on the opposite seat. I asked why she didn't sleep inside but she said she was fine. I went fast asleep. In about an hour, I felt the breeze pick up, and it started raining. The cockpit cover was up but with the wind blowing we were getting wet. As the rain started I sat up, and saw that Nancy was also getting wet. I put my hand on her shoulder and told her to go below, she asked if I was coming and I said yes. We were both wet, I removed my shirt and when we got down into the cabin we both jumped under the sheet. When I woke up at about 6:30 Nancy was cuddled up next to me. Saturday and the rest of Sunday went just fine with Nancy saying as she left that she'd love to do it again soon. Joe, Carlos and even Karen said I was nuts for not jumping all over that. I liked Nancy but she was no Cat.

Again the week went fast and before I knew it Friday was here. I looked forward to Cat coming home. Cat did show up Friday afternoon, we first went by the apartment and then out to dinner. At dinner Cat said that Jacob had asked if he could continue to stay at the beach house with both Wendy Michelle and Johnny. Jacob was looking for two women to live at the house, one to take care of the kids and the other the house. Betty said that she would only stay another week and would then return to Miami. Cat said it was her idea to move into the beach house and take care of the children. I didn't mean it as it came out but it did. So, I said, you have decided that caring for those kids is more important than us. Cat looked at me and said that I was welcome to live in Nassau where she could be the wife she wanted to be and us both raising Deanna's children and several of our own. Cat said that she would be there waiting for me whenever I came to visit. She said she just had to do this.

The next morning, I went to work and when I returned to pick her up to go sailing, she was gone. Cat left me a letter saying almost the same thing as the night before but this time there was no question what she was going to do. The children were going to be her priority. Not just Deanna's children but all the children. Cat said with my permission she would continue with Michelle's trust money to service the children of Nassau. Cat said I didn't need to give any notice of my visits, I would always know she was there waiting for me. She said that she looked forward to the day when I sold all my businesses and came back to where I belonged.

There and then I saw no hope for Cat and I, at one time I could have raised Wendy Michelle as mine but having a second that wasn't mine would be out of the question.

CHAPTER XII

DIANA

Joe wouldn't be going today; I really didn't know if anyone would be at the dock. I called Karen but didn't get an answer so I just went on down to the boat. To my surprise there were several people there and the party had already started. Karen said that she had called and left a message on my answering machine and didn't know if I was coming or not. Karen said since they already had the drinks and food that they would just sit on the boat and have a good time. I said well let's get the show on the road. Karen had been at the 1800 club the night before and invited all the girls that were off tonight. There were seven girls and me, and yes one of them was Nancy. We cast off from the dock, motored out the channel, raised the sail, shut down the engine, and were off. When Karen got the chance she asked about Cat, I told her that Cat was out of the Picture for now. Karen asked what another divorce so quick? Karen quickly announced to everyone that I was now single again. The girls cheered. I glanced over at Nancy and she didn't seem happy with the news. When I got the chance I asked Nancy what was on her mind. Nancy looked and said that she was told that I had a girlfriend and that I would be bringing her on the trip. Nancy said she came to see what she was like. Was she your wife Nancy asked? No I said Karen just likes to kid around about it as I always say that Joe is her husband. So I asked, you're not happy that I don't have a girl friend? Nancy said that she had enjoyed holding me last weekend. So I asked, what was wrong with that? I'm engaged she said. Wow I said, why not bring him along with us? Nancy said he lives in Jamaica. Sorry I said but we didn't do anything wrong last week. She said oh yes, I know. Who will you sleep with tonight she asked? I don't have to sleep with anyone I said, I can sleep in the cockpit like last week. Can I sleep out there too she asked? And what if it rains again I asked? Oh I hope it does she said. We arrived down at Elliot's just before dark. We anchored and barbecued our Scotty's stakes on the grill that hung out over the water from the stern railing. When it looked as though the party was winding down, I took Nancy's hand and led her to the front cabin and shut the door behind her. The next morning Nancy asked me what she would tell Mark? I said you don't have to tell him anything. Nancy wasn't a talker but from that moment on blended in with the others on the boat.

The next week while Joe was in town Nancy invited Karen, Joe and I to dinner at her house. I spent the night as she said her father was out of town on business. It was about 6:00 AM the next morning when we heard, Nancy I'm home! Oh my God Nancy said, it's my father. I jumped up and got dressed like a fireman and headed out the door. Her father had seen my car and was blocking my exit in the hallway. He held out his hand and asked, who the hell are you? I said my mane is Jim and I'm a friend of Nancy. Still blocking the hall her father called for Nancy. Nancy came walking out with her JPs on. Her father then asked what the meaning of this is. Nancy said Jim's my new boyfriend. Her Father said no! You have a fiancé that your pledged to marry. He then looked at me and asked if I was planning to marry Nancy. I just turned and looked at Nancy. I'm sending you back to live with your mother, her father said. He then looked at me and asked me to leave. Nancy walked me out to my car and was apologizing the entire way. Look I said you don't need to apologize for anything, the meal and night were great. I kissed her soft lips and left.

That same day I would fly to Andros to check on the crane problem that Lee was having. Lee had sent several messages that we were ahead of schedule until last night. The crane operator had locked up the rented crane and said the owner said he was not to work until we were up to date on his invoices. According to our numbers we had paid every invoice in full. I called the owner and he said that they were missing five months of rent. I told him that those invoices were to be paid by Gianetti, the man said their crane wouldn't move until he had his money. I called Miami Crane and arranged for another crane. I called Rodger at Bob's office and told him that I needed a barge and tug to move a crane to Andros.

Once all was confirmed for the new crane, myself and another crane operator flew to Andros. The new operator said he knew the other crane and could move it as he had a key that would fit. When we arrived the original operator wasn't there and our new man moved their crane well out of our way. I told Lee that our people were to place large boulders on all four sides of the crane so as it could not be moved. I said, not so that's it difficult to move, so that it can't be moved. Lee understood and did what I asked. The Navy's man asked what was going on and I told him.

The new crane didn't arrive for two days, but it did arrive. The last contractor had called back telling us he was willing to negotiate a settlement. I sent the message that for him to come and pick up his crane but not until he had paid its storage in full. Storage was $500.00 per day or part thereof.

The overall work at the job site looked good, I was pleased with Lee's attention to details. The local men also liked Lee and were happy that Lee had chosen a Bahamian to be the mother of his children. This and the way he treated them meant a lot to the men.

Our new dock was almost finished and looked like a million. Well it cost almost $90,000.00 thus far. This without the caterpillar generator that would be setting on the dock when finished. The generator would run everything, including lights, an ice machine, a live fish tank, fuel tanks, and a small dock house that could sleep two. At the land side end of our dock, there was only a fence and a dirt road. Captain Mike and his crew would be by this afternoon to ferry Lee and I to Nassau, this plus all the crawfish they could carry. Presently any crawfish tails they had would be given to the Navy's dock master. It was just before 4:00 p.m. when Captain Mike showed up. The faster we got going the faster we'd reach Nassau. Lee was anxious to see Janie. For Lee there wasn't much to do on Andros except work.

The trip would take us a good three hours at ¾ speed. The sea was calm with a light chop and when over the deep channel a roll of about 3 feet. It was 7:00 p.m. when we docked in Nassau. Our other boats were in and either being washed or refueled. Janie was on the dock waiting. No one knew I was coming, not that I would expect anyone to be waiting. The men were happy to see me and I them. Captain Mike had his stuff together as when he arrived he went straight over to the city bar. His two men would work the crawfish delivery then the clean up. They would fuel up the next morning. In about 30 minutes I followed Captain Mike over to the bar to visit with him and Willy. Captain Mike was on his second beer when I walked in. Willy said he was happy to see me; he had heard that Cat was living at the beach house taking care of Deanna's kids. Willy knew it wouldn't sit well with me. Willy asked if Cat was expecting me. I said no. Well she'll know soon enough Willy said. It wasn't long before the bar got a call, it was Cat asking Willy if I was there. Willy past me the phone, Cat asked if I was coming by the house. I asked if she could get away and she said that the women that was helping her out with the children had already left for the night. I said I would catch a taxi to come and see her. After I finished by beer I walked on over to the apartment and dropped off my small bag. I caught a taxi out to the beach house. Cat met me at the door, I asked for Jacob? Cat said he was somewhere in town working. I said working on Friday night? Cat just raised her shoulders. Cat asked if I was hungry and I said thanks but no. I asked how it was going with the kids and she said that Wendy Michelle spent most of the day running down the beach, in and out of the water. Johnny was getting bigger every day and would soon be walking. Cat asked if I missed her and of course I said yes. She said she too missed me. We talked until there was a knock at the door, it was the women that was helping Mary and Tim with their children. Cat had called around looking for someone that could come over and stay with the children. It was a pleasant surprise for both of us. Cat made a quick change and we were off. I was again pleasantly surprised that we first stopped at the apartment. Cat said I looked like I needed a good shower. Yes! From there, we went to eat at my favorite restaurant and ended up back at the apartment. When I reopened my eyes Cat was gone. It was only 11:30 p.m., I walked over to the closet and looked what I had to wear. In moving what I had in there I noticed a suit that looked like it had a note attached. The note said "Dear 007, I hope you don't mine. I picked this up from the cleaners for you. I want it always ready so you can put it on and visit me again soon. Love Michelle" Wow I thought, I remembered the last time that I had worn this suit. Michelle had said I was better looking than 007. It wasn't long after that when we lost her. It was the last time Michelle had seen me in a suit. I didn't pull the suit out and replaced the note where I had found it. I pulled out the next suit and put it on.

I had heard that there was now a playboy club on the island. I

had been a playboy member since I was 18 years old. Well, the name on the card was Robert as my oldest brother and myself looked alike. I had used my brother's Military ID to obtain the membership card. I presented the card at the door and one of those nice Bunny's escorted me in. The Bunny asked what my pleasure was, I said I just wanted a look around. Would you like me to accompany you or would you prefer someone else? You'll do fine I said. We walked arm and arm through the club until I spotted what I was looking for. There she was, sitting behind the Black Jack table. I went straight to her table and asked if I could be seated. The girl said to sit, you must play. What's the minimum I asked? She said $5.00. I pulled out a few hundred and handed the Bunny $200.0 and asked for chips. I stood until the Bunny returned and said here are your chips Mr. Robert. I asked for a chivas rocks and sat down placing a $5.00 chip on the table. She dealt me two cards which totaled 21. With a five dollar bet my winnings weren't very much. I asked her name and she said Diane. I asked another questions, and she said the dealers weren't allowed to have conversations with customers. I said well, then shake your head. Are you married I asked? She shook her head no. I then pulled out one of my Traveling Cat cards and put it plus $500.00 on the table and pushed it all to her and said to call those numbers any time she arrived in Miami on Chalks and she would be picked up by myself or my secretary. You won't need any baggage I said. She quickly took the card and money and said thank you Mr. Robert. I said my name is not Robert. My name is Captain Jim; some people call me the

King Fish. I then turned to the Bunny and gave her the rest of my chips and said thank you. As I walked to the door I noticed the man standing behind Diane was following. Excuse me Sir he said. Did you say you were the King Fish? I slowed down and turned and said I did. The man asked if I was the same King Fish that was partners with Ms. Michelle? I then stopped in my tracks and turned to him. Yes, one and the same I said. May I welcome to the Playboy club he said. I thought you'd be much older he said. I was just a boy back then I replied. A boy the man said with a smile. Can I possibly offer to buy you a drink he asked? No thanks I said I was just looking. Looking for something particular he asked? Yes, I'm very particular and found what I was looking for. Excuse me, Sir, he said. If it's Diane, I can make some arrangements for you to meet with her. I just met her, I said, but thanks anyway. I walked out and caught a taxi back to the apartment.

The next day I was up early and after eating conch fritters at Angee's, I met Otis at his boat. I would spend the day pulling traps with Otis. Otis talked a lot about Maggie and the Thompson's. Otis said he didn't like Mr. Thompson and that his attitude toward him had changed since Deanna passed away. Otis said that Mr. Thompson had told Maggie that he didn't have a future. I asked Otis about collage and getting a better education. Otis looked at me and asked about my education? Before I could answer, Otis said he wanted the same. Otis 's pay was the same as the other junior Captain's.

That afternoon, Cat had arranged for her nanny to be there so we could spend a few moments with Otis, Mark and Peter before Peter would leave out with his tourist on the Hatteras. After that Cat and I went and ate aboard one of the cruise ships and then would take out one of the Bertram's and anchor over the treasure site. The weather was great and we had a good time. I must have asked her two or three times to return with me. The last time I asked she said she'd come if she could bring the children. I didn't comment.

We got back to the dock early Sunday morning just in time for us to eat some fritters on one off the carts. Cat would go home and me well I would go out again with Otis. Cat dropped me off by the apartment to pick up my small bag just in case Otis would have to drop me off on the way in at the Seaport. It would do my heart good to once again get on that same seaplane smelling like crawfish. I thought, wouldn't be something if that same woman was traveling to Miami on that same flight. When Cat dropped me off at the apartment she had promised to come visit for a few days next month.

Our days outing pulling traps went good, on the trip back I informed Otis that I was promoting him to full Captain immediately. His pay increase would be retroactive as of the first of the year. Otis was jumping for joy.

Even though I might have had time to shower and still make the flight I had Otis drop me off at the seaport dock.

I checked in early and then went and sat on the dock. When it was time to board I climbed the steps and went to get in my seat but before I did I took that quick look for the Bahamian women. To my big surprise there she was sitting Looking at me. No, not the Bahamian women; it was Diane. I slowly walked up to her and sat across the aisle. Hello I said. Hello Captain Jim she said. She then said I guess I know why they call you the King Fish she said and we laughed. Then from behind my seat came a familiar voice, oh my lord the voice said I'd know that smell anywhere. I stood and looked behind me and there she was. Hello Mam I said sorry about the smell. She said it's good to see you Captain. I overheard the young lady say that you are the King Fish, is that so she asked? The flight attendant then asked me to be seated and to put my seat belt on. The big Bahamian women from behind said it all made perfect since now. The woman didn't stop talking all the way to Miami. I could hardly get a word in to Diana, but it seemed Diana was on her way to Miami to call those phone numbers.

Neither one of us had much of a bag, we got a taxi and went straight to my apartment. I showed her the spare room and where there was a good supply of clothing that she could change into. I then I got a shower and called down stairs for them to bring around my car. Diane almost couldn't believe her eyes when she saw the Vet. Joe's on the beach was now closed for the season and the studio was closed on Sundays so we went to the Prince Hamlet to eat dinner. From there we stopped by the 1800 club where we ran into Carson and Karen. Both were surprised that I was with a new girl. Diane was a beautiful girl with dark black eyes, brown hair, and silky dark tanned skin. Carson was a good 30 years older than I but that didn't stop him from doing his best to move right in on Diane. Karen reminded me that we were to take the 2:00 a.m. red eye to Savannah, I had completely forgotten. I asked Karen if she could handle it herself but she said she just rather move the trip to Wednesday morning. She then went to the phone and made a few calls. Diane and I stayed until almost midnight. We planned it that Karen on her way to work would stop by the house in north Miami and turn on the charger switch on the Donzi. Karen would pick up Diane after 11:00 a.m. and they would shop and have lunch. I would stop by the apartment at about 3:00 p.m. to change into a bathing suit. Diane and I would meet Karen at the house to do some skiing out on the lake. When I got to the apartment Diane was ready to go. Except for what Diane was wearing I didn't see any of the clothes she had gotten. We met Karen at the house and skied until just before dark. I had invited Karen to dinner with us and said for her to bring a friend.

Diane came out of the spare room looking great. Wow what a difference. How do you like it she asked? She said that Karen had helped her pick it out. I went to the safe and opened it and took out some jewelry, I walked up behind Diane and said we were going to barrow a neckless, bracelet and a ring. Diane was quite impressed with the jewelry. I told her it was part of a collection that dated back to the late fifteen hundreds. Karen had made reservations for 8:00 p.m. at the Studio.

When we arrived we found Karen sitting at the bar with Carson. I had thought that yesterday had been a coincidence but again today knew that it wasn't. I asked Karen right up front and she said that Carson was like me at 65 and laughed. Carson said I was just jealous. The night went good and Diane seemed to fit right in. The second night at the apartment was much like the first. Diane and I talked for hours out on the balcony. I again told her to lock her door and again someone would pick her up by 11:00 a.m. for lunch. I met Karen and Diane at the seaport just before Diane was to return home. We got to talk a few moments and she asked if she could someday return. I said to call one of the numbers and we'd set the date and pick her up. She asked if she could kiss me good bye and I said of course. The kiss was great and she said she wished she had done that much sooner. I mentioned that if she wasn't using some kind of contraceptives then she should look into it when she got home. Is that something I will need if I come back she asked? I said most definitely. She smiled and said that she would visit her doctor the first time she got the chance. She hugged and kissed me and boarded the flight.

The next day Karen and I visited Savannah, from there Karen went back to Miami while I went on to Washington DC. The Department of the Navy had invited me for some kind of briefing on the Andros project. I also carried two invoices for the Navy, one for the materials and one for a section of the construction on Andros. The Andros thing was just more changes and more work. I spent Thursday night in DC and would then take a morning flight to New York to see Benny. I hadn't spoken to Benny since all the FBI arrests were made. The meeting with Benny was interesting as it seemed the New Partner that I had in Savannah, Mr. Harrison was going to testify on behalf of the state. Benny asked if I could in any way influence him to change his mind about his testimony. I told Benny that I barely knew the man, that Mr. Collins of BBS had put us together. Benny said the State's case looked solid and that many of his friends would be going away for quite some time. Benny told me that I should stay clear of Harrison and Titlebaum as both men would get special protection from the Government because of their possible testimony. Benny asked if I was interested in solving any of his friend's problems, I said no. Benny said that there was a party that was interested in buying the Container part of my business. I said that I wasn't looking to sell but if the price was right I'd sell. Benny said he let them know. Benny invited me to stay the weekend but I said I thought I would be visiting Jamaica. Benny said he had heard that I had visited the New Playboy Club in Nassau. Benny said that I had come in on a borrowed card. I laughed and told him the story of the card. Benny also thought that funny. Benny said the club thought you'd be bad for business because of my reputation. I laughed. I asked when Benny was coming south for a visit and he said he was in his low profile mode. I was driven to the airport in one of Benny's limos and caught the next available flight to Miami.

Nancy's father was sending her to see her mother and of course, Mark. Nancy asked me to go along and meet her mom and Mark. I had told Nancy that all she had to do was to see Mark and find out if she still had feelings for him. Nancy knew that we were and would continue to be just friends.

CHAPTER XIII

JAMAICA

Nancy and I left that next morning for Montego Bay. It was a beautiful Saturday mooring in Jamaica. Nancy's mom, little sister and Mark met us at the airport. It was a little awkward but we managed. Mark had flowers and hugged and gave Nancy quite a kiss. On the way to their car Mark told Nancy that there was a big hobby cat race on Sunday and he wanted her to be his co-captain in the race. When he said that I noticed Nancy's sister's disappointed face. I looked at Nancy's sister and asked if she sailed? Nancy's sister said she was the best hobby cat captain in Jamaica. Their car was small and I asked the sister if she would ride with me and show me the sailing club. I could tell she didn't want to, but she agreed. We had gotten a short introduction but I didn't catch her name. As we got seated in the taxi, I introduced myself as Jim she said I'm Beverly, my friends call me Bev. Within 10 minutes we were at the sailing club, I had my bag in the trunk so I asked the driver to wait. Bev said that wasn't a good idea, I asked why and she said that he would charge a fee for the wait. I said I agree to the fee. We walked in and I asked if she would be in the race. Bev said she was going to be Marks co-captain until he offered it to Nancy. Why did she come back anyway Bev asked? Oh I don't know maybe she was just homesick, I said. I doubt it, said Bev. I asked if she could get another hobby could you still race tomorrow. The dead line to inter is today at 3:00 p.m. Bev said. Well is there another hobby that you could barrow or rent I asked? No rentals she said but my uncle has one for sale. Where is it I asked?

It's right behind the club Bev said, come on she said, I'll show you. The hobby looked as if it had been there for years. I said it looks like its 20 years old. Bev said it could be more, my uncle won his last race in this hobby. Have hobby's changed much over the years I asked? No she said there exactly like they were. Well I said why not ask you uncle if you can barrow his hobby for the race. That's a waste of time Bev said, my uncle is an old sourpuss. Where is he I asked? Its Saturday, he in the club bar getting drunk she said. Let's go I said, no I'm not going to ask him besides that old boat might not even float not to mention sail she said, No I won't do it. What's his name I asked? McGregor she said David McGregor. Come on I'll do the talking. We walked to the clubs bar with me in the lead. Bev stopped at the door and said she couldn't enter. Why I asked, well for one thing, I'm under age. Which one is he I asked? The one with the hat she said. I walked right up and said, good afternoon, I'm looking for the owner of the fine-looking hobby cat out back. Mr. McGregor looked up at me and said you're looking at him. Sir do you think that boat could ever race again I asked? That's the fastest hobby cat in Jamaica he stated. Well Sir I said your nice Beverly wants to race tomorrow but she's without a boat. Oh yeah he said whatever happen with her racing with that boy Mark and his hobby? Well, I said her sister came in from Miami today, and Mark pushed Beverly to the side so that Nancy could race with him. Well he's a damn fool to do that if he wanted to win Mr. McGregor said, a damn fool, Beverly is a better captain than he is. Then he said the hobby is for sale, ifin she wants to buy it. How much are you asking I asked? Mr. McGregor said $5,000.00. That's the price for you nice I asked? That's the price for anyone he said. I said that I figured that the hobby was worth about $2,500.00 but that if he could have the hobby in the water and ready to race tomorrow morning at 7:00 a.m. I would pay the amount of the $5,000.00. I said I needed everything to be in good shape and the bottom and sides buffed and waxed. Mr. McGregor agreed. I stuck out my hand to shake his, He stuck out his hand to receive money. I said I would advance $1,000.00 so that he could ready the boat, and the balance to be paid at the time, 7:00 a.m. tomorrow morning. Once Mr. McGregor received his $1,000.00 in cash, he then shook my hand. Are you a betting man Mr. McGregor I Asked? On occasion he answered. How about a bet that Beverly places in the race, say $1,000.00. If she doesn't place I pay you $1,000.00, if she places you pay me $1,000.00. If she comes in second you pay me $2,000, and if she walks away with first place you pay me $3,000.00. So Mr. McGregor said if she comes in 4th or worse you'll pay me another $1,000.00? Yes I said, he said it's a bet and we shook hands. From his bar chair Mr. McGregor called in Beverly and told her to go fetch Joseph and little George, they're around back working on the Englishman's boat. Yes, Sir, Beverly said, and she was off. How about a beer young man Mr. McGregor asked? No thanks I said I have a taxi waiting out front. Beverly came back with the men and Mr. McGregor handed them the key to his locker and said they were to go over his hobby and have it ready to race and in the water by 7:00 a.m. tomorrow morning. I said and don't forget the wax. The wax I said must be 100% covered on the bottom and sides, then buffed with a cotton buffing wheel that fits on a disk grinder. Whatever you don't have let me know now so we can buy or barrow what we will need. I handed Beverly money for their lunch and said I'd be back as soon as I checked into a hotel. They all agreed to start working now and not stop until finished.

As I walked up to the taxi, the driver he said I owed him a bunch of money; I handed him a $100.00 bill and told him to drive to the best hotel in town. I told him to tell me when I spent $80.00

I had no problem getting a room and asked the hotel to get me reservations for dinner at two different restaurants, the best in town for tonight and tomorrow night at 8:00 p.m., dinner for two. The hotel said their restaurant was the best in town, but I told him no hotels and something with a view. Once in my room I called the office looking for Karen. Karen had gone for the day, so I asked the girl to find her and have her call me at my Hotel after midnight. The plan is that again we would change our Monday morning trip to Savannah for Wednesday morning. I needed my return flight changed from tomorrow evening to Monday morning. I'd be back in Miami then.

I changed clothes to jeans and a T shirt and went back to the front desk. I asked where to buy nice young women's wear and the woman gave me the name. I told the taxi driver to take me there. I guessed about Beverly's size and picked out clothes that I liked. I spoke with the shop's owner and left a deposit on my credit card. I then took one of his Taylor's, and we left with the clothing and shoes I had picked out plus the Taylor.

Once at the club I found Beverly and marched her into the women's bathroom. The Taylor worked with her almost an hour before they came out. Bev walked out and right by me without a word. The Taylor said that Bev was difficult but he had the information he needed to work. I said I needed it all today and rubbed my fingers together. The Taylor left with the Taxi driver. I then took a look at what was going on with the hobby, Bev and her Uncle were there with the two men that were doing most of the work. Bev walked over and asked what the clothes were for? She said her mother wasn't going to like it very much. I asked if she liked the clothes and she said she liked the clothes but she didn't think she should accept them. I said that she would dine with me tonight, but she said she didn't think her mom would let her go with me anywhere after dark. Besides she said I have plans for tonight. I'll talk to your mom I said.

I asked about gloves, a stand out seat and line. Bev said that she hadn't ever used the seat. I asked where a boat supply store was and we both got another taxi and left for the store. At the store I found everything I was looking for. Gloves, the seat and line, hats and two smart looking life jackets. We then returned and placed the purchased items in her uncle's locker. I asked to see Marks hobby, the boat looked new and the bottom was without any wax. Bev said she had never seen anyone put wax on the bottoms of the boats.

It was about 5:00 p.m. when Beverly's uncle said, he was calling it a day. He came and said that his sister would say yes if we promised to stop by to visit his mother after we were dressed. I told him thanks and we'd see him tomorrow morning. No he said I'll see you both tonight. Beverly's grandmother lives at my house.

The original taxi soon arrived and Beverly and the Taylor were soon back in the bathroom. The Taylor came out and gave me thumbs up. Then he handed me the bill for which he charged on my credit card. I asked what I owed him and he said that he had made the most beautiful girl in Jamaica, which only cost me $500.00. This besides the cost of the clothes. I told the Taylor $200.00, and he said $400.00; we settled at $300.00, which I thought was fare. I threw in another $20.00 for a taxi back. Our taxi was full of boxes.

It was now almost 6:00 p.m. and the reservation was for 8:00 p.m. We were cutting it close. The taxi took us to Beverly's house where the three of us carried in the boxes. Her mother was cooking dinner, Nancy and Mark were out somewhere. I explained to her mother that I saw the look in Beverly's eyes when she heard Mark ask Nancy to sail with him tomorrow and decided to do something about it. And the boxes her mom asked? Well, mam, I'm asking if Beverly can dine with me at the Sea Shore restaurant. I purchased some clothes just in case, I'll have her home before 11:00 p.m. and I promised your brother to come by and visit your mom on our way to dinner. Please mom Beverly asked? Ok her mom said, but I want Beverly home before 11:00 p.m., you understand young man she asked? Yes mam, I said. I told Bev I be back in an hour and to be ready. I returned to the hotel, showered, and changed into my black suit.

I was back at Bev's house a few minutes longer than I expected. I did tell the desk person to call the restaurant and tell them that I'd be 30 minutes late for dinner. When I knocked on the door, Beverly opened the door. There standing in front of me was a Princess. Bev's mom was right there when Bev opened the door. Bev's mom said she had told Bev that it was customary to make me wait before she came out. I couldn't help but say it, "I've never seen anything so beautiful before" and I wasn't lying. Bev's mom started to tear up. Her mom said you'd better go before I change my mind. We got into the taxi and were off to her grandmother's house.

I didn't know that her grandmother was very sick and bed redden. Mr. McGregor had let us in and we went right into her grandmother's room. Gramdmother's eyes lit up the entire room. She was so happy, she called me over to her bed and looked at me while holding my hand. She looked at Beverly and said, now this is a man that you shouldn't let go of, this is a real man she said. Her grandmother asked Beverly where was her little girl that came to visit her almost every day? Are you happy her grandmother asked? Bev as nice as she looked, said I'd be happy when I win that trophy tomorrow! I understand your name is Jim but what do your friends call you her grandmother asked? They call me the king Fish, I said. Her grandmother looked at her son then they both looked at me. Beverly's grandmother asked her son to bring in her jewelry box. As he came back into the room he handed his mom the large box. Open it please my son she said. Beverly nor myself could see inside the box but her grandmother pulled out a beautiful neckless. Your grandfather gave me this neckless when I was just about your age. All of us back then also called him the King Fish. My David, your grandfather found this and much more at a ship wreck that he found while diving on a black coral head that came up from the sea bottom and ripped the bottom out of one of those Spanish ships a long time ago. I remember my David said surly those Spaniards must have thought they were in deep water, my David said that in all his years of fishing and diving's he had only seen one rock like that in our waters. I was saving this for you in my will, but looks like it would go mighty fine with what you're wearing. Put it on her would you David she asked of him. The jewelry sparkled around Beverly's neck. The center piece was something similar to what I had seen before. Well, her grandmother said, you run along and have a good time. I know I'll be seeing more of you young man. She kissed Beverly and whispered something in her ear. Beverly's uncle walked us to the door and said that the neckless was genuine and that Beverly should take it to a safety deposit box on Monday. She kissed her uncle and we were off in the taxi.

We arrived at the restaurant another 30 minutes behind the time, I apologized to the maître, and he said our table was still waiting. The view was breath taking. I'm talking about Beverly. The window view at the restaurant was Montego Bay. Beverly was all smiles, she said she had never been to one of these fancy restaurants. Beverly said both her mom and grandmother liked me, especially grandmother. Bev asked how I got the name the King Fish, I told her it was a long story but that I was a fisherman when I was a boy. I wanted to hear about her. How about, you I asked any boy friends in the picture? How old are you and what grade of school are you in, what about hobbies? Well she said, I'm 17, no boyfriend, lots of boys that are friends, a senior at school and I like sailing. What about you Bev asked are you married or engaged. No I'm single. I have several girlfriends, I too love to sail, fish and dive. So she asked, have you ever sailed a hobby cat before? No mam I never have even been on one. I sailed a small wooden sailboat to Nassau when I was 15, I now own a 35 foot Morgan. We ordered our food and talked and talked, ate and talked some more. The food was good but the company was better. The time had passed by quickly and a glance at my watch indicated that we only had 15 minutes to get her home on time.

We made it to her door at 11:00 p.m., the door step light was on and Beverly opened the door. She thanked me for a wonderful day, all the nice things and dinner. I said it was me that thanked her for her company. I said I would be there at 6:30 a.m. and to please have eaten a good breakfast.

At the hotel I received my midnight call from Karen and she confirmed my airline changes. Karen asked about Nancy and told her that I hadn't seen her since arriving at the airport.

The next morning Bev and I were at the Club at ten minutes to 7:00 a.m. The boys were still getting the Hobby ready. It was in the water but looked like they were doing some rigging adjustments. Mr. McGregor was here to collect his money. He had a big smile on his face as I counted out the 40 $100.00 bills.

Our hobby was the only one in the water, once I hooked up the hanging seat, I said we were ready to shove off. Bev said that the race didn't start for another three hours. I said for us it had already started. I told her to use the bathroom, get a drink of water and let's shove off. We sailed on out to the bay and I asked Bev to show me what she had. The boat was fast and Beverly sailed with confidence. After 30 minutes I said let's now try it with using the seat. I had two lines, one in each hand. One that held me to the boat and the other in the chair that was hooked to the top rigging. I could literally stand on the hobby's side rail molding shifting my weight where it was needed to produce the most speed. Of course it wouldn't help if I slipped and or fell over. We practiced and practiced me shifting my weight and coming about. Once we had this down pat, we worked on having the hobby at the starting line right at 10:00 a.m. The markers were placed right at 9:00 a.m. Still we were the only boat out there practicing. We both had watches and the 9:30 a.m. cannon sounded off to set everyone's watches by. The next cannon would be the three-minute mark. We had practiced this 3-minute drill over and over. If the wind didn't change before then, we would be right where we wanted to be at the 10:00 a.m. cannon. It worked just as we had planned and practiced. At the shooting of the 10:00 a.m. cannon we were the first to cross the starting line. The race was on. Both Beverly and I were wearing matching life jackets. Bev had on a bikini top, shorts and tennis shoes, me I was wearing an American flag speedo bikini and tennis shoes. Both of us had on a USA hat. Around my neck I worn a small pair of sport binoculars and a whistle.

Looked like Marks boat didn't get a great start but they were moving up toward the front of the pack. We were out front but Mark was catching us. Why, I couldn't understand how it was possible. Beverly also saw them moving up and yelled that she had told me he could sail. Stay to the port as much as you can so he'll have to past on our starboard I said loudly. Let them pass she asked? The way their coming we might make the next marker before they catch us I yelled. I then jumped up on the port side rail almost standing at a 45-degree angle. Our new speed slowed their gain but they were still gaining. Mark's boat was now only 10 feet behind us. We were going to just touch the turn marker at our port. Mark saw that he wouldn't be able to go to our port so he stayed on our starboard. As we came up on the marker Marks hobby was right alongside of us. Mark was so close to us he had to know we couldn't come about without hitting him. Mark had Nancy on their port side, if we came about our boom could hit Nancy. I then saw his plan was to get us to pass our turn and then he would drop back and cut us off. At the marker I slid across the stern taking the tiller and started blowing my whistle warning of a possible collision, then coming about. It looked like our boom was going to hit Nancy but instead I caught the line not permitting our boom to cross the line over to their boat. Our boat didn't lose a beat and I was back out on the starboard side rail.

We had startled both Nancy and Mark. As we had come about Mark had to go off to their starboard then come about to head for the marker which they had missed by 50 feet or so putting them a good 75 feet behind us. Mark must have been boiling that his plan didn't work. Beverly new what I had done and knew that she wouldn't have done what was required. Now with a good lead I used the binoculars to study Mark's sails. I was sure his jib was over size. If so that could explain his speed. What was going on now was that he and maybe Nancy too had been a bit shaken up with almost getting hit by our boom. Beverly still hadn't said a word. As we made the final turn marker Beverly knew that Mark's nor any other boat could or would catch us. Bev looked at me a said in a loud voice, I know Mark, he will protest. Don't worry I yelled we were in the right. I'm sure the judge's boat heard my whistle. Our last leg of the race didn't require my weight in the chair. As we went over the finish line the cannon roared. We were first by a good 100 feet.

We then made sail for the club. Bev wasn't quite as happy with the win as I was. I was sure that Beverly didn't like what we had to do to win.

Just as Bev had said, just as soon as Mark's boat made it back to the dock he went into the office to protest. Bev said that she didn't think we had a chance even if we were in the right. As Mark came out of the office. I met him half way. Good sailing, I said. Yes he said, and in the end I'll have my trophy too. I said, according to the rule book we had the right to come about at any time to make the marker just as long as our pass was clear. I also blew my whistle to give you fair warning of our turn. I didn't hear any whistle Mark said. I'm sure the judges heard the whistle I said. We'll see Mark said. Mark started walking away and I said, don't make Beverly protest your over size jib. You will be disqualified for sure, you still have time to remove your protest and receive a second place. Mark stopped in his tracks. He turned and looked at me, paused and said one on one I can beat you. You taught Beverly well, why not take the credit for that. Eventually if the teacher is good enough the student will always one day beat the teacher.

Mark went and removed his protest. Beverly was declared the winner. Beverly was still not happy until her uncle made it back to the docks. Mr. McGregor was aboard one of the larger boats watching the race. Just as soon as he hit the dock he walked straight over to Beverly and congratulated her on the best sailing that he'd ever seen! That whistle he said and that move, where did you learn that move he asked? Mark and Nancy were right there too, Beverly looked at me and then Mark and said that Mark had taught her. Mr. McGregor looked at Mark and said well young man you've done a great job teaching my nice to sail, good job son, well done and shook Marks hand. Well then came the trophy. While Beverly had the trophy in her hands I had Mark help her up and I held Beverly up over my head with her body parallel with the ground. While up there several photos were taken. Pepsi was one of the sponsors and once back on her feet asked us again to get her back up there with a can of Pepsi. Of course we repeated the seen, this time being bare footed, wearing only our bathing suits and Beverly holding up that Pepsi with the boat and trophy in the background. The photos were just incredible. With Beverly now feeling better about the win she was happy. Her uncles pleasure came to a halt when he had to count me back 30 of the 40 $100.00 bills that I had given him in the morning. Thank you I said, what will you do with the hobby he asked? Why not ask the new owner I said, pointing to Beverly? The hobby is mine Beverly asked? Yes mam, you earned it. For the first time Beverly jumped into my arms and kissed me. Her uncle gave me thumbs up while I could see Nancy saying oh my God. Mr. McGregor said drinks were on him. The hobby still had to be taken out of the water and put away. We then passed by Beverly's grandmothers to show her the trophy. Her grandmother was just as happy as Beverly. We then went by Beverly's house to show her mom. It was now 4:00 p.m. and I again asked her mom's permission to take Beverly to dinner. Her mom said that Beverly had school tomorrow and needed to be home by 10:00 p.m. at the latest. Nancy and Mark were also there and Nancy asked that we all go out together. Beverly looked at me like that is what she wanted. Yes, the four of you their mom said. Nancy said that Mark and she would give a ride to Beverly not to make me have to come by in the taxi. I quickly said I'd be there at the house at 7:30 p.m. sharp to pick Beverly up. I asked Nancy to call and increase the reservation to four from the two we already had. Beverly walked me to the taxi and asked if bringing Mark and Nancy was ok. I looked at her and said that with or without them, I wasn't going to be able to keep my hands off her. I looked at Beverly's hands and they were shaking. How do you mean that she asked? I mean you're the most beautiful creature I've ever seen in my life and I just want to touch you, kiss you and hold you. Her hands shook even more. I open the door of the taxi and stepped into the seat. At that same time, she pushed me in and also sat and closed the door, when the door was closed she kissed me and said that she too wanted to hold me and not let go. The taxi started to pull away and I said to stop. We kissed again and then I reached over and opened the door. I looked at her and said the short dress, no pantyhose. See you at 7:30 p.m. I watched as she walked to her front door where her mom was watching.

I of course wore the same black suit and that same cologne that I always wore. This time when I got to her house she wasn't ready, but she certainly was worth the wait. This time just looking at her took my breath way. Beverly had a short black dress with a low cut top, the same neckless but this time a diamond ring on her right hand. The ring was her grandmothers that her grandmother had passed to her today when we visited her. Today I thought that Beverly couldn't have looked better under any circumstances but I was wrong. Her mom walked us out to the taxi and said to have her home by 10:00 p.m. Her mom said that she probably wouldn't be seeing me again and that it was nice of me to bring Nancy back home.

Once in the taxi not 100 feet from her house Bev was about sitting in my lap. She said she wanted to go anywhere but to the restaurant. She said take me back to your room. I smiled and said we wouldn't be going anywhere but the restaurant, you don't want me she asked, that's the problem? I said I do want you. Are you ready to go home with me tomorrow? I asked. She said yes. No you're not, you don't even know me. I don't care she said. Let's do this right I said. Going home with me would turn your entire family against us I said. Now we're going in and have dinner with your sister.

As we walked into the restaurant everyone stared at us. What are they looking at Beverly asked? You I said, their all looking at you. Table for two the Maître d' asked? No its for four I said, the Maître said of course right this way. Our table as under a light, I looked at the Maître and asked for a table with less light, he understood right away.

We sat on the same side and when we were seated my right hand was ¾ up her dress. I ordered the waiter to bring his best bottle of champagne and put it on ice alongside of the table. He was to open it when the other couple came to the table. As we were kissing, I heard Nancy's voice say, I see we're just in time. As they were seated the waiter came and open the champagne. My toast was to the best two hobby cat captains in Jamaica. With the toast Mark said that Nancy had said I was quite the Captain myself. How many fishing boats do you have he asked? Five I answered. And a girl in every port Nancy said. Before I could answer Beverly said and he now has one here too. That answer stopped Nancy from saying anything more on that subject. Mark asked what other businesses I was involved in? I said I also had several other businesses that kept me more than business. Mark then said that Nancy wouldn't be going back to Miami, he said they had decided that she would look for work here in town. Well that's a surprise I said. Nancy's boss will be lost without her. It seemed my hand was being moved upward on Beverly's leg. It wasn't me it was Beverly. Nancy said well I might need to go back until my boss finds a replacement. Mark said that won't be necessary. We ordered our meal and talked about life on the Island. Beverly said she always dreamed of settling down and having lots of kids. Nancy said Jim's dream is to sail the world looking for adventure. And your dream Nancy I asked? The time passed by so fast. It was going to be difficult to get Beverly home on time. We'll take her home Nancy said. No I said that displeasure will be nobody's but mine. Just blocks from Beverly's house I told the driver to park and take a walk.

I asked Beverly if she could come to Miami on Friday, Beverly said that would be impossible until she was 18 and that would be 4 more months. Bev said I could come back every week until then. I told her I be back but didn't know when. Beverly said she didn't even have a passport to travel on. We stayed in the taxi until almost 11:00 p.m. Bev didn't want to leave me and I didn't want her to go. I left her door at 12:30 a.m.

The next morning, I was up early, my same taxi was waiting at the hotel's front doors. The driver said he was sad to see me go, not for just the money he said, it was for my style. I said I would miss him too, but to be sure I would come back soon. This time when the driver gave me his card, I put it in my wallet. I paid him his charges and then gave him a handsome tip. I then also gave him another $200.00 hundred for things like flowers that he was to deliver to the McGregor's house for grandmother and of course flowers for Beverly and her mom.

At the airport I got two surprises. One Nancy had decided to return to Miami, and the next that Beverly had come to see me off. What, no Mark I asked Beverly as I held her. Mark doesn't know Bev said. Nancy has decided to break off the engagement. Beverly said that in Miami Nancy had made lots of friends and their father well he would just have to live with that fact that Nancy won't be marrying Mark. Beverly then asked me what I had said to Mark for him to withdraw the protest. I told him that we would protest his oversize jib that he was using for the race. Mark's jib was 25% larger than the rules permitted. What we did was use the rules to win, Mark was breaking them to win. Beverly asked if Nancy had known about the sail. No way had Mark told her I said. Nancy wasn't talking much and had boarded the plane. I boarded at the last call. Before I left Beverly took the ring that her grandmother had given her from her right hand and moved it to her left. I'll wear this until you give me one or you don't come back Beverly said. Everyone will know I'm spoken for, she then kissed me and said she would wait for my return.

Nancy didn't save me a seat, this even though there were lots of empties. I found her and asked the women sitting next to her if she minded changing seats. I sat down next to Nancy and said that it was just the way things worked out. Nancy put her head on my shoulder but didn't say a word the entire trip home.

I had an amazing weekend and it seemed unreal that I had found such a girl and felt the way I did. Nancy would be alright; she would have to deal with her father. I knew too that at least four months from now I would have to deal with him too.

Karen and I went to Savannah and then to Norfork to talk with the BBS representative there. BBS had told them that I was looking to open a New Facility up there by years's end. This wasn't true but I didn't tell them this.

The work week went well with Interpol Leasing calling for a meeting, they wanted me to purchase one of or both of their Miami depots and make one out of the two. They had visited our other locations and said they would just add to the already crowded yards. Seemed that their New York office wanted to distance themselves from the mob investigations that were going on. That Friday I would meet with both owners of their depots and it looked like I could come to an arrangement with one of the two. The owners that were willing to sell were the Garcia brothers. Both brothers had served at the Bay of Pigs and one I was almost sure was either CIA or had worked with them. It would be fairly easy for me to find out from Carson and or Bob. Both brothers were a part of the FBI's indictment.

The other owners were a part of one of the New York families, they treated me well at the meeting but said they could be partners but would not sell. The owner here was Vinnie Catroni. Vinnie was a bit older and had two grown daughters and a grown son working at the Family business. The second daughter was the only one of the four that hadn't also been indicted with that same group. Vinnie said he would like to stay in touch as if for any reason he or his son were to be wrongfully convicted then the company may then be on the table.

Here it was Friday night, I hadn't heard from Cat nor Diane. Seemed funny that I thought I had three girls but it looked as if I would be spending the weekend alone. I decided to wait and see what might come up. I had decided that the following week I would go back to Jamaica.

Friday night I went to the club and was sitting with the usual group when Nancy walked in with Beverly. What a surprise it was, Beverly had called Nancy and asked for her help, they planned it so Beverly would come over to visit their father for the weekend. Beverly's uncle had a lot to do with the Jamaica side of the family. Beverly's mom and dad didn't talk, about anything. Nancy had given in and was helping Beverly get to see me. Nancy later commented that she had done this for Beverly and not me. Beverly said that she and Nancy had until 2:00 a.m. to stay out. I hadn't mentioned Beverly to Karen but Karen picked it up just as soon as Nancy and Beverly walked in the club. The group was going dancing at the alley in the grove at about 11:00 p.m. I got up and took Beverly by the hand and said we see them at the Alley. I could see Nancy's concerned face but I said we'd meet her there. Beverly didn't ask anything she just held my hand as to not let go.

We left the club and got in the vet and headed to my apartment. It was two of the best hours I had ever lived. Bev was amazed by wow I lived. She said that she knew just what she was going to do for the next two days. She said we were going to stay in bed. Beverly asked if I had ever taken Nancy to my apartment. I said no. It seemed that Nancy and Beverly had talked quite a bit. Bev said her father wasn't to know anything about our relationship or that she and Nancy had seen me. I agreed for now but not for long. We arrived at the dance club at about 1:30 p.m. with Nancy looking relieved and saying we had time for just one dance. Nancy said she would do her best to be at the Morgan at 2:00 p.m. It was understood that if Nancy and Beverly didn't show I wouldn't be leaving with the others. Joe was on his way driving from Savannah and would be here at any moment. I walked the girls out to Nancy's car and got my kiss good night and said I would either see them at the boat tomorrow at 2:00 p.m. or I' be at the 1800 club waiting for them starting at 6:00 p.m.

I waited until their car disappeared and then went back into the dance club. Karen was dancing but when she saw me come back in she stopped dancing and came and sat down next to me. What you going to do with that girl Karen asked? Why don't you just you find a girl from Miami she asked? Karen said that if Nancy and Beverly showed up tomorrow that I should give money to Nancy for her to stay in a hotel. Karen said that she had spread the word that no one was to show up tomorrow at the boat so she could be alone with Joe. You and Beverly would be fine she said but not Nancy too. I agreed and told Karen not to worry.

The next morning, I met Joe at the Dunkin Donut and then visited our three facilities. Nancy and Bev didn't show up at the boat. Joe and Karen would get their small honeymoon. I told Karen that I would most likely see them down at Elliot as I would come in the Donzi if we could. Joe said he'd be ready for some skiing by that time.

I met Nancy and Beverly at the club, we agreed that I'd return Beverly at the 7-11 four blocks from their father's house at 1:00 AM. Beverly had told her father that she and Beverly would go sailing Sunday morning. We agreed that Sunday morning Nancy would drop off Beverly at the Dinner Key Marina at 7:00 a.m. Beverly's flight home would be at 8:40 PM Sunday night. I thanked Nancy for all her help, Beverly and I went back to my apartment, then dinner at the Studio and then back to the apartment. Besides the obvious we talked and laughed a lot. She said her mom had taken her to the doctor and they, her mom and she also had talked. Bev's mom wanted her to study in Jamaica after high school. Not get married but study. I said that once she was 18, I wanted her here with me. The UM was as good as any of a University. Beverly asked about marriage. I said at the end of the first year we would marry. That was good enough for Beverly but she would talk to her mom. What's to talk about I said. Beverly said her mom and grandmother would want her to be married before living with me.

I somehow got Beverly to the 7-11 on time. I was up early Sunday, I had changed Joe's truck for my Vet. I picked up the Donzi had it fueled up and was waiting at the marina by 7:00 a.m. Beverly asked if Nancy could come along. I said, of course. We motored on over to and stopped on Key Biscayne and had a champagne breakfast. From there we were at the Morgan's side by 9:30 a.m. giving Karen and Joe lots of time to sleep late. The skiing was great, Beverly loved the Donzi and the sailboat. Joe and Karen had liked Nancy but they could see this thing with Beverly and I was quite different. We pulled up anchor at about 2:00 p.m. and we were towing the Donzi. At 3:00 p.m. Nancy, Beverly and I left in the Donzi back for Miami. We would arrive and had the Donzi back on the trailer by 4:00 p.m. Beverly and I took the Donzi back to my house in North Miami and Beverly got the chance to see the house. By the time we got back to the apartment it was time for our first shower together. My that was nice. By the time we showered and caught a short nap it was time for Beverly to be at the airport. At the airport we said our good-byes and agreed that I would come to Jamaica in a few weeks. I would go from the airport to Joe's house to change cars.

The next morning a caught the red eye for Savannah, Karen would ride back with Joe helping him to drive, Savannah was an 8-hour drive from Miami. They would leave at midnight and arrive before 10:00 a.m. Karen asked if she could spend the week up there and I agreed.

The Savannah depot was now doing good; in a short time, we had turned the depot around from a $10,000.00 a month looser into a $20,000.00 a month winner. Sales had almost doubled from when we started; our 2% charge for managing was now like $8,000.00 plus a month.

I would be back in Miami early this week, George Barone the ILA president that had also been indicted, had called for our once a month lunch. At the lunch George said he was happy to see that I wasn't afraid of the dogs that were hounding him. George said he wished he had been as lucky as me to have had so much wisdom at such an early age. George asked if I knew that there had been a New York play called West Side Story that he was portrayed in the play. I said that I had heard of the play but hadn't know they had him in it as one of the main characters. George was proud of this. George said that he had been betrayed by the same people that he had helped make rich and powerful. Your different Jimmy he said, seems you made your own luck. The only difference between you and I he said is that you're smarted than I was. Be smart he said, get rid of that Harrison, he is bad news. If you don't get rid of him first, he'll get rid of you. George seemed proud that he felt that law enforcement was watching us eat. We didn't talk much business except for Harrison; George was keyed in on Harrison.

Lee had sent a message that our dock was ready and 100% working as we had planned. Lee said that the Navy men were now requesting that he take them fishing and diving, no more bar fights. Janie and Betty were now at the apartment as Janie and Lee wanted their new born to be born in the USA and besides Lee was concerned about the Nassau hospital. This weekend Lee would be flying from Nassau to Miami. The Chris Craft and Captain Mike would be adding an extra day in Nassau to accommodate Lee. The Navy had nothing but good things to say about Lee and his work. It would have been a good weekend for Cat to come visit but she said with Betty being gone she was shorthanded. She asked that I travel to Nassau. I would go to Jamaica instead. I stopped by Miami Diamond Exchange and picked out some things, not so big and not too small. We would now be able to return her Grandmothers ring. My visit would be a surprise; I didn't even tell Nancy. From the Montego Bay airport, I went straight to Beverly's house, where I found the house empty. I then went to grandmother's where their car was parked outside. It was quite late for them all to be at her grandmothers and I worried as to what was going on. Turned out that Beverly's grandmother had another stroke and was paralyzed on her left side. Grandmother was awake and her eyes lit up when I walked in the room. Beverly was feeding her as I walked in and kept right on doing so. I walked up to her grandmother and pulled the fine box out of my jacket. I looked at her grandmother and said I had come to return the ring that she loaned to Beverly. She immediately closed her eyes and starting shaking her head. I then opened the box and said that I would exchange her ring for mine. When her grandmother saw the ring a smile and tears rolled down her face. I walked around to the other side of the bed and kissed Beverly. I took her grandmothers ring off her left hand and placed it on her right. I then took my ring and put it in her left. Now all three of the women were tearing up. The first words that her grandmother had said then came out, "I'm happy" she said. Beverly said, me too grandmother, me too.

It wasn't going to be one of those weekends where Bev and I got too spend any time alone together but we did become closer. I also became closer to her family. Beverly said she would come to Miami in a few weeks and stay with me the entire time. I left Sunday night.

This Monday morning it wouldn't be Savannah; it would be Norfork. This was again one of those meetings that Mr. Collins of BBS had put together. This time Harrison wouldn't be involved, this time it was the BBS agent there in Norfork. This time it was build the facility and the clients would come. Who was to build the facility? Us of course. The agent would provide the land, us the money and BBS would be the customer base and we would manage. This time there was no offer of a management fee. The property at today's market was most likely worth the $1,000,000.00 but they had owned the property for over 30 years. For the agent it was like they might win the lottery. BBS only had to move their business from one place to another and us well, we would need to invest cash and the time it would take to build and manage the company. We only owning 33 and a 1/3 % meant that we could be easily moved out. To top all this good news, the agent wanted to put their son in as president of the new venture. It took these good people 6 hours to explain their offer and only took me 3 minutes to say no. Actually it was no thanks. The agent acted as if I had wasted their time, Mr. Collins said that he wanted to speak with me alone. Mr. Collins said they had done allot to come this far and needed this to work. Mr. Collins said that BBS would put their profits from Miami and Savannah to make up half of the $1,000,000.00. BBS had already received their share of the profits from Miami for last year and I didn't control the money from Savannah. I said I would agree with a proxy of the BBSs vote until we had received our investment back plus 25%. This meant that BBS's profits would go to us until we received $500,000.00 from their profits plus their vote until we received 125% of our money back. BBS would also agree not to move or share their business with another facility. We shook hands and we walked back into the meeting with an agreement. When I left the meeting we had all signed an intent letter plus Peter and I had signed our side agreement. Mr. Collins didn't want their agent to know the details of our side agreement until after the signing of the contractual agreement. I was ok with this. Roth senior the owner of the agency invited me to stay the night. He said there were no flights out of Norfork after 6:00 p.m. I asked if we would be going to dinner and he said that they were all eating aboard a BBS ship that was in port. It didn't sound like an offer, so I though about maybe catching the train into DC or New York for the night. Roth said to suit myself and we all parted. Mr. Collins said that I wasn't missing much as there was always a lot of drinking at these kind of things. I called Karen to somehow get me out of town. Roth's office was locking up when she called me back saying for me to get to the airport and a helicopter would pick me up in the parking lot. Norfork was a small town that looked like it closed down at dark. The helicopter took me to Washington DC where I caught a flight to Atlanta then back to Miami. I told no one of the plans or agreement of Norfork. George Barone called our Miami office first thing in the morning. I was late getting into the office Tuesday morning. Monday afternoon Diane had arrived in Miami and called the office number, me not being there and Karen either, so the office manager had picked Diane up and took her to my apartment where he knew that at least Betty was there. By the time I got home Janie and Diane had gotten well acquainted. Janie hadn't sold me out and when I got home Diane was on the coach watching TV. Betty had left a note on the outside of the door. It read Boss there's a girl in your bed name Diane. Betty drew a skull and cross bone on the bottom of the paper.

Diane was in the pajamas that I had brought for her. She was happy to see me and said she was sorry that she didn't call. Really she said I couldn't believe that you didn't have a wife here. Janie had explained all about the women in my life to include Janie's and my short time together. I was beat and while Diane had moved into my bed and turned on the TV. When I was ready for my shower I came in from the bathroom, turned off the TV, took Diane by the hand and led her into the shower. That was that.

Like I said I was late getting into the office and the first thing I did was to make a protocol about what to do if any girls showed up!

I then called George and we would meet for lunch. George wasn't too happy about my Norfork visit and asked about what was going to happen. George had his head down and was whispering. He said that the present depot of BBS owed them money and he only collected if BBS stayed. I put my head down and said to him that it sounded like he should talk to BBS. George lowered his head again and said we are talking as friends. I won't lose our money up there he said. I won't look like I'm getting lacks in my old age, do you understand he asked? With my head still down and a serious face I asked how much they owed him. George looked both ways and whispered $90,000.00. I whispered back, do you need someone to help you collect your money? Then George's head straightened up and he slammed his fist on the table and said we're not playing here. I didn't flinch. The waiter came and asked if everything was alright. I said we're ready to order our food. George then calmly looked at the waiter and placed our order. George smiled and said sometimes I lose my temper. I knew this was going to get me one of those long awaited visits from the FBI. We had a good lunch talking about such things as sports and fishing. George said he liked to fish and said he had heard that I had a nice big yacht and wanted to know when we could go out and catch a few. I told him my Christ Craft was being used in Andros. George asked where Andros was. It's just one of those islands off the coast I said. I got to pay the bill this time, George said to think about what he had said.

I went back by the office and there was a call from Cat that said she would be here Friday for the weekend. She most likely made that call just as soon as Janie called her about my visitor. I thought that could work out just fine or maybe not. Diane would be leaving tomorrow, Wednesday afternoon and Cat coming in on Friday. Cat and I had never discussed other women before. If I had to choose from Diane and Cat, Cat would win every time. If it were Cat and Beverly, I would have to do quite a bit of thinking. Let's hope that doesn't happen. Besides, really I didn't have any of the three. I was still sleeping alone most of the time.

Diane and I would go out that night and be home early. Diane had made it clear from the first night that she had visited the Doctor's office. Diane said she was from the Grand Bahama Island, which we all knew as Free Port. Diane had gone to school to learn how to deal cards wanting to get a job aboard one of the cruise ships. Diane said the cruise ships wanted mostly married couples to work the ships. Most men taking a cruise were married or brought along their girlfriend. The management didn't want the wives to feel that their husbands were on the ships for the girls. Living in Nassau was kind of boring as the only thing to do was water sports. I asked her about the money she made and was surprised that it wasn't more. Diane said the manager asked a lot of questions about me. Why me I asked? She said that she didn't know why but they said if she needed more time to take it with full pay, please don't let them know I mentioned that to you she said. They can play rough when they want to. Gambling is a rough business I said. Any celebrities come into the club I asked. The club has invited several heads of state like Baby Doc and his mother. I also dealt for an older blind man from Dominica. Although I didn't see them, I was told that Castro himself and his brother Raul had been there. They said the security was tight. Well I said I would like to run into either Baby Doc's mother or any of the Castro's. Then I laughed. Diane was nice to be around, I would pick her up for a late lunch the next day, do some shopping and then drop her off at the seaport. Diane said she wouldn't come again without calling. I said to take up her bosses offer on spending more time here the next trip. Come in on a Friday and spend the weekend going back Wednesday afternoon. Diane asked if I would call the next time I was in Nassau, I promised I would.

Karen showed up on Friday afternoon, I asked her how the honeymoon went, she just smiled. I said that Cat was coming in the afternoon and I wanted her to pick her up at the seaport and feel her out. I told her about Diane coming in while Janie was here. Woops Karen said, I'll do my best. Karen then asked where she should take her, I said I'd meet them at the 1800 club. Karen gave me the thumbs up.

I was at the club by 6:30 p.m., no Cat or Karen. I guessed that Cat's plane had been late. Since it was Friday there were lots of people including people that worked in our offices and customers too. Nancy was there too to brief me on her grandmother's health. Nancy said that her Grandmother wasn't doing so well and that Beverly was actually staying at her uncle's house. I didn't hang very long with Nancy as Cat would soon be there. It was almost 8:00 p.m. when I saw Karen coming around the corner. Karen had this big smile on her face. Two steps behind Karen was Cat. Cat looked like a million! Her hair was cut and done up and she was sporting a new dress that made my mouth water. I had been sitting, but by the time Cat got to me I was there with my arms open. Cat gave the kind of kiss was that normally saved for the shower or in bed after the shower. If there was any question of how she was before that kiss there was none afterwards. On Cat's first bathroom break Karen came and asked if she did well? I asked how much I owed her and she said Cat had paid everything with cash. I said it was a job well done and asked if Cat knew about Diane? Karen said that Cat hadn't mentioned it.

Seemed everyone was going dancing. I couldn't remember the last time Cat and I had danced. Cat and I got home at about 3:30 a.m. Somehow we didn't make it into the shower. Cat hadn't yet mentioned anything about Diane. We fell asleep and the next morning Betty fixed me breakfast and I was out the door by 7:00 a.m. Lee had come on the same flight as Cat. Janie was due any day now and Lee wouldn't go back until the baby came. When I got home at lunch time Cat still had on PJs. Cat said she'd just like to stay home with me today and tomorrow. She took my hand a pulled me back into the room and shut the door. It was shower time. I knew she knew but something was different. Cat was much more intense with her affection. Don't get me wrong I was enjoying every moment. That night we dined out at the Studio and then back home. Sunday I got up and was reading the newspaper out on the balcony while Betty cooked breakfast for us all. I was expecting Betty to bring me my coffee but is was Cat. Cat said it was the first time she had seen me reading the newspaper or stay home. Must be the company I said. How about doing this more often Cat said. What, I said reading the paper or staying home? Both Cat said. Where here or over there I asked? By ourselves or with kids? I was thinking if we had our own then then having Wendy Michelle and Johnny close by wouldn't be so bad. What do you think she asked? Are you saying that you'd like to move in here without the kids? I'm saying that we could build a house for Jacob and the kid's right next to the beach and you and I and our kids could live in the beach house, Cat said. And this is when I asked? Now Cat said. You staying or leaving today I asked? Cat turned and walked back inside. When I went to look for her I found her crying in our bed. Why did Deanna have to leave us she asked? Why? Can't you see Jim if I don't take care of those kids, they'll be separated. Jacob is a mess and drinks every day now. It's getting harder and harder to control his drinking. Get him to sign a paper and bring the kids here for havens sake. I rather have you here with the kids than not to have you here I said. Cat then said that she knew about my other women and that it hurt so badly. She also said that she knew it was her own fault. Come I said get dressed, were going to eat and then go show you the house. Lee and Janie also wanted to go. You'll have to take your car I told Janie; with that big belly you'll need all the space you can get. Cat did laugh at that. We all ate and then we were off to the house, as I shut the door Betty asked if we was moving again?

The house was a little musty but clean. Most of the furniture was just as it was when Mare and I had lived there.

Cat said the house was fine as it was. The kids wouldn't have the beach but they would still be able visit Nassau. While Cat and I were in the master room she asked if I could be happy here with her and the children. I said if she could get awarded the children and if she could get permission to move with them in and out of the country then that would be acceptable with me. I reminded her that my intentions were to sell the container business in two years. Then we could move back to Nassau. We would buy a larger sail boat and do some cruising with or without the kids. Two years I said I still need two years. Cat shut the door and pushed me on the bed. I bet if you gave me the chance I could talk you right out of that two years she said. Ok Lee said were leaving now. Saved by the bell she said. I got up and called out to Lee. Hey, I said just because you can't doesn't go for both of us . What about the Donzi Lee asked, still run like a top? No I said it runs like the wind. A hurricane to be exact I said. Lee said Janie was getting tired and they were heading on back. Cat reminded that she needed to catch the afternoon flight. Well I said looks like the fun is over. Cat said she wanted to do some shopping at Public's for some things she would take to Nassau. I dropped Cat off at the seaport at about 3:00 p.m. I said we had kind of left things open, Cat said you will come next week right? I'll be there if I can I said. Cat said and oh yes you can take me to the new playboy club. I hear you're lucky at Black Jack. She turned to walk away and I gave her a hard slap on her butt. Cat turned as she walked and said she loved me. I stayed until the seaplane took off.

CHAPTER XIV

THE ATTEMPTED KIDNAPPING

Yeap, from there I just had to stop at the 1800 club. As I walked in there was Carson sweet talking a new girl. Carson saw me come in and told the girl I was his father. Dad, Carson said out loud, how about a drink before you have to get back to the old folk's home. I sat down and the girl had already made my drink and had it waiting, Carson looked at her and said I thought you were new. The phone rang and one of the girls on the other side said it was for me. I took the phone; it was Larry from New York. Larry said that Benny was away on a hunting trip, Benny's mother was on a cruise and Jena's guard hadn't made his 4:00 p.m. check in and the phone seems to be off the hook. I said I'll be there in 10 minutes and hung up. As I ran, I said to Carson lets go. Carson was right behind me, we jumped in the vet and took off. I told Carson to turn around in his seat and open the box. In the box was an AR-15 with a 40 round clip inserted and a pump 12 gage riot shot gun. Carson also pulled out a vest of which I told him to put on. We hit the causeway doing about 100 MPH. we slowed to make the Starr Island turn. As the vet slid around the corner and flew across the bridge we passed by a Miami Beach police car parked facing us. By the time he put on his lights we were sliding into a left turn two blocks up. I took a right at the next street. We could see a late model car making a right at the next corner. There was a White panel van parked across the street as we pulled up to the house. I pulled up as to block the van from driving forward. Both Carson and I jumped out, him with the shot gun and me the AR-15. The vans side door was still open as if someone had just gotten out in a hurry. I yelled to Carson to tell the police to have someone block the bridge. Cover the front I said as I ran around the left side of the house. When I got to the pool I saw Jena in the pool with a young man. Jena could see my concern as I yelled to keep low, get out of the pool and get behind me. I ordered the young man to stay in the pool and not to move. Me facing the back doors of the house and Jena at my back we backed up until we were at the pool house. We entered and I put Jena in the bath room. I took off my jacket and told her to put it on. I drew my Beretta and asked Jena if she remembered what I had taught her. Jena said yes. She saw me put a bullet in the chamber and take off the safety. I told her to lock the door behind me and to button up the jacket. Don't open the door for anyone accept for me. Anyone that tries to open the door shoot 5 times at the door and wait, if they come back, shoot another 5 times, remember you have 15 shots. I then started heading across the yard to the back door. As I went in I saw the guard asleep on the couch watching TV. With caution I shook him but he didn't move. I relieved him of his gun and headed for the front door, before I opened it I called Carson's name. I opened the door and Carson said it was all clear. I waved him in and I ran back to Jena. Jena I said, it's Jim. Don't shoot me. Put the gun on safety like I showed you. Jena then opened the door and I took the Beretta and holstered it. I asked whom the young man was, she said she had met him last night. I asked if he had slept here, she said yes. What's his name I asked, Jena said John Roberts. I sent Carson to check the house. When he returned with the all clear I told Carson to watch Jonny Boy while Jena and I went stairs to check Jonny Boys ID and get Jena some clothes.

Just as I thought, his name wasn't Roberts. By now the Beach police were at the opened door and I could hear sirens coming. The police knew Jena as I thought they would. I said that we were family friends that came when the body guard didn't answer the phone. The phone lines had been cut. I said to call an ambulance for the Guard as he was still out. I was sure he was drugged. When the first Metro police officer showed, Carson asked them to call the FBI and report an attempted kidnaping and to notify Big Ted. I keep an eye on the man in the pool reminding him not to get out of the pool. I asked Carson if he had this as I wanted to get Jena gone from there. Jena quickly told Carson and me that she had met he young man in a bar in Fort Lauderdale the night before. The policemen didn't like me leaving with Jena but they didn't stop me. Carson walked us to the car returning the shot gun, pumping out the un-used shells. I said I would take Jena to my apartment until Larry got down here. I also told Carson that in my opinion the Beach cop that was sitting at the bridge was serving as a lookout. Carson said he would do what he could here and get a ride with Big Ted back to his car. Carson said he'd stop by on his way home.

I took Jena straight to my apartment. Oh well _____ happens I thought. Cat was not going to believe a word of this. I guess I could have taken Jena to a hotel or even to the North Miami house but I thought that Jena would be more at ease at the apartment. After all she had once just about lived there. The door man that parked the car saw me with the AR-15 and didn't even flinch. Once on my floor we entered the apartment and Jena walked right to my room saying hello to Janie and Betty. As she shut the door I told her to get Larry on the phone. Janie called Lee when she saw me with the rifle. Lee was napping and came out and asked what was going on. I said that someone had just attempted to kidnap Jena. Jena then called me into the room where she had Larry on the phone. Larry I said, Jena is fine. You should get down here ASAP as it was an attempted kidnaping. Your man at the house should be at the beach hospital. I believed they drugged him. I told him what I knew and that I thought that at least one police officer was involved. The main thing is that she's ok. Larry asked if he should use the jet and I said to just catch a flight. She's ok here for tonight I said. Ok I'll be there tonight and pick her up tomorrow morning at about 9:00 a.m. Jena had shut the door and when I put the phone down grabbed me with a hug. I pulled back the sheet and turned on the TV, rest for a while, your safe here I said. I went out and shut the door. Janie asked, why bring her here? I said because it's the safest place I know of. Lee if you want you could take Janie to the house and spend the night but it's a much closer drive to the hospital from here. We'll stay he said. I walked into the kitchen and asked Betty what was for dinner. Cooked goose she said, yours just as soon as Ms. Catherine hears about this. Cooked Goose.

Carson showed in about two hours, dinner was just being served. Carson said he loved a good home cooked meal. Jena slept though dinner. Carson was acquainted with Janie but not Lee. Carson made the crack that he knew of Lee's father's partner Mr. Gianetti or as Carson called him Mr. "G". Carson and I excused ourselves to the baloney. Carson said Big Ted had arrived at Benny's mom's house maybe 30 minutes after we left. The young man said that two men had given him $2,000.00 in cash to go home with Jena and then today drug the Guard, cut the phone and open the front door. They said they wanted to rob the place he said, I didn't know they wanted to take the girl he said. Carson said the young man was told that most likely they would have left him dead at the scene. The FBI had arrested the man, and said he had several arrests but no convictions. Carson said he could spend the night if I thought I needed him. I told Carson that I'd see him during the week and to please keep his ear on the ground.

Betty made the cot for me saying she didn't think I'd use it. Betty as always when guest were here slept on the couch. It was 2:15 a.m. when Lee came out and said that Janie's water had just broken. Lee and Janie left for the hospital and I was going back to sleep when Jena came out and said she was hungry. There were left overs. Then Jena wasn't sleepy and wanted to talk. At 5:00 a.m. Lee called and said it was a little girl and they maned her Deanna. Lee also said she was white. White I said, how disappointing I said. Lee laughed and said he had also called his mom. I hope she knows she needs to book a hotel I said. Lee understood what I meant by that. Lee said mom and baby were doing great.

I called Karen and said I'd be late to work. Karen said I was making this a habit. Karen said if you can't pay the fiddler then I shouldn't dance. I wondered where she had heard that before.

Larry knocked on the door at 9:00 a.m. He asked Jena if she was ready and Jena said she wanted to stay. Larry said that she would go back to New York for a couple days. Larry said that her father was on his way back from his trip and wanted her home. Jena went into the room to get her things. She called me in and shut the door behind me.

She said that she had never gotten over me and now I had surely saved her life. I'll never feel safe again she said. It's all my father's fault. She then kissed me and said she would call Cat and tell her I was a perfect gentleman. Anytime you wish to misbehave please call me she said. Jena and I then walked out into the living room, Larry then opened the door and he and another man walked down the hall way with Jena.

Betty said she wasn't going to praise me for behaving myself with that woman. Betty said, it would be like swimming with a hungry shark and throwing in a bucket of blood. You'd just be asking to get eaten Betty said. Ifin you were going to sleep with that woman I was going to throw in the bucket of blood, Yes I was Betty said.

When I got to work there was a telex saying our Norfolk agreement was ready to sign, they would send several signed contracts and needed me to sign two originals and to transferee the money to the listed account. Karen asked what to do? I said that when we received the contracts to copy one and hand deliver to Roy. Nothing more nothing less.

Karen wasn't told anything about yesterday's little adventure but she took calls from the Miami Beach Chief, Benny, the FBI, Big Ted and if course Carson. Then Karen buzzed me and said that the FBI was there asking to see me. I thought it was about Jena but it wasn't. These guys wanted to know what was talked about during my lunch with George. I told them that it was a thing that he and I did every month. He's the president of the union and provides me with labor. As most law enforcement duals do. One was the good guy and the other the bad guy. I didn't like either. The bad guy said I wasn't to get smart. I said that third grade was my three favorite years of school. Then I told them one of my favorite jokes about the boy that picked up rabbit pellets all the way to school and sold them to his friends telling them they were smart pills. Some of my friends finally said they didn't believe the pills were making them any smarter and that the pills also tasted like crap. The ones that kept buying them all year did graduate and all went into law enforcement. The ones that said the pills tasted like crap had gotten smarter. Neither agent liked the joke. The one agent stood up and said let's just send over the IRS, the other told him to sit down and give me a chance. He then asked what had made George so mad as to pound the table. Well I said George wanted his money back. You see I said George also said the pills tasted like crap. Then the first one walked out but the other stayed. My friend doesn't like you very much he said. I said threatening me with the IRS is illegal but send them if you must, I prepay my taxes.

You won't help us he asked again. George has never asked me for any help or money I said, our relation has always been on the up and up. He may be guilty of whatever he's charged with. But you know what, I would be with him just like I'm with you. The answer is no. The last time you gentlemen didn't like the truth, you did send in the IRS and it did cost me about $300,000.00 whether I owed it or not. But since then I hired out my accounting and they have guaranteed me that if I need to pay something additional they we'll pay it. I'm a straight forward business man that employs lots of the local people in town. I'm not a crook so stop treating me like one. The man got up and left. As he walked out I couldn't believe my eyes. It was Benny sitting in my waiting room. I wondered if he or they had noticed.

Benny I said, so nice to see you. I opened my door and he came on in, please have a seat. Benny asked was that the, and I said yes. Sorry he said I should have called first. Don't even mention it I said. Well Benny said what do you know? I know that your daughter picked up some guy in a bar and took him home. They didn't have to take her from your mother's house they could have done it much easier. They wanted to make a statement. The beach police was there as a look out. That SOB must have radioed whomever was at the house that we were coming. I'd start with him and you should make it quick. They won't leave any loose strings if you know what I mean. This is odd you coming to the rescue Benny said, I think these people are the ones that want me and you out. Wait just a moment I said why mix you and me. Well Benny said my spot is always waiting for some ambitious group that wants what I got. In your case you have the only waterfront business thats not run by the mob. They'd like to have you on board but if not they'd like to have it without you. Word is that you've wrapped up Norfolk and the group that's losing the business say their contributions to the funds and more important the insurance money will dry up like it did in Miami and Savannah. I heard, Benny said, that it might be easier to get rid of a standing President than you. How many misses have you had? Well I said there's not too many people that can say they've been shot by one of the men that shot JFK. And there's another reason you're not liked Benny said, you think you know it all. I hope you still like me Benny! Come on Benny said this is serious. Well the last time I told you I could be interested in selling, I didn't get any offers? Maybe they think it's cheaper to just get rid of you Benny said. Are you armed Benny? No he said my parole doesn't allow it. Well I said I want the names of the people that want our jobs. What for Benny asked? Let's take a walk I said. Outside I told Benny that I liked him. I don't have to trust you to like you but I'd rather have you where you are than someone else. I have obtained lots of information, some of it is not worth much, but some, however, could be used to change the thinking of others. Most of what I have is in film and photos. Many of your associates are caught on film that they wouldn't want anyone to see. Benny said that black mail wasn't a good business. I said it's not black mail. If anything happens to me all that film goes to the FBI. I also have how and why the waterfront is so important to for the mob to control. All is irrevocable evidence. This includes a sitting Senator too. Even you Benny, I said. Your parole wouldn't be worth the paper is was written on. Drugs, underage girls being sexually abused with them screaming to stop hurting them. Benny said to stop. That was long ago Benny said. Yes, and you too were being black mailed by Michelle. Yes Benny said, yes she was black mailing a lot of us. If I thought, you had her killed I'd kill you myself I said. But here we are and someone's already paid that dept. I want the list. Once I have it I will work to keep you on top and me alive. No black mail just samples.

I told Benny that I had found film of Deanna's sister Wendy at just about the time she disappeared. She was with a very well know man that was being pretty ugly with her. At one point she seems to have stop breathing and she's wrapped in a sheet. Wendy was 18 at the time but there is another underage girl in another film too. That girl was located and we have her description of what happen on an additional tape. Seems the King Fish did have something to do with Wendy's disappearance. Michelle could have had good reason to want to get rid of the King Fish I said. Whether the King Fish fire was an accident or not, no one missed him and I'm sure that no one has or will lose any sleep over it.

Benny asked if I rescued Jena for her or him. Benny I said if they took her you would be without, without whatever ransom you paid, without your daughter and without a Job as the head man. He looked at me and said for whatever the reason thanks. I'll get you your list. Benny said he had heard the story of when I was younger, people use to ask if I was part Bahamian. Now that you've grown up that Italian blood has taken over.

That night at the 1800 club, Ted, Carson and I met in the back room. Ted had security sitting just outside the door. We talked about the attempted kidnaping and what we knew and didn't know. We knew that the officer that we thought was being the lookout had called in sick this morning. The FBI had gone to the Beach Police Office in the morning but the officer hadn't come in to work. They visited his house and neighbors said he had come home and left again yesterday at about 7:00 p.m. I said I thought it was early for Benny's men to have gotten him. It was most likely the kidnapers that had him, if so we agreed that he'd be found as a suicide or they just wouldn't fine him at all. The young man was a different story, he was still in jail as of this afternoon. He had confessed to being a part to what he thought was going to be a robbery to include he admitted drugging the guard. The Guard was still in serious condition from the overdose that he was given. The Doctor said the Guard was lucky to be alive. The FBI said they were going over the $100.00 bills that the young man was paid, this to check for any matching finger prints. The van was stolen and whomever drove it wore gloves. The only thing found in the van was sand on the passenger's side's floors. The sand was like dredged up sea bottom. The FBI had checked and there were only two spots on the way from Miami on the cause way that a car could pull over. One of those spots had the van's tire marks plus another car's tire marks and what looked like one set of shoe prints coming from the one car to the van. It wasn't much but it was something. Judging from the tires and the weight of the vehicle it was a large car with firestone tires. Carson said by tomorrow they may have the breakdown of what cars use those tires. The shoe size and weight suggested a man of about 240 pounds and most likely over 6 feet. Damn Ted where were you yesterday I asked jokingly.

I told them about my visit from the FBI and Benny. I couldn't believe it I told him, they passed right by one another. I mentioned to them that It reminded me of the movie, The Longest Day when the German soldiers were marching one way on one side of a small hedge and the American soldiers were walking on the other side going the opposite way. In the movie the last soldier in the American group only noticed at the very end that they had just walked right pass one another.

Ted said they had tried to keep a lid on the attempted kidnaping but that the word had gotten out and that everyone on the Metro side was talking about it. Ted said the word was out that heads were going to roll at the Beach office. I told them that I had asked Benny for a list of his enemy's and it looked like we would have it soon. Ted said that Jena should probably be on Benny's list. What Ted meant was that Jena was just looking for problems. Ted still had 11 men that were in our security group. Our fund paid them like a reserve check of $500.00 per month. For that money they would train together at least once a month. When activated on an hourly basis they receive $30.00 per hour. The daily combat rate was between $1,000.00 too $5,000.00, depending on the risk. Ted was on duty so he didn't stay long. When he left the security stayed.

I asked Carson that he take the lead in the Kidnaping investigation. Carson said that he was called by Benny and that they had also met before Benny returned to New York. Carson said he hoped I didn't mind. Carson said that Benny had offered him money for his support yesterday, I didn't take the money Carson said. I'm glad you didn't as I'm about to start pushing back. Benny claims he's being pushed by the boys whom were collecting from the business that can no longer pay up. I have told them I won't pay anything but the union dues that's in my contract. I looked at Carson and asked if he had a third safe at his home? Carson said no and that has garage safe was full. I told Carson that he would be the only one that had access to the Michelle films. The ones that he was working on were copies that I had made myself. I let Carson know that I had now taken all three apartments on my same floor. I would be moving into the three bedroom. My new master bedroom had two walk in closets. Now it only has one. The entire closet was made into a safe. The new safe is bomb and fire proof and I don't think even Houdini could get in. I have a will that would allow you to get in with two other people at the same time. I told Carson that the will states that when I die all the information and film I have goes public. I'm going to start to use the information I have, no black mail, we don't need money we need security. I'll be waiting for that list. Carson said that Benny had a lot of respect for me but thinks you stick your neck out to far. I noticed that your vet had has some modifications. It's a lot heavier than it was, I could hardly open the door, am I right Carson asked? Yes, it's slower too I said. I have a new BMW being worked on right now I said. Maybe I won't be able to out run them but I will be able to out gun them I said. Carson and I wrapped up our business meeting and went to sit at the bar.

Lee would be bringing Janie and little Deanna home tomorrow and on Friday they would be heading back to Nassau. Janie was planning on staying at the beach house with Cat and Jacob with Lee returning to work. Betty would stay with me. It would be good to have my place back. Carson was the first to know that I was moving, well sort of. The safe in the two bed room would be dismantled and moved to the North Miami house. This would be the second safe in the house, both were good but the safe from the apartment I considered my first masterpiece. Miami safe was doing the new insulation and two of the three locks. The base would be there for the third lock but I would do the insulation personally. Betty would move in the following week. Even though Betty would have more work, there she would have her own room and bathroom. No ocean view but her own room.

At the bar I told Carson that I would most likely go to Nassau over the weekend. It would be my last scheduled trip for a while. Carson said he was going to stay put to see what happened with this kidnaping thing. The bar phone rang and it was Larry, the little pain in the butt had escaped from the house. Larry said she could be headed back down here. What a Bitch I said. Larry said they would have people posted at both airports. There was also a man posted at Benny's mother's house, grandmother whom didn't know anything about the attempted kidnaping was still on the cruise. I thanked Larry for the news and went and sat back down and told Carson the good news.

The next day I few to Norfolk to sign the two agreements. The first with BBS concerning the money advance and their voting proxy, then signing the agreement with Roth Sr., BBS and myself. Before signing either of the agreements I informed them both of the concerns of the ILA and the Mob that everyone including Mr. Collins said didn't exist.

We also agreed that all three groups would finance all the equipment required having all three groups sign on the dotted line. Once we had everything signed I called Karen and had her transferrer the money from a US bank. The property that we would be building on was an ex Bus factory that was closed many years before. The ground was 90% pavement or concrete and the buildings all still in fair shape. Joe would love this place in the summer but the winters would be bad. I told Karen that she should find a place out on the beach with at least three bedrooms.

The week went by quick, no word on the kidnapping or the where Jena was. If someone had her they hadn't called yet wanting to pay us to take her back. If they had her and she could talk, they'd soon be calling.

I had been regularly calling Beverly, her Grandmother was still doing poorly. Beverly's birthday was coming up in two weeks. I told Nancy I would gladly pay her flight so that she could relieve Beverly for three days. Nancy said she would ask for the time off.

Lee and Janie were already in Nassau and Lee would go back to Andros with Captain Mike on Sunday. I flew out Friday afternoon and Cat was there to pick me up. We went right to the apartment; our shower was like a honeymoon. After the shower while getting dressed, Cat mentioned that Jena was staying at our boarding house. Cat said she should have called me but Jena said you knew she was here. Janie had told Cat of the whole kidnap thing and Cat thought maybe I was hiding Jena out here. No way I claimed, I didn't know and her Father is worried sick over where she might be. That bitch I said! I called Benny's New York office but got no answer, I called him at home but he hadn't reached there as yet. I tried to contact Larry and the same, I couldn't reach either of them. I left messages for them to call me in Nassau.

From there we went to see Willy, Willy said that Jena had been in to see him several times. She talks too much Willy said. She can't stop talking about you Captain. Willy said she kept saying she couldn't understand why you would pick Cat over her. Pardon me he said but, what a no brainer. I asked Cat to call the boarding house and try to reach Jena. Cat gave me that I don't want to look but she called any way. Cat left a message as Jena was not in. Cat and I started talking about us and the kids. Cat said she was ready for me to talk to Jacob as she was worried and even a bit scared of Jacob's drinking. His drinking had become an every day and night thing. Willy said not to look at him because Jacob didn't drink there. Jacob was no longer working and eating very little. Cat said maybe he'd listen to me. Jacob's father had recently been appointed a judge. Cat said that he too was concerned about Jacob but when asked about getting permission for the children to leave Nassau he barked and said he would not allow it. Nor would he allow for Jacob to sign over John Paul over to us. The Judge didn't approve much of me or for that matter for Cat either. The part about Cat was sad because the Judge knew it was Cat that was taking care of the kids. Cat repeated that she wasn't going to permit the children to be separated. Here we were right back in the same place.

It wasn't another 10 minutes before Jena walked in in shorts and a bathing suit top. Jena said she had been at the beach all day. I asked if she had talked to her father and she said no. Jena said she was paying everything in cash, not using her credit cards. Jena said her father most likely knew where she was as she had seen Pilar at the playboy club just last night. Jena said she asked Pilar not to call her Father but she was sure she had. One of my father's men checked into the Boarding house at midday. He was waiting for me at the boarding house when I returned from the beach, she said. I asked if she knew the man, and Jena said oh yes, he's one of my Fathers men. Where is he I asked? Sitting on the bench outside she said. He's ok he saw you in here. Jena said she was having dinner tonight with Pilar, Baby Doc and Baby Doc's new girlfriend. I'm sure Pilar wouldn't mind seeing you Jim, your all she talked about. No thanks I said Cat and I have plans tonight. Cat then said we'd love to go. Jim promised to take me there this weekend and I'd like to meet Pilar. Cat asked what time the dinner was and Jena said the show started at 10:00 p.m. Jena asked if she should wear her Voodoo outfit, then laughed. Jena said that last night Pilar was wearing the Ring that I gave her.

We only had one boat that had come in so far, Mark was now making three weekly crawfish trips to the west side of Andros, they would be returning tomorrow afternoon, and Mike should be coming in at any time now. I wanted to see our new dock on Andros but I would like to take company and spend the weekend. The next weekend was free so far and then the following week I'd be going to Jamaica or Beverly would be going to Miami. The boat that returned first was Otis with the "Johnny". The crawfish numbers had dropped a bit so we had decided to move the traps away from the reefs and see how long it took for them to come back strong. The new spots had fewer crawfish in each trap but we were pulling more traps. Otis said he had a full load but had pulled 23 traps. The crawfish size was about the same.

Standing on the dock's side walkway, looking down into the boat and remembering the old days, I could almost hear Michelle call out, "all clear, no boats," as I came up from a treasure dive. The "JOHNNY" had been the first boat Michelle and I purchased to hunt down our first treasure find. I'd be diving alone while Michelle was topside, watching that other boats were not around to see what we were doing.

Otis brought me back, asking you alright, Captain Jim? Yes, Otis how's that girlfriend of yours doing I asked? Otis said if it wasn't for this job he and she would run away and get married. How does the job stop you I asked? Cat had walked up and heard the last part. Cat said not to encourage the boy. We'll talk later I told Otis.

Peter had ordered and installed two new engines. The Johnny had now changed out motors three times. The Cuban working in our shop behind the tourist store had proved to be a wise investment on my part. Not once in eight years did we lose a single motor while out on the water. In fact, we repaired motors for others too. The Cuban worked wonders with wood and fiberglass too. While Cat was talking with Otis the second and third boats came in. They, too, did well. Peter and the Hatteras were gone; they had made a trip with a family from Canada which had been pre-booked for over six months ahead of time. Harbor Island was their destination. Cat said that one day she'd like to Captain a boat like the Hatteras. Cat said I would be the only crew member.

When Cat and I got back to the bar, Willy said that Jena had left to start getting dressed. I asked Cat if she had her long black pleated pants. Cat said she had them ready at the apartment. Cat said I would have to wear my 007 suit. Yes Cat said, she had read the note that was attached. She then mentioned to Willy whom had written the note and what it said. Willy didn't comment, he just smiled.

I wasn't too happy about going to the Play Boy Club for dinner. But maybe, just maybe Pilar would keep Cat's mind off of wanting to meet Diane.

We went back to the apartment and talked a bit more, I wanted this thing with the children solved before I left Nassau. What was Cat going to do? If she wasn't coming to live with me in Miami, then maybe Beverly would and if not Beverly then maybe Diane. The truth was I just didn't like sleeping alone. Seemed I was always rolling over reaching for a warm body and finding an empty bed. Not all the time of course but most of the time.

At about 9:00 p.m. Larry called and I told him the news, he said they found out Jena was here and sent someone right away. Are you going to come get her I asked? Larry said no that Benny said she could stay as long as she didn't make too much trouble. Trouble I said! Her middle name is trouble. Larry said that if I wanted I could bring her back with me. Ha ha I said that's so funny.

CHAPTER XV

BLACKMAIL

Larry said that Pilar had called earlier in the day looking for cash as Jean-Claud and his girlfriend were into the casino for $300,000.00 and Pilar said it was going to be difficult to raise the money. What was Benny's answer I asked? Larry said he was sure that Benny didn't say it to her directly but that he was tired of them asking for money. Benny had business with them and was always advancing them money. Any way Larry said that Benny said he would send $100,000.00 on Monday.

I asked Cat how much cash she had in the safe Cat said that she had maybe 7 or 8 thousand. Other than that I asked? Cat said she had never looked at or counted the other money. The safe had three sections. One was two loaded guns, my 32-20 long the other a 357 magnum, both revolvers from the old treasure days. One section was jewels of which Cat would pick something out for tonight. The other was cash and papers. I pulled out the cash box and started counting the stacks of $100.00 bills that were rubber banded in ten thousand. There were 22 packs or $220,000.00 in there. I then looked for my old sack that I started moving my first gun back and forth from Miami to Nassau and back. I first put my Beretta in the bottom hide away and then the $220,000.00. Cat saw what I was doing and asked if I was going to gamble with the money. Nop, I said, but I might buy some beachfront property. I told her what Larry had said about Pilar asking for money. Cat had heard that Pilar and I had traded favors in the past but asked? You don't trust those people do you? I don't need to I said. I asked Cat for her purse and put my 9MM Browning in the bottom, and asked her to put her cash on top. Just before we were ready to go I looked at Cat for the first time that evening. Cat had on a satin gold short sleeve shirt with the arms edge folded up once. Under that a black bikini type top, the shirt was out and unbuttoned. Holly molly I said. I grabbed her and told her that we might not be going, Cat said she wanted to meet Diane. When we get home if I'm still talking to you Cat said. Walking out, I had my stainless mini 14 Ruger in one hand. In the other hand I carried the pouch with the money. We wouldn't be driving, we walked out the store front and hailed a taxi. Once the taxi was at the door, I placed the ruger inside the store door out of sight and locked up.

At the Play Boy club doors, the door men made a quick check on me for a weapon. He opened the pouch, saw the money and waved us on, once inside there was mention who we were, and I was rechecked. This time they asked Cat to open her bag. She did and a women stuck her hand in touching only cash. I asked to be escorted to the Baby Doc table. As we walked up to the table Pilar got up and greeted me with a hug and two cheek kisses. Fat boy Baby Doc didn't bother to even stand. Pilar said, so this is the young lady I've heard so much about. Please she said be seated. As the seats were arranged, there were not two empty seats together. I asked to rearrange the seats and Baby Doc objected. He looked at me and asked me to sit next to his mother. I pulled out the empty chair that was next to Baby Doc for Cat and whispered that if he touched her to slap the crap out of him. I could tell Pilar was happy to see me, but Baby Doc was not. Someone said the seating was so, as Baby Doc was uncomfortable sitting next to Jena as he thought she was an evil spirit. I told Pilar that, it was the nicest thing that I had heard anyone say about Jena in some time. Baby Doc liked that. The sad part was that I wasn't joking. Pilar asked what I had in the pouch? I told her it was my shopping bag. She asked what I was shopping for tonight. I replied a bargain. The show was starting and Pilar stood and took my hand, come she said let's walk. Pilar looked at Cat and asked for permission? Cat said to bring me back in one piece. I stood and passed by Cat to kiss her, as I bent over to kiss her she dropped the Browning in my coat pocket. I whispered she was so smart and to watch the bag and not the show.

Pilar took my arm and we walked outside of the show room. The Club was crowed, this I thought because the club was new and most likely taking customers from Benny's groups club. Pilar asked if I had brought money from Benny? I said no I brought my own money. Pilar said that Baby Doc had brought with them $100,000.00, but him showing off for his new girlfriend ending up in debt almost $300,000.00. I said I had $220,000.00 with me. I said that Bob had once told me that Papa Doc had loaned him their Villa on the beach and that it was for sale. Is it still for sale I asked? Pilar said, that for $300,000.00 it was mine, however she needed all the money tonight. I told her I was almost sure I could get more but that I would have to go to the club. I walked her back to the table and whispered to Cat that I would be right back.

I then made my exit and got a taxi to the club. As I walked up the stairs at the Club Royal, a man stopped me to check for a weapon. He took my Browning. I said I needed to speak with the manager. I went to the desk and waited. The girl at the desk handed me the phone and I explained who I was and why I was there. You want us to give you $80,000.00 to pay a debt at the Play Boy Club, No, hell no he said. I asked him to please call Benny for his approval. He still refused. I then called Benny's house number and got ahold of Benny. Benny asked if Jena was in trouble so quickly. I said no it's me that needs the help. I need $80,000.00 in cash. I told Benny that Jena was with Pilar and that I was going to need the money to give Pilar. I told him I could return the cash in New York or transfer it back to him anywhere out of the country. Benny said I'd have the money in ten minutes, and that a transfer would do just fine. Within minutes I was escorted to the cashier and given the $80,000.00. I took the money in a cash sack and walked out. The man at the door handed me back my gun and I caught a taxi back to the Play Boy Club. In the taxi I again put the gun under the cash. I got out, the security made a quick check, and again only saw more money.

The show was still going on when I got back, I excused myself and took both bags to the bath room. I went into a stall and removed both guns. I then put the browning back in my right coat pocket and the Beretta tucked between my pants and underwear at my back's center, under my coat. I then took the bags and went and got Pilar to follow me to the cashier.

Once there we started handing in the money. The Cashier gave me a receipt for $300,000.00. I pulled out ten $100.00s and requested $900.00 in chips. The extra $100.00 was a tip for the cashier. Pilar and I then went up to her room where she wrote me a bill of sale for the Chateau of Port-de-Paix . The description read as a walled 10 acer site on the beach and bay, a two story main house of 8,000 square feet, two guest houses, servants' quarters, tennis court, both salt and fresh water pools with bar and kitchen, and horse stables.

The bill of sale was marked paid with the seal of Haiti and the signature of Pilar. There was also a spot for Baby Doc to sign which Pilar said we would get signed at the table. Pilar said you were looking for a bargain and you have one. Come she said let us see if this will change our luck.

By the time we got to the table the show was over. Pilar walked over to Baby Doc and put the bill of sale in front of him and said to sign it. He didn't even look at what he was selling. He signed the paper, Pilar gave it to me and said let us celebrate. She turned and said champagne. We toasted to our good health. I gave Cat the paper and about half of the chips. Cat said she was headed to the black jack tables, Pilar and Jena were right with her. I was sure that Diane knew that I was in the Club. Cat was pulling me by the hand. When we got to the table there were two empty seats Cat and Pilar sat down. Diane looked at them and said place your bets. Pilar looked at me and I gave her a hand full of chips Cat didn't waste any time she asked the dealer her name. Diane Mam she answered. Cat said I'm Jim's wife. Diane looked straight at Cat and asked Card? Cat said hit me, Diane said as you wish mam and smiled. With that Pilar turned and looked at me and said you men are all alike. One more seat was emptied and Jena took it and held out her hand. I said you women are all alike. All four women smiled. Pilar looked at

Diane and said I'm just a friend, then Jena said I'm Jena I'm Jim's ex. Then they all smiled again. I emptied my pockets of chips and put them all on the table and said help your selves' girls. I'll be in the bar.

No one said wait and no one joined me. I sat at the bar thinking if I was going to be sleeping alone tonight. I was asked several times if I was looking for company but each time I said no thanks. On my third drink Cat appeared and said she was ready to go home. She said they had spent all my money. I said you got plenty more and Cat said she just couldn't beat that girl. She took my arm and said let's go. I looked in her purse and the papers where still there. Cat said, whatever you put in my purse will stay there until you remove it. Cat didn't say a word about Diane during the drive home. The taxi stopped at the front door of the store door, I opened it and took the mini 14 in hand and walked on in.

Once upstairs I got the answer to my question, about sleeping alone. Cat didn't or said she wouldn't get into the shower. I watched as she took off her shirt then top and then those pants. It was great to take my clothes off at the same time and jump in the bed. Oh what a Friday night.

Saturday morning was already here, I got up to take a shower and received company, great company. I said it should be like this every day. Cat didn't talk. We dressed and went down stairs to eat at Angee's. Ah that food, crawfish fitters and conch salad. Oh yes and a cold coke.

Angee was happy to see us, I was happy to see her. Cat sees her all the time. As we sat eating in walked Diane with whom she called her uncle Tiny. Good morning Diane said, looking at Cat. I knew last night you wanted to talk to me, and I couldn't sleep good thinking of you. Tiny wanted to meet Jim so here we are. I was already on my feet but went and gave Tinny as she called him a big hug, Angee was right behind me. To Diane's surprise Tinny seemed to know Angee and I. Uncle Tiny Diane asked do you know these people? Tiny was holding back his answer, so I answered for him. We knew Tiny some time ago, we or I called him Goliath. We are all old friends Angee, Goliath and myself. Cat, I said, this is your uncle Goliath that you have heard about. Cat was now also on her feet. Diane asked? We're related, yes I said in a very special way. Come on Tiny I said let's take a walk and let these girls talk.

I walked outside with Tiny or Goliath as I knew him and tried to put my arms around him. It's been a long time I said. How is your brother and the children I asked? There all fine thanks to you Captain Jim he said. Sorry he said but this isn't my fault he said. Yes I know, I said, I just had to see her and when I did I just couldn't help myself from not getting to know her better. As we were talking Angee came out and brought Tiny some of her cooking. Angee asked how he lived so many years without her good cooking. I sees you haven't lost any weight Angee said.

I asked Angee how the girls were doing? Well Angee said they aint fighting as yet. So what's going on here Angee asked? Well I said when Ms. Michelle died Goliath's brother had done some dangerous work for me. Angee said I does that every day around here. Anyway I sent him to Freeport to live. We found Diane in a bad spot and I sent Goliath with Diane to live with Goliath's bother. Goliath and Diane have been there since then until recently when Diane got a job dealing cards at the new club. Sooo I said Goliath is back in Nassau for a while. Goliath said he too had gotten married and had three kids of his own. Angee was quick to say that she didn't get married and she too has an almost grown boy, Goliath you remember little Otis don't you, Yes mam he said, I do. Well he's the Captain of the "Johnny "now. Well I'll be darned Goliath said. Goliath said he was sorry to hear about Ms. Deanna and that he had found and visited her grave. Ms. Deanna had helped move Diane to Free Port Goliath said to Angee. Angee then hugged Goliath and myself and said we were good men. She then turned said she had to get back to work. As she opened the door Angee said she expect to see Goliath a lot more in her restaurant getting some of her good food. I turned and looked into the restaurant and Cat and Diane were gone. Goliath said that she's in love Captain Jim. She don't know everything yet but what she does know that she's in love with you. She was heartbroken when Cat gave her the news that you and she were married Goliath said. Hell Goliath we're not married; Cat just tells people that. I wonder where they went to, they'll be alright Goliath said. I went back in and finished my food and had some more. After eating Goliath and I walked down to the wharf to see our boats off. Captain Mike met us as we walked. I introduced Goliath to Captain Mike and explained what he was doing. Captain Mike was on the way to get some fixings from Angee. Otis's boat had already pull out and the other Bertram was just doing the same. I was happy to see Cat was down here with Diane. They almost looked like friends. I looked at Goliath and he just smiled. The girls noticed us and came up walking. Diane came and kissed me on the cheek took Goliath's hand and started walking. Cat then looked at me and asked just how many of us are there she asked? Like you and Diane I said, only two. How many girls have we tried to save, more than I can count. Cat then took two steps toward me and hugged me hard enough to yes, take my breath away. I love you Jim she said but I must put Wendy Michelle and Johnny's needs before mine. Cat then still hugging me started crying. She just didn't let go.

Once her emotions calmed she said she wanted to go back to the beach house. She asked if I'd come with her to see the kids and speak with Jacob. We went to her truck and were off to the beach house.

It wasn't quite 9:00 a.m. as yet, when we got there, Wendy Michelle was out on the beach playing with a neighbor's kids. The nanny had little Johnny out on the porch feeding him. Jacob was still asleep. I'm sure I was a rude awakening for Jacob. He was still wearing the clothes from the day before and not only smelled like alcohol, he smelled bad. I told him to get in the shower or I'd do it for him, he didn't fight me he went and showered. The house woman had coffee ready for him but no breakfast. I asked about food and she said that Jacob didn't eat it when she cooked it. He'll eat it today I said. She said yes Sir and went into the kitchen. The house was clean all except Jacob's room. Cat said again that the house women refused to clean in there because of the smell. I looked around his room and found empty bottles of beer and liquor. I looked at Cat and said there was to be no more liquor or beer in this house. It wasn't a request. I started making a pile of clothes and trash that I wanted burned. When Jacob came out of the bathroom he asked what I was doing with his stuff. I looked at him and said he was going to stop drinking and going back to work. I told Cat to call the store and get some clothes over here now. I want someone from the store here in 20 minutes by taxi with underwear, socks, pants, shirt and a pair of shoes. The house women then came to the door and said Jacob's breakfast was ready. Jacob said he wasn't hungry but my reply was he either ate it or I was going to stuff it down his throat. Jacob didn't like me too much but he knew I meant what I said. We all went into the kitchen and watched Jacob eat. I told Jacob that I had purchased a house in Haiti and I wanted Him and Goliath to go to Haiti. Jacob said he hadn't seen Goliath around here in years. Well he's here now and you and he will be leaving tomorrow I said. Cat asked what's the property like? I said I hoped it was as nice as Bob had described it to me. It was actually Michelle who told me about her and Bob's visit there. So counting the years that had passed, it could have drastically changed. I need you to go and register the property in one of the company's names. All I have is a bill of sale, but it is signed by the President of that country. Jacob only ate a few bites but at least it was something. One of the girls from the store showed up with his clothes and I wanted Cat to take him to town and buy more clothes as I was serious about burning what was in the pile. While you're at it I said, buy a new bed too. I took the Taxi back with the store girl, Cat told her to be careful of me and for her to sit in the front. The girl looked at me and asked, she's kidding right? I said apparently not.

I kissed Cat and asked if I would see her tonight? She looked and said she didn't think so. Sorry she said I have my hands full here. Besides she said Diane is waiting for you to call her. Cat said she had told Diane that we were not really married. Cat took my hand and walked me to the taxi. Where does this leave us I asked? Cat said she would always love me and she'd always be here waiting. She kissed me and swatted me on the butt. I got in the taxi and the girl asked again, Cat was kidding right?

Once at the store I went up to the apartment and opened the safe and took out three tapes. These were good copies that I had made myself at Carson's house. With the tapes and a small projector in hand I would walk to Jacob's father's house. Once there and at the gate, I called the gateman. First he told me to go away, but I told him who I was and that is was urgent. The gate man came back and opened the small door in the gate. The Judge met me at the house door saying he wouldn't give any permissions to move custody of John, no custody and no travel. Sorry to bother you Judge on a Saturday I said, but it has nothing to do with the children. Its Jacob correct he asked? Well I'm working on Jacob but what I'm looking for is some justice.

The judge looked at me and said the way he had heard it was that I took justice into my own hands. For an example I asked? The King Fish he answered, everyone knows it was you he said. And who's was always pushing that rumor I asked? Mr. Thompson I asked? Well the judge said Thompson always said you had the motive. And you are always causing trouble here on the Island of one kind or another. What if I could show you it was Mr. Thompson that had the motive. I have here the films and a projector, I'm sure you will find these three films of interest. The Judge said to come in. I was set up in a moment. I turned off the light and rolled the first film.

I told him the first film with the girl was taken on the night before the King Fish reported Wendy Johnson missing. In the film Wendy appears to be very near death or dead. A man was having sex with her body. The man starts slapping then punching Wendy trying to get her attention. At this point Wendy with her eyes and mouth open appears lifeless. The man is angered and kicks Wendy off the bed onto the floor. Throughout all this, the film shows several flashes of a camera. Please note the camera's man face as he moves in for a better shot of Wendy lifeless body on the floor. Yes I said, it's your own Mr. Thompson. The man that did the pounding on Wendy is a standing US Senator. The Senator's face is bloodied but when finished with the girl, his face is then cleaned with a towel. Wendy was placed back on the blood soaked bed and rolled up into the bed sheet and carried away dead. Please note the man that carries off Wendy's body, it is none other than the King Fish.

I then turned on the light, and while changing films told the Judge that there is said to be a living witness, that on the night of the Fire on the King Fish's boat Mr. Thompson was aboard the boat and a shot was fired into the King Fish's back. The girl in this next tape was aboard that night and had run and locked herself in the boat's bathroom. Mr.

Thompson then opened the engine compartment, poured gasoline into the bilge, then set it on fire.

I then again turned off the light and rolled the second tape. The tape again showed the same Senator having sex with a younger girl. When the girl does not return his kisses the Senator then starts the beating. The girl is beaten into unconsciousness. Even when the Senator sees she is unconsciousness he continues to have sex with her. Again the camera man is Mr. Thompson.

I then turned off the light and played the third film. This was the tape where Mr. Thomson was in the same room with Michelle and once Michelle fell asleep Mr. Thomson then takes the two derringers from Michelle. One from her purse and the other from a box in her top drawer. These guns were given to Michelle by Papa Doc of Haiti, who also was a regular visitor of Michelle. The Film as you see shows Mr. Thompson leaving the room with both guns.

At the end of the film I noted that Juan Carlos the drug dealer that sold the drugs to Mr. Thompson's son was killed with one of these same guns. The gun along with this tape has been in the custody of the Nassau police for quite some time. Mr. Thompson's fingerprints were found on the gun and both discharged shells. Yet he is still out there. I turned on the light. The judge was horrified! Judge, the two films have been turned over to Interpol, the FBI and the US Justice Department. The International community will soon see the films I said. At the time for some reason the Nassau police chose not to prosecute Mr. Thompson for the murder of Juan Carlos. But given the newly release film I think it prudent to reopen the investigation. If not, it will look like Nassau just turned a blind eye to it all. I stood up and the Judge asked what I got out of all this? Well like you said Judge everyone thinks I got rid of the King Fish. Now they can have someone else to think about. I may cause a few problems here and there but I'm not corrupt, I said. What do you think all those photos have been used for all these years? How long do you think this has been going on? Black Mail I said, even the Mob thinks that Black Mail is a bad business. The judge was still just sitting there staring at the wall. I got up and showed myself out. As I walked back to the apartment I thought, now that gave him something to think about. I wondered to whom would be his first call. Let the games begin.

I had a phone number for Diane and called about meeting with her before she had to report for work. She said she'd meet me at the park by the church. I also asked to speak to Tinny. Goliath came to the phone and I said I wanted him to accompany Jacob to Haiti tomorrow morning. Goliath asked me about Diane and I said I was going to talk to her at the park. At the park I asked Diane to quit her job at the Club and come to Miami with me until Goliath got back from his trip. Diane said she had worked hard to get this job. How about a job in Miami, I asked? Working with you she asked? Maybe I said. Will you go with me to talk to the club she asked? I will I said. Diane asked if I was going to see Cat tonight. I said no. Diane said she felt badly about Cat and I, I told her it didn't have anything to do with her. She said she understood but still felt badly. Diane asked where Tinny was off to. I told her that I was sending him to Haiti. She asked me if Tinny had worked with me before. I said that he had. I often wandered where Tinny got his money from, did you send it? In a way, I answered. Were you the one that saved me from the fire she asked? Yes, it was me I replied. With that Diane hugged me crying. She said, I knew it was, I just knew it. I pushed her back a bit and sat her on a bench. What do you remember about that night I asked? I remember everything until all the smoke she said. The next thing I knew I was in a fishing boat that was on shore on Andros Island. I was scared but my pocked had money in it and the people that found me were good to me. Sometime later Tinny came looking for me and said I had been lost overboard in a storm. I didn't remember Tinny but he was so big and kind I went with him to Free Port. Tinny said that a Guardian Angel had sent him to protect me from Evil. I said two things were very important here, one is that you do not repeat anything that had happen to you without me asking you too. The second was that our relationship started the night I met her in the casino. Please don't love me for anything that happened in the past. We had a fresh start that night and that's what is important. Since you were 14 years old you have lived from a trust that was set up way back then by a woman that left her fortune to protect children like you. You now turning 21 that money is yours to do with as you please. You don't need anyone, especially not me. Diane then hugged me again. And asked when we would go to the club. We caught a taxi and went to the club. There we asked for the manger and Diane thanked them for the job but said that she had gotten a job in Miami. They asked her to stay but I said that she would be leaving Nassau the next morning. The manager wished her luck and we all shook hands.

It was now almost 9:00 p.m. and I said perhaps we should call it a night. Come on I said I'll walk you home. Tinny had a small apartment in town. When we got there Tinny was there waiting. I said for him to be extra vigilant as the games had started. Diane asked what time we would be leaving I said we'd catch the 9:00 a.m. flight. Meet me down at the wharf for breakfast I said. Diane kissed me and I was off. I wasn't using a taxi I needed the walk. I wasn't hungry or sleepy. I walked on over to the city bar and sat with Willy. Willy said that Cat had called asking if he had seen me; Cat said you were acting a little strange and wanted to know if you were alright. Well here I am and I'm good I said. What's going on Willy asked? Well I said I'm about to go on or have already started my biggest adventure. I got up and went into the bathroom. I came back with the mirror from off the bathroom wall. I went behind the bar and set the mirror just where I wanted it. Willy not understanding what was going on asked? Why did you move the mirror he asked? Give it a while I said. Within 10 minutes two men walked by the bar looking in. Willy I said, when I say get down, do it. The two men re-approached the bar, with my back to the window I said to Willy get down and turned on the stool firing my Beretta at the men. Both were hit in the legs dropping to the ground. Both had guns in hand. Both returned fire as they fell. By the time they had hit the dock I was on top of them pointing the Beretta at them telling them to drop their weapons. As they did I kicked the guns into the water. I asked who sent them and the one said no one. I took a quick look then kicked him at his wound. The other one said Jose, Jose sent us. Jose Diaz. I looked at his arm and there they were, tracks marks. By now Willy was out of the bar and I asked if he had something to wrap around their leg wounds? You smart guys aren't thinking of pulling out maybe a knife are you I asked?

No, no they said. Willy came with two lines and I threw one to each so they could attempt to stop the bleeding. By now two policemen were at the scene. Both men were known to the officers. Within 10 minutes or so an ambulance came and took both men accompanied by one of the police to the hospital. By then several people had stopped by. I was back sitting at the bar. I didn't get the chance to drink my first beer while it was cold so Willy gave me another. I pulled out $500.00 and put it on the bar. Willy I said I hope this will cover the glass. Leave the built holes I said it adds character. Willy still a little nervous said that he could have been killed. He said you knew they were coming. Well I didn't know for sure but I did have an Idea. I then asked Willy for the phone. I placed a call to the Judge. Good evening Judge, this is Captain Jim. Whom did you call today about the film? I called the prosecutor, Mr. Hernandez he said. Well I said two heroin addicts just tried to kill me. They said a Jose Diaz had sent them. Anybody see the films I asked? Hernandez did the judge said, he came right over when I called him.

Deanna's father Mr. Johnson soon arrived at the bar. He said he would go talk to the prisoners and then pick up Mr. Diaz. I then asked whom didn't want them to go after Mr. Thompson for the Juan Carlos murder. Mr. Johnson said it was Hernandez. By the way Mr. Constable, the men's two guns are just off the dock in about 5 feet of water. Oh yes Mr. Diaz is armed with something much bigger that a 5 shot revolver. How about if I come along I asked. You've caused quite enough trouble today, thank you, he said. The one police that stayed had Willy and myself make and sign statements. Ms. Angee had come, Tinny and Diane too. As I looked in the mirror, there stood Cat. As she walked in, Willy said you should have seen him in action Cat. Cat said I've seen it all before. Someone made the seat on my right available and Cat sat down. I knew something was bothering you, Cat said. The Police were still there with big lights fishing out the two guns from the water. Cat asked if I was alright. I said I was just fine. Cat also saw the mirror that had been positioned and said you knew they were coming. Well I said I wasn't sure but did think it was a possibility. Who was it Cat asked? I'm afraid it comes from Mr. Thompson I said. That SOB Cat said. He'll probably be in the front row of our church tomorrow she said. Well I said at least I have an idea who he's working with. Diane was sitting on my left. I looked in the mirror and saw the three of us sitting together. Cat was the first to see the mirror and seeing me looking at us. Cat then said that if I was planning on sleeping alone tonight to forget it. Diane hearing what Cat said, quickly said,"I got this one".

There was no doubt that the police would find the guns, but as they brought the second one up the small crowd clapped. It was Saturday night, Cat hugged me and kissed me and said that if Diane couldn't learn the shower routine to just give her a call. Cat then looked at Diane and asked if she liked American football. Cat said that she should study up on the linebacker's role. When Cat said that the tears rolled down my eyes, they were tears of joy.

It was getting late, Diane said she be staying with me tonight. Tinny said he see us at breakfast at 7:00 a.m. I was pretty sure that there wouldn't be a second attempt during the night. I was wrong about the second attack, it happened in the shower.

The next morning, I gave Goliath the bill of sale for the Villa in Haiti, besides making the change of ownership, I wanted an on sight inspection. He was not to trust Jacob nor let Jacob nor the bill of sale out of his sight. Any signing of papers needed to be me not Jacob. I would fly in on Thursday or Friday to take possession of the property. I told Goliath that he should find a bank and I would send money that he could turn a part into cash.

Diane and I left Nassau on the morning seaplane flight to Miami. Betty when opening the door was surprised at my companion. Betty with her own way of showing displeasure asked Diane what she liked for breakfast. Betty said she was sorry but she just couldn't keep up with the traffic. We were now in the new apartment. The only things left to move were the things in my safe. It wasn't much and Diane and I would complete the move by 4:00 p.m. By five I was putting the finishing touches and then locked it up.

Diane and I would visit the 1800 club, we had not discussed Diane being my live in Girl friend and I wanted Diane to understand this. I told Diane that we would look for a place for her to call her own. Diane had enough money to buy an apartment or for that matter a house. Ted showed up and I briefed him on the situation in Nassau. When Diane understood that Ted was the security man she expressed her wanting to know how to use a weapon and learn self-defense. She said she wanted to start at once. I said who would should give her the shooting class would be Carson. Carson will surely want to teach the hand-to-hand defense course. Ted said that way Diane could also use what she was learning. It was still early so I called Carson and said that I had a student for him. I'm too old for that crap he said. Ok I said I'll just tell her that you're too old. Her you said, yeah you remember that girl that I had at the club a few weeks ago. The dark shin girl he asked? Yes, Diane I said. Carson said he was on the way. Carson was there shortly and training would start tomorrow. Don't you have some important business tomorrow Ted asked? I do now Carson said. We all left the club around 11:00 p.m. At the apartment Betty had Diane's things in the second bed room. Diane walked in and got on her PJs and carried her bathroom things to my bed room. Betty asked where she thought she was going? Diane said that she was now my personal body guard. Diane said that meant at night too. I looked at Betty and raised my shoulders. In bed I mentioned that she was the best body guard that I ever had. After saying that, I thought it but didn't say it, besides Cat.

Monday morning there were a rash of phone calls that I didn't return many of. I informed Karen of my purchase in Haiti and the need to replenish money in Nassau's safe and send Benny back the money he had lent me. Karen was to give any support to Goliath that he needed. I called Cat and said to have the bank hold the fish money for the next month. We would move at least $80,000.00 to the apartment safe. I also told cat that I would send a contractor to do some upgrades to the Hurricane house so we could install a good safe there and make it my living quarters.

Karen talked me into her going with Diane and myself to Haiti on Thursday. It was all set, we would stay until Sunday morning.

I then return the most important calls. Interpol whom also received two of the anonymous film clips, had matched Wendy's face to a missing person's report. They had contacted the Justice Department and the FBI and found that all three had received the films. The three identities talking together put the crime scene in Nassau. They had called Carson for a meeting at FBI headquarters in Miami. I was also being called to this meeting. Both Carson and I were prepared for the call and the eventual meeting. The film had been sent from somewhere in New York City.

At the late afternoon meeting I was questioned as to what I knew about the disappearance of Wendy. They did not mention the film and I was not under oath. I said that I had met Wendy once at a disco in Nassau. I said the next day while sitting on her father's porch swing I had seen her walk in, have a spat with her Father and walk out. I didn't ever see her again. The rest of what I can tell you is here say. The man in charge asked me if I had set the King Fish's boat on fire. I looked him in the eyes and said, no sir. After some time, they showed a still photo of Wendy that was surely taken from the film, the man asked if that was Wendy. I said she looks bad but yes that is her. They then showed me a photo of a man holding a camera and asked if I recognized the man? I said yes. Who is he the man asked? That Sir is Mr. Thompson of Nassau, I said. Are you sure he asked? Yes Sir, I replied. Then the questioned turned to a photo of a much younger Diane, also from one of the films. How about this girl the man asked. Sorry I said I don't know anyone that looks like that. Take another good look he said. Nop, no one that looks like that, she sure does look scared I said. We are told that you have had a few disagreements with Mr. Thompson, is this correct he asked? Well, I said his son raped my girlfriend while I was away in the Military. His son soon died of an overdose in his father house. I had warned his father that his son was a heavy Heroin user. Was his son murdered the man asked? If you consider that he did it himself, then yes, I said. The man looked at me and said that he thought I knew more than what I was letting on. That's funny I said I get the same feeling from you. But then again you're the one asking the questions. He looked at Carson and caught him smiling. The man asked me several other questions about Michelle and Deanna's father. Questions like how well did I know each of them. He asked me how Michelle had died, I told them that although Michelle's death certificate said she died of cancer, she was murdered by a man known to Chicago law enforcement as

Doctor Death. The man asked where this Doctor death was. I said he was murdered by a mob hit man while out on bail for killing the wife of another mobster, and oh yes the mob hit man then committed suicide in the same apartment that he killed Doctor Death in. The same mob hit man had also killed the mob man that had Doctor Death murder his wife. It's all quite interesting I said. Mr. Johnson, Wendy' father the man asked, do you think he was capable of setting the fire on the King Fish's boat that night? No I said that would be impossible. Why the man asked? He just doesn't have it in him I said.

The man looked at me and said it says in your FBI file that you have a top secret clearance from the Navy. Can you tell me anything about this he asked? You must have the wrong person I said, I've never been in the Navy. Again he looked at Carson and this time, Carson said, nop he's never been in the Navy.

Along with the film that was sent there was a note attached which said. "if no arrest is made within two weeks the films will be distributed"

At the meeting they never mentioned the Senator. They didn't show me the films so I figured they were still trying to sort things out. Carson didn't leave when I did, they kept him another hour. Carson had gone down to Nassau at the time of Wendy's disappearance. He wasn't down there for that reason but he did stick his nose into it.

Later that afternoon Carson stopped by the office. We talked about a few related things with him saying that the interrogator said that I knew a lot more than I was telling. Carson said he told them to be honest with me and that they could count on me to do the same.

Carson said he was picking up Diane from the apartment and would have her home by 10:00 p.m. I mentioned that we had changed apartments to the south west corner on the same floor.

I heard from Goliath late that afternoon, he put Jacob on the line. Jacob said that the only property they had found papers on in that area was 50 acres and not 10 as the bill of sale said. I asked who was the owner of that properly and he gave me the given name of Papa Doc which was Francois Duvar. Jacob and Goliath were in the capital and I asked them to call me in an hour. I then put a call in for Pilar, Pilar said that she had just made an over sight on the amount of land, that yes it should be 50 acres. Pilar said she would send a hand written note over to the deed office. I also mentioned about the property still being in Papa Doc's name and she said she would also cover that in the note to the deed office. Pilar said she was looking forward to my visit, this time for pleasure. When Goliath and Jacob called back it was now too late to do anything. We agreed that they would be back in the deed office tomorrow at 9:00 a.m.

Before I left the office the FBI called again to ask if I would return tomorrow morning for more questions. I said I would see them at 9:00 a.m.

It was just before 10:00 p.m. when Diane got home. I asked how it went and she said that Carson was a good instructor but made her feel uncomfortable. I asked how and she said I think he likes me. I laughed and asked well who wouldn't? She said that I of all people should know that the look in a man's eyes when they want something can be very worrisome. If you want I'll find someone else, she quickly said no, I'll work it out.

The next day Carson was also there at the FBI office. This time the interrogator said they were going to put everything on the table and wanted me to do the same. He said they had received two film tapes the Friday before. The films of which they would now play had a note attached that threatened that if they didn't make some arrests within two weeks the film would go public. The lights went out the film began. At its end the lights came back on. Well he said what do you think. Do you have the Senator in protective custody as yet I asked? The man said no. Well I said whomever has those photos must have have been Black Mailing him for years. Just as soon as they know about this film the Senators life won't be worth much. The man then turned and said to find the Senator and get him in protective custody. Tell the Senator we have a serious threat. I said they should trace and listen to his calls, this because whomever is the Black Mailer will need to know from the Senator about the extra security. It will most likely be his first call. If they know about the tape they will try to stop him from talking. Also check banking records and travel spots, Cayman's for money and Dominica for sex. Bad habits are had to break I added. They then played the second tape. What else the man said do you see. Do you have a date when the second film was made, I asked? Yes, the man said, its March 11ᵗʰ 1971. I quickly said, the same night of the fire of the King Fish's boat fire. The man answered, yes that same night.

Durning my investigation, I said, l had spoke with a source that said on the night of the King Fish boat fire that Mr. Thompson had visited the King Fish's boat with a young girl. The source said they saw a flash and heard what they thought was a gun shot. They then saw the boat on fire and Mr. Thompson leaving by himself. The source said the flash came from inside the cabin. A short time later the boat was on fire. Whatever the case the fire on the March date at 2:00 a.m. caused the boat to explode. I checked the tides for that night and at that time the tide would have been moving out to sea, if there were body's and any associated blood the sharks would have torn up the bodies.

So you think that it was Thompson that killed the King Fish? If you're asking me and I guess you are, yes I'm sure it was Mr. Thompson. I also believe that it was Thompson that killed Juan Carlos a Nassau drug dealer. This for two reasons, one, Juan Carlos sold Mark the drugs that killed his son and two, Juan Carlos was the one that supplied the young girl to Thompson. Juan Carlos most likely wanted a fee for the dead girl as he was selling her at the bar. Thompson killing Juan Carlos was like killing two birds with one stone. It's too bad you don't have the King Fish's body I said. Mr. Thompson had a two shot derringer. Juan Carlos was killed with Thompson's gun which had both empty shells in the chambers. One shot for the King Fish and one for Juan Carlos. Thompson' fingerprints were found on the gun. The man asked the question, the constable knows of Thompson's finger prints on the gun? I said yes. Well then why not arrest Thompson? Well Juan Carlos was just a drug dealer and prosecutor Hernandez wouldn't press charges because he said there wasn't enough evidence. Another taped film was given to the Constable showing Thompson with two guns that he had stolen from Michelle. The twin guns were given to Michelle from Papa Doc of Haiti. So where is the other gun the man asked? Maybe Thompson still has it. No, he doesn't I said. Who has it then he asked? I do I said. Anny, Thompson's youngest daughter came aboard my boat one night and tried to kill me with it. Anny said that her father had said it was I that was responsible for her brother Marks death. I still have that gun and it too has Thompson's prints on it. And what did you do with the daughter that attempted to kill you he asked? I sent her off to college I said. She's now working for your Governor in the Attorney's Generals office in Tallahassee I said.

The man looked at me and said, it was you who sent the films right? No I said. I then asked? Can I ask two short answer questions? The man said go ahead. When you were in high school or college did you ever use drugs? Absolutely not he said. Carson laughed. The man looked at Carson and said, we don't need you here, Carson said you already fired me and laughed some more. And the second question he asked? What is it? Oh yes I said, who killed JFK. Lee Harvey Oswald of course, he said. Now both Carson and I laughed.

The Justice Department man then asked if I was antigovernment. I asked him why he thought that and he said that he noted in my FBI file that I was uncooperative with the waterfront investigation. I said that when I first got into the waterfront business I knew nothing about its works only that I needed an ILA contract to work. That was it. Your two FBI bozos came looking for me at my Dad's shop and scared him half to death. They wanted me to tell them something when I didn't know anything. When I couldn't tell them what they wanted to hear, they threatened me with the IRS. My IRS audit cost me $300,000.00 and according to the same friendly FBI agents I was no smarter after paying that money.

The other thing is the JFK assignation. You people know Lee Harvey Oswald was set up. Yet you can sit right there and say that he did it. If I could figure it out, why couldn't you people? You didn't because the truth wasn't convenient for you.

So I said, I love my country and it's not that I don't like my Government, it's that I don't trust them to do the right thing. Will the good Senator go to jail for his crimes, somehow I just don't think he will. He most likely will be forced to resign. What would you do if you were the father of one of those girls? Fortunately, I think things will work out so that he's punished.

Now, do you have everything you need? Yes, one more thing he said. How did you know ahead of time about the pending death of the King Fish? I understand you worked very hard to have an alibi, Key West wasn't it he said. Let's just say I knew one way or another he was going to get what he deserved. At the time I was sure he had killed my friend Johnny and figured that he had also done away with Wendy.

Carson said that after I had left they said that I was still holding out. They told Carson that they were sure that I was somehow connected to the New York Family that Benny headed up. They believed that the film was real but that it was released now to somehow take one of my enemies down or remove some of their power. Carson said he was about to leave when another man brought the Justice Department man two folders with an information sheet. Carson said the Justice Man first read the note, "oh my God he said, the Senators daughter has gone missing from her dorm at collage". Then he opened the next folder and said "Jesus! Where did this file come from?" The man that brought the folder said it had just come in from Langley. The Justice man then looked at Carson and said to get me back in there. Carson said he looked at the man and said, I don't work here anymore. The man from the Justice Department handed Carson a paper that was in the other folder and said you do now, you've been reinstated. Carson said he looked at the paper and through it back to him.

The justice Man asked if Carson had known about my shooting two men Saturday night in Nassau. Carson said it was self-defense. The Police report said that Jim was waiting for them! Whose men are they he asked? Carson said that I thought that Thompson is smuggling drugs from Nassau to Miami aboard his ships. Jim visited a Nassau Judge Saturday afternoon trying to get him to take action against Thompson. Jim knew that whomever the Judge would call would send someone after him. My God the justice man said, he rescued you from Angola? Carson said I did. The justice man then said and what about this radioactive money, where did that go he asked. Carson said he didn't know about and radioactive money. The money the man said, the money he gave the Cubans was radioactive! Anyone exposed to the money even for a short time would die. Here it says that your friend got off a Lear jet belonging to the Mob at JFK and traded a duffle bag for the brief case. The limo driver who did the trade was stopped and the duffle bag had $1,000,000.00 cash in it. The CIA showed up at the limo driver's booking and took the driver and the money. Says here that radioactive money had been in storage from years back on an attempt to get Castro the money. Your friend is no ordinary guy he said, he's got connections everywhere. There's just no way that radioactive material is going to be release without it being approved by the director himself. Carson said the Justice man said he wanted a tail on me 24/7. Carson said he mentioned that would be fun, Carson said he'd give it less than the same day before I picked up the tail. The justice man told the FBI to send their best men.

When I got back to the office Carson had called to tell me about the Senator's Daughter being missing. We agreed it was not good news. I then called Nassau to get Jena the message to catch the next flight to Miami. She'd be safer staying at my place than where she was. Diane wouldn't like it too much but like my Mom always said "that's the way the cookie crumbles".

I wouldn't see Carson until the next day. He did come by and take Diane shooting. Goliath had called the office that day but we had missed each other. The last word was that he would call tonight. Goliath's call came in just after Diane had returned from her session with Carson. Goliath said that when they had got to the deed office no papers had been sent but by the time he had called me and was waiting, they were surprised that Pilar herself showed up at the office. Jacob then got on the phone and said that everything was done as I instructed. Jacob said that if I wanted they would use a private plane tomorrow and visit the property.

I told Jacob that if they could get there and back the same day that would be fine. I also asked him to check with Karen because I would be flying into Haiti on Thursday and didn't want to spend time changing planes to get there. I said If so I'd rather contract a plane from Miami and fly direct into Port-de-Paix. I also told Jacob that there would be six of us coming to visit staying until Sunday morning.

I called big Ted and told him about the trip and that I would need two fully equipped men to make the trip with us.

I told Diane that Jena would most likely be going with us to Haiti. Diane said that was ok but that if she put a hand on me she would give her a whooping. She wasn't kidding.

The next day the same Department of Justice man called the office requesting my presents at the FBI headquarters. I didn't call him back. Then Carson called and asked about the same and I said that I couldn't or truthfully didn't want to return. In two days, I said nothing positive was accomplished. I also said that since this morning I had a tail with a government tag, if you want I said I can provide film. As for the Senators daughter being missing whomever had her would most likely not bring her any harm unless the Senator started talking. Follow the money trail I said.

While still in the office we received an overseas collect call, Karen buzzed me that it was Deanna's father. When I answered he asked how long I had known. I said I was sorry but that soon we would have those involved punished. The Constable said that he hadn't just dropped the case and that yesterday they had issued a warrant for the capture for Mr. Thompson on several charges. The reason I'm calling now he said, is that I believe Mr. Thompson is aboard his cargo ship that left Nassau late last night. This could be at our advantage as here in Nassau, if arrested he would have just been let out on a small bail. Thompson and his people have been under surveillance for quite some time. Aboard the same ship there are 14 illegals but more important there are about 100 kilos of drugs aboard. The drugs are in two empty refrigerated containers of which I will send now via telex the container numbers. The drugs are located in the evaporator panels of both units. Please Mr. Johnson said don't let that SOB get away. I asked if he had informed the DEA about the drugs and he said that they had been working with his group for some time but that they were in the investigating mode. Ok I said I'll keep you informed.

With that I called the FBI office to see if Carson was still there. He was and I said that I would be over in 15 minutes.

Once there the Justice Department man asked if I had finally come to my senses. I just looked at him and shook my head.

I didn't tell them where I got the information, but did share it with them. The FBI he said, basically had nothing to do with the ship matter and if Mr. Thompson was the holder of a good a passport there was nothing they could hold him on. They did call the DEA and said they would appreciate them making the bust with Mr. Thompson on the ship. Carson could see I wasn't too impressed with the actions that were taken. I told Carson that Thompson wasn't running from the warrant but the Mob. Like the Senator, they would do what they could to stop him from talking. While there the FBI man that was following me in the morning thanked me for his two tickets and 4 flat tires. I told him anytime.

Back at our office we had heard from Goliath and Jacob. They had reached the chateau and wanted to speak to me. Jacob left a phone number where they could be reached. I called right back and both men said the place was beautiful but the phone and telex were down and the electric was on and off in that zone. Jacob said that the town and airport were about three miles away. The town was small and didn't have many services. There was a poorly supplied general store that included a small clinic. Food was mostly purchased in open markets in that same town. I said they should do what they could to restore communications before they returned. Jacob said they had chartered a plane for the day as there was only one daily flight in and out of Paix. Karen was with me as we talked with the men, them being on the speaker. When we hung up I asked Karen to see about chartering us a flight out of Miami for the next day and picking us up Sunday at about noon. If she could get the charter, then she was to cancel the other air travel reservations. Karen was to call Diane and Jena to start making lists of what we needed to take with us. Food I said to Karen, and if we get the charter don't forget ice. I then called Rodger at Bob's Import export company and told him to see about getting a new Cat Generator and fuel tank sent over there. I realized that it wouldn't get there for this trip but to start the ball rolling. I wanted at least 350 kilowatts and a 5,000-gallon fuel tank. I then called Mr. Makee and asked if he could spare one of his men to do the trip with us as I was sure I wanted to do some future construction and electrical work there.

About an hour before the Thompson ship arrived to its dock on the Miami River someone had called the Miami Herald and tipped them off that this ship was coming in carrying drugs, illegals and a fugitive of justice. The Herald called the DEA, Immigration services and law enforcement. The best call was to Interpol. TV Channels 4, 7 and 10 were also called. I wasn't going to be there but I was sure that it wasn't going to be ignored.

Jena had arrived at the apartment yesterday evening and was staying in the room set up for Diane, of course Diane wasn't staying in that room. So far Jena and Diane have been getting along just fine.

Karen confirmed our charter and said the two engine prop airplane would stay parked at the Paix airport until we needed to depart. There would be seven of us traveling.

Guess what made the nightly news? A cargo ship arriving on the Miami River was carrying drugs and illegals. There was no mention of the ships name or owners or whether or not any one was arrested. My buddy Bob which I hadn't heard from in a while apparently saw or heard the news and called in at the apartment that night. Bob said the ship wasn't his, so it must have been Thompson's. I told Bob about Thompson's warrant in Nassau and that we were told that Thompson, too, was aboard. Bob knew the Feds could be listening and was careful what he said. Bob mentioned that he'd like to see me on the weekend but I said that I would be out of town. He asked if I could meet him at the Sailing club, Bob said there were too many ears at the 1800 club. I said I'd be there in 30 minutes. Diane and Jena were in watching TV and I called Diane and told her I was headed to the sailing club. I said that if she went it would be nice to take Jena along but only if she wanted someone to talk with. We all three went. I called for the New BMW to be moved up to the front door.

Bob met us at the Sailing Club's bar, Bob was a little confused as the last time he saw me I was with Cat. He knew Jena but it was the first time he had seen Diane. I introduced Bob to Diane. Yes, Paul was still the bartender there. I asked Paul if he minded keeping the girls occupied while Bob and I went for a walk. Paul was more than happy to oblige. It was good to see Bob again, he still had one of those big Cuban cigars in his hand. I asked him what had happen to the little Cuban girl he had and he said that he had her stashed away where I couldn't find her. Bob asked about Jena and what I was thinking? You're not with that crazy broad are you he asked? Didn't I hear that you and Carson just saved her from a kidnapping? No I'm not and yes we did I said. Bob said I always did like playing with fire. Bob asked what about this film, don't tell me it was one of Michelle's? Yes I said. Michelle's not involved right, he asked? Do you have to ask me that I said? No Sorry. So what's going to happen Bob asked? We'll have to wait and see I said. I can't imagine that at least Interpol doesn't have Thompson at this very moment. What about the Senator Bob asked? I told Bob about someone having the Senator's daughter. Bob said it was the way our Justice Department worked. If they would have been serious they would have protected the entire family. Of course the Senator's present wife wouldn't be touched by the boys. The daughter is from his first marriage. His first wife died in a car accident. Bob then looked at me, knowing what I was thinking, and said, I have no idea. I told Bob of my new purchase and that we were heading over there tomorrow. Bob said he hadn't talked to Pilar lately due to their finances. Bob said every time he spoke to Pilar she asked him for an advance. I said that she was also calling Benny. Bob didn't ask and I didn't say anything about how much I had paid Pilar for the chateau. The only thing Bob said was that it was beautiful and that Michelle loved it there when she was young. Bob said that when he closed his eyes he could still see Michelle riding down the beach with all the children running alongside her. Ah Bob said those were the days.

Well, I said we got room for you on the plane; why not join us? Bob said, are you nuts? Being around you for an hour or two is dangerous enough. But with you and that crazy bitch for a couple days, no thanks. Hey by the way he said you do remember me in the will right. Then that old laugh of Bob finally returned.

As we returned to the bar we could hear them all laughing. I paid up and Jena said she was going to stay with Paul and that Paul would bring her home. I said some other time. Jena wanted to argue with me but Diane took her hand and pulled her on pass me. As Jena passed me, she stuck out her tong. Jena yelled to Paul, I'll see you when I get out of jail. Bob looked like he was going to stay and on my way out I looked at Bob and Paul and told Bob to warn Paul about playing with fire. Bob laughed.

❧✦☙

CHAPTER XVI

PAIX

The next morning, I went by the office, Karen had already come and gone. I saw her BMW in the parking lot but Lourdes said that Karen had borrowed a pick up from one of our supervisors. The charter was going to meet us all at Opa Locka airport at noon.

When the three of us arrived at the airport the plane was loaded and ready. The only person I didn't already know was a nephew of Mr. Makee. Once Jena saw him on the plane she said, now you're talking. As she sat down next to him, although I was just kidding, I said Jena he's married and has three kids. Jena said what happens in Vegas stays in Vegas, Diane said but we're not going to Vegas. Jena said oh yeah will just don't tell him that. The engines roared and we were off.

We hadn't heard back from Goliath or Jacob but in two hours we should start finding out things for ourselves.

The flight was good. When we arrived the pilots flew low over the small landing strip then circled around and landed.

There was no one to receive us not even customs. Yes, not even a taxi. I called the phone that Jacob and Goliath had used and a man answered at the general store. He was very pleasant and said he would find a taxi and someone with a pick up. The story here was that the only time there were people here at the airport was during the once a day flight in and out using the same plane.

We waited about 30 minutes when here came the Calvary. A taxi, pick-up and a military jeep with two solders. At first the solders acted like they wanted to be in charge but backed way off when they noticed that they were out gunned and found out where we were headed. In fact, they helped with the baggage and acted as if they were our escort. Once loaded up we were on our way.

It was a short ride along a long beach that was spotted with wooden shacks, the closer we got to the Chateau the more boats we saw. Here it looked as most of the boats had sails.

As we arrived there was an old man at the gate with a double barreled shot gun strapped to his back. He came to the cars and asked if I was Captain Jim his new Boss man? The old man who looked to be in his seventies saluted like he was in the military. He opened the gate and as the three vehicles passed shut it behind us. The placed looked like a dream. Kids started running up to us screaming with joy. People started walking out from the main house as well as the barn and something that looked like a small barracks. They must have known we were coming because their dress was clean and colorful. Flowers were given to the girls. Everyone talked at once. Then a woman clapped her hands and all became calmed. She came and said the she was the head master of the house, her name was Sharon and she welcomed us to the Chateau. I walked through the big double wooden doors and was amazed by the beauty, it looked like it was all 100 years old but still in almost like new condition. It was clean and well kept. Sharon directed me upstairs to the master's bedroom. It was quite big with three sets of double French doors that opened to a large balcony that had a view of the ocean and the bay. The curtains that hung from the high sealing also looked 100 years old but seemed new. The Bathroom was equipped with cold water only French stile. Sharon said that when we were ready for a bath they would heat the water and bring it up. In all, upstairs there were 4 bedrooms all with bathrooms and baloneys. Down stairs was a great room, the kitchen, the study, the living room and a porch that almost encircled the entire house. The girls were on their own exploring the house with Mr. Makee's nephew, Andy. The security we brought along settled into one of the rooms and then went to work. My biggest surprise was the house barn. Here there were several beautiful horses, possibly a little under fed but beautiful. As I walked into the barn there I met Salinas. Salinas whom was brushing one of the horses stopped and introduced herself. Salinas was born on the property not ever leaving. When I asked how old she was she said she didn't know. As I was talking with her the girls walked in behind me. Karen said right away she smelled trouble. Diane said no trouble as she walked up to Salinas and said that she was the woman of the house and to stay clear of me. Jena said she was a friend of family and Karen said she was the Secretary that was in charge. Andy said he was here to design any changes. Up walked one the security man and introduced himself as such. The security man said that I should come and visit the barracks. The girls stayed with Salinas while Andy and myself went with our security.

In the barracks there was a large locked door. We called the old man to open it. The key which was the only one he had, opened the door. Here we found a supply of arms that included two colt 45 pistols, 20 M1 rifles, two Thompson machine guns, four boxes of hand grenades, two bazookas and two sniper rifles with scopes. Of course there were boxes stacked with ammunitions for all of this. The security man using a powerful flash light noted that the ammunitions were stored in a separate room below ground level that looked like it was at least double walled. Enough for a small war the security man said. The security man laughed as there were oil lamps mounted on all the walls. I wouldn't want to light a match down here he said. We left and relocked the door behind us. The barracks looked like at one time had housed more than 20 men.

We spent three very nice days here, Andy made lots of notes that included a generator house that would be able to house a large generator and fuel tank. Andy said that air conditioning was almost out of the question. The electric was limited and the rooms with their high ceilings were too big. He suggested adding lots of ceiling fans.

Horseback riding and the beach is where we spent much of our time. The three girls and Salinas seemed to do good together. Looked like Jena may have found her first friends. Andy whom wasn't married showed his interest in Karen. The food was great! Karen and the girls had done well with their shopping. Andy suggested two refrigerators and a big freezer. The second refrigerator was to be propane, used when the electricity was down. While we were there, the electric came on and off, staying off from midnight until 6:00 a.m. in the morning. The two pilots also slept at the house them even flying myself and one of the local fisherman looking for what could be a future good diving spot for myself. The fisherman said there was lots of fish but there were not too many buyers. No one in this zone had money, most, over 90% were poor. No ice meant that the fishermen could only feed the family their catch. We had found a small reef and even spotted a wreck in shallow water. Crawfish seemed plentiful. The fisherman said he had furnished many a big fish and crawfish to Papa Doc. The fisherman remembered Papa Doc's son as a spoiled little fat boy. The fisherman said that Pilar didn't ever come with Papa Doc. Papa Doc either came with several women or visited the women that worked at the Chateau. It is said the fisherman noted that Papa Doc had fathered two children at the Chateau, both girls he said.

Diane and I didn't spend a lot of privet time as she, Karen and Jena spent all their time with Salinas and the horses out on the beach. Salinas not only took care of the horses, she could ride. Me sitting out on the balcony would see Salinas riding down the beach standing on the horses back.

Sunday morning, I wasn't ready to go back. The girls, all of them asked to stay. That wasn't going to happen but I did promised Karen that she could bring Joe down here anytime. When we left I had a clear mind of what I was going to do here including coming back soon.

CHAPTER XVII

JUDGEMENT DAY

Once back to Miami and at work I called Carson to get any new scope of what was going on. Thompson had been taken into custody by the Interpol personal as I had hoped. The Senator had resigned with some lessor charges being mentioned. The pressure on him to give information on the blackmailing and the where abouts of Wendy Johnson just went away. The Senator's daughter showed up saying she had gone camping with a friend and didn't think of telling anyone.

Diane had never seen the tape but once she did it was relived so horrifically! We were about to drop a bomb shell on both the Senator and Mr. Thompson. Diane would bring a civil law suit of rape on the Senator and as well as offering testimony to Interpol on the murder of Wendy, the King Fish and the attempted murder of herself. The film tape would only come out on the Senators side if it went to trial. Diane was asking for $5,000,000.00 to settle. As far as Mr. Thompson was concerned his goose was cooked! Diane would also bring suit to Mr. Thompson for the pain and suffering he had caused her all these years. Mr. Thompson was charged with two murders, endangerment of a minor and one count of attempted murder.

I would testify that on the night of March 11th, 1971, I arrived in the Nassau Harbor in a 28-foot Donzi that belonged to Don Arron. As I was passing by the King Fish's boat I saw Mr. Thompson and a women get aboard the King Fish's boat. I then saw a gun flash in the cabin and then saw a fire being set by Mr. Thompson. After lighting the fire Mr. Thompson then got aboard his boat and left. I then pulled the Donzi alongside of the burning boat and using a fire extinguisher as I went, first saw the King Fish on the cabin floor with a built hole in his back. I heard coughing coming from the head, I broke the door in and found Diane then unconscious on the floor. I then carried her and put her aboard the Donzi. I then went back for the King Fish's corps. As I put his body aboard, I casted off and gave it full throttle, the King Fish's boat then exploded.

Once I got out of the harbor, I put the boat in neutral and checked on Diane, she was breathing and seamed unharmed by the fire. The King Fish was dead from his wounds. I raced the Donzi to the south end of Andros where I buried the King Fish's body in a shallow grave. I then put Diane into one of the fisherman's boats. I sounded my boat horn and when I saw several lights come on. I left my flash light there on the boats bowl shining on the first house with its light on, got back into the Donzi and went out of the channel at full speed.

Of course the defense drilled me as to how and why I was there at the scene. I said I was out sightseeing, the jury laughed. The defense painted a much different picture saying it was me that killed the King Fish. Clearly I had a motive and I had the opportunity. Thompson's defense said that I had made an elaborate alibi in Key West during that same time.

The prosecution was doing their best not to use the film in the court room. The two clinchers were the testimony of Diane and the fact that I had led Interpol to the body of the King Fish. The bullets that killed the King Fish came from the same gun used to kill Juan Carlos. Mr. Thompson was convicted on one murder count and the attempted murder and acquitted on the other charges.

After the trial the two Miami detectives that were originally chasing me for the King Fish fire visited me at the 1800 club. They wanted to know how I had made the Key West trip to Nassau and back so fast. As I had said once during my scouting days, I told them that a Great Bald Eagle had swooped down and had carried the Donzi and I to and from Nassau.

What had actually happened was I had adjusted the throttle and timing for my trip to reduce the available engine power and thus lowering the running temperatures and saving fuel. Before returning the boat I raised the throttle and timing to the maximum. That Donzi was designed to intercept another fast boat, not to run a long-distance race.

With the court battle won with Mr. Thompson, the Senator settled with Diane for $3,000,000.00. The settlement from Mr. Thompson would be much less, Diane would be awarded 50% of all his assets. The judge left open the opportunity for the family of Wendy Johnson to follow suit and file their own law suit. With this, it ended up Diane and the Johnsons becoming partners in Thompson's shipping line and the tourist shop. My friend Bob made his way into their shipping business by him joining the two shipping lines into one.

Me well it didn't change me much. During those long court battles that lasted almost a year. I had one of the most romantic adventures in my life to this point.

Beverly had turned 19 years old. The first trip I made with her was a short trip to you guessed it my French Chateau in Haiti. Beverly and I rode horses down the beaches day and night. In all we made four weekend trips there, we watched as it changed to having full time electric that allowed the place to shine. Beverly and Salinas became good friends with it being no surprise to us to learn that Salinas was Baby Doc's younger sister. The rumor about two children was said to be unfounded. By now, Salinas had caught my eye with her looking back at me almost every time she walked by.

Beverly 's grandmother remained sickly but what changed our relationship was that during a trip that Bev and I had made to see some of Europe, Beverly's mom had a terrible heart attack. That brought us back at once. Beverly was never the same, she was then taking care of both her mother and grandmother. She said she was sorry but that she would never leave them again. You remember that 10 caret diamond ring of Pilar's? Well I had bought it from Pilar and had planned to ask Beverly for her hand in marriage during our Europe trip. Of course that now wouldn't happen.

After the down fall of the Senator, Benny got stronger, my business had also expanded. The Garcia brothers had come to me offering their Miami container business. They needed the cash to fend off the FBI Ricco charges. This gave me Interpool leasing, one of the last container company holdouts.

Diane, about to become quite wealthy was still living in my apartment. She used her room more and more as we romantically drifted apart. Don't get me wrong. We still had our moments with a good shower now and then. Diane was now studying and wanted to be a one of those lawyers. Why she didn't just get her own apartment I didn't understand. Karen said it was because Diane had terrible nightmares, and if she wasn't already in my bed, she could get there by just running across to my room.

CHAPTER XVIII

COLUMBUS DAY REGATTA

Joe and Karen didn't see one another much. I too didn't see much of Joe. The last time I had seen Joe we had rented a 47 foot Morgan sailboat and invited anyone that wanted to come on a Columbus Day Regatta. We would leave from the Miami Marina. Joe had driven in from Norfolk that Thursday night to prepare. Prepare you ask? Prepare for what. War, prepare for the Mad Water Balloon Wars. Joe would construct balloon launchers. Two such launchers would be placed, one on each side of the boat connected to the stainless steel stays. We had our office girls filling and freezing balloons. Invitations were sent out weeks in advance. To my great surprise Cat had called in and made reservations for Janie, Lee and herself. We decided to inter Cat into the race captaining our own 35 foot Morgan. Joe had more work load than he thought. That Friday night everyone was to meet at the 1800 club for a pre Regatta party. Janie, Lee and Cat would also be staying at the apartment. Even Jena showed up at the door of the apartment. This was certainly going to be odd. The party at the 1800 club started at about 9:00 p.m., there were more than 100 people at the party to include Carson whom was also going to take his sailboat. My friend Carlos and his girlfriend would take the Donzi down. At the party I finally came face to face with Cat. It had been more than six months since we had even spoken. She came into my arms and she kissed me and said how much she had missed me. I was sure that Diane had noticed and I would soon hear some remark. Cat still had the marriage ring set on.

The night and the party went on and from there we went dancing. I was dancing with Cat when Diane cut in. Diane said that I would be on loan just for the night and to be sure to leave my door unlocked just in case she had a nightmare. Everything was cool, Jena cut in on Diane.

Once back at the apartment I got one of my favorite showers with Cat. Cat wanted to first apologize because what she thought about me meeting Diane at the Play Boy Club was way off. She also told me that Deanna had believed that it was me that had started the fire on the King Fish's boat and that I had did away with him. And of course they both thought that I had her old boyfriend killed in the shanty town bar. Cat said she would never misjudge me ever again, unless it was something she saw with her own eyes.

Cat said that the children were doing great and getting big. Jacob, she said hadn't had a drink since his return from Haiti. Goliath was around to keep him straight. Jacob was now working and had taken over his father's Law Office. Cat said that Jacob had recently asked her to marry him. I asked what her answer was and Cat said that she hadn't said yes but that she also didn't say no. Cat said the children were calling her mother and that she liked it. Cat said she was tired of sleeping alone. Cat noted that Otis had moved the Thompson girl in with his Mom and him. Cat said she had contracted a new house to be built on Ms. Angee's old properly. The neighborhood had changed. Now there was city water and lights in that zone. I hope you don't mind but I was thinking of you giving them that house as a wedding gift. As for you and I she said it doesn't look any better than it did a year ago when we talked. Maybe you'll be ready to settle down when Martha is of age. Cat said that Martha was almost 14 now. She is the prettiest girl in Nassau. Martha now even goes out pulling traps and is using your old scuba gear diving your old wrecks with Otis. Just as I was falling to sleep Cat mentioned that the money that Michelle had left was about gone. She said that to keep everything in motion it would take about $7,000.00 per month. That put me right to sleep. Before we knew it the sun came up.

Betty cooked a good breakfast, Cat took the BMW while Diane and I took the vet. Cat would go south and I north. Our boats would meet somewhere near the starting line. Yes, even Jena would be aboard our boat. Everyone had been given a ticket with which boat they would be going on and directions. It was never our thought to win the race or even race for that matter. We were there for the party and the wars. The starting gun would go off at 10:00 a.m. We were throwing and launching balloons way before that. We even bombarded the starter boats as we sailed through the starting markers. Cat had started her engine to catch us and then we let each other have it. We then would coordinate attacks on other boats. All of our crews were dressed like pirates. Both sailboats flew the Jolly Rodger flag. We would do our best to catch a boat in between us and let them have it. Many boats raised a white flag of some kind. After passing the finish line and dropping the sails, a large yacht was coming up on our stern with all its occupants on the bridge. They were throwing balloons down at all the sailboats as they passed. Joe and I got ready and as they got in range we had several direct hits on their occupants but one hit and knocked out their front windshield. They were so busy firing back, they didn't even notice.

Once the first leg of the race was over and we were at Elliot's Key the custom was to tie up as many boats together as possible. Our boat was tied up in reverse. I dove off the stern with the anchor and swam it out about 30 yards. I then dug in the anchor's wings into the sand. Anchoring with the stern into the wind was so that we could use our spinnaker for some fun. We would connect our bowman's chair to the spinnaker and let the spinnaker catch the wind and raise whomever was sitting in the chair into the air. Cat's boat wasn't right next to ours but was in our line. Carson too had found us. Once anchored and secured the party started. Each boat would host any and all visitors. Food such as fish fitters would be served and of course a cup of rum punch. We had an old rubber drum on deck that every so often someone would poor in more rum and maybe some additional fruit juice. Then we put a foot in and stir it all up. Sometime this was done bare footed and sometimes while wearing a tennis shoe. It was however, bring your own cup. We also had the Donzi anchored off our stern. Carlos offered skiing to whoever wanted to go. Most people just wanted to ride in it. Cat had brought with her 100 pounds of fresh Crawfish from Nassau.

Needless to say our boats were very popular. There were girls that were going from one boat to the other whom had lost their bathing suit tops. Some didn't even notice and some didn't care. The party would go on until people just got so tuckered out they just had to sit or lay down anywhere they could. Somehow Cat managed to stay close by and was able to get me back to the Morgan's cabin. It was about an hour later when we had a loud knock on the door, it was Diane whom just came on in and locked the door behind her. The next morning the whole place was a sight. I wondered just how many we had lost, maybe still drunk or even had gone over. We had this one girl that worked in the office that everyone said was kind of prudish. I had to look for her. When I found her she was curled up with two young men, all three without clothes. She looked up at me, sat up, looked where she was and screamed. I threw her a towel and she left with me. On the walk back crossing from boat to boat she picked up her bottom two boats down and her top down another three boats. When she found her top while putting it on she asked me not to look. She begged me not to tell the others.

Breakfast would be the Scotty's stakes that we didn't remember to cook the night before. Our Sunday morning orange juice had vodka in it. Someone said it helped with a hangover. Lee said he had never remembered a party like that at FSU. We still were missing crew members, Carlos made the rounds in the Donzi and found one of the girls that was two boat lines over. She had no idea how she had gotten there. On her back there was an arrow pointing to her butt. Under her bathing suit bottom a note was written in magic marker. It said my name is Hank call me and had a phone number. That's it, both boats were complete. We finished up breakfast and all the boats started to untie for the race back.

The trip back was more fun than on the way down. Now there was no one on board that was shy. Everyone work as a team. There most likely wasn't more than a few boats out there that didn't see several balloons coming their way. As we crossed the finish line Cat took the Morgan west to the Coral Gables water way and we went east to the Miami marina. Carlos would take the Donzi out at Dinner Key. Cat,

Janie, Lee and Jena would all spend one more night at the apartment then head home in the morning.

For years my Dad had designed and produced the medallions that were given to each captain of the race. This year my dad did the design and my shop produced the bronze medallions, I was quite surprised that the Race committee invited me to present the trophy that my dad had built and donated, this almost 20 years before. I did present the trophy but it was a setup, as almost everyone in the audience had been given a water balloon to throw at me up one stage. I must have gotten 50 direct hits up on stage. The crowd and myself though this was so funny and of course deserving. Before I left the stage they awarded me with a full size Jolley Rodger Flag and a plaque that said "Best Pirate Ever". Karen and Diane had both played a part in setting me up. Even Carson was among those that hit me with a water balloon. What a night it was.

❧✦❧

CHAPTER XIX

DEATH OF THE DON

I had just gotten home from the trophy banquet when the phone rang, it was Jena saying her father had died of a heart attack and she needed me. Yes, Benny was dead. I would leave on the next flight to New York. I knew that by the time I arrived there would be a New Don. Big Ted wanted to travel with me but I went alone. The funeral was held that same day. The church was standing room only. I sat with the family, Benny's mother and Jena. We left the funeral, Jena insisted that I attend the wake that was arranged at the house. Once there at Benny's house, I was asked to join a privet meeting in the study. It would have been an insult not to attend. I was introduced to the new Family Head. He said in small speech that he was going to bring things back to the way they were. He looked right at me and said everybody pays. When the meeting looked like it was about over he waved me over. Jimmy he said, I like to make you and offer you shouldn't refuse. The offer was $5,000,000.00 and I walk. I take nothing and no one with me. The payment I asked? Two million in cash he said, then $200,000.00 per month. No I said if I sell I want it all up front. There's more than $4,000,000.00 in receivables I said. You don't need me to finance I said. $6,000,000.00 clear I said. You pay all the taxes, ILA dues and bills I said. The construction business and fabrication go with me I said. No he said the Construction on Andros stays. I'll be finished my first contract on Andros within two weeks I said. That money is, yours he said. Ok I said once my bond money is returned and I'm paid in full for Andros the construction is yours. Deal he said, we have a deal. $6,000,000.00 and your gone he said. We shook hands and I returned to Jena's side. Jena asked what happened. I said I'm out. Jena said she was scared what was going to happen to her. She whispered that her father had called to her before he died. He gave me the combination to the safe and had me empty it all into a sack. The sack in is my Mercedes trunk. When I returned he was dead. He said you would know what to do with it. Where is your car I asked? I dove it to a self-parking place and took a taxi back. When I got back home I called 911. Do they know I asked? I don't think so but they asked me not to leave the house she said. Ever since they heard the news there's been a man standing at the study door. Well I said if they open it while you're here and it's empty they'll know, they just will. Do you trust Larry I asked? No she said. Well I said there's at least 50 guns in the house. I'll say my good byes and you walk me to the car. If it's a taxi you jump in when I say. If I can get Larry to take me to the hotel, you walk me to the car, I'll ask Larry to let me steal his car. If he lets me we're off, if he doesn't we'll somehow take it any way. Where are the Mercedes keys I asked? There already in your coat pocket she said. You won't leave me here will you she asked? Act normal I said while I do my thing.

I said my good byes and asked Larry if he mined taking me to the Hotel, he said no problem. I'll pull the car around front Larry said. I found Jena and asked her to walk me out. It didn't look good there were men everywhere. Larry was waiting in the car. He must have thought it strange that I opened the back door. I asked Larry if he minded that Jena ride along with us. He turned and looked at me and said are you sure? I said yes. He turned and said get in and we'll see if they open the gate. Jena got in slowly and I after her. Larry pulled out the car nice and slow. The gate opened and we drove through the gate Larry looked at his mirror and asked what hotel. I said the Waldorf, he nodded his head. So Far I still had my right hand in my coat pocket with my Beretta 9mm. I reached over kissed Jena, she understood and kissed me back. When we got to the hotel I opened my door and pulled Jena out of the car and asked if Larry could wait for an hour or so? Larry said he needed to get her back, and we continued to walk, saying I needed an hour, Larry jumped out of the car, and he saw I had my gun in hand. I said sorry Larry but I need an hour. Larry stood there as we walked in. I watched as he got back in and drove off heading for the house. We walked through the hotel and would exit the side door on the other street. If Larry didn't stop and make a call, we might have a 45-minute head start. On the way through the hotel I asked Jena what was close by the parking garage. We got in a taxi and directed him to a small restaurant near by the parking garage. Just as the taxi drove off from dropping us at the restaurant we headed to the garage on foot. We walked to her car and popped the trunk. I opened the bag and saw that it was still full. I then took out my Swiss army knife and removed her car's tag. I then exchanged her tag with another parked car's tag. We then walked out the other end of the garage with the sack. We caught another taxi to the train station. We got a locker and put the sack in and locked it. A train was leaving and we got on it. Where it was going we didn't know. It was headed south. I left Jena sitting and went and got a sleeper. The train was headed to Miami we would be there by 4:00 p.m. the next day. Once in the sleeper Jena wouldn't leave the room the entire trip. At one of the short stops I got off and called Karen. I needed Ted to get on our train in Fort Lauderdale with a black sack with about 30 pounds of newspaper inside. I'll be waiting for the bag in the number 5 car. After delivering me the bag he should then exit and drive and meet us at the Hialeah Amtrak station. Tell him that once in Miami we'll need at least one patrol car and some back up. Call the leer jet Pilot and have him get Benny's mother back to Miami ASAP, tell him, no other passengers. Karen knew not to talk to anyone.

During the trip Jena said she felt guilty about what she had done, not calling 911 right away. I told her that this is what her father wanted. Jena said there was a copy of her fathers will in the bag. I told her that everything would go to her.

Jena shed her dress, I didn't even remove my jacket or shoes.

Ted did what I asked, when we arrived in Miami Ted and our back up were there. As we got off the train I didn't recognize any of the new Don's players but I knew they were there. I put the sack in to the trunk of one of the police cars. Jena and I got in a car with Ted. Then we were escorted by the police car with the bag too my apartment. This should have the boys thinking that I had the bag in my apartment.

Once home at the apartment, Jena asked how long she could stay? I told her in front of Diane and Betty that she was welcome as long as she followed the rules of the house. Betty growled and when I looked at her she said it was her stomach. Diane said that Jena could use her room. I knew what that meant. Ted was still there and we talked on the balcony for about 20 minutes. The next morning, I would call Benny's attorney and get a read on the timing for Benny's will. Benny had told me once that he would leave 100% to Jena. Benny had said something about a trust for his mother and Jena. I would also call Roy about my selling the Container business. Roy was going to be happy for me to get out while I was still able. Roy would call the new Don's attorney and get things going. I wouldn't tell Karen or Joe until I had at least a date of sale. Joe wouldn't be happy with to whom we were selling to but at least he could come back to Miami and maybe even settle down. Karen wouldn't lose anything as she could keep her job or quit and come with me. Karen had heard several times how I'd one day just sail off into the blue.

Ted would leave, him being on stand by for him and me going to New York. I called Carson and asked him to stop by. I was going to use Carson to retrieve the sack that we left in the train station. Carson and I would separately fly into New York, me without guns and looking almost like a bum would fly under another name carrying a bag with my good suit. Carson would fly as the FBI agent that he is. Carson had been reinstated when the Thompson film was sent in. Once in New York Carson would meet me in the men's room at the train station. Me still looking like a bum would go sit at the Train Station near the Lock box seeing if anyone was watching and when the coast was clear. Carson would use my key and take the sack out of the lock box and catch a taxi. I would follow close behind. Carson would get a hotel room at the airport. I would come up and we'd investigate what we had. Carson would take the money and me the documents. I would fly back in my good suit using my real name.

Our trip was successful. Once again Ted met us at the Miami airport and escorted us to the apartment. Once there with the now two bags I went into my room with Jena and closed the door. I then opened my new safe and had it standing by. First we did the money. The money came in rubber banded stacks of $10,000.00. There were 327 such sacks. We counted each pile then placed it one by one back into the sack and then placed the sack into the safe.

The paper work was very organized. There were letters for Jena, her grandmother, Benny's attorney, Larry, Benny's secretary at the bank and me. None of the letters were sealed except mine. Jena took hers and read it while sitting on the floor. I opened mine and read it sitting at my desk.

Benny's letter was very businesslike. Most of everything he owned would be left to Jena. I would be the Trustee of all moneys and businesses. His attorney, Benny said had one of two originals of his will, Benny said the attorney had asked him to give me the will before now as it was widely known that others would want in on the moneys and businesses. Sell or dismantle the Bank, Benny wrote. Its purpose was to move the money. Do this first. The financials are in the file marked BANK. Sell the jet, it cost money, offer it to the pilots first. Make them a good deal you may need them in the future. Sell the limo business as it also was useful but a write off for taxes. The New York house, sell it too unless you want to live there with Jena. Ok sell it. The real estate market isn't so hot right now so do what you think is best with all the other real estate except for Mama's house. Of course you will take care of Mama through the trust. I have a business with Bob and Pilar, there, that ship that goes in and out of Cuba and Bob's general purchasing business. Bob will want to buy it cheap, whatever he offers you buy it. Oh yes the club on Paradise Island. There I own 51 percent; I have left a list of buyers. The present manager is the one most likely not to cheat you but by now, since my death he has most likely stolen most of its operating cash. He too is on the list of buyers but won't have the money. As you'll notice the property is still in your name. Yes, I paid you for it but didn't take you off the ownership. Sorry, it was convent for me. I did pay the taxes every year. Use this property as leverage on whoever takes my place. Since I cheated you on the price it's yours again to do as you see fit. If I would guess it will be Guido that's takes my place, but who cares none of those punks will be able to manage the entire business. I have 25% of two Vegas casinos sell that too. There are small checks and notes for Larry and my secretary. And last but not least my old friend. If you want, take it all but marry my Jena, I always wanted a son like you, signed Benny. Benny had well over 100 other businesses all over the world and stocks in almost every major company.

I looked over at Jena and she was just sitting there crying on the floor. She looked at me and asked how long it would take to be free. She said I've always been his daughter and now he's gone. Who will watch over me now? First of all, I said you need to stop that crying right now and help me finish putting this stuff in the safe. Are you really selling out to Guido she asked? I gave him my hand I said. On my part it's a done deal. We packed up the rest of the paperwork. I shut and locked the safe and I told her to go get a shower and put her PJs on. She looked at me and said oh boy I've just changed fathers. I then opened my door and saw Diane setting there at the table studying. She picked up her books and came right into my room and took over my desk. I had left Benny's letter on the desk and she asked to read it. I said she could but that it was none of anyone business but mine, she looked at me and said she understood. I walked over and shut the door. While reading she stopped and asked if it was true that I once owned the property that the Club Royal was sitting on? I told her it was a long story. She kept reading until she said "over my dead body". She then looked at me and asked? You don't need the money that bad do you and laughed. If you want she said you can marry me and have my money. She stood up and came to me face to face and said there's not one, not one chance she sleeping in this bed and I better not hear that you've been with her. Well I said I've never once locked my door to you but still to often I sleep alone. I'm sorry she said how unthoughtful of me, I never looked at it in that way. Diane then hugged me and for the first time said she loved me.

Ah saved by the knock on the door. Diane said he's busy. Then Betty said there's a man at the door asking for Diane. I opened my door and went to the door and opened the glass look out. My man was there and a young white male was with him. The young man was holding two bouquets of flowers. Frank, my man at the door said it was all clear. I said just one minute and walked to my room and put on my jacket and tucked my Browning between my pants and skin with my jacket hiding the gun. I went back to the door and opened it. Good evening the young man said, my name is Marco and I'm here looking for Diane. Come right in Marco I said. These Flowers are for the lady of the house Marco said holding out some daisies. Betty was right there and said it would be her as she took the flowers. Diane hadn't come out of my room as yet in fact she had closed my door. I went and knocked on the door and said she had a visitor. I believe Marco is his name. Jena quickly came out of her room in a pair of Diane's pajamas. Hello mam Marcos said. When Diane heard Marco say hello to Jena, Diane came right out. Hello Marco Diane said, what beautiful Roses she said. Come and sit with me on the couch. Captain Jim, Marco has come to asked me on a date Diane said. Diane said that she had told Marco that I said her studies had to come first. I don't know I said, Marco do you sail I asked? No sir he said but I sure would like to learn. Diane told me of her wonderful weekend of being a pirate and having water ballon wars. Well I said, Diane has been taking some courses on how to solve social difficulties with a friend that would love to teach you and Diane to sail. And in case Mr. Carson is occupied the sailing club gives free sailing lessons. Why don't you and Diane talk about that, I'm sure that Diane can find the time if you can. Yes Sir Marco said. Well, I said I have some calls to make, it was nice meeting you, Marco, I look forward to seeing you again soon. When Marco wasn't looking Diane stuck out her tong at me.

Actually I got a shower and went to bed. When Diane came in she got in bed and asked if I was asleep? She asked me why I wanted her to go out with Marco? I said he looked like a nice young man and that she needed to get out more. Besides I said you need to learn to sail and having Marco along should make you feel better about being with Carson.

Diane asked if I didn't want her? I then rolled over and said that I was planning to sell the business and do some traveling. Traveling by sail I said. Think about it I said, you would have to put off school for at least a year. So if you're interested, learn to sail and take scuba lessons at the YMCA like I did. Can't you teach me she asked? Yes, but its best that you don't pick up any of my bad habits. Like long showers Diane said. Something like that. I don't think I want to share myself with anyone just yet she said. Just give it a try I said, and get along with Jena. I believe she'll be around for a while. At least until I sell her businesses. I told Diane that during the next few weeks I'd be traveling to Nassau, The Caymans and maybe even Switzerland, all with Jena. If you're interested in joining us we could make 3 weekend trips of three days each. Diane said she wouldn't miss it. Diane said it was a good time to ask me about Cat and what my plans were. I told her that Cat was asked by Jacob to marry him. The kids were calling her mom and that I wasn't going to be taking the kids on my trip. Diane said that sounded good to her. Diane said she had told Cat that there would be no more loaning me out. Just a moment here I said, she didn't let me finish.

The next morning when I got up Jena was on the floor at the foot of my bed. She had a pillow under her head and a blanket over her up to the same. I hoped she woke up before Diane or she just might get a swift kick in the butt. My days would now be full of calls and meetings. I first called Roy to inform him of what was going on. He said Jena would need someone to represent her down here other than him. Roy said that she, or maybe even I being the trustee would need a financial planner. Roy said he would need to talk to Guido's attorney to get my agreed sale going. Roy said rumor of a sale would make the customers nervous. Roy wanted me to pass by his house later where we could talk. My list of incoming calls included. Guido, Guido's attorney, Larry, George Barone and Vinnie Catroni. The manager from the Club Royal was now on the phone, I took his call. He wanted to fly in today. I just told him that I would hold him personally responsible for any losses at the club and to keep the place going. He wanted to present me an offer to buy Jena out. I told him if he had the money and the price was right we would consider. I also said there wouldn't be any financing. I got a hold of Guido and he was now on the phone. Jimmy he said when you can come up. Sorry Guido I can't make it any time soon. You still buying I asked? Yes, he said. Ok I said have your attorney call mine and let's get this done. Guido said he'd like the bank, and the gambling shares too. I told Guido one sale at a time. He said no I want them all.

Well if that's what you want then make a cash offer. But after we first close on the agreement we already made.

Next was my call to Benny's attorney, he would fly in today for last will and testimony reading tomorrow at Jena's grandmothers house on Starr Island at midday. He confirmed that it was the same will that I had one of two originals of. Benny's attorney said that he had three offers for the bank and one for the casino business. I told him to bring the offers with him and we'd take a look.

George Barone wanted lunch and lunch he would get. George said that Guido had called him to get his assistance with me selling him the Benny's holdings, all the holdings. George said that Guido had said that he didn't know how but I had emptied Benny's safe. I told George that I didn't think that Guido had enough money to purchase what he wanted. George said that Guido wanted he and I to fly up and meet and talk things over. I said I wasn't going anywhere. Look I said if someone's got the money then make an offer, if its cash and a good price, I'll sell. My beeper kept going off while with George, he didn't like me even going to the men's room. I paid for lunch and like the last time George didn't go away happy.

I called the office and it was Bob that was calling. Bob wanted to meet over dinner. Bob still liked the Studio, he said it was best for the food and talking. Bob said he wanted to buy Jena out, you've already got me involved with two of your girlfriends and now all of a sudden I got involved with another one. Bob was made a 40% owner of the ex-Thompson line for next to nothing. Bob had the customers and contacts and was managing the new combined lines. The girls would manage the Thompson store of which Bob was not involved. Bob said he would offer $1,000,000.00 in installments. What about Pilar I said, why not buy her out? No can do he said. She doesn't have any money in it, just what she brings to the table. Pilar gets 10% of what we buy or sell that goes to or from Haiti. What about the silent partner I asked, the 25%? Who is the owner there I asked? Bob said he didn't even know. He just deposited the money in the bank. The Castro's were much like Pilar, but they got 50%. That left 25% for Benny and I and we paid the expenses! Poor Bob I said. How much did you send Benny per month? About

$300,000.00 per month Bob said. So you're offering Jena less than what she would make in a quarter. Bob said ok $1,400,000.00 but no more. I'll take her the offer I said. But if she takes it, it will need to be cash. Do you have it I asked? Bob asked, with a 10% discount? I laughed.

Bob said he had lost his Cuban girl, she found a younger man. What about you Jim Bob asked, I hear thru the grape vine that you're going to sell out. Now where did you hear a thing like that I asked? You might go on that sailing trip that you dream about but you'll be back Bob said. I, Bob said I chose the center, from there I can bend either way. You, Bob said, it looks as if you're against the both sides. You know whom ever buy's your business won't be able to keep it together. They're not you Bob said. You know Benny wrote me the same thing about his business, I said. Benny wrote that it didn't matter who took his place they wouldn't be able to keep it together. I asked Bob if it was alright with him if I gave the beach house to Cat for a wedding gift. Why ask me he said, if you would like me to return it to you I will I said. No my days there have been long gone. It's only a memory now Bob said. So I asked, where will you go when you retire? Well, somewhere that I can have a nice young girl sleeping by my side each night he said. You see Bob said, you have that right now but you're anxious to get out of that bed every morning not knowing if you'll be back at the end of the day. I once told our Michelle that you would never settle down. That's funny, I said; Michelle told me you and I were alike. It had been quite some time that I didn't pay for a dinner, but Bob did get this one.

Bob hadn't mentioned or even hinted that he might want me for a partner, I guessed it could have been that he didn't want the attention I drew. Anyway, I wouldn't accept his offer to buy Jean's 25%. Me buying at that price was still very much an option.

As I had mentioned to Guido the Andros contract was coming to an end, at least we hadn't received any additional requests. Lee and Janie would be getting married soon. I had heard that Lee's father would be getting out of jail on parole soon. It was understood that the wedding would take place once Lee's father was released. Lee's mother was spending a lot of time in Nassau. I had talked to Lee to keep the crew there on Andros to build a house to match the dock we had built.

I didn't want a big house, something small. It too would have to be built to withstand a direct hit from a Hurricane. Lee had done the design on his own. A two story three-bedroom house with a balcony all the way around the second floor with a small pool. I figured with that reef the fishing there would be good at least another 100 years. The closest neighbor on the south side would be the Navy. I didn't really talk to Lee about his future, if he and Janie played it right they should be just fine with money.

Tomorrow would be another long day. Benny's will would be read at Jena's grandmother's house at noon. It shouldn't take long and I didn't know if Larry was going to show, I hoped he would.

At home Jena was watching TV and Diane was studying. I asked Jena when she was going back to school. She said she wasn't planning to go back. For what she asked? For one thing I said to learn and meet people other than in a bar. Find a husband start a family. Jena looked at me and said I have a family. Diane looked over at Jena and said that we may be family but that she wasn't going to have any children with this family. Jena said after tomorrow she'd be able to buy a husband. Diane said yes but not the one you might want. Jena then looked at Diane and stuck out her tongue. I reminded Diane that after the will reading I'd be taking everyone to Joe's Stone Crab for a late lunch. Jena was quick to ask if Diane was going to be there at the reading. Diane will be at the house; the reading will be done in the study. I hope you girls have special clothes for Saturday night. We'll be leaving here Saturday morning and Saturday night visiting the Club Royal. Diane said they could stop her at the door because she was a Bahamian. Jena said don't worry little sis I'll make sure you get in. Ok I said just a warning about the clothes, I'm wearing my Tux and am going to pitch the Michelle charity. I'd appreciate you both on the stage with me looking your best. I'll be matching any donations.

Friday morning came and went, we were at the Starr Island house at 12 noon ready. Larry and Benny's long time secretary Ms. Larson both showed up. Larry was frisked at the main door and relieved of his gun. The attorney asked me for the letters for Larry and Ms. Larson. Both opened the letters and silently read them. Both received a gratitude check for their service. The attorney read the will without stopping. At the end the attorney asked if there were any questions. Ms. Larson asked if she was to continue working. I handed her a letter from me as trustee of the bank and asked her to stay on at least until the bank was sold. She said she would be at work Monday morning. No other questions were asked. The will was signed by Jena's mother, Jena, myself and the attorney. That was it. Larry asked if he could have a word. Larry said he had stopped the car that night and waited one hour before returning to Benny's house. Larry said he acted dumb but Guido didn't buy it. Larry said he needed a job. I told Larry that he could start at once as the security for Benny's mother. I was sure Larry wasn't too happy with that but he took the job.

Jena rode with us and Benny's mother in her limo. We all went to Joe's for lunch. At lunch Jena, Diana and I decided to see if we could catch the afternoon seaplane flight to Nassau. Jena asked if she could invite Karen to join us. My first call was to Ted to see if his people could make the flight. Ted said that he'd have one man waiting at the seaport and two more that would fly over tonight. The hurricane house only had one bedroom so we would need at least one room at the boarding house and maybe someone could stay at Cat's. The four girls said they would all sleep at the hurricane house with me. Oh boy I said there goes the neighborhood. I mentioned that there was only one bathroom and the place would be a mad house, them getting ready for the club Saturday night. They didn't seem to mind. The flight was short and as we got there our crawfish boats were pulling in. Peter was getting the Hatteras ready and invited Karen and Jena to go out with the tourist that had contracted the boat for the night. At first Karen said no thanks but then Peter said it was four Miami Dolphin players, Karen quickly changed her mind. Jena wasn't too impressed but said she would go a long to keep Karen Company. This left Diane and I to visit the other boats even meeting Janie down at the wharf waiting for Lee. Janie looked darn good for now being a mother. That put a thought in my head that all the girls could assist tomorrow night with raising money for Michelle's charity. I wouldn't ask Janie's help without first speaking with Lee. Otis's boat "Johnny" had been the first boat in. He and his girl were down there cleaning. It would be normal that Maggie wouldn't be too friendly as she most likely felt me responsible for her father being in jail. Otis on the other hand stopped what he was doing to come and greet us. As Otis spoke to Diane and I, he mentioned that he was glad that since Cat was off the market for a husband at least I was still with a Bahamian girl. I didn't think anything of his comment at the time. Otis said his catch was good but wanted to return the traps to the reef. I mentioned that in my opinion they should wait until the area that they were in, the crawfish started getting smaller. I said it was good to have Maggie help clean the boat, Otis said that Maggie was going out with him every day. She reminds me a lot of Deanna Otis said. I asked how Angee liked her? Otis said that Angee loved having her with them. Otis said they would marry sometime in June and to keep that month open for the wedding. There won't be any wedding unless you're here Otis said. I asked about Mark as I didn't see his wife on the wharf. Otis said that Mark would be returning tomorrow afternoon as we were getting the largest hauls from the west side of Andros. The last Bertram was pulling in as we spoke. I said hello to that Captain and then Diane and myself walked on over to Willy's bar. Sitting at the bar were Karen and Jena. Karen said those football players were all old married men and that she and Jena decided not to go. Jena said they would later hit the disco. It was good to see Willy; he was happy to see us too. I borrowed his phone and called Cat to let her know we were here and to say that she needed to go with us to the club tomorrow as we were going to raise some money for the Charity. I'll need you looking your best. Cat said she be in the center by 9:00 p.m. Cat's voice didn't seem the same, the excitement in her voice wasn't there.

The four of us would stay at Will's until about 8:30 or so then we'd walk on over to the Bahamian Cuisine for some dinner. Diane said she was still full of stone crab. The hurricane house would be cramped but at least Karen and Jena each got a couch. The girls had talked Diane into going with then to the disco. Karen said I was an old fogey for not wanting to go with them. Diane came into the room and shut the door behind her to kind of ask permission for her to go to out with the girls. I told her she didn't need my permission to go. She said she did; this is something new I said. Yes, Diane said ever since you're trying to get me to go out with Marco she said. You're my man she said. I said I'm your best friend, I wanted her to see me for what I am, not what she wants me to be. You need to get out and do things, I didn't say you need another man. What if I get scared she asked? That's why your need to go I said. She hugged and kissed me and got ready to go. I would send the only security man I had with them and told them to stick together. Karen knew she must be the leader and that Jena needed watching for one thing and Diane needed her to watch for any signs of uneasiness. I would walk on over just as soon as the other security men showed.

The girls left at about 10:00 p.m., the two additional security men came in at about 10:50 p.m., the two of them and I walked on over to the disco. It had been quite some time since I'd been there, years in fact. The wall where Deanna sat while we started talking hadn't changed much, sure did bring back some memories. Darn good ones. We made our way inside and met the other security man. Mack was the first and then there was Patrick and Sam. Mack pointed out the girls, were all dancing together. Over there Mack said is trouble, I figure one Columbian and three Cubans. The Columbian is armed. They approached the girls as they came in but Karen chased them off. They've done nothing but watch the girls ever since. Over there Mack said, that one wants to ask Jena to dance so bad but so far can't. I said you can't be afraid of rejection in a disco. But not to worry if he's looking Jena will see him. If she wants to dance with him she'll do the asking. Mack said the bar tender made a call just as I walked in. Mack ask Patrick to keep an eye on the girls while he went over to speak with the bar tender. I watch as Mack asked the bar tender who he had called. The bar tender must have said something smart and Mack slapped him with the back of his Hand. Mack came back over and said that we might be getting company of some kind. Mack told Sam to go outside and see whom might arrive. Mack said that he thought that if more than a couple showed up that we should leave. The bar tender then made another call. Mack told him that if there was any trouble the bar tender would be the first to receive his displeasure.

Sure enough Jena walked over to the shy one and took his hand and led him into the group. The Columbian didn't like that and started at the girls. Mack went to intervene but I stopped him. Give the girls a chance to handle it I said, they know you're here. The Columbian entered the group dancing. The girls then formed a circle with the shy one in the center blocking out the Columbian. The Columbian just threw up his hands and walked back to his group. Good call Mack said. If he goes back, then you should step in I said. Soon Sam came in and said a taxi had showed up with three tough guys. They all look to be high Sam said but they didn't come in as yet. He then went back outside. It was only 5 minutes later when Cat showed up. Mack didn't know Cat, she walked right up and kissed me, and asked if we could go outside to talk. She took me by the hand and led me outside. Cat looked like she had been crying, she didn't waste any time. Cat said she had decided to marry Jacob but didn't want me to hear it from someone else. She said she still loved me but that the children and Jacob needed her. I told her not to cry and that it was ok. As I hugged her Sam pointed out that now there were four and they were headed in. I told Cat that I still needed her for tomorrow night and that I was needed back inside. Go home I said. We'll talk tomorrow night, it's ok. I turned and walked and when I looked back she was gone. Once inside the four that just came in went first and sat at the bar. They were chatting with the Bartender. I said ok let's get the girls out of here. Mack went for the girls while Patrick, Sam and I watched the Bar. By now Mack was on the way out with the girls while we watched the bar. Patrick pulled a small Uzi from his backside and was holding it with both hands looking at the bar. As I looked around here came Cat in holding a gun in her hand. Cat walked up and said I know that look. Buy now Mack had exited with the girls and we started backing toward the door. Once we were out I stepped back in with Patrick following. I went up to the bar and said good evening gentlemen, is here anything I can help you with. None of them said a word. I then said looking at one of them, don't I know you from somewhere? The man looked back at me and said I don't think so friend. You own this place don't you I asked? Why yes he answered. You own that bar in shanty town too I said. Well the man said a matter of fact I do. What's the name of that bar I asked? The Cat House he answered. Actually the man said, I was called alerting me that you were in the bar maybe looking for trouble. We came just as quickly as we could, thinking someone might need our help. I was behind the bar that night you shot up Miguel he said. Miguel still doesn't walk to good he said. I hear he doesn't walk at all I said. I hear that he's in a wheel chair. Yes he said, Miguel is my brother. Well I said, now I understand the interest. The Columbian and the three Cubans with you I asked? I know them he said. Well here I am if you're looking for some payback I said. The man swallowed and said not tonight friend, some other time. I then said that now that we know each other this was the best chance he was going to get. Patrick pulled on my jacket letting me know it was time to go. As we backed out the man said see you real soon gringo.

As we stepped out the door Cat was right there with her gun in hand. I looked at the gun and saw it was my very first. It was my grandfather's 32-20 that I had found in has attic. Patrick said he had wanted the girls to start walking home with him but Diane said she was staying with Cat, Jena and Karen said they were staying with Diane. Patrick said they were the four musketeers. Cat still with the gun in her hand, looked at Diane and said you need to learn to handle a gun and tackle like a linebacker. Cat walked to her pick-up got in and as she pulled away said she'd see us tomorrow night. We then started walking for the house. That young man that was dancing with mainly Jena was walking with us. What's your name Jena asked? My name in Johnathon. Jena introduced us all. Johnathon said he was from the cruise ship. He was on the ship with his grandmother. They were from Norway or something like that. Jena said she'd like to walk Johnathon back to his ship. Patrick said he had it. It was just after 1:00 a.m. when Diane and I got into bed. Diane asked what Cat had come for and how she knew we were at the disco. I said that she had come to tell me that she had decided to marry Jacob. She wanted to tell me before I heard it from someone else. She had stopped by here and guessed that we were at the disco. What did you say to her? I wasn't listening, I was occupied with watching those jerks. Cat understood that I couldn't just stop what was going on and talk to her. So Diane asked? What would you have said? Well I would ask her if she was sure. If she was I would support her 100%. If she wasn't sure before tonight she is now I said. Not too many women need to go back to their car and get a gun to help your husband get out of a bar or disco. I really don't want that for anyone but I've built a reputation here and I believe I need to keep it in tack. Reputation caused us not to have had to fight tonight. Diane said I think the shower is free. The last thing that Diane said that night was, learn to shoot, sail, scuba dive and tackle like a linebacker.

Morning came and I was out and about early. I had breakfast with Angee. She brought me up to date on Otis and Maggie. Looked like everything was moving right along. I mentioned to her that it was Cat's idea and I agreed to make the house that was being built on her lot a wedding gift. Angee hugged me and said we had both come a long way from that first night at Mr. Bob's. God took my Johnny she said but brought me Otis. I don't know what I would have done without him.

Lee and Captain Mike had come in last night, once again as I was walking to the wharf Captain Mike was walking up for breakfast. You still sleeping on that boat, you old sea buzzard? Mike said it was like home. Beer in the fridge and a pillow under his head and the sound of the ocean moving under him. I asked how the catch was coming a long and he said he'd never seen anything like it. Captain Mike said that he too was going to find himself a woman and rent the house that Lee had started on Andros. Not a sole to bother me he said. He shook my hand and walked on to find something to eat.

Otis, Maggie and their crew were just about ready to shove off. I told Otis that I had heard that he and Maggie had been diving my old treasure spot. Otis acknowledged that they were spending two Sundays a month at the sight. Otis said that they had found several coins and a few small jewels. Otis said they were practicing to get ready to start searching for that second ship that could be out there. Deanna had once told him that I had found a small boat near where we night fished. I told Otis that diving on the west side of the channel wasn't safe, and I would have never taken Deanna in the water there under any circumstances. If you want to dive there I will go with you after I sell my mainland business. Diving there we will need four men in the water and two look outs on board. Maggie could very well help aboard. Otis asked when that would be because he wanted a house and boat of his own. It's not that I don't appreciate what I have here, but I want to one-day work for myself, he said. I said I was sure he'd have the chance one day and to keep dreaming.

Marks crew would work the east bed traps today and take Sunday off. Mark was still making those overnight trips to the west side of Andros. I told Mark that it was possible that we could start selling fish, conch and crawfish using the small air strip near the Navy base. It's just a thought I said, think about it some.

The girls had finally woken up and had eaten at Angee's. Jena said she was ready for some beach time. I said let's go. The girls all had to be back early as they all had appointments at the hair salons. Johnathon showed up at the house. Jena had invited him to go to the beach with them.

We took two taxis and went to the Paradise islands east side beach. No one there to bother anyone. From there, we walked west to the Holiday Inn. That $20.00 tourist ticket was now $25.00. The girls loved the pool bar. The time passed and we all headed back to Nassau. The girls did there thing and I sat and spoke politics with Willy. Willy said a lot could change with Mr. Thompson out of the picture. I said the drug dealers were still out there noting that the disco was now owned by the same group that owned the shanty town bar. Ever think about owning a disco I asked Willy? Oh no Sir don't even think about it. Ok I said but if you know someone that would be interested in owning a disco that didn't permit the drug trade in to let me know. Having that Shanty town drug dealing bar is one to many, but having it right at our back door is something else. Well Willy said if you think about it, life could be a lot better if we could elect some strong officials. Maybe Cat could run for mayor Willy said.

The girls were dressed, Cat arrived and we all went to my favorite restaurant to eat. From there again, we took two taxis and again crossed that skinny bridge.

We arrived at the club and at the desk asked to inform the manager we were there. Within two minutes the manager was there and introduced himself and his top personnel. I informed him that we wanted a front table and that before each show I was going to make a pitch for the Michelle Charity and was hoping that the club would participate as they had in the past. The manager said that Jena had the last word.

As we walked through the club seemed that every eye was on the girls, I had one on each arm and two walking behind. It was almost like we were Royalty. We were seated and champagne and flowers appeared. It wasn't two minutes when a couple came to the table; as they walked up, Cat stood up first and greeted them. The couple had gone on one of the Hatteras trips. They remembered Cat and said how they had enjoyed Cat's company. Cat introduced them first, Mr. & Mrs. Kline from New York, then us one by one me being the last. Mr. Kline then said that I must be the famous King Fish that they always heard about. Well Sir don't believe all what you hear I said. Well if Cat said it we believed it he said. I asked if they would like to join our table but the Mrs. said they had guest with them that they must attend to. Mr. Kline looked disappointed, and hugged Cat saying that they would like to take that trip again soon.

The curtain then opened and the announcer stepped out. Tonight he said we have the honor of having one of the most famous fisherman of our islands. Ladies and Gentleman the King Fish. The crowd clapped as all five of us walked up onto the stage. I took the mic and said that we also have a very special guest tonight, I introduced Jena as the majority owner of the club. Jena then made a curtsy like I had never seen before. Each of the girl had top hats in their hands. Tonight we are asking for your support in a very special cause for our Bahamas. When this club opened in 1966 our greatest entertainer was Michelle. Michelle was just 18 when she became the symbol of this club. Before she passed away she had started a charity that has built a school, a clinic, a community center as well as over 50 homes for the poor. When Michelle died she left her entire fortune to her cause. Tonight we are asking for your support thru donations. For each dollar we collect I will match two for one. A man stood up and asked that if he gave $10,000.00 then I would give $20,000.00? I said yes Sir. Well bring that hat over here then. All the girls then started passing the hats. Karen then quickly sat at our table and counted the checks and cash. Karen came back up to the stage and whispered in my ear the number $33,000.00. Ladies and gentlemen I said. Your kind hearts have donated just over 33,000.00 dollars, and the Michelle Charity will have an additional $100,000.00 to work with. Please a well learned applaud for yourselves. While the crowd applauded Jena came and took the mic. I have an announcement to make she said. I don't know if the club has this much champagne but I would like to celebrate with you all. Waiters please pour as much champagne as you can until everyone has a glass or we run out. The club adds $100,000.00 to the Michelle Charity and $100.00 dollars in clips to every table for your kindness. The crowd then stood and there was more applauding. I took back the mic and thanked them all and said to enjoy the show. As we walked down the stairs I said to Jena that she just gave away $115,000.00 of her inheritance. Jena turned and said no only about $58,000.00. The other $57,000.00 came from the other stock holders. Cat almost in tears said she was greatfull for all the support and also gave Jena a special hug and thanks. Cat said that this money would keep the charity going for two more years. Well I said let see what the second show brings. I said that if anyone wanted a break we would meet just outside the room entrance just before the next show. I looked at Jena and said my number of $115,000.00 will be correct by the end of the night. The second show will have people standing outside the room to get a look at you girls.

I was right, the next show brought in more money. The club had to run out and barrow 100 bottles of champagne for the second show. The night collected well over $425,000.00 for Michelle's charity. When looking and recounting the donations the club manager had donated $10,000.00 of his own money. Cat was so happy that she just couldn't stop crying.

It was a good night; we had collected enough money for Michelle's Charity that should keep it going for a least 5 years. Sunday morning, we all would return to Miami.

Jena was now very wealthy, and asked for money to buy a new car and said she would buy an apartment on the same floor. I suggested my old apartment for which I still had the old safe. Jena would buy that apartment from me and we became neighbors, Jena then said she had invited Johnathon to come and visit.

I sold the container business and a lot of what Benny had left Jena, Jena was no longer holding any percentages of any clubs nor any mob related business. It all happened so fast. The new owners offered Joe to stay with them. Surprising so Joe went with the English company Sea Containers. Joe wasn't happy about the sale but he would receive his share. BBS and Harrison were stunned by the sale. They said I should have offered my share to them first. I noted that BBS hadn't asked my opinion when they attached me to Harrison or the Norfolk people. Guido had paid me only $2,000,000.00 of the $6,000,000.00 due to the amount of cash he paid Jena. We didn't finance any of Jena's money as I didn't want to get caught up in any problems me being trustee. Bob had given us his best offer and as Benny suggested I deposited my cash into Jena's account buying her shares of Bob's shipping business. After all these years, Bob and I were finally partners.

I delivered the Morgan to Merrill Stevens to replace the engine, having them make some other repairs and improvements. This as I was getting ready to finally go on my trip.

Diane was studying and taking shooting lessons with Carson on Wednesday nights and sailing lessons on the weekends. Marco was also taking sailing lessons with her.

Diane, after talking to Cat on the phone one night asked me if I knew someone named Dick Butkus? Cat had asked her to ask me. I told Diane that that he was a famous linebacker. This got a smile from both of us.

Since Jena had gotten her own apartment, Diane and I had lots of time together.

Cat and Jacob did get married in a small service at the Nassau Methodist church. I sent Jacob paper work that if he signed would give Cat the beach house as a wedding gift. I still wasn't sold on Jacob.

It wasn't long before I got a call from my friend Robin. Robin had been the latest Miami branch manager of Sea Containers. Robin was pissed! He said I had betrayed his company and him personally. He said I had sold out to the devil himself. Robin was right, I did sell to the devil. I went to Robin's office and we made an agreement. I would open a facility just for them, no other customers. I would stay one year and then they would buy the facility from me. Robin agreed. I was now thirty years old, putting off my retirement off for one more year. I asked Robin to pick the name of the depot. Robin called me the next day, Omni Terminals. Within the week the depot was open and running. Since this was a small business I was thinking I would have lots of free time. Sea Container was only moving about 230 units a month. Container control would be done by a girl named Evette while her father Papo would work the yard.

The computer guy that was now working with the group that I had sold out to was sent on vacation, while gone the new owners hired someone to steal all Tim's programing. I had explained my arrangement with the new owners before the sale. Any programs that Tim built while working with me would be 50% his. The new owners thought it would be cheaper to steal the programing than buy his half. At least Tim had saved all the programs before he left. When Tim came back they then fired him. We kind of figured they wouldn't keep their word so we had worked a plan before his vacation. We obtained a used IBM model 34 and once Tim was fired he would run the office and systems for Omni. We wouldn't make so much money due to the small volume but we could pay good salaries and provide a top service for Robin's Sea Containers.

We didn't see Jena very much after she purchased her apartment. Jena and Johnathon had hit it off and Jena was spending a lot of time traveling. I worked it out so she had a generous amount of money to spend every month. If she didn't spend it, then it just added to the next month. Jena was well off.

Diane was out of school for the summer and seeing, Marco, at least while Carson was teaching them to sail. I said something to Diane about getting away for a week or so, she said ok but didn't seem too interested. Once again we seemed to be drifting as lovers.

The Navy hadn't paid my last invoice so I made arrangements to fly up and visit. Of course I thought it was going to have something to do with a budget overrun. If so I was willing to do some horse trading.

The drugs that were coming into Nassau were being shipped in from Cuba. From Nassau, shipments were being made to Miami. The shipping line now doing the moving was part mine. I wanted it stopped. I also wanted to rid Nassau of that Shanty town bar and Miguel's brother. When I left the Secretary of the Navy's office, it was all agreed, the Admiral would get what he wanted and hopefully I would get what I wanted. The navy would form a blockade form Cuba to The Bahamans. Even one of the sonar units that we help build would be used. The Commodore guaranteed that for two months nothing would get through.

Out of nowhere a man showed up in Nassau offering a large supply that could be brought in from Columbia. It would a onetime shipment but it had to be all cash. Tomas, the brother of Miguel and owner of the shanty town would need to borrow the money. I figured that Tomas would go to the casinos for the money. Funny how things work out. Tomas got his money and would purchase the same drugs that the Navy had seized. The exchange was done just one mile off Nassau. Tomas himself was aboard when the Navy stopped him, and the drugs. Tomas used the papers of both the bar and disco to pay an attorney to help get him out on bail. Tomas made bail and vanished from sight. Guess who purchased the bar and disco? The bar was dismantled and bulldozed the very next week. The disco was donated to the City of Nassau under the agreement that they would manage it as a disco for young people. No alcohol was to be served. I didn't think the Law would ever see Tomas again. The mob was short millions and I was sure they would get their man.

After that mission was complete I was ready for some free time. I mentioned to Diane that I was thinking of taking some time off, Diane said I deserved it but didn't ask to go. I told only Karen where I was headed and said she was to tell no one. I could be reach by only her. I hadn't been shopping on my own in years, Burdines was still my favorite clothing & make-up store, Scotty's my favorite food store and Big Daddy's my favorite liquor store. I purchased stakes and two cases of Dom Perignon champagne and got crawfish from Nassau. The same two engine airplane was hired and I was off for Haiti. No security just me.

We scheduled our arrival with the timely arrival of the once a day air service from Port a Prince. I hired an old pick up and was off for the Chateau.

My plane was not hired for the return; it was a one-way trip. I wanted to see how long I could stay away. When we drove up to the gate there was old man Pablo with his shot gun. I didn't bring any heavy arms as I knew that I had plenty on site. The house hold looked happy to see me but were surprised I was alone. The food I brought with me was put in the new refrigerator. I told them the beef and seafood was not to be frozen. I went up and changed into my bathing suit and took a towel out to the beach. I said I wanted an iced pitcher of Rum punch brought out to me. I must have looked funny carrying a briefcase out to the beach, inside were my two guns with extra clips.

It wasn't 15 minutes; I was still it the water when I saw what was coming my way. I started walking to my towel and said. Good morning Salinas, I thought you only worked with the horses. She wasn't smiling when she said, it was my mother's idea. Well I don't want to keep you from your horses. Their ok she said, would you like to go riding later when it's not so hot she said. Too hot for me or the horses I asked? She smiled, how about a swim I asked? Oh no she said I don't have a suit. Go upstairs and look in the large suit case. There are bathing suits in there that I believe will fit you. Salinas set the tray down and started walking and then the walk turned into a run. I was wearing a hat and sun glasses with the sun directly overhead. Several minutes passed but there she was walking toward me. I couldn't see her face only her outline as she walked. I thought the sand must have been burning the bottoms of her feet but her walk didn't show any hurry to it. The shapely silhouette turned into a beautiful reality, she stopped within 3 feet of me and smiled and said this is my favorite one. Yes I said, it fits you perfectly. The other clothes she asked? Are they all my size she asked? I hope so I replied. Did you come for me or the beach she asked? I came for the horses I said. But whatever doesn't fit them I guess you can have. And where are all your women she asked? Presently you are the only girl that I'm thinking about. Why should I believe you she asked? Well for one thing I'm here alone, just you and me. My mother said you will make love to me and then leave and come back with another. My mother said, when she saw you had come alone, she knew that you had come for me. And she sent you carrying that rum punch anyway I asked? I came to change you mine she said. I will make you love me and not want another. The only door that your men placed a lock on was mine, my mother said that was to keep me safe.

Salinas then walked right pass me and to the water's edge turned and asked, are you coming with me? She held out her hand and I took it.

The trip seemed short but I was there for ten of the shortest days I could remember. I had never wanted to stay somewhere before so bad. Karen had sent me five or six telex's asking if I was ok. The last telex back I said to send the plane for the next day. I did want to take her with me but didn't, I wanted to see how I did without her. I had never had better care from any woman, Never! Salinas didn't cry when I left, she just said that she be there waiting for me to come back. Maybe I'll have a surprise for you when you return she said. I don't like surprises I said. As I left in the old Taxi, Salinas raced alongside on her horse. The dust had made her pull back. I turned and she was there waving.

Back in Miami, the IRS had visited the Omni office looking for me twice. Karen said she didn't want to bother me with it. I thanked her. The IRS had left a card so I called and made an appointment for the next day.

Seemed that Omni was getting bombarded by customers that wanted to leave the facility that I had sold. The new Owners raised pricing, cut services and hours of operation to include not being open Saturday. Every inquiry was turned down.

My IRS appointment did not go well. They were starting an audit on my old business. I showed them a copy of my sales agreement that stated they, the new owners were to pay all taxes to include any audits. The IRS said that agreement was between them and me and had nothing to do with the IRS. The NICE IRS lady warned me not to try to hide any of my money.

I called the companies new manager and informed them of the pending audit. The manager said he already had the IRS visit and received the official notice. The manager said that Guido had ordered to stop all payments to me until the audit was finished. This didn't sit well but I figured that I might had done the same. I didn't need the money so I didn't even bother to call Guido. When opening Omni, I put the stock in Karen's name. Karen was also listed as the President. I had no problem getting Karen an ILA contract.

Guido had given me 60 days to find other personal transportation. Both my cars and even Karen's were in the old business's name. I told Karen to go out and buy us three more vehicles. One for her and two for me. This time around I wanted the same model BMW and a pick-up. The BMW would need to be armored but not the truck. Karen would get another BMW too.

Two days later my Miami banker called and said my bank accounts had been frozen by the IRS. My North Miami house had a levy filed on it, my Morgan too. I went back to the IRS with my accountant and asked what was going on. The IRS said their audit personnel had reported illegal activity in the reporting and in my investment fund reporting. We explained that we were making pre-tax payments on all accounts and as far as we knew there was over $2,000,000.00 in an account for any additional taxes. The IRS lady said that our reserves account had been depleted. And according to the new owners that money was now theirs and any outstanding taxes were owed by you personally. We again showed her the contract and she said again that the contract we signed was with them not the IRS. At this point I called Guido. Guido, I said our contract clearly states that you would pay any taxes due using the $2.000.000.00 tax reserves and the over $4,000,000.00 in receivables. Guido said so sue me and then hung up.

It was now Friday afternoon. I called and asked Tim to wait for me in the office. Tim was there when I arrived. Tim had told me that he had a way to erase the memory off all our old computers and make the programs disappear. Tim said if they hadn't made back up when they stole his programs and hadn't changed the eternal phone numbers for the computers then he would only need to make a phone call to each computer and type in the cross bone message. If I wanted, he could do it now and by Monday they would have nothing. I said, do it. I then called a school buddy that worked with Southern Bell. My friend with Southern Bell would meet me at the 1800 club. I also called Ted to send one of our group to the club so I could also chat with them. I called Diane but she was going to an early movie with Marco. Now this was a first. Diane said they would stop by the club after the show. Damn maybe I could have brought Salinas home with me after all. Maybe not yet.

I was still driving my vet but if my plan with the computer failures went well, then for sure I would be dropping off the Vet tomorrow morning. Karen had already dropped her BMW off. She already had her new BMW but mine wouldn't be ready for another week. The pick-up would be ready tomorrow.

I stayed with Tim until he had called each of our old computers. We wouldn't know if they had made back up until next Monday. But they hadn't changed their phone numbers so Tim was able to get in and by Monday morning their computer screens would be blank.

At the club I spoke with Jeffery who worked with Southern Bell. I was looking for telephone disruption for Guido's two largest Miami terminals on Monday morning starting at 9:00 a.m. for as long as possible. Jeffery said he'd see to it, he asked if 3 or 4 hours would do I said that would be great. Steve our metro police friend also showed up. I told him that the traffic was going to be terrible Monday morning at all my old facilities and if he could arrange to divert the trucks not to block the street or ticket those that did. Steve too got the message.

The idea behind this was that on Monday with the computers down, none of the facilities would be able to receive or dispatch containers. What a mess it would be and with the phones down it would even be worse. The Police would be sending their trucks on their way so not to block traffic. WOW, if they had made backups for the systems they wouldn't recover for three or four days. If they had no backups they would not recover.

I felt good about the plan. I sat and thought about how much money I could be losing over this. The IRS could capture about $650,000.00 worth of cash and bennies plus the almost $6,000,000.00 Guido owed me. I already was thinking on how to recover part of that money. Most of the container lift machines I had purchased under the name of Miami Machinery which was not incorporate so maybe just maybe the IRS wouldn't touch them. I intended to include the lifts in the sale but if Guido wanted to play, well, let the games begin. Then there was always that "ACE" card that I was holding.

Tim and his wife showed up as well as Karen. Karen didn't know about the plan. She was more concerned about the IRS. I told her not to worry. Steve and Jeff didn't stick around past 10:00 p.m., they were family men. At 10:30 p.m. Diane and Marco showed up. Karen said what's up girl and went and gave Diane a hug and kiss. Who is this Karen asked Diane? Diane said this is Marco he's just a friend. Karen being Karen asked Marco to stand up. Marco did and Karen walked around him and said, well honey when you get through with him you just let me know. Diane nor Marco liked the comment very much and we could see it made Marco uncomfortable. Marco finished his drink and said he'd be getting home. He thanked Diane for the movie and started to walk out. Diane looked at me and asked what she should do. You like him I asked? Diane said yes. I said then get after him. Diane took off running. Karen looked at me and said, aren't you going to keep any of those girls, what are you afraid of she asked? It happens to everyone. Oh yeah I said, where's yours. I haven't found him yet she said. Well I did try it and it didn't work out to good. You just give them away Karen said. I'm just not ready I said, getting close but not ready. Well Karen said when Diane moves out I'm moving in. Don't even think about I said. I got the next one all lined up. Well Karen said she can use your room and I'll use Diane's. You going dancing tonight Karen aske? Nop, I think I'll close the bar down or go on over to the sailing club and see what Carson is up to. You didn't call him back? Karen asked. No I thought I would see him here tonight. Well she said, call him as he said something about taking a trip to Grenada. Why would he go way down there I asked when he has Nassau so close? I went to the pay phone and called his number. With no answer I decided to pass by the sailing club. Karen said she'd meet me there but from there we would stop by the Alley to dance.

At the club there was a note for me that said that "you just missed me, on the way to Grenada on a fishing trip, will call when I return, Carson" I didn't think too much of it and was unhappy in missing him. Now I would have to go dancing. I danced a few with Karen and then Karen picked out something she might like for the night. She came back to the table with a big smile and said ok you can go now. It was almost 1:00 a.m. when I got home and I decided to move some of my money and Jewelry to Jena's apartment. Jena it seemed hadn't been home for at least a week. Jena had left me keys to both the apartment and her safe. The safe was the one I had taken out the guts when I moved and put back when she moved in. I was worried that the IRS might show up with some kind of search warrant looking for valuables. I fell asleep in Jena's bed.

When I woke I made the bed and went back to my apartment for some breakfast. I told Betty that I didn't think anyone would come over the weekend but that by next week, the IRS might show up. If they have a warrant then let them in, if not don't even open the door. If they want in the safe they'll have to bring a lock smith and maybe, even then they won't be able to get in. Make sure you tell them it's bobby trapped. When they ask you how just say you don't know. Tell them that you heard something about needing a gas mask. The safe had a sticker that read "Beware Nitrogen Gas under Pressure", it should be fun to watch. I had installed a valve that if someone pushed in the rod that needed to be pushed just a hair too far, air pressured would sound off and a harmless gas would be sprayed out the same hole.

I asked Betty what time Diane had come home and she said she didn't know. I asked if she was in her room and she said that Diane was in my bed.

I went to work, it looked and felt strange being so few workers and so little work. It even felt stranger not having a boat in the water, for that matter not having a boat. The only thing I could even think of doing was to catch the afternoon seaplane over to Nassau. Karen was at the office and I mentioned it to her and she said let's do it. Evette was there too and asked if she could come along. So I called Diane and she said she and Marco were going to visit his parents that lived Orlando and at the same time see Disney World. I thought that was moving right along.

It would be the three of us, Evette, Karen and myself. I wanted to take the girls out on the Hatteras on Sunday when Peter returned from his Saturday night fishing trip, the boat should be back at about 10:00 a.m. We didn't take any fancy cloths just swim wear and jeans. When we landed, we went straight to the Holiday Inn. We rented a cabana and spent about two hours on the beach. We then went from there to the Hurricane house dropped our bags and headed to see Willy. Willy said he was happy to see Karen again especially in what she was wearing. Evette was a short pretty girl that Willy said barely made the criteria that he could serve her alcohol. Willy was talking about her chin barely reached over the bar top. Willy just had to tell that old story of Rusty's and my first bar visit. I don't know how it came up but Evette said she was the best fish cook in the world and she wanted to cook some fish. Willy and I just laughed. Evette's father and mother were from Cuba. I don't think Evette even knew we were fishermen from way back. Willy said there was this famous fisherman in Nassau that they called the King Fish. Evette said she wanted to meet him. Willy said you're sitting next to him. No way she said, then asked can we go fishing? I said, I catch them, and you cook them? Evette said you got a deal. The boats had already come in so we walked to Angee's and asked about Otis. Angee said they were upstairs. Otis, and Maggie were going out in the morning diving the old wrecks. When Evette and Karen heard they too wanted to go. Neither of the girls could scuba but both said they could skin dive using masks and snorkels. Otis said he would have enough gear on board. We said we'd use the Hatteras and meet them there at the dive site at about 11:00 a.m. This would only give us about two hours in the water. Otis said he would call a few hands to assist us with the boat. Evette asked? We're still going fishing tonight right? I said yes indeed I wouldn't miss it. Karen said she would catch the biggest fish. We walked to the store and purchased what Evette said she needed. There were plenty of drinks on either of the Bertram's. The first Bertram we jumped on was gassed up and ready. We picked up ice and Karen shoved off, and we were on our way. The three of us were on the bridge heading west south west. It was now almost 9:00 p.m. I told the girls about the red sky at night sailor's delight. The sky had been red and the weather should be good. We pulled up a nearby trap and took out its 5 crawfish and put back the crawfish heads and two cans of cat food. We then headed to the reef's edge. As we used to do, I anchored 30 feet from the reef. Evette was raring to go. I baited her first hook showing her how. Then cast it out just short of the reef and I laughed. Karen had watch me do Evette's and she did the same. Evette had one on the line before Karen's line hit the water. You should have seen that little girl fight that fish. As I swooped it in with the net I said well there's supper. No Evette said I want to keep fishing. I walked back to the stern and connected the salt water pump system to one of the ice boxes. Then I took out the hook out of Evette's fish and threw it in the box. Karen was next and they went back and forth catching fish. I thought they would never get tired. Finally, Karen was getting tired and stopped fishing. Evette just kept right on going. I then unhooked the last one and took the reel away from her. I looked at her and said I was too tired to eat and I was going to bed. I looked around and Karen was gone. I went to check the front cabin door and it was locked. I knocked on the door and got nothing, I then turned and Evette was getting in the only bunk left. Evette too looked like she was now asleep. I looked at the space in Evette's bunk and said no way. I grabbed a sleeping bag from the closet and one of Evette's pillows and went out on the deck. The deck had a strong smell of fish but then so did my T shirt and feet. I turned out all but the running lights and went to sleep.

The sun was just starting up when I got up. I recalled sleeping like this many time while on the "Princess". Even though the sun was just starting to peep through I could still see the stars. I started the engines and gave a little forward push and then put it in neutral and went and pulled up anchor. I walked back to the wheel and turned away from the reef and then climbed up the ladder to the bridge. After about 45 minutes into our return Evette came climbing up. She sat next to me and asked where I slept. I told her on the deck. You could have shared my bunk she said. I had heard you are married and that certainly wouldn't have been proper I said. My husband is in jail and will be for another 7 years she said. Papo isn't my father he's my father-in-law. I've lived at his house since I was 16 she said. I will move out just as soon as Karen gets a place or my divorce comes through. I was only married three weeks when he got arrested. My mother won't take me back. I've filled for a divorce and I hope you don't mind but I used the office address on the filings. So I'm stuck for now. How old are you I asked? I'm 17 she said. Please don't tell Karen you slept on the floor. I told her I would take care of you. As we came into the harbor Karen came on up. How'd everybody sleep she asked? I slept great I said. Evette said me too.

As we docked I said we would sell the fish and buy breakfast. After breakfast we cleaned the boat and waited for the Hatteras to come back in. When it did Karen and Evette helped clean her too.

Only one man showed to help us with taking the Hatteras out and just as soon as we finished cleaning we were off. The Bertram was no comparison to the Hatteras. The Hatteras was the cat's meow. Again the three of us sat up top and the two engines roared as we headed to the wrecks sight. Using binoculars, I could see that Otis was already anchored over the sight. Looked like they too had spent the night on the boat. As we came up to the Bertram I placed bumpers to keep the boats from rubbing and tied us off to the Bertram. Otis was ready to pass us the diving gear. Karen and Evette were quick to get their equipment on. Tommy our boatman would sit up top with the air horn and watch for sharks and or other boats that got to close, I pointed this out to Otis too. Otis said he hadn't ever seen a shark in these waters. I haven't either I said, but just two miles from here there are lots and lots of sharks. The other thing I wanted to point out to Otis and Maggie was that should one of them have problems while diving, could either of you get the other out of the water and on to the boat, I think not. So unless you can prove to me otherwise, from this point on you will need a third person aboard to use as a lookout and that will be able to assist you when coming out of the water. Otis was quick to ask who watched me while I was diving? I said I dove alone. In the beginning Michelle was the look out. We had a system that we used. On several occasions Michelle had to assist me out of the water. I was shaking so bad I could hardly hold on to the boarding handle. And let me tell you about physical shape, I was stronger then but I can still whip your butt. All the girls laughed. When Michelle started diving with me we had Deanna aboard. All of this is about team work.

Even now you don't want another boat getting to close while you're in the water. When you in the water there is no defense. You're at their mercy, don't put yourself in that position. Always have a plan, think what if, a good plan always has a good backup. I've been in a lot of situations that if I hadn't planned it out, I wouldn't be here today. When I look at you and Maggie I think of Deanna and me in our young years. When I look at Karen, I see Michelle, you look and act like her, always taking care of me.

Ok who's ready for some diving I asked? As I went over I got this rush like I hadn't felt in a long time. I didn't know until then I had missed it so. The ocean bottom was covered with boat shells. There were all kinds of fish everywhere. Evette was in right behind me. I looked at her and saw her eyes were as wide open as they could be. She then looked at me and gave me a thumbs up. Evette swam alongside of me, side by side. I pointed down and I took a breath and dove to the bottom looking under and old wreck and seeing crawfish on top of crawfish. I went up and pointed for her to go down and she did. She looked almost natural in the water. We then swam over to where Otis and Maggie were digging. I looked around getting my bearings. Otis was nowhere near where we were digging years before. I dove down for a closer look and saw what looked like a cannon ball. I went up and got my bearings again and Evette and I would swim about 30 yards to the south. I was sure this was the last place where Deanna, Michele and myself found our last load. It was here I was sure. The thing was that the boat shells had moved. What could have moved everything around so. The only thing I could think of was some kind of storm. My mind raced just as it had years back. Then I smiled and we headed back to the boat. From the tower Karen said all clear no boats and I could see that big smile of hers. Karen came down and she and Evette went in off the stern. I stepped down into the cabin and got myself a coke and took it on up the tower. As I drank the first swig of coke the memories came running by. Had it really been 16 years ago when Johnny brought me here. I would stand and watch the water. It could be quite possible that a shark could get by me without noticing. I remembered that first shark that swam a long side of the "Princess". If Rusty hadn't been standing in the small cockpit he might have missed seeing that shark. Rusty was never the same from that day on. From that day he was always looking and thinking about that shark, any shark. It was about 1:00 p.m., we needed to start back. Otis said that today they didn't find anything of interest but a few cannon balls. I told him that they should take the cannon balls back with them and investigate when and where they were made. If you knew what cannons they were made for and what ships used that type cannon, then maybe just maybe you could find some kind of information of what ships went missing that used that type of cannon. Maybe it was a military ship, maybe a pirate ship. Could be it was carrying gold or silver or both. Karen and Evette said they wanted to learn to scuba dive and come back.

We untied the Hatteras started the engines and headed on back to Nassau. By now the girls had got acquainted with the Hatteras. The Hatteras wasn't new anymore but she looked like it. At full throttle she was running at a speed of almost 40 MPH. Of course at that speed you could almost see the fuel gage moving. We made it back by 2:30 p.m. giving us time to do some cleaning. As we docked there was Little Martha waiting for us. When I say little that's not the right word. Martha wasn't little anymore. Martha was about 5'8" at 14, she was the most beautiful girl on the Island. Captain Jim she yelled waving. Marta caught the bowl line and tied us off. Martha asked permission to come aboard, she had with her a folder. Inside the folder were certificates of her excellent school work and a scuba diving certificate. What Martha was looking for, was to go scuba diving with me or anyone. I couldn't believe that this was Rusty's Martha. Ok, oK I said we'll go scuba diving. When she asked? Karen and Evette there too asked, yeah Captain Jim when? Well, I said, looking at Karen, you will have to get lessons and your certification just like Martha. I looked again at Martha and said we could give them one month. Martha then gave me hug and said thanks uncle. I'm almost late to make a delivery she said as she ran down the dock. Delivery Evette asked? What does she deliver Evette asked? She runs a launch service that includes shopping for the yachts that anchor in the harbor. Evette asked how old is she? I said 14. Evette said she's 14 and bigger everywhere than me. I said all accept the cushion area. Evette asked you don't like my cushion? I said I didn't have any comment until after the divorce. Evette looked at me and said fair enough. The four of us cleaned the boat then Karen, Evette and I walked on over to the house, the girls showered and we were ready for a taxi ride to the seaport.

Before we had left Miami,, Karen followed me to our old terminal and I had dropped off the vet. I had the guard sign the paper that Karen had written up for the delivery. Karen picked me up and we were off to the Seaport.

Now back from our trip Karen dropped me off at the apartment, Evette asked if I wanted company. As I stepped out the door, I said, yes of course I do, you know any nice single girls? I then leaned in the door way and mentioned that tomorrow and maybe all week was going to be tough.

As I opened my apartment door, Marco who was sitting on the couch stood and said good evening Sir. He had that guilty look all over him. I returned the good evening thing and as I did Diane walked out of her room and came and kissed me on the cheek. That said it all. Diane took me by the hand and led me into my room. Diane said she was going to move in with Marco on campus. She said they had a great weekend and Marco had told his parents that he had found the girl that he was going to marry. So I asked, he asked you to marry him? Not yet she said but he will. When I asked? Whenever I'm ready she said. Are you sure about this I asked? She looked at me and said no and that's why I'm going now. I don't think he's scared of me enough yet, I said. I better have a talk with him about this, Diane asked me to please don't. This is my idea she said not his. She hugged me and said she would keep in touch. I asked if he or the family knew of her money. Diane said they did not.

I walked out and walked up to Marco and extended my hand and once had his didn't let it go. Just remember Marco if either of you change your mind about this you best return her here just as you found her. Now go to the desk and write me all your phone numbers and addresses too include your parents. Marco did what I asked and sat back down. Looked like Diane was in complete control.

Diane had several bags packed and I helped carry them down to the valet door. I said not to forget my number and wished them luck.

On my way up in the elevator I thought about it. When I walked in the apartment door, I made the call. The connection wasn't the best but I got ahold of Salinas. How about you coming for a visit I asked? With my mom she asked? I said no. Salinas said she'd ask her mom. Sharon picked up the phone and asked me to repeat what I was asking. I want Salinas to come for a visit. Her mom asked who would chaperone and I said not to worry that I would take good care of her. Her mother didn't say another word to me. Salinas took the phone and asked if I was coming for her? I said I would be sending my attorney to get the permissions and that then, I would come for her. She said my mother says yes! Ok I'll see you soon. I then called Cat, the connection was good. I asked how everyone was doing and she said everyone was good. Cat said she had heard I was here with Karen and a new girl. Cat asked if that was my new girl and I said no that she was a friend of Karen's. I asked for Jacob and said I had some additional work for him and Goliath. Jacob came to the phone he was friendly. I said I wanted himself and Goliath to go back to the Haiti house and get all the papers that would be required for Salinas to come and visit. I told him that I didn't know what kind of papers she had or what would be necessary. Salinas's mother was there and could give permission but that her father was dead. Jacob asked her age and I said 16. Jacob said that could be a problem. Ok I said whatever the problems were I wanted it taken care of. I told him that I wanted Goliath to go with him and to have Cat's father put someone there to watch the beach house while they were gone. Jacob asked commercial or privet. Fly over there on a commercial flight and then use a privet plane over to Paix. If you would put Cat back on the phone. I told her what I was asking of Jacob and asked her to get $10,000.00 out of the apartment safe. She didn't ask any questions and said she would. I said my thanks and we hung up. I took a shower and went via taxi to the 1800 club. It was quite and I ate and returned home early.

Monday morning, I got up as usual and taxied to work. Tim was there and asked if I wanted to take a car ride by the old Terminal. I said sure and away we went. The trucks were backed up for 5 city blocks. We could see the dispatches were also stopped. Normally the delivering trucks waited as the dispatch was the priority. Traffic was completely blocked as the trucks wanting to pick up a container had formed an additional line. There were police on foot directing traffic but it didn't seem to help. We too got in the traffic as there were trucks and cars everywhere.

As we got free we headed back to the yard, before we got there my beeper started going off like crazy. The first call back I made was to call Ted, he asked if there was any way I could help to fix the traffic problem. I said it was now out of my hands. The next call that I returned was to Robin of Sea Containers, his question was what I though was going on over there and how long it would take them to fix whatever problem there was. Our problem Robin said was that there were trucks in the line over there that were dropping off over there and then the same truck would be picking up at Omni. I suggested that if they could reach the dispatcher then they could temporary drop off the empty here. We would charge the lift and storage to the transport company and we would dispatch the Sea Container units. Robin liked that and said that was a great Idea. I talked to Karen and instructed how to write up a bunch of equipment interchanges that said that we had no responsibility of damages and that the transport company would pay the charges. Karen would call Sea Containers and tell them to have the transport company send a telex authorizing the handling and storage cost for each unit. The yard personal would just off load and stack these units. The only way we would unload a container that wasn't sea containers was if they were picking up a sea container unit. Robin called me back and said that everyone that had an order to pick a contained from our old Terminal now wanted to change their order to a Sea Container. We started getting busy at about 11:00 a.m. and by 1:00 p.m. Robin called and said that he was authoring all units to be repaired. We had about 300 available units and almost 600 damaged units. Robin's authorizations would give us a lot of work. The calls that were coming from our old facilities, I didn't bother to even return their calls. By 3:00 p.m. even Guido had called, his call too wasn't returned. Every other call was a customer wanting a container for Freight. We just told these calls to call sea containers. We were very busy but I did have time to call Carson's people to ask when he was coming back. I was worried about that old fart! Robin called about dinner, I said what about the club.

Tim had gotten lots of calls from different programmers looking to buy his programs. Tim said he had nothing to do with the break down, and could not help them. We ended the day closing the gates at 8:30 p.m. And dispatching about 80% of our available containers and receiving over 200 units, only 27 of them belonging to sea containers. We wouldn't leave work until after 9:00 p.m. I went from work to the club, Robin had driven by the old terminal and said that there were still trucks in the street. Robin asked what had happened? I said I had torn my $2,000.00 suit. Not the suit he said their systems. Oh I said, I guess they had some kind of problem. You think they will have it fixed by tomorrow Robin asked? Well I said if they haven't fixed it by now I don't think it will be fixed. Any way I said, we appreciate the approvals, we had several of our past best people stop by after work hours asking for a job. We don't need any office help but we did hire six more yard men. Robin said he hope this boom would last for his office. I said it would, I said it seemed that the new yard boss that they have over there panicked and told the dispatchers to dispatch units from the wrong stacks. Today my old business dispatched containers with holes in them. Meaning that if the exporter finds the holes while loading cargo they will be returning that container back to the same terminal tomorrow. If they didn't find the holes and loaded the cargo, then there's a good chance the load could be damaged during shipping.

Today's problems are just the start of the problem. The leasing companies will withhold moneys owed to the terminals until they understand what the damages have cost them. Robin had reached the club before me and had a good head start on the scotch. He said I was the biggest SOB he'd ever met and he was glad to call me his friend. Tuesday was much the same with work, fortunately for Guido's facilities it was much the same for them too.

Wednesday Bob stopped by the office and said the Navy had called and asked if I was happy with my Sonar equipment payment. Bob's question was if there was any doomsday code that I could feed the units to stop transmitting. You know like what you did to Guido. I told Bob that the Navy had lived up to their word and I was happy. And no there was no such code or device.

Bob said he'd heard I was single again, but like really single, like living alone, Bob asked if I'd like to go on his next trip with him. No thanks all those wild tigers you are hunting are all yours. I have a work in progress. Bob said if I changed my mind just to let him know. I asked about the business, and he said it was never better but that the Soviets had considerably dropped their oil shipments to Cuba. Hopefully it's just some glitch he said. If you're asking because of money Bob asked, we made the quarterly payment two weeks ago

CHAPTER XX

SALINAS

Wednesday night, Jacob called and said that the Salinas thing was as ready as possible. Meaning that Salinas now had a Haitian passport but no exit permission from the Government. Ok I said, fly on back and get her a Bahamian passport. Jacob understood and said he'd send both passports, hopefully by late Friday. Saturday morning Jacob arrived in Miami delivering me a large envelope. Inside was Salinas's Haitian and Bahamian passports. The Haiti passport had Salinas's mother's signed permission to travel. The Bahamian passport had Salinas leaving Nassau two weeks ago.

I called Karen and said to get me the charter plane that I used for Haiti, I wanted to be leaving at 7:00 a.m. tomorrow, from Opa-Locka.

I told the pilots what we were going to do, so they wouldn't have any surprise objections. We flew to Port-au-Paix. I found a taxi if you called it that and went to the Chateau. Old man Pablo was there at the gate. When we drove in I got a low key greeting. Salinas actually looked sad. Her mom had started crying the moment I showed up. What is it I asked Salinas? My horses she said, I will miss them, I stood and turned and started walking to the taxi. Salinas's mother came out with one bag and said to please take good care of her little girl. Please when you don't want her anymore send her back to us. I promised we'd be back soon to visit. Salinas kissed each of her favorite horses and then her mother. Still looking sad Salinas got in the taxi. We were off to the airport. When we arrived the plane was ready for takeoff, we got aboard and the plane took off for Nassau. Salinas had never been on an airplane before. She was glued to the window. Hey pretty girl, are you ok I asked? She looked at me and asked where we were going? I told her we would first go to Nassau and then to Miami. Where will I live she asked? With me I said, you don't have a wife she asked? No wife just a beautiful Haitian girl. I think it was the first time that she realized that this was really happening.

We landed at the main Nassau airport, we both went through customs Salinas using her Bahamian passport. The plan was from here we would fly back via Chalk's on the afternoon flight. The chartered flight would go on back to Miami. Salinas and I would catch a taxi and pass by the Hurricane house and drop of her bag then walk down to the wharf. It was now just pass 2:00 p.m. The only boats there were the Hatteras and the Chris Craft. I gave Salinas a short tour and she didn't want to get off the Hatteras. She wanted a boat ride. I told her that we didn't have the time but that the next week I'd do my best to bring her back. She smiled at the thought of getting to ride in this big boat. Until that moment, I was a bit worried until I saw that smile. We walked back up the dock and she took my hand. We walked into Willy's bar and Willy was just shaking his head. Reminds me of more than 15 years ago. Hello, Salinas said, my name is Salinas. Mines Willy he said. You Captain Jim's girl Willy asked? Does he have another she asked? Well Willy said you be asking Captain Jim that question. Willy said she's a looker that's for sure. Willy asked where she was from and she said Haiti. Salinas said Captain owns the Chateau that we live in. I bet its beautiful Willy said, Salinas said it's the most beautiful of all the land. Salinas said she had 10 fine horses that she is or was the care taker for. I just watched Salinas and Willy talk. I look at my watch and said that we must be on our way. Salinas said it was nice to meet you Willy, we'll see you next week. Willy gave me a thumbs up when she wasn't looking. Did you tell her about the sharks Captain Jim Willy asked? I said she had met a few of them. We went back to the house and retrieved her bag and caught a taxi. As we went across that skinny bridge Salinas grabbed my arm and closed her eyes. Now that wasn't that bad, I said. We got to the seaport, got our tickets and got aboard.

Salinas's second air ride started on dry land then the plane rolled into the water, then took off from the water. Salinas wasn't a bit scared, she was glued to that window.

I didn't anticipate any problem at immigration and didn't get any.

Salinas's Nassau pass port said she was 18. We caught a taxi and headed to the apartment. As we drove up in the taxi Salinas had her head out the window looking up at the tower. You live here she asked? We live here I said. We took the elevator and got off at our floor. As I put in the key, Betty opened the door. Well hello, young lady Betty said I'm Betty. I said this is Salinas. Welcome Salinas Betty said. Salinas walked right for the balcony. It's so beautiful she said. Betty asked where the bag went. I said my room. Betty said yes Sir.

Salinas walked in my room and when Betty walked out I shut the door with us finally being alone. Betty had cooked us up some dinner, we ate and then returned to my room. The next day Sunday we went to a champagne breakfast next door at the Brickell Town House. I told Salinas it was here on this very location that 25 years earlier there were caves all along the seashore. I loved telling Salinas the old stories and she loved hearing them. It was even hard for me to imagine us putting my little 8-foot dinghy on the wagon that my Dad had built and pulling it down to the bay. Seemed like a hundred years ago and yet it was just a quarter century ago. From breakfast we went to Vizcaya, I hadn't been there since they had restored it and opened it to the public, Salinas said it reminded her of home. Well it did look French I said. The twin Islands that had been right off Vizcaya's sea wall were no longer there. The Tiger Shark that twirled at the entrance to Key Biscayne was still there. The bus bench that I was sitting on when that first policeman stopped me skipping school was most likely the same bus bench. This was supposed to be for Salinas to see but it was me that was enjoying it so much.

We reached back to the apartment and decided to go shopping. Burdines here we come. Salinas was thrilled with the young women's section. Every dress she tried on looked better than the last. The sales attendant had called the manager because she saw something that she just couldn't put her finger on. Salinas was a natural model. The manager said she could put Salinas to work modeling for their magazine. I said the only thing was that she was a real princess and they would have to hide her Identity. The manager said oh my. Well, Salinas liked everything and that's what we bought. The girl at the makeup counter was also impressed with Salinas's skin. It was the color and texture that the girl said was perfect. It was the bed ware that Salinas picked out that I couldn't believe. I asked where she would wear that? Salinas said walking around the apartment. I laughed and said it might stay on for two minutes, then I said not even that long. I realized that it wasn't the first time that I had to pay two taxis to get us home.

It was funny everybody wanted to help with her things. Back in the apartment it was the soft PJs that Salinas put on. It was funny, I didn't want to go anywhere. Staying home with her was just fine.

I didn't want to leave Salinas home thinking the IRS might show up and scare her, so I took her to work with me. We taxied in and Karen was there to greet her. Karen said my car was finally ready so we went and got it. The car looked normal. It was of course much heavier but comfortable. Karen said she could keep Salinas busy at work. Evette came into my office and said that Salinas was pretty but she still was going to get her chance. I called in Karen and she knew what I was going to say. Karen said she would take care of that. I told Karen that I didn't want anyone making Salinas uncomfortable.

Tim said there were rumors that the BBS terminal was going to close. The damage to the clients was irreversible. I called Karen and asked if she had found all the paper work for us to recover the Lifts that were in the two big yards. She said she had paperwork for five of the eight. I had her meet with the W.E. Johnson sales person. Before the apparent collapse they probably wouldn't have been so willing to assist. Upon our call they would arrange the five lifts to be picked up. The five were valued at about $800,000.00.

Our Omni container shop employees had doubled in size and had the ILA asking us to take more ILA personal.

The daily mail brought with it an order of Levey on my wages. The IRS wanted all but $50.00 per dependent, in other words they wanted me living on $50.00 per week. I told Karen to stop writing me a paycheck. I quit. Karen laughed.

I had called Langley several times about Carson but hadn't gotten any answers. I asked Karen to get me on the red eye for Langley tomorrow morning. I said that I would be back the same day. Karen was to use the day to take Salinas to see Doctor James and have him install a T for Salinas. I wanted Karen to also to take Salinas for her first haircut and nail job. The hair was to stay long. When we closed at 5:30 p.m. or so we went home and then later went out to eat at Joe's. Salinas had on one of her new dresses that showed her figure. It was a simple dress that was worn with sandals. Salinas hadn't worn shoes much and heals, well that would be something she could learn about sometime in the future. We were home early: Karen would be picking her up at about 8:00 a.m. for her 9:30 a.m. appointment with Doctor James. Me, I left for the airport at 12.30 a.m. Tuesday morning. I was headed up to Langley to see what was going on with Carson. Once there I waited two hours before a vice director came in to see me. He said that Carson was in Grenada checking on Soviet and Cuban activity. Although the Government was socialist the Brits had granted monies for one of the two runways on the Island be extended to allow a bigger plane to land. At present the biggest airliner that could land on the Island was a 727. At present none of the large Soviet planes could land there do to the length of the runways. The Grenada Government stated that the Cubans had offered to supply the labor and expertise to extend the run way at no charge.

Carson had already sent back valued intelligence data. I objected them sending Carson as the Cubans could very well know who he is from his Angola days. The Vice Director said Carson asked for the assignment. Unless something changed Carson should be returning within the next two weeks. Have some patience Sir, Carson is in good health. I said that when Carson got back he wouldn't be.

I flew back that afternoon arriving back in Miami at about 7:00 p.m. When I got home Salinas wasn't there but the IRS had been. Betty was still laughing. Captain Jim she said. I told that Lady and those Gents that you were up in Washington DC today on business. I don't think they believed me. Here's the warrant Betty said as she handed me the papers still laughing. They came with the same man that helped you install that safe. That safe man read what you wrote on the safe and backed right out of the room. The safe man said you were crazy enough to have booby trapped the safe just like you said. They left one man here watching the safe then came back with two other men. The other men put in some kind of camera in the hole and said it looked like there was a bomb in there. They also left. By now Mr. Roy showed up, I had called him like you said. Mr. Roy said that the warning on the safe was a joke. The IRS lady said that she would hold me under contempt. That Mr. Roy he's smart, he told me to get some alcohol and a scotch paper. Mr. Roy wiped off the warning, then he said, now you can open it if you want. Betty still laughing said that Mr. Roy then told that woman, " I'm sure its fine, but give me 15 minutes to get out of the building". The lady told the two men to open the safe. It wasn't 10 minutes when I heard the horn blow and the gas came out. Every one of them were on the floor. They all went running out of the apartment. They came back and still they couldn't open it. They said they were going to get a court order for you to open it. Those men they were shaking something fierce. It was one of the funniest things I ever did see Betty said.

In a few minutes Betty still laughing opened the door for Salinas and Karen. Karen came in and I looked at her and gave her the thumbs up, Karen returned the same and said everything is good. Salinas had her hair cut shorter than I would have liked but it looked great. Salinas had her nails done top to bottom. No makeup I asked? Karen said they put it on and Salinas would wipe it off. Salinas said you wouldn't like it, and raised her shoulders. Betty asked Karen if she would stay for dinner. Karen said she'd let the love sick and the sick spend the rest of the night alone. By love sick I guessed she meant Salinas and me the sick. Karen asked about Carson and I repeated what the CIA had told me.

Salinas said she was starved and was ready to eat, As Karen left I asked her if she didn't feed Salinas lunch. Karen said that Salinas had eaten a good lunch. Salinas hugged Karen and thanked her for her help and being a good friend. Karen said she was sure this was going to be a lasting friend ship.

For being hungry Salinas didn't eat much. She said she was tired and would wait for my showed before going to bed. That sounded like an invitation, we showered and went to bed. Once in bed I asked Salinas how she liked Dr. James? Salinas said that the good Doctor said it was to late for whatever he was going to put in there. Salinas turned on the night stand light and took my hand and put it on her stomach. Right here is our baby she said. For some reason, I wasn't surprised, I asked if she was happy about that and she indicated she was very happy. She said she knew she was with child from the first time. She asked if I was happy and I too indicated I was. She said what was why her mother let her come. I even told my horses she said. I should have figured; it was the first time I had uninterrupted relations twice a day for ten straight days with anyone. Plus, I did remember Salinas's last words when I left her were that she would have a surprise for me the next time she saw me.

I didn't sleep well, I just kept staring at her while she slept. It was strange, the only person other than Salinas that smiled while she slept was Deanna during our early days.

Salinas had said that Karen, Evette and her were going to start scuba lessons Tuesday night. They would have lessons two nights a week. I thought I had them three nights but it was quite a while back.

We got up early and went to work together, Karen was going to be in charge of Salinas's activates. Early Tuesday Karen handed me the list of things that Salinas should eat. Karen noted that Salinas should get lots of rest and shouldn't get warn out or too tiered. Karen looked at me and said I should let her get some sleep at night. I knew where she was going.

I had been thinking a lot about us not being able to use the Hatteras in Nassau when we wanted. It was booked every day. I called my sales guy at Merrill Stevens and asked about another Hatteras. Same size maybe a little more range. The man quoted me a discounted price of $187,000.00. I asked where it was, he said at a boat show in Jacksonville. I asked if we settled on a price if they could have the boat delivered in Nassau by Friday night. The salesman said that this boat had a travel range of over 1,000 miles. He'd have to call me back on the delivery and I said I would make up and offer. Before I could do anything the Merrill Stevens manager called and said that he would give me a 10%

discount for cash payment. Can you deliver it to Nassau on Friday I asked? The man said yes. I said to start the paper work and send me the bank information so I could transfer the money. No taxes, it's for export the company name is Blue Ocean LTD. I called Cat and said for her to please get Janie and go to the bank to transfer money for a new Hatteras. Cat asked about that sailboat that we had always talked about having in Nassau. I said she was right and I'd look into doing something about that too.

I called the sales person back and said we were ready we now just needed their banks information to make the transfer. I also asked if it would slow the process down If I drove up and took a look while they were readying the boat. The salesman said not at all. I informed Karen what I was doing and said that Salinas and I would leave at about 4:00 a.m. and drive up and back the same day. The salesman sent the transfer information and we in turn sent the same to the Nassau bank. Karen reminded me that we hadn't received the balance payment on the Andros project. I asked her to call the Admiral's Secretary and ask her if they were missing anything that was holding up our payment. While I was thinking about it I asked Karen to make reservation with Chalk's, the last time I used them they were quite busy. Karen asked if she and Evette could go along. I said that I would be delivering some bad news to the Club, so the club, would be off limits. If the New Hatteras arrived Friday night, we would be spending most of our time aboard. And you know who would have to behave. We could travel to Andros to see how the house was coming along. Karen said they still wanted to go. Make the reservations for Friday afternoon and coming back Sunday afternoon.

The girls would go to the YMCA and I went to the 1800 club. Salinas got home before I did and was waiting in bed. I told her that if she wanted to go I would be driving about 5 hours north to see the New Hatteras we were buying. Salinas wanted to go. We left for our trip at 4:00 a.m. and returned right when the traffic was at its worst. Salinas was tired from the ride. The boat was beautiful. Salinas couldn't wait to get aboard. Thursday morning, we went to the Miami Diamond Exchange. I think these people knew that when I came in it was because

I had a new girl. We were shopping only for a diamond solitary. I found a nice one carat and had it fitted and I carried it out in a box.

After Salinas returned from her scuba lessons, we went walking on the beach at the now Biscayne state park. This is where that old light house was that my Dad had taken us to so long ago. On the beach, right at about the end of the key with the light house within sight, I walked Salinas into the water at knee deep and asked if she would marry me. Salinas said yes. I put on the ring and she tackled me into the surf. We then went home and showered and were planning to go out to celebrate. Once out of the shower I noticed a massage on the phone, it was from Carson. I called him back, he was headed to the sailing club. I said we be there in twenty minutes. Salinas and I were already dresses, she looked like a million. Once at the club we went into the bar, of course we were overdressed. Carson stood and gave a hug and also kissed Salinas, Carson looked at Salinas and said some things never changed. Paul asked if he could get in on the hug and kissing part. Salinas looked at Carson and held up her hand and announced that we had just got engaged! The entire club then applauded. Carson asked for real and before I could answer Salinas said she was going to have our baby. Finally, Carson said a woman that can out maneuver him. Salinas said we were on our way out to celebrate when Jim saw his call. Like always Carson and I asked Paul to keep Salinas occupied while we took a walk on the dock.

Carson said that he was sure that the Soviet and Cubans were planning to take the Island. The Cubans already had at least 100 strong and he saw more than 20 Russians. The Cuban Government had offered to supply the labor to extend the runway. Carson said they had hundreds of workers there that are actually regular army. Carson said that while he was there a Soviet supply ship was there and had anchored in the bay. I had to look real close to see if it wasn't Bob's ship, Carson said. Now that would have been something He said. Carson said the US should do something before it's to late. That ship anchored there could just as easily have military gear as supplies. Carson then said that there were two universities down there, one being a medical school that had quite a few American students. I asked if he had met any that liked older men. Carson said, quite a few actually.

Carson asked if I was going to get married? I said yes and that I wanted him to be the best man. Where you going to have this wedding Carson asked? Well I said I think under the circumstances it will be Nassau. She's here on a Bahamian passport that says she 18. She's Baby Doc's 16-year-old daughter. Well she sure is beautiful. I wish you'd start sharing some of these girls. Then Carson laughed. Ok he said just let me know. I told Carson about those nice IRS people and that I was going to kick and bunch all the way. Carson said he hate to be on the other end of that.

Cat doesn't know it yet but she just bought me a new Hatteras for a wedding gift. It will be delivered to Nassau this Friday. Now there will be a boat there just waiting for us to fly down and enjoy. Carson pointed and said here comes trouble, it was Salinas walking down the dock. Carson she said will you join us for dinner, Carson said sorry mam for keeping him so long. I want to congratulate you both on both getting engaged and the about to becoming parents thing. Will you come to our wedding she asked? Carson said I better be there I'm the best man. Join us for dinner so I can get to know you better she said. No mam you both go on without me. Well then how about joining us for the weekend Salinas asked, we're going to try out Jim's new boat. Carson looked at me and asked where did I find this treasure? Thanks for asking mam, Jim never invites me anywhere. I got a special project that I'll be starting this weekend. Oh mam, Carson said, Jim likes to sneak off and go on fishing trips every now and then, you keep him close to home. Thanks Salinas said, its ok if he goes fishing with you right. I laughed.

Salinas and I headed on over to the 1800 club and had a good dinner. Jan the manager and all of the girls came over to Salinas to speak with her. Of course Salinas gave them the update of us getting engaged.

The next day was Friday, Salinas took a small bag with her too work. We would leave from work to the seaport for our Nassau trip. Salinas was fine with Karen but looked a little nervous about Evette going.

I had made several calls to Jacob to insure all the paper work was ready that I had spoken to him about. At 3:30 p.m. Jacob called to confirm that all was ready.

My apparel would consist of the suit that I was wearing and some clothes I threw into Salinas's bag. I would travel to Nassau in my suit for the first time that I could remember.

Once we landed the girls as they did last week wanted to go directly to the Holiday Inn and rent a cabana. I would take a separate taxi and go directly to Jacob's law office. Jacob's father the judge would also be there. From them what I wanted wasn't an easy task. Jena had sold Guido the club but I owned the property. What I would deliver to the club tonight was a notice to evacuate the premises. The order would be signed by the judge. The order said they were given 30 days in which to evacuate. The notice said that any attempt to extend the order would revert to a 72-hour notice. The judge said they couldn't prove they owned the property but would attempt to extend the deadline. A separate notice noted that rent hadn't been paid in over three years and that money $740,000.00 was due on demand. Once the receipt was signed tonight, the club would have 72 hours to respond before the order went public. It was a possibility that the club wouldn't want to sign the receipt. In that case I would put on the front desk and take a photo. I would visit the club at 10:00 p.m. accompanied by Jacob as a witness. When we were ready the time and place was set for us to meet, Jacob would bring the paper work.

From there I walked to the wharf where two of the four boats were already in and cleaned. Mark would be coming to in a bit late, coming back from a two-day trip from the west side of Andros. Captain Mike would also be showing up from Andros. Otis and Maggie saw me and came to ask about the new Hatteras. Is it true captain Jim? Well I don't know what you heard but we have a new Hatteras that should be arriving tonight. This will not be a work boat I said. This one's for pleasure. Otis asked if we were going diving at the treasure site. I told them that I wasn't sure what we were going to do. For one thing I was going to speak with Lee when he comes in tonight. I wanted to know how far along we are on the new house on Andros. We might just take a run over to take a look at the house. Otis said that Martha had mentioned that you might be here this weekend to take her scuba diving. Martha has gone out pulling traps and says she can out work us all.

I headed on over to speak with Willy, Willy asked what was up with the suit. I said I had some business later at the club. Willy asked if I was here alone and I told him I was with the girls. Willy had also heard about the new boat that was coming. Cat had called and spoke to Pete about the slip we needed. Willy said that Peter was already down on the Nassau Queen getting ready for tonight. You give the new boat a name yet Willy asked? The name is "Salinas" I said. You going to keep that girl Willy asked. Yes I said, and added that if everything went as it should I'd be a father in about 7 more months. Willy said he was happy for me. In a few years we'll have all these kids running down the docks. Yes, I figure that Cat will be with child soon too. The next generation started with Martha. When I saw her last week I couldn't believe she's so big. Yes Willy said, it won't be long before she finds a man and starts her own family. Pete stuck in his head in and said that the new boat was about an hour away. That was about the radio range that we could receive transmission from their ship to shore radio. This would put the Hatteras in 30 minutes after dark. Heck when I thought about it we could have three boats all coming in at the same time. The girls arrived and Willy congratulated Salinas on the news. I told the girls that they could go to the house and get showers. Salinas said she wanted to take her shower aboard the new Hatteras. I asked if anyone was ready for some couch salad and all raised their hands including Willy. As I was walking to the wharf, I ran into Mary and Tim. They both said that Martha was anxious to see me. I told them the new boat would be here within the hour and if they wanted they could bring or send Martha on over to the city docks to see the boat. They said they would see. I picked up conch for us all and headed on back to Willy's. We had just finished when Peter came to the bar and said the new Hatteras had just entered the harbor. The boat was given the slip number by Pete and we walked and waited at slip #32. The Hatteras swung around and came in stern first. Across the stern it said "SALINAS". Salinas was the first to see the name and yelled out Salinas! She was so thrilled to see her name on the stern of that boat. The boat came with four boat bumpers; we would need more. The place inside looked like a hotel complete with sheets, pillows and towels. The Captain that made the voyage said they had only used about half the tank of fuel. The captain also said the weather was beautiful the entire crossing. The people that were taking out the Nassau Queen saw the new Hatteras and said they were happy to see a second boat as that should decrease their waiting time between trips. This trip would be their third time going out fishing on the Nassau Queen. They said they loved the boat, the service and of course the best fishing they had ever experienced. They said they kept us a secret as they didn't want their friends to come, fearing that their trips could get pushed back. They said they had requested and were promised that Cat would be going along with them. I looked at Peter and he was nodding his head yes, that she was coming. I hadn't even thought about Cat still making these trips. In speaking with Peter, he said that many of his repeat customers ask for her. Peter said it was at least once a week and sometimes more. Peter said that he once heard me say that salt water ran in her blood.

Cat showed up. When we saw her she was jogging down the dock to the boat, she first said hello to her clients and then came to see all of us and the boat. Cat noticed Salinas and her ring first. Cat looked at me and asked if that was for real. She said I didn't waste any time. She hugged Salinas and congratulated her and then me. All I can say Cat said, was that we'd do fine if she could stay with it. Salinas knew whom Cat was and all, well almost all the history. Salinas didn't give Cat the news that she was with child. Salinas saw Cat's face when she saw the boats name.

It was almost time for my taxi ride over that skinny bridge. I kissed Salinas and I was off. I had told the girls that I wouldn't be long. Jacob had ridden back to town with Cat and was waiting at the dock's entrance. We both got in a taxi and were off to the club.

Jacob and I pulled up at the club at about 9:20 p.m. We got the normal service and stopped at the front desk. I asked for the manager and we were asked to go up the elevator. I asked that he be so kind to receive us at the desk for which he took only minutes to appear from the elevator. Captain he said with a smile, not another shake down? Referring to the last fund raising we had performed there. Well, yes and no I said. We're here to serve you notice that you are trespassing. With that I handed him the papers. I'd appreciate you signing my copy as received, the manger read the notice and signed its receipt. Could you come up and talk a moment in my office he asked? I said I'd be happy to talk over a drink at the bar. He said thank you. I handed Jacob the receipt, the manager and I walked to the first bar. Jim he said the property is for real yours, he asked? Yes Sir, I've owner it since 1971 and paid its taxes ever since. And Guido, does he know this he asked? Well you're the one that gets to give him the news I said. Any way you're looking for a partner the manager asked. No I'll be looking to sell. I think I could get a pretty penny from your competition I said. What will you have the bar tender asked? Before I could answer, the manager said the house. I'll have a Chivis rocks, double. The manager said the same. Once we both had our drinks I said here's to a hand shake. I downed my drink and stood up and offered my hand. We shook hands and I walked out.

Jacob was waiting at the taxi and we went on back to the wharf. On the way Jacob said he didn't think the manager would sign the receipt. I mentioned that he signed because he thought it would please me. Guido will kick his butt for signing. Jacob asked what I thought would happen. In the end I said they will pay what they need to. Guido will lose face with his peers, Guido has made several bad calls since his taking the head spot. I asked how things were going with Cat and the children. Jacob said things at home were better than he had ever hoped for.

Jacob dropped me off at the wharf, he would take that same taxi on back to the beach house. The Nassau Queen had departed and the girls were sitting with Willy. Karen said that Lee had come in with Captain Mike and would be at the apartment. I said I would go talk to Lee, Salinas went with me. Lee and Janie hadn't met Salinas, Lee quickly brought out their daughter and said they had named the baby after Janie's sister Deanna. Salinas gave Janie the news about her and I and that she was with child. With that Cat would hear the baby news just as soon as she got off the Nassau Queen tomorrow morning.

Lee said the house on Andros was just about finished. He said it probably looked better than what I thought it would. Lee also had brought a letter from the Navy which he said was requesting additional work, mostly repairs of items that we hadn't ever worked on. In fact, the list was almost identical of the list we had given to the Navy that the cement was or would shortly fail due to the poor sand used in the cement mix by the previous contractor. The letter didn't say one way or the other that they would pay for these repairs or if they intended pay at all. Lee said our end of the job sign off sheets were complete. I took the letter and said that I would contact them Monday or Tuesday with some kind of reply. I told Lee that our getting out of the construction agreement was no longer in force.

I went back to the bar and the girls and I discussed our options. We could all go visit the Andros house or we could just go diving at the treasure site leaving tomorrow morning and spending the night over the wrecks fishing. Evette said she still owed us a cooked fish dinner and could do that at either location. We decided that we would go to Andros early tomorrow morning and then spend the night over the wrecks fishing and Sunday morning dive the wrecks. Captain Mike had appeared at the bar, what a surprise, I asked him to make the trip with us. The Captain looking at the girls agreed to go along. I then called Martha's mom and informed her of our plans, she said Martha could go and would be ready. I said for her to bring all her diving gear. Mary asked for me to please be careful and to take good care of her daughter.

Salinas and I walked Karen and Evette over to the hurricane house. They would sleep there and meet us at 7:00 a.m. for breakfast at Angee's. I removed money from the safe that we would spend on gear for the new boat plus a little shopping for the trip. Salinas took clean sheets from the house. Salinas and I would sleep aboard the Hatteras. All three girls were beautiful but walking behind Salinas, everything just seemed to move keeping my attention. If you know what I mean. Salinas was gaining on me every hour. I could hardly wait to get on the boat and take that hot shower. Yes, the Hatteras did have hot water. The bath and shower weren't so small like the Bertram's. The master bath was a good size. The bed was a Queen size, and our Hurricane house sheets didn't fit. Of course we didn't need much space. After our shower and now in bed, Salinas wanted to talk about Cat. Salinas said she saw my eyes when that man talked about Cat. Salinas said she could see my feelings. I said that I would have married Cat years ago but she had chosen to stay close to Nassau, her ill sister and know her sister's children. I told Salinas my long history of women. Yes I love Cat, and would do anything for her that was within my power. This however was limited. I reassured Salinas that she was the center of my attention and my love. I said that my adventurous spirt would live on but I would do only what I must. I was a little worried about what was going to happen when she had that big belly that would soon be there. Salinas told me not to worry she'd keep my interest.

The morning came quickly. We were up at the crack of dawn; well I should say awake at the crack of dawn. We met Karen, Evette, Captain Mike and Martha at Angee's for breakfast. Captain Mike was to receive the Hatteras from the Captain that was delivering the boat. He and his two-man crew would then move her to the fuel dock to cap her off. Karen and Evette would go food shopping while Salinas, Martha and myself would go to the Fisherman's Paradise and buy boat stuff. The boat store would then deliver the purchases to the slip. Once my group left the boat store we stopped by the Dive shop. All was coordinated that we weren't going to wait very long for the equipment to de delivered to the boat. By 8:30 a.m. things started to appear at the slip. By now we were all back to the boat. It was fun receiving the gear and putting it in its place. We would pull out from the dock by 9:30 a.m. on our way to Andros. Captain Mike said that the delivering captain had mentioned that we would need to stay within that ¾ throttle range for another 12 running hours or so. This would put us at our Andros channel at about 12 to 1:00 p.m. The day was beautiful and so was the trip over. This was the new Hatteras's first trip to Andros, Captain Mike could now do this crossing with his eyes close. Moving up to and through the channel we could see the reefs ocean side straight drop off. The channel was a section that looked like it had just dropped into one of those massive caves that were under the ocean bottom. The channel went from a depth of 50 feet at its outer end to low tide of 10 feet at its mouth. The channel was a good 60 feet wide. On our starboard was the Navy docks. We would go south another half mile to reach the house. As we came up to the dock it all looked very different. Having a house attached to the dock changed the look quite a bit. We docked and after tying off, the girls were almost at a run for the house. I followed with the keys. The house looked like a fortress. Its concrete base was built up from the sand a good 5 feet, the pillars on which the house was standing on looked to be 6 feet in diameter. The house itself was 10 feet above the base putting the house's first floor a good 15 feet from the ground. The fully screened 10-foot wide balcony circled the entire first floor. The 10-foot wide steps were located at the center of the house. The doors that were at the top of the steppes were three large windowed French doors. There were two bed rooms on the first floor and one on the second floor. Like Lee had mentioned it was more than what I had asked for but it was incredible. In walking the baloney on the island side I could see that Lee had planned well. The fence wasn't quite finished but there was no wall for intruders to use as cover. The south side of the house had imbedded fuel tanks and a second generator that it too was located high above the ground. Any electric here at the house, as the dock would only be coming from generators. The kitchen as was most of the house was fully equipped and ready to go. We had only been there a short time when a Navy truck pulled up from the road side. It was the base commander that had heard about the house but hadn't seen it. The commander said he had only planned to look from the outside but since we were here he asked to come in. I introduced the entire gang. The Commander was impressed with the house and wanted to know if it was for rent. I told the Commander that we hadn't decided what we were going to do with the house as yet. The commanded said he had dispatched a letter requesting work be completed on our project before he released the last payment. I explained to him that when we took over the project we had noted the problems that they were facing with the first contractors work, mainly being that they had used sand from the Island that had a high salt content. The commander had only been here on the Island for the last 8 months. The Commander said he would investigate to see if what I was saying was correct. The commander said the Navy had decided to expand the Base to the south and that would make the house that much closer to the base. I mentioned that I was sure that his expansion plans would be to the north as we owned the property from here northward right up to the base. The Commander said that he was sure that I was mistaken about the property line. I was sure about the boundary line, and I didn't want the Navy base any closer than they were. The Navy would need to go north putting them closer to that small hotel and the bar that was used almost strictly by the base.

The Commander also had noticed that the boat now at the dock wasn't the Christ Craft that he had seen many times. That's a nice Yacht you have out there the Commanded said. Yes Sir I said, we offer trips out of Nassau with our other Hatteras the NASSAU QUEEN". What about fishing around here he asked? Well here the reef just drops of. I'm sure the fishing is great if you're trolling, but we offer night time bottom fishing. Could one of your boats pick us up from here he asked? No problem I said just call our Miami or Nassau office. The girls were asking if I was ready, they didn't like having the navy personal staring at them. Salinas came and took my hand a pulled on me. Ok everybody please clear the deck as I'm locking up. The Commander blew his whistle and his men were rounded up and headed to their truck.

Once on the boat the girls said they loved the place but it needed to have the fences completed as to keep the unwanted out.

Captain Mike looked at me and I nodded to get the show on the road. In less than a minute we were pulling away from the dock. As we went through the channel I asked myself just how a pirate ship would have anchored here. With no channel, they couldn't have come in at all, they would have either came ashore on the west side or either the southern or northern ends.

The trip back to the east was at a good ¾ speed, this was about 25 mph. The girls took turns at the wheel. They all seemed to get along together great. Since we would arrive earlier than I expected and the girls wanted to swim, we went straight on to the treasure site. We anchored, set up the watch and Martha and I put on our scuba gear with Salinas, Karen and Evette would be using snorkel, mask and fins. Martha was excited as this was her first dive at the wrecks. The water was as clear as glass. I had told the girls that we would pick up a few crawfish to use for bait tonight. This Hatteras wasn't set up for live fish so as we caught them tonight they would have to be cleaned and iced. All the girls would be taking fish home with them, yes including Salinas. Martha and I had the mop and bag. I shoved the mop under one of the wrecks hulls and would pull out a crawfish or two. It was so easy before I knew it the bag was full. As we were doing this the girls had moved too far from the boat. When I brought up the bag Captain Mike told me they were too far. He pointed their way and I told him to sound the horn. As he did, I dropped my tank and belt and just as one of the men got Martha's hand I took off swimming in the direction that Captain Mike had pointed. I swam with my head up and once I got around the boat I could see that they were almost at the currents edge. I heard the horn but they didn't seem to be heading back in fact they were getting further. I was half way there before I realized that they were fighting the current. I also heard the boat's motors start. When I reached them we were all in the current. Maybe I could have fought the current helping one but not all three. They were all glad to see me but by now they were too tired to continue to fight the current. We were now riding the current along a reef that I didn't know. I told the girls to all hold hands and the boat was on its way. As we moved to the east with the current I kept an eye on the boat and the bottom to make sure we didn't get too close to the reefs edge. As the boat neared on my last look at the bottom I noticed that it had gotten deeper and had become quite rocky. The rocks were large, some in groups and some quite spaced. The Hatteras was now close enough to throw us a line. I caught the line and we were pulled to the boats stern. Still moving with the current but now with the last girl now aboard, I wanted to see the bottom better but decided to return tomorrow.

Once aboard I told Captain Mike to head to our fishing spot. I then looked at the girls and asked, ok girls, what went on back there? Salinas spoke up first saying it was her fault, she said that she, they were following a large turtle and before they knew it they were caught in the current. I told them it could have been serious; the current could have taken them into a spot that the Hatteras couldn't have gotten to. I didn't mention the shark part.

We arrived at the fishing spot early. Evette was set on cooking us fish. One could catch fish here at any time of the day. Using crawfish tails we baited two lines, one for Salinas and on for Martha. Karen was going to help Evette get things ready in the galleys. Both girls got fish on the lines; both had a great time reeling them in. We had purchased two large ice boxes and one bucket. The bucket would be used to keep what was left of the fish after it was filleted, this to keep the sharks at bay. The girls had caught two big hog snappers, more than enough for Evette to cook for us all. Evette and Karen had already started some kind of crawfish chowder. Salinas and Martha would continue to pull in the fish. The Captains men kept on cleaning. When dinner was almost ready, we stopped fishing and threw the fish scraps overboard, then cleaned the cockpit and deck. We then pulled up anchor and moved to another spot. As we re-anchored, Evette said dinner was served. The dinner table was set for six, it was the first time I had a sit down dinner on any of our boats. The food was serve with a chilled white wine. Salinas would only be given one glass. Dinner and the company were great! Martha volunteered to wash the dishes, Salinas would help. Captain Mike was in haven with all his attention and questions about the boat and his life as a sea Captain. We fished at the new spot until 10:00 p.m., Captain Mike's men finished filleting and cleaning up. The girls and I sat up top on the bridge for about another hour counting falling stars. There were no lights anywhere except the stars. It was time to hit the sack. Once in our cabin Salinas said she was sorry about getting caught in the current. I told her that sometimes things happen for a reason but she needed to pay attention to life, if not it could lead to death. I also told Salinas that something had caught my eyes down there in the rocks. I told her it wasn't the first time something caught my eye and I just had to return. I told her about the cannon and about a young girl that I once noticed brushing a horse. We were in the dark but I knew she was smiling.

The next morning before the girls woke up, Captain Mike, his men and myself had pulled up anchor and were our way back to the old wreck spot. I hoped that Otis would show up early enough to have breakfast with us.

It was still not 7:00 a.m. when we anchored. I taped on Evette's and Karen's cabin door. Karen opened the door and I mentioned that it was time to get up and start cooking. Today Breakfast would be our only meal aboard. Salinas also got up to help cook. Salinas said she was the French chef. Salinas said that pancakes were invented in Haiti, we all laughed.

Otis and Maggie arrived just after we finished eating. I wanted to go back to the rocks but I didn't want Otis to be diving there with Maggie. Those rocks mixed with a heavy current would be tricky. I hadn't dived there but from experience the visibility, shark wise would be limited. Even if you had a lookout, a shark could move within the rocks without being noticed. No I would wait and come back hopefully with Carson.

Today there would be four of us scuba diving the old wrecks. Martha was again anxious to begin the dive. We would have three teams, Otis and Maggie, Martha and I and the three musketeers, Salinas, Evette and Karen. I was sure that the girls would be careful not to leave the circle. Otis and Maggie were mostly digging for whatever they could find. Again today Otis had found a few items including a musket, a belt buckle and what looked like some kind of tool. Martha and I mostly explored the site. We saw lots of big fish and might have even found a good size shark sleeping under a large hull. If so this disproved my theory that there were no sharks here. What we saw was only the tail that certainly looked like a shark. We weren't going to wake it to find out. The four of us had used two air tanks each and the girls were getting tired. The three musketeers were already back aboard. I had told Salinas that two hours of skin diving for her would be good exercise but I didn't want her to overdo it. It was noon when we headed back. We would need some extra time to get the fish and crawfish packed up for the Flight home. Martha was happy about the diving and thanked us all, Martha also took Crawfish and fish home to her family. The girls and I helped clean up and I asked the men and the dock master Pete to keep an eye on the boat. We all stopped by to drop off Willy his grouper and to say good-bye, we then caught two taxis back to the seaport. Like in years passed that thing that I might have seen in the rocks bothered me to no end. As soon as we got back, I would call Carson to meet us at the sailing club or the 1800 club, where ever he wanted. The girls had a blast! The three of them got along so well together, I was surprised. Karen and Evette would take one ice chest while Salinas and I the other. Betty would be happy especially that she didn't have to clean the fish.

Once we got home to the apartment Salinas wanted to take a short nap. Before she went to sleep she asked the possibility of Karen and Evette moving into the spare room. I said that for me Karen would be fine but that Evette might make her feel funny. Salinas said she knew Evette would like nothing more to tangle with me but that she and Evette had talked about it and Evette gave her word that she would not make the first move. I replied that should have said it all. Salinas said she trusted me. Salinas also asked about a date to get married. I asked what about December 7th? Salinas said that would be great and then asked why that day. I said if we got married on that day I wouldn't forget the date. Salinas didn't know anything about Pearl Harbor but she said not to worry about ever forgetting our marriage date, she would remind me every day. While Salinas slept I called Carson, he answered the phone after about twenty rings. Carson said he knew it was me because no one else would let it keep ringing so long. Carson said he couldn't make it because he was too busy working on a project. He said he would see me during the week. It sounded like a push off so I went and called the valet to pull my car around front.

In 20 minutes I was pulling up in Carson's drive way. The old Mercedes was parked outside on the cement. I looked inside and the steering wheel was missing. I could hear noises coming from the garage, so I pounded on the large door. He, yelled go away. I walked to the front door and put in my key. As I turned the key and pushed the door it jammed. I yelled, Carson open up its Jim. Carson came to the door and opened it. Ok I asked, what's going on? I walked into the garage and there I found an older pick-up truck with the fenders and side panels missing. I saw that Carson was building some kind of aluminum boxes that were going to hold something under the fenders and panels. So what are you fixing to smuggle I asked. Carson said he had gotten a job at the medical university in Grenada. As he talked I looked at the tires and saw that they were heavy duty and that they had a code that indicated that were built proof. Carson was going to smuggle in arms. Arms I asked? He answered yes and a radio. I'm going to keep an eye on those g__ d___ Cubans he said. When are you leaving I asked? This coming weekend he said. Carson said he was going down on a freighter with his stuff and of course the truck. They'll see you coming I said. I don't care Carson said, I won't make it easy for them. Carson said that Washington's plan was to let the Cubans finish the runway and then they'd move in on them. Carson said he feared that the Russian ship that was anchored was full of heavy weapons including tanks and anti-aircraft guns, hell maybe even a helicopter or two. If so it wouldn't be such a walk in the park. Besides he said if the Russians landed a force on the west southerly end then Regan would have a full blown war on his hands. No he said I'm going over there and stay until help comes. The navy's big guns could take out any big guns on the ground I said. Carson said yes if they knew where they were. Carson I said I think I could have stumbled onto another wreck. Carson looked at me and said I was just trying to get his attention elsewhere. He looked at his truck and then back again back at me. Well it's been down there two hundred years, I guess it can wait until I get back from Grenada. Carson we're looking at an early December wedding I said. Now that's something I don't want to miss Carson said. I promise to be here for the wedding he said. Nassau I said, the wedding will be in Nassau. Ok Nassau it is Carson said. Now don't get shot and or captured I said. I don't plan on it Carson replied. Now I said can you stop a few hours and meet Salinas and I for a sandwich at the sailing club I asked? It will have to be the 1800 club Carson said, the sailing club closes early on Sunday. Ok I said see you in about an hour.

I went back and picked up Salinas, she was ready to go. We had a nice meal and a few drinks and I wasn't to see Carson for some time.

On Tuesday I had an appointment with the Navy in Washington. The Admiral apologized for the letter that we received from the

Commodore and the way that it sounded. He acknowledged that I had sent a letter noting the damages before we started. He was looking for a way out because he hadn't done anything with my original letter that was sent certified. We walked into his planning room and there he had this huge model set up on his table. The Admiral said that this was in the works and that he wanted us to do the construction. In fact, he said here, pointing with his pointing stick, in this blank spot its all TOP SECRET and as yet, even I don't have a copy of the plans. I was hoping that you could add in your cost to do the repairs that you had previously noted. I also trust you will keep this between the two of us. Well Sir, I said if we get the project and it's as big as you say it is, we will do the repairs at no cost. I will not add any additional cost to my bid. I will also do my best for this not to come up and you have my word not to bring this up to anyone. Fair enough the Admiral said. I then asked about my full payment. You will be please to know that this check covers 100% of your final payment. The Admiral said that they would keep the same bond in force. I took the envelope without even opening it and put it in my brief case. Once I had my check I walked back to the model that he had of the expansion. I picked up his pointing stick and pointed to where the southerly existing fence is today. This is your present properly line, would you agree? Yes he said, but the Bahamian government said we can expand with a new 99 year lease. Well I said I just want to make it clear that our property extends to this fence. It would be 100% illegal for the Bahamian Government to add that properly to your Navy property. Yes Captain, we understand you own this property. We're sure you will understand the importance that we go forward from here. The Admiral said there was a helicopter on the Heli pad waiting to take me to Langley. It looked like this was a part of their plan not mine.

I went along, with the flow of things, I was curious to see what was going on. The copter took me to Langley and the pilot said they would wait in the parking area. I guess that meant that there were several Helicopters running back and forth. I gave the pilot a thumbs up and started walking. Once inside I got the usual check in, this time receiving a stack of papers that the receptionist said I was to sign and have witnessed. I then was led to the director's office. The man was pleasant even thought I could tell he didn't approve of me. He said that they were going to upgrade my TOP SECRET status and he wanted me to understand just what that meant. He said this project's stage two would be similar to the first one, but that stage three would need to have each worker classified and cleared by the CIA before their knowledge of and or participation. I asked about the project and was told that the Navy had lost one of my sonar devices, they sent a two-man sub down and lost that also. The sonar had reported something moving down there at about one mile below the surface. I asked the director if he had ever heard of the LUSCA? He said he had not. I told him of the stories that the locals told of the monster that lives in the blue holes. The locals call it Lusca I said. It has been said to swallow up entire vessels in one bite. The Lusca it seems is more than 75 feet long and looks like the head of a shark and has the body of a giant octopus. Maybe that's what's down there I said. Captain he said you don't believe that do you? Well I said the locals don't swim in any of the lagoons. The Navy sailors have said that they found caves with piles of bones, some human.

The director said that the new facility would be directly over one of these blue hole caves that they believe having direct access to the TOTO. I asked if the caves were natural or man-made. The director said the cave appears to be natural, however it appears that someone or thing had been working to widen this particular cave.

The director said that the liquid from that small sphere that I opened had a small trace of radiation. He said that they had found that same radiation signature in the caves. Are the two connected I asked? We don't know as yet he answered. We plan to use the new Facility and caves to camouflage what we bring in and out of the facility. We need to know what's down there and who or what widened the caves, and for what purpose. Once you return the signed agreement we will deliver the plans and provide you with more information.

I then asked what Carson was doing down in Grenada. To my surprise the director said Carson had resigned. We know he has gotten a job at one of the universities down there and he most likely plans on keeping an eye on the Cubans. We just hope he doesn't stirrup any or get into any trouble down there. We most certainly don't want you going down there with you group rescuing him. The director noted that If Carson got into trouble, he'd be on his own. I didn't like what I was hearing; it all sounded all too familiar.

Once in the waiting room waiting for my helicopter's turn, I opened the envelope with my check. I truthfully didn't know what the amount owed was but the check was bigger than I was expecting. Once in the helicopter I thought about all that I had going on. Not that I was counting but the weekend would bring my 33rd birthday. Tonight the girls would be taking their Scuba certification exams. Oh my, it was hard to imagine taking the three of them scuba diving. No I wouldn't even think about it.

I was delivered to the airport and before I knew it I was on my way home. From the airport I drove to Roy's office. I left all those papers at the reception desk and asked the girl to ask Roy to call me when he got a chance.

The day was about gone but I wanted to get word to Lee to ask what else he had heard. When I got to the office I had Karen make that call first. The girls were awful quiet and I told Salinas that if they were planning something for my birthday to please don't.

Roy called and ask what I wanted done with all this bunch of papers. He said he had looked it over and would only let me sign what wasn't relinquishing my rights to a fair trial. He said I could send someone by tomorrow and he have everything ready.

Karen said that Jacob had called with some good news about the Nassau property. She said he would be expecting my call tonight at home.

The girls were excited about their exam, I would go and watch. Afterwards we would go out and celebrate. I had Karen call Carson but there was no answer.

The exam for the girls went fine; all passed. Their two middle-aged male instructors were sorry to see them go. We went out to dinner, and then Salinas and I went home. My first call was to Carson, again there was no answer. I then returned the call to Jacob, it had now been almost three weeks since we had given Guido's notice to vacate my land. As the judge had mentioned, the first that Guido would attempt to stop any eviction order. After the 72 hour mark we had published the noticed in the Nassau newspaper. That created lots of interest to include the owners of the playboy club. I called Jacob and he said we had a cash offer from Guido's main competitors. Jacob said his father said there would be no way we could be stopped from a sale of the property. The offer was less than the value, however it would fit my requirements and would add to the damage that had already been put on Guido. Without any further thinking about it, I said to sell.

My next call was to Big Ted. I first mentioned that I had seen him and he had put on a bit of weight. I was still spending the money to keep up his team and asked how the men were doing. Ted said he only had seven men that were still training every month but they were ready. I informed of the current situations and wanted Salinas covered at all times. We also talked about Carson and that I was aware that we had donated some of our wears. Big Ted said that Carson had asked for the donation and he said I would approve the gifts. Its stuff we had for years Ted said. I told him that we'd have to keep up contact once Carson departs. I asked Ted to check if he knew of any ex-Navy Seals in south Florida that might be interested in joining our little group. Ted said he'd inquire around.

Before I went to bed I called Carson's number one more time. Again no answer.

The next morning, I went straight to Carson's house. The Mercedes was no longer in the driveway. I knocked on the door and with no answer I let myself in. On the table there was a note for me. The note read "Sorry old friend, I know I mislead you about the date of my departure but I thought you might want to stop me. Like another old friend once said don't send the Calvary. Looking forward to being with you in December, maybe we can do some of that diving that you were talking about, sounds like fun. Your friend Carson." That buzzard bait I said to myself.

I decided to stop on by Roy's office and pick up the clearance papers. I would sign at the office and Karen would be my witness.

Once the papers were signed, Evette would drop them off to Federal Express. After lunch Karen said that the IRS had been back looking for me, Karen told them that due to the levy on my pay, I had quit. We both got a laugh about that.

Karen said that the Navy check was just over $1,600,000.00 and should be deposited in Nassau, I agreed. Karen volunteered to go. Fat chance I said, it's my birthday and I'm going diving. We decided that we would all go to dinner at Joe's Friday night and then dancing. Saturday morning we'd all fly on over to Nassau. Karen said she had contacted Bob, Big Ted, Carlos and Robin to join us for dinner. With our office, Jim the yard manger and with Tim bringing his wife we would have 15 for dinner.

I had told the girls a story about flying to Nassau, but I had no intention of doing so. Merrill Stevens had called the office and left a message to return their call. I did not, I went by. The manager walked me out to the dock on the river. There sitting was this beautiful 54-foot sailboat. It was the Hunter that I had been waiting for. I jumped aboard and inspected the boat, it was unreal. Merrill Stevens had thought of everything; the boat was fully equipped ready to go. The only heads up with the Hunter was its draft. The draft was about 6 feet. This boat wasn't meant for Biscayne Bay; it was meant for the Bahamans. As I inspected the interior I noticed right away that the Hunter had a lot more space but seemed the Morgan had more bunk space. Here with two cabins there was sleeping space for six. The boat was built for cruising and speed. The boat would be titled in the Bahamas but we'd take delivery here in Miami. My plan was to take her out Saturday morning and sail her down to Ocean Reef in Key Largo and then back Sunday. Anyone that showed for dinner Friday night would be invited to join us on the sailboat for the weekend. I had already sent Merrill Stevens a deposit and would have the balance transferred within the week. I named the boat "CAT".

This was my dream boat. I could see it sitting at the city docks in Nassau or anchored at Harbor Island or even sitting in the water at the Chateau in Haiti.

The new container business, Omni, was doing well, its sales had increased as the container business that I had sold to Guido was slowly but surely disintegrating. We were not taking any of their business. Sea Containers was taking their customers business. Sea Container was now in high demand. Omni had doubled in size and the facility was now crowed. Tim the computer guy and Karen would now be running the business. Tim was to own 50% of the company. Tim was a good man whom became a good friend and a perfect fit for the business.

Salinas was starting to show but even with a small belly she was still the most beautiful girl I had ever known. She got along with everyone. She was smart, outgoing and reserved. I was happy as could be with her. Things in my life where good.

Friday night came, the three musketeers left early to do what girls do. Dinner was to be at 7:00 p.m., Joe's didn't take reservations for anyone. Salinas had left early with Karen, I got home at 6:00 p.m. and Salinas was almost ready. When I saw her, I wanted to remove that dress and stay home! I just had to sit and watch her continue to get ready, Wow.

Karen and Evette were now living in the third bedroom in the apartment. They too looked great and had knocked on our door saying that they knew what I was thinking but that we needed to go.

Dinner at Joe's was great! Everyone showed up. As dinner was being severed I stood up and announced our new purchase and plans for the weekend. All said they would join us. Karen and Evette would go grocery shopping first thing in the morning with us planning to eat dinner at the Ocean Reef club the next night. I had already reserved three rooms at the club for Saturday night.

From dinner we went dancing. Salinas was looking tired at about 1:00 a.m. so we left early. It was good to get home and into that shower.

Saturday morning to my surprise everyone showed up. Carlos brought along a new girlfriend so that made 16 in all. We did wait a few minutes for Karen and Evette but we were on our way by 10:00 a.m. We motored out the river having the 2nd street Bridge open for us then out into the Bay and again the Port of Miami Bridge opened for us and we were headed out the channel. Once out of the channel we raised the sails and headed south. The boat sailed like no other I had ever been on, it seemed to just slice thought the water. It was great, Salinas took the wheel first, and her smile said it all, she was happy. We all were happy. Robin was the next to take the wheel, Robin whom was now the vice president of Sea Containers had brought with him a Captains hat that said was his when he was given his first ship. The Hunter 54 had 16 aboard and everyone was comfortable.

We arrived at the Ocean Reef club at about 4:00 p.m., by the time we got into the dock and tied up it was 5:00 p.m. We then all headed for the pool. We had a nice dinner, Karen, Evette, Salinas and I would sleep aboard and the others split up the three rooms. The next morning, we ate breakfast at the club house and then departed for Miami. Everyone had a great time. The only other birthday I could remember was at seven when my Dad had given me my first bike.

During our sailing trip, Salinas had mentioned that she wanted to visit her mom and her horses before she got too far along. I said that I would sent a security person along and suggested that she take along Karen and or Evette, Salinas liked that idea and would ask the girls.

Monday morning brought the news that only Evette would go with Salinas and that they were ready to go whenever the transport could be arranged. Karen said she would arrange the charter and inform Big Ted for the security requirements. Salinas would go on Tuesday morning and return the following Sunday. This would be the first time we spent the night away from each other since I had brought her to Miami. Salinas said for me to behave while she was away.

It was Tuesday night at the 1800 club that I asked Karen if she wanted to go to Nassau Friday afternoon and do some scuba diving. I told her that I had planned to do this dive with Carson but that he had run off to Grenada. Karen asked if it was business or pleasure, I said both. Karen said she would go. It was like I needed her, I didn't have anyone else that I could trust. Sure I could trust Otis or Peter and or maybe Mark, But Peter was busy and Otis, well I was afraid that he would go back with Maggie and get one or the other hurt.

Tuesday night once we got home we got a call from Salinas saying that they had arrived ok. The telephone connection was poor and the conversation got cut off. At least I knew they were ok.

Wednesday I purchased new scuba diving gear including wet suits. Ted would provide security, I said it had to be Steve. Steve now had two kids of his own. We weren't expecting trouble we just needed him to keep look out for sharks and boats and assist us on and off the boat. A walk in the park, a paid walk in the park.

Thursday there was a call from George. Since I sold the container business and resigned as a trustee on the ILA fund I hadn't heard from George. George wanted to meet in privet, I agreed to lunch in public at the same restaurant that we used to go to. George said that if we had to go to a restaurant and I was paying he'd like to go to Joe's on the beach, so Joe's it was. George didn't seem himself, this was the first time he looked worried and tired. He asked if I was going to take back the container business that I had sold to Guido. I said no. I told George that I was retired from that type of work and all the responsibilities that came with it. I told George that I had sold Guido a working business without problems and that Guido blew it. George said that Guido was going to close the doors at the end of the month. This to include Savannah and Norfolk, this George said was going to cost him personally a small fortune. I looked at him and said talk to Guido. George said Guido blamed it all on me. George said that Guido also was told that I had sold the Casino property right from under him. I informed George that Guido had plenty of time to respond but didn't. In the end George didn't pound on the table he just warned that Sea Containers may have problems with their ships while working on the east coast. Not my problem I said, I'm not involved.

I went from lunch to the Sea Containers down town office. Robin had just started a two-week vacation and was in England. I had his secretary send him a telex letting him know of the pending closers and implied treats. It was most likely late at night there and I wasn't expecting a quick reply.

Thursday night we tried to call Haiti with no luck. We telexed and found everyone doing fine. I let Salinas know that Karen and I were going to Nassau to, for one thing, to deposit the Navy check.

CHAPTER XXI

THE SECOND OF DRAKE'S SHIPS

Karen, Steve, and I left Friday at 7:30 a.m. As we arrived in Nassau we dropped off our bags at the Hurricane House and went straight to the bank. Karen deposited the check and we then walked to Angee's for some of that great conch salad. Angee was so happy about Otis and Maggie and said that there was to be two December weddings in Nassau. Yes, Otis and Maggie were going to get married. Their house was finished and they would move in after the wedding. Angee said she'd be a little lonely but that she'd just be waiting on the grandchildren. Angee kept asking about Salinas over and over. Everything's ok Angee I said, Salinas is visiting her mother. Angee also kept looking at Karen. I also told Angee not to worry about Karen. Angee asked? How could anybody not worry with a woman like that around? I looked at Karen and said that was Angee's way of giving her a compliment. Karen said she wanted to take the Hatteras out, can we she asked? We stopped in to say hello to Willy and then walked down to the Hatteras. Karen said she just wanted to ride. I noted that we needed to be back so I could speak with Otis. We would be using the "Johnny" Saturday and Sunday. It would be hard but he wasn't going to be invited. Karen did all the Captaining. I worked the lines. Karen was comfortable behind the wheel. I think I had mentioned it before but Karen reminded me of Michelle. I could just imagine Karen up on that stage, those poor souls, all those drooling men.

We stayed out until almost 4:00 p.m. I got back just in time. Otis and Maggie were cleaning up the boat. I went aboard and told Otis I would need to borrow the "Johnny" Saturday and Sunday, they could go out with the other Bertram or take the time off. Otis didn't ask any questions he just said that would be fine. We still had time so we walked on over to the dive shop and asked for 8 tanks of air. Karen was happy to show her certificate. The man, now not as young, told Karen of his first experience with me renting tanks. Karen said yes that's our boss. I was concerned that people would think something of so many tanks but it had been some 14 or 15 years since we had starting bringing up the treasure. It didn't seem to catch anyone's notice. Karen went shopping and checked the boat for sleeping and cooking gear. The plan was to just go out once not to attract any suspicion. Karen must have thought I was paranoid. It was Friday night, the three of us ate at the Bahamian Cuisine Restaurant then Karen wanted to sleep on the Hatteras. Yes, right at the dock. Of course it was hot and she had the AC going but we slept on the Hatteras just the same, Karen had the front cabin and Steve got the smaller one, I got a bunk. We got an early breakfast and then headed out with the "Johnny". With Karen at the wheel we made the same false headings at the beginning and then changed course to head for the old treasure sight. Steve was in charge of constantly checking that we weren't being followed.

Once at the sight I explained to Karen and Steve what we were going to do and how we were going to do it. We should get at least three slack tides during our two days out there. The boat would either tow me behind or the boat and I would go with the tide. The first day we started at 9:00 a.m. No air tanks, just mask, snorkel and fins. The water here being so rocky, I now had with me a bang stick with a 12 gage shot on its end. One hit with this bang stick and any shark would lose all ambition to bother anyone or thing again. By the time the first slack tide rolled along I hadn't seen anything but the normal beautiful bottom. It was rocky with scattered sandy and grassy spots. At the slack tide we anchored and Karen and I skin dove using the old circle system that Johnny had taught me years ago. We weren't looking for fish we were looking for signs of a wreck, it could be a canon, a plank of wood or even and anchor. When the girls had been taken by the current, while assisting them aboard, I thought I had got a glimpse of something that had the shape of a large anchor. We had made two large circles without spotting anything that looked like something like it was from an old wreck. We looked all day, nothing. At 6:00 p.m. we moved to the center of the circle and anchored. I dove and got six big crawfish for dinner, Karen cooked. Just after dark we went to sleep, again Karen taking the small front cabin, Steve and I lying out on the deck.

The next morning Karen cooked pancakes, eggs and bacon. We got an early start. On our very first drift of the day I spotted what I had seen several weeks before. I yelled for Karen to drop the small anchor. She did. I then got aboard and started the engines and went back against the current moving past the anchor about 50 feet, and then had Karen drop the main anchor off the bow. I then cut the engines and went to suit up. Karen wanted to go to but I said it could just be nothing. Beside the current was still strong. I once again tied a line to the anchor line that I could use to slide along the anchor line. I went in at the bow, grabbing the anchor line. I pulled myself forward until I was right over what was now clear was a large anchor. No I didn't actually see and anchor, what it was, was green algae that was in the form of an anchor. The anchor was sitting on and between two large rocks. If it had been in the sand, I might not have ever seen it. I went up and said we would wait another few hours when the current died down. I said we would do two things. One, I would scrape off some of the algae to see the metal and if there were any markings and check to see if a chain was attacked and where it led us. I noticed that I wasn't in the same physical shape I had been in so long ago. I promised myself that regardless of what we found here I would start running when I got back.

We waited two hours, I couldn't wait any longer. With Karen on a tie off line, we both went over. The current wasn't too bad but I wasn't having too much luck scraping off the attached growth. We did however find the chain and it pointed us to the reefs edge. Karen couldn't go past her tether line but I followed the chain for about 100 feet. As I got closer to the reefs edge, the water was becoming quite alive with fish. I was still fighting the current and something in my brain was sounding an alarm to go back. I quickly got to Karen and when I got eye contact I put my index finger over my mouth. She gave me a thumbs up. We boarded and dropped our gear. Slack tide would start in about 30 minutes. We started the engine and pulled up both anchors. I took the wheel and moved the boat to where I thought we were just about where I had been when I turned back. This time we faced the boat west dropping the bow anchor then using a little reverse to go against the small remaining current. I then had Steve drop the stern anchor and cut the engines. I asked Steve to go up top and keep a good look out and be ready to sound the alarm for other boats or sharks. I pointed out the direction of the channel at a distance of about two miles. Any boats should be going to or heading in from that channel. Steve said he understood.

Karen suited up with new tanks. This was our third tank each since yesterday morning. There now was little or no current. I took my bang stick and a hand tool. We went overboard and I located the chain. We were now 50 feet from the reef, the water was about 20 feet deep with still a rocky bottom with those same spots of sand and or grass. The chain was actually easy to spot and follow. As we got closer to the reef I could see Karen getting a bit nervous do to the large fish. All of a sudden we could see what was left of a ship and its debris. It had been a large ship, it looked like it rammed the reef sideways and sank on its port side. I say this because almost half of the ship, the starboard side was sitting on the rocks. We could see the broken masts in parts some sitting atop of the rocks. The ship was literally sitting next to and alongside of the reef. We could see all kinds of fish swimming in and out of the structure. Karen was now holding on to my weight belt strap. It was only a matter of minutes before we saw our first shark. It didn't mind us but I heard Karen make a loud noise and point to it. Obviously Steve couldn't see it as it went along the bottom weaving through the rocks. I could tell Karen was uncomfortable and maybe just a little scared. I looked for our boat and couldn't see it. Steve should be watching our bubbles but we went up to the surface so I could get my bearings and insure that Steve knew where we were. As my head came out of the water Steve acknowledged us with a thumbs up. I asked Karen if she was ok and could keep going or she had enough. Karen being Karen gave me the finger. We went back down and got even closer to the ship's carcass. The intact part of the ship was actually well kept. Only in a movie had I seen such a sight. There were planks and items all laying on the rocks, looked as if items that reached the bottom had disappeared. If there was a treasure down there, its weight should have put it very close to bottom of the ship's hull. I knew that to claim the site we should go back with some kind of proof even if it wasn't treasure. I counted only four canons that looked very similar to the one that Johnny and I had found. They were either laying on the rocks or somewhat sticking in the sand. As we reached the ships stern I saw something, as we got closer I recognized what looked to be a part of the wheel. Yes I was sure, I looked at the tank gage and we were done. I signaled to Karen and we went in a straight line for the boat. We got aboard and I changed to my last tank. I wouldn't have much time before the already turned current got too bad. I grabbed a line with an empty water jug and went back over. No bang stick, no tool, just a jug tied to a line of about 40 feet with the other end of the line free. I swam right to where we had seen the section of the wheel, found it and tied it off. The jug was floating and I headed back. We pulled up both anchors and would move the boat to the jug. Once there with the current heading out, I rapped the line around the hoist and started winding. I was surprised on just how heavy it was. As the section of wheel lifted off the rocks the winding got easier. As it came up out of the water the boat was tilting to the starboard from the wheel's weight. By now we were moving with the current. I stopped what I was doing and went up top to get a good idea exactly where we were along the reef. Ok I said to Karen, give us a hand getting this thing aboard. The wheel was so big that even having it winched to the top of the roller the wheel wouldn't clear the boats starboards side. I quickly took the rubber mats that were on the floor and put on the side of the boat in order not to cut into the fiberglass. All three of us now with gloves would now try to pull this thing aboard by dragging it over the side. Once we had the top part well into the boat I winched it down on the remaining rubber mats. Now with part on the deck and a part still resting on the side. I changed the location of the line to the center of its weight and again, using the wrench we raised the wheel up off the side and swung it into the boat and on the mats. What is it asked Steve? It's the wheel of a ship Karen said. That's it for the day, let's get back to Nassau I said. I started the engines and we were on our way back. When we got close enough I radioed in asking Pete for a slip at the city dock. I asked him to get me three slips side by side. My thinking was that I would cover the wheel with blankets and park a Hatteras on each side not to have people looking down into the cockpit wandering what we found. Pete was ready when we got there. I had to do some moving of the Hatteras's but when we finished it was like I wanted it. Steve would stay with the boat while Karen and I went to Willy's and used the phone. I called for Cat but the woman answering said that Cat and Jacob were in town attending church. I walked to the church and it was just getting out. Cat saw us and came to asked if there was some kind of problem. I waved over Jacob. We walked into the park and I told them both that we had found the second ship. I told them that I had sitting on the "Johnny", part of the ships wheel. I wanted Jacob to start the paper work to register the find. We would use the Blue Ocean LTD Company. Jacob agreed and would start at once asking his Father's help. Cat of course asked about Salinas and I let her know all was good with us. I was going to surprise Cat with the sailboat but decided that she might want to make its first crossing with us. When I told her face lit up and couldn't stop asking questions about it including the Name. When she asked, Karen smiled and said CAT the name on the stern is "CAT". Cat tried to hide the tears put she could not.

Karen would travel back to Miami with Steve on the 3:30 PM flight. Someone had to work I said. I would stay and assist with marking the chart for the registrar and when the coast guard was ready assist with marking the area. This might take a few days and the "Johnny" would need to be out of commission until the papers were signed for the claim. Karen said she telexed Salinas and let her know I was here and alright. I said not to mention anything about the ship find.

Monday morning, I got a surprise, now days there was a fee that went along with the registration. The fee $25,000.00 was not returnable, however should you find something of worth the Bahamian

Government would get 25% and that $25,000.00 fee could be applied to that 25%. Cat would have to come down to the bank and arrange the payment of the $25,000.00. It was Wednesday before we had everything signed and the Coast Guard went out there and put down buoys.

I thought that Otis thought I wanted to keep him away from any treasure, I explained that I was concern about his safety. His and Maggie's. I let him know that I considered this dangerous work. I was also thinking of Angee, losing one child to the sea was hard enough. Otis said he understood but still wanted my permission to dive the wreck. We agreed that when we dove the wreck, Maggie would stay aboard and that he'd need an experienced diver with him in the water at all times. The "Johnny" had been sitting there all this time. Otis moved the "Johnny" over to the ship yard and then they hoisted up the wheel and it was taken to our shop behind the store. Otis, being days behind would now have lots of catch up work with the trap. The other Bertrams had pulled more traps every day but only an extra 15%. The other 85% of the "Johnny's" traps had gone untouched.

Bel's son Dave had died in an accident in 1977. The tug that Dave, his wife and their top diver were staying on sank during the night, surprisingly all three lost their lives. Just months after Dave's death, Bel found one of the biggest treasures that had ever been found. I didn't have such a good taste in my month for that whole Dave experience. No I wouldn't call Bel. I would do this myself.

I flew back and informed Karen that when Salinas got back we would be sailing the Hunter to Nassau. Weather permitting, we would leave the following Friday. Anyone wanting to go for the sail was welcome.

I did call Bob an ask him to find me two barges with a size of 20 feet wide by about 40 feet long. Both Barges would have to be modified with living quarters, a generator, an air compressor and fuel for each. Bob was to donate two 20-foot shipping containers from the old Thompson line. One of these would once have been refrigerated. This for its insulation, keeping the air-conditioning in and the noise of the generator out. The center of each barge would have a cut out and an electric hoist. The two barges could be bolted together at the ends or sides this to create a large space from which using a seahorse type hoist would enable us to lift even a canon. Once ready the barges would be towed by a Tug boat and anchored at the wreck's site. Time wise we were talking a month or more before the barges would be ready. Our permits for the wreck would last two years and depending on what we found could be extended for another year.

Friday the Navy sent via an armed currier the plans for the new Andros project. We put in a call for Lee requesting for him to fly into Miami instead of going to Nassau for the weekend. We said it was urgent. Lee would arrive late today or tomorrow morning. This ship wreck thing was happening in the middle of several things.

The Navy plans wouldn't be left in the office, I would take them to the apartment, the covers of the plans booklets and every page was marked TOP SECRET. When I got home I had a pleasant surprise, Diane had come to visit. She had heard I was going to be a father and wanted to come and congratulate me. Just as soon as I walked in I opened the safe and put the plans and locked them in with only one key. The safe was still empty awaiting the next visit from the IRS. Diane looked good, we sat on the couch and she caught me up on the news. She and Marco were getting married in April and although she didn't have to ask, she did. She wanted me to give her away. I of course said yes. As we'd talked Karen and Lee arrived. Betty asked if we be eating in and Diane said she would be leaving in just a few minutes. When she said that I knew that there was something else. We walked out onto the Balcony and I asked her what was on her mind. Diane said she hadn't told Marco the truth about her past. Diane had told Marco that her parents had died in an accident when she was young and that her Uncle Tinny and I had raised her. Diane said that Marco also didn't know about her money. Well I said, it will be hard but you will have to tell him. If it was me it wouldn't matter, but there's always the possibility that someone else finds out and tells him first. I don't think you will have to go into all the details. But you need to tell him. If you want my help in doing so just let me know. Sorry, I know it's hard but you have managed a lot tougher things than this. He might back off a bit and if he does, just come on back home for a while. He'll come for you I said.

Diane gave me a hug and kiss, told me she missed me, said good-by to everyone and left. Karen asked what all that was about? I said just a family thing.

Now for the fun part I said. I got out the two sets of plans. Lee and Karen sat at the table. Only laying out one set of plans keeping the second set closed. The very first thing that Lee saw was the blank space in the center of the plans. I told him that was even more secret than top secret. We all laughed. I told them both that I did have on the table the other set of drawings, but they weren't to see them as yet. I must say this will be and adventure. Lee asked if he'd still be boating from Island? I told him that I'd like to have Janie and his daughter living on Andros, but that wasn't likely, so we would arrange to have a small leer at our disposal. I told Karen to contact Tommy and offer him the contract. He must have a new plane by now I said, if not help him out with a little push. How much of a push Karen asked? Up to a million, I said. It wasn't late so I called Mr. Makee and told him that we had an urgent need. Mr. Makee asked if 7:00 a.m. in his office would be fast enough. I said that I would have coffee at my apartment ready at 7:00 a.m. He said they'd be here.

When I hung up Lee had some observations. His first was the line up with the large Blue hole and the center of the new project. Looks like he said the Blue hole will have a lot to do with this project.

Remember he said some of the Navy personal said they had lost a sub down in the channel there last month. They lost a maned sub and one of our Sonar devices I confirmed.

That rumor that they have traveled from that Blue hole to the channel is also true I said. What do they think happened to their sub Lee asked? They don't know I said. They are working on the possibility that someone or thing had worked on the cave to widen it from the channel to the blue hole. Well, Lee said you wouldn't get me diving down there. That's why I hired four ex-Navy seals to do some exploring before we actually start working down there. They will work diving the blue hole until the barges are ready, and then those four and a possible two more will work the wreck site. When we need the divers for the underwater construction part of the contract you can pull four of them back and forth from Nassau. The construction will obviously have the priority. Lee said that I was talking like we already had the contract. I said I was counting on it. Lee said if I didn't mind he would catch the next flight back to Nassau to spend some time with the family. I told him to go but that the Divers would be at Andros in two days with their gear. I will need Captain Mike to move air tanks back and forth from Nassau. When you go back to Andros take at least ten full tanks. I'll ship 20 tanks or so down to Nassau via the shipping company. Karen please take care of this early tomorrow. Karen said she would.

I said we'd be in Nassau sometime late next Saturday sailing the New Hunter over. I said that I wanted the divers to start working just as soon as possible. We shook hands and he kissed Karen and he was off.

As Lee shut the door behind himself Karen noted that he has worked out quite well. Yes I said, then asked, when are you going to find someone like that? Karen laughed and said she was having too much fun working and playing the field. Karen said that I should get some sleep. Salinas and Evette would be back on Sunday. Karen said she hadn't told Evette as yet but that her divorce papers had arrived at the office. She looked at me and said that I was off the hook but watch out all the other men out there. Karen said the girls would be at Opa-Locka at about mid-day. I said I'd pick them both up, Karen gave me a thumbs up as she walked into her room. I picked up the plans and re-locked them away in the safe and hit the sack.

The next morning, I was up early making things ready, Betty cooked Karen and I a good breakfast and the coffee was ready for Mr. Makee. Mr. Makee was right on time. He brought with him the two young engineers that had worked on our first Andros project. All three men got a look at Karen in her pajamas. Karen gave that double look to all three. Mr. Makee mentioned something about quite a woman. Coffee please he said shaking his head.

The plans were laid out on the dining table. After a minute or two Mr. Makee asked about the other set of drawings that must fit within the blank space. The blank space, I said would be priced on a cost plus percentage. Mr. Makee said cost plus 20%, Ok I'll go with that I said, what about this group?

Mr. Makee asked if everything equipment wise was still down there. I said it was as Lee had just finished the house that went along with the dock that he had built. You really want this job Mr. Makee asked? Yes Sir, I'm counting on it. Ok he said, he looked at his two men and asked if they needed anything else? They said no. Mr. Makee said they would have the quote and return the plans by Tuesday morning. I said that would be fine and reminded him that these plans could not be let out of his site nor copied. As marked, I said, they are TOP SECRET.

One of the engineers asked if Karen might need a ride somewhere? This as Karen walked out of her room ready to go. Karen smiled and said that most Fridays nights we visited the Alley in the grove. Maybe she'd see him there some time. I walked them to the door and thanked them and said we would be talking to them on Tuesday. I then asked Karen where she was off too and she replied that I was going teach her how to handle the Hunter today. I laughed and said I be ready as soon as I locked up the drawings.

The Hunter was a breeze to sail. Like I had mentioned the only thing was its draft. The Morgan's draft was two and a half feet less than the hunter.

Karen had been aboard the Morgan once when Joe had run us aground on the Biscayne Banks. Back then we ran aground at 2:00 a.m. during high tide. By daylight the Morgan was sitting on the bottom at a 45-degree angle on its starboard side. We had to wait until the next high tide to get her off. We tied an anchor to the main sail line coming from the top of the mast, then walked the anchor out as far as we could to the starboard side, placed the anchor, then winched in the line healing the boat even more on its side freeing the keel. Then Joe and I were in the water pushing the Morgan forward. It took us all day to get her free. Anyway the story here was if the hunter ran aground we'd be in deep crap! Karen got the message she was a natural sailor. In fact, Karen could do just about anything! I didn't tell her, but I was fortunate to have such a good friend.

We had a good day sailing and Karen literally learn the ropes including the basics details of the engine room.

We returned to the marina at about 7:00 p.m. and from there went to the 1800 club for dinner. Karen was going out that night with some new guy and me will I hit the sack early as Sunday would be a big day for me.

Sunday morning at 11:00 a.m. I left for the airport to pick up the girls. I was there as the small plan rolled up and out came Salinas running into my arms. I missed you so much she said as she hugged me not letting go. Then stepped out Evette looking browner than ever. What about my hug Evette asked as she also came and hugged us both.

We got their luggage, went through immigration and were off to the apartment. I carried Salinas's bag into the room and she shut and locked the door behind us. To the shower we went. It was great having her back, I didn't realize just how much I had missed her.

From the shower to the bed we went. At about 5:00 p.m. Salinas was ready to get dressed, we were going out to dinner. As we were getting ready I noticed blood spots on the sheets. I asked Salinas about the spots and she said that it started two days prior. I quickly called Doctors James's office and left a message on the answering machine. I told Salinas that we were on hold until we heard back from Doctor James. Doctor James called back within the hour. I told him what I saw and he spoke with Salinas. She told him that they had been doing a lot of horseback riding, yes she said I ride bare back. She then handed me back the phone. Doctor James said I needed to bring her in first thing in the morning and to keep her in bed. Nothing but rest he said, nothing. I said I understood and agreed that we would be there at 9:00 a.m. I looked at her and said it would have to be dinner in bed.

Our baby's alright isn't she, she asked? I said for one thing our baby is a he not a she and yes everything will be just fine. Now I said do as the good Doctor said and get back in bed.

I went to the door and called for Betty. I asked if she had something cooking or if we should order out. Betty asked what Salinas was in the mood for? Salinas said steak. Betty said well maybe I should run down to Scotty's and pick up some of those heavenly stakes. Betty said she'd start some baked potatoes.

The next morning Salinas and I were off to see Doctor James. Just as I figured, the Doctor told us that we were looking at a possible pre-abort. Salinas would need to stay in bed for at least two weeks maybe more. Doctor James said he'd see us again in two weeks.

Salinas was worried but I told her it would all work out. Just do as the Doctor ordered. I told her that I would cancel the Friday's sailing trip to Nassau but she wouldn't have it. Salinas said she would use the days I was gone to rest. Salinas said I should go just as planned. I took her home and made sure she was in bed and then took off for work. Karen had already called to have 20 new scuba tanks delivered to Bob's Shipping Terminal on the river. I told Karen to purchase two new Boston Whalers too. One that we would tow down behind the Hunter the other to be shipped aboard the cargo ship. Karen also called Rodger to make sure the tanks and the whaler would go out on the next trip. Karen said Rodger said he'd take care of it personally.

Karen had also tried to contact Carson, again without any luck. By 2:00 p.m. Karen came to me and said the Tommy thing was a done deal. Tommy could start tomorrow. I asked her to make arrangements for Tommy to fly the new divers and their gear to Andros that same day he started. I also had her to call Lee and tell him when the divers would be there. The divers will stay at the beach house with Lee. If he can't get there in time with Captain Mike have Tommy pick up Lee too. I want the drivers to start working by Thursday.

The week went by quickly everything seemed to be going as planned. Tuesday Morning Mr. Makee called and said the quotation for Andros was ready. Karen sent Evette over to pick it and the drawings up. Once she returned I looked it over and had Karen get our quote ready for the Admiral.

Tommy flew from New York to Nassau and then came back for the divers. By Tuesday night the five of them were at the house on Andros.

Karen and I would fly up with Tommy to see the Admiral Wednesday to present the quotations. The Admiral was happy to see Karen again. He had us sit down and wait while he opened both large envelopes. After 30 minutes or so, him having several interruptions, the Admiral said everything looked to be in order and said he be calling us soon. He walked us out and again said he would call.

Karen and I few back to Miami with Karen saying she didn't think there were any other contractors involved.

I spent Wednesday night at home with Salinas and would be ready for a busy Thursday.

Thursday was a shopping day for Karen, Evette and myself. They would buy all the supplies for the trip. I was shopping for a ten-man life raft and would pick up one of the Boston whalers and motor it to the marina.

Karen's confirmed count for the sailing trip to Nassau was 8. The girls had this big pre-voyage post-divorce party planned, Karen had of course given Evette her Divorce papers which finalized her divorce. Everyone would meet at the 1800 club then go dancing in the Grove. We would be leaving Friday morning from the Miami Marina at 4:00 a.m. I was sure that Karen and Evette would show up in their party clothes coming directly from dancing all night. This is why they had everything aboard by Thursday afternoon. I was at the club for a few hours Thursday night and then went home to be with Salinas. Salinas was in good spirits and seemed to appreciate me being home with her. I would leave the apartment at 3:00 a.m., Salinas didn't even wake.

CHAPTER XXII

THE SAILING OF THE "CAT" TO NASSAU

Once at the Marina, I walked down the dock to the Hunter. As I turned down the side dock I saw a body lying on the starboard cockpit seat. Just like old times the voice said. It was my old friend Rusty! He stood up and when I stepped aboard we hugged. When did you get in I asked? Well Rusty said, Karen had called my mom and my mom called me Wednesday night. I talked to my two bosses and I left yesterday after work and drove straight down. Two bosses I asked? Yes Rusty said, I got remarried and have a son too. Another Russell Eugene I trust, I asked? Rusty said right on.

We talked as I opened the cabin door and Rusty looked around. A little different than our last trip Rusty noted. Not too many sharks bigger than this boat he said.

As the time got closer to 4:00 a.m., only Carlos was late. Some things never change. As I saw Carlos and his girlfriend walking down the dock. Rusty met them half way and gave Carlos a big hug. Evette was half drunk and gave Ralph a pat on the butt saying she liked what she saw. Ralph asked if she was alright in the head.

I told Ralph that she just got divorced and had been with Karen all night celebrating. Karen said Evettes a light weight where it comes to drinking. Karen was already changed and ready to get the show on the road. She then went and got the whaler which was about three slips to out to port.

The whaler would be towed behind the Hunter. We had checked the weather and there were no storms in the Atlantic. With all aboard we were ready to get started. We shoved off and motored up to the Port of Miami Bridge and sounded our horn for the bridge to open. The Bridge went up and we went under the bridge and motored out the channel. As we passed the Chalks seaport I received a funny feeling in my stomach. I closed my eyes and for a moment remembered all the times I had flown in and out from there. It all had started 18 years ago on that trip that Rusty and I had made on the "Princess," a wooden homemade 21-foot sailboat.

When I opened my eyes again we had passed the parked Sea Planes that had been on our port side and were now passing a large cruise ship on our starboard. When we came out of the channel we hoisted up the sails and shut off the motor. We were on the way, next stop Nassau.

By now Ralph was an advert sailor. Carlos could sail and both Stann the man and his wife could sail. That would make six of the nine that could sail that I would trust behind the wheel. We had four groups that we would take two hour shifts. That would allow everyone to get some sleep. The sun would be coming up soon and we'd see how the sky looked.

As the sun rose the sky was clear with hardly a cloud in the sky. I said out loud, Red sky at night, sailors delight. Red sky at morn sailors take worn. Rusty looked at me and smiled.

Rusty and I had lots of time to talk about Martha. I told Rusty he wouldn't believe she was almost 17. She looked like a grown woman but her mom was still very protective. I told Rusty that I had promised that I wouldn't tell Martha that Mary and Tim weren't her real parents. This unless Martha asked me. Rusty said he had no intention of telling her but that he wanted to make sure she had an American passport. Rusty said that it should be left for Martha to decide. I agreed and said that I would bring it up to her parents after he went back to the mainland. I told Rusty that Martha had her own business of moving tourist to and from the anchored boats and doing things like shopping for them. Just the week before Martha had gone scuba diving with me. Rusty got choked up a bit and said that he came on the trip with hopes of seeing her.

The day went by fast with us all poring salt water over our heads to keep cool. There was also hats, sun block and tanning oil. Starting at 11:00 a.m.the girls took turns bartending. Lunch was sandwiches and chips. Karen told everyone the story of the time that she, Joe and I were having a guacamole fight while sailing to Elliot. We were sailing the Morgan and our Banker with his wife were out sailing and had spotted us and wanted to visit. We anchored just off Elliot and they tied up with us.

Our boat was full of guacamole everywhere, even our ears and hair were caked with guacamole. The Banker's wife looked at us like we were wackos, she didn't even want her husband to put a foot on our boat. We all had a big laugh.

By night fall all had taken turns at the wheel. All had heard Rusty's story of us almost being run over by Bob's freighter. Although the Hunter had radar all were told to look for other boats. We did have a few boats appear on the radar but nothing came even close to us. By morning we had passed the north end of Andros. From that point on every 30 minutes we would try to raise Nassau on the ship to shore radio. At about 9:00 a.m. we received our first answer. It was Pete from the City Marina. City Docks calling the sail boat "CAT" he said. Pete is that you I asked? Captain Jim, is that you? Yes sir, I replied. I trust you're not sailing that 21-foot sailboat he said. No, we're bring in a 54-foot Hunter, you got space. If we don't I'll have to kick out one of these 42 Hatteras's that are sitting here, one is collecting salt dust. He and I both laughed. What's your ETA Pete asked? About two hours I said. Ok I'll have everything ready. By any chance you don't have that rascal Rusty with you do you, Pete asked? I handed the mic to Rusty and he said, Hello Pete this is Rusty, got any girls lined up. Oh my Lord Pete said I'll have to go walking down the docks warning all the mothers to keep their daughters on board.

We all got a laugh out of that. Ok we'll see you soon. Rodger that Pete said.

Within the hour we got another call, this time it was Cat calling. Cat calling the sail boat "CAT", Cat calling the "CAT", she said. We hear you loud and clear Cat I said. Hello Captain Jim when you getting my sailboat here. About one hour over. Be on the lookout for a whaler that's coming your way Cat said. That will be Martha correct, I asked? That's correct Cat said. Rusty was quick to grab the binoculars and start looking. Then another Familiar voice came over the waves. City Bar calling the sail boat "CAT", that you Willy I asked? Hell yes Willy replied. You got anyone on that vessel that their chin won't each the Bar. No Sir I replied, we do have someone that might not be able to sit very long on one of your stools. Then Evette took the mic and said, Willy this is Evette, you know I can hold my liquor right.

Oh yes mam Willy said yes mam. Ok then I hope you got plenty of cold Polly Girl in your frig. Yes mam, I got plenty. Ok Willy I said we'll see you soon. Ok Captain see you in the bar. A motor starting had me turn to the stern. In the Whaler were Karen and Rusty. Ralph untied the tow line and they were off to meet Martha.

The next voice we heard was Martha's, she had been listening and it was her turn. "CAT" this is the "Tide Runner" do you read me? Read you loud and clear "Tide Runner".

That Whaler coming at me yours, Martha asked? Then Karen interrupted saying, hello litter sister this is Karen calling. Big sis Martha replied. Good looking Whaler Martha said. By now both whalers were within clear view and heading our way. Permission to come aboard Martha asked. Permission granted I said. Both Whalers were now tied up to our stern. Martha, Karen and Rusty came aboard. Martha came to me and hugged me. Martha introduced herself to all aboard. Rusty couldn't keep his eyes off her. Rusty walked by me and whispered that she was more beautiful than I had said.

Once we entered the Harbor, Karen and Martha took the Whalers and went ahead. They would tie up both boats and meet us at the City docks.

Pete was on the radio and gave us the slip number. The current would be working against us but the reverse on the Hunter was much stronger than the current. Pete and Cat were there to catch the bow line.

As we were tying up, Karen and Martha came running down to help with the boat. The docking was a piece of cake. Cat was on the side dock and asked permission to come aboard. Permission granted I said. Cat took one step over the side rail and the other on deck. I introduced Cat to everyone she didn't know. Cat looked around once and asked where Salinas was? I said she didn't make the trip. Oh Cat said.

The Hunter was secured and we were ready to all go up to see Willy for those cold beers he was talking about. As I was about to step of the boat Cat took my hand and asked me to show her the cabin. Cat started down and I followed. Once we both were standing on the cabin floor she turned and kissed me. When she stopped she took my hand and was heading for the front bunks. I stopped and pulled back my hand. We're not going there I said. Why not Cat asked? For one thing you're married, for another I couldn't look Salinas in the face if I did. You still love me Cat said I know you do. Yes you're right, but we'll both have to settle for being best friends. Cat then turned walked to the front cabin and shut the door behind her.

I heard her sobbing but I didn't go to her. I walked off the boat and joined the others at Willy's. When I walked into Willy's Karen gave me the evil eye, Willy was telling everyone about the first time he saw Rusty and I. Willy said Rusty still has a bruise under his chin. We all laughed and laughed. Willy said, my how things have changed, it's too bad that Michelle and Deanna couldn't have stayed with us.

Cat had just walked in and jumped up and sat on the bar. A toast I said, to those who helped make this all possible but aren't able to be here. We all raised our beers and said cheers. Willy said we've had good times and bad times noting that I had shot two men through that very window.

Only Cat knew that story. Cat said that those two weren't the only ones that I had shot on the Island. He doesn't shoot to kill she said, he just amines to hurt them really bad. Cat then jumped down from the bar and walked out. I had never told the story of when Cat lunged at the man that took my gun. I told the group that a man had broken a chair over my head and shoulder. When I came to the man was standing over me pointing my gun at me. That was when Cat attacked him saving me. What happen then Evette asked? Well, I said that gave me enough time to draw my leg gun and shoot him in both knees. I was a little blurry eyed and missed him my first shot. I bet that hurt she said.

At this point Cat was coming back in carrying a large basket of fresh crawfish fritters. I looked at Karen and she gave me a thumbs up. It looked like Cat would be fine. Cat then announced that tonight we all were going to eat dinner on one of the cruise ships. Dinner will be served at 8:00 p.m. sharp. Please she said, everyone will need to bring an ID that can be left at the ships main door. This was an unexpected pleasure that Cat arranged on her own. Karen said that Cat had sent word that everyone would need to have dress clothes for dinner but nothing about eating on one of the cruise ships. Karen said she had called Salinas to make sure I had such clothes in my bag. Everyone except me would be flying back Sunday afternoon on Chalks.

I would be staying until Monday as I would be signing the paperwork for the sale of the property on Paradise Island. Also collecting and depositing the payment.

Karen had arranged for Tommy to fly into Nassau's main airport to pick me up on Monday afternoon.

The crawfish fritters were great! Everyone enjoyed them. Cat said that our first crawfish boat, the "Johnny" would be coming into the fisherman's wharf at 4:00 p.m., Cat invited all to visit the boat and see the catch. Cat was now acting like a tour guide. Ralph had passed by me and asked about Cat. Is she single he asked? Nop I answered she's married. That's too bad Ralph said she's quite beautiful. Yes I said, I agree 100 %.

It wasn't long before Otis and Maggie were docking. We all headed over to see them, the boat and their catch.

While there, at the "Johnny" our two Bertram's also came in and docked. Captain Mike's Chris Craft was out delivering air tanks to Lee on Andros and should return that night. Everyone was impress with the boats and their catch, each boat brought in between 160 and 180 crawfish. Our crawfish were delivered to Mr. Johnson's people alive. From there the crawfish would be delivered directly to the cruise ships. If there were no cruise ships in port the crawfish would be kept in live well cages under the docks. Fish heads would be thrown in several times a day to keep the crawfish nice and fat.

From there we walked back to Willy's, got a fresh beer and went to visit the two Hatteras's. Both boats were much the same. The "Nassau Queen" was the only one of the two used to take tourist fishing and or for that two or three-day trip to Harbor Island. The "Salinas" was to be used for days like tomorrow when we would all go out to the wreck for a look see. The "Salinas" has an over 1,000 miles of cruising range and could be used to jump on and go. The two new 19 foot whalers that I just purchased were to be used to ferry things out to the barges and permit us to have a 24 hour a day presents at the wreck site. The Chris Craft would still make its two per week crawfish runs to Andros along with carrying air tanks to both Andros and our wreck site here in Nassau.

Every one of our group were impressed as to where we were with our operations. They seemed to question why was I still living in Miami.

Cat offered that she had several rooms reserved in her Boarding house for anyone that wanted to sleep on shore. She mentioned that sometimes the mosquitoes made themselves unwelcome. Rusty asked if we still used those green burning rings that stayed lit all night. Cat said we could now run the air-conditioning to kept the mosquitoes at bay. Rusty said he remembered many a night hearing that bussing sound of mosquitoes in his ears all night. Of course Rusty said we didn't have any air-conditioning back then.

Carlos and his girl Julie, and Stann the man and his wife Mary-Ann would take Cat up on her offer. Cat said she'd drive them on over so they could use the rooms to get ready for dinner. Tonight we would be dinning aboard the "Ocean Princess." The rest of us would either use the showers provided by the Marina or on board the "SALINAS" or the "CAT". Cat looked at me and asked if friends shared showers? She smiled and as she left saying she'd see us at the on the cruise ship. As Cat left, Karen and Evette said they claimed the main Cabin in the "SALINAS", the boys she said could sleep on the "CAT". By now Martha had walked on home as she too was invited for dinner. Martha would meet us back at the city dock and walk with us to the cruise ship.

Rusty was quite happy with himself about coming along for the trip. He said that he just couldn't help from staring at Martha. You know Rusty said, I've never bragged or even told anyone about the story of our trip. The story he said should be told to our children and our children's children. I agree, but added that the story's long from over. Rusty just smiled.

By now we were all getting ready, it was a shame that Salinas wasn't here she would have enjoyed meeting Rusty and being with the group. I missed her.

Most of us met at the cruise ships stairs. The people at the stairway radioed up and we were all allowed to go on up. Once up on deck they took an ID from each of us and we were escorted to the dining room. Cat accompanied by her husband was at the table waiting. Cat introduced everyone and we were all seated. Several bottles of champagne were then brought to our table. I asked we all stand and I proposed a toast. To the new addition to our group, may the winds be steady and the weather be bearable.

Karen asked how the kids were and Jacob replied that they were big enough to run down the beach and swim all day. Cat said she would soon have them out on the Hunter sailing. We invited Jacob on our tomorrow's sightseeing trip but he said that he would be spending most of the day with the children. Cat said she be going from tonight's dinner to work the "Nassau Queen" giving Peter the night off. In that case I said we should order dinner.

The food and company was fantastic. I had four childhood friends there that hadn't been together in quite some time. We told stories that made me laugh more than I could have ever remembered. Ralph said that we should plan a super reunion and get all of the Boy Scout troop together. We started naming them off, at least the ones that we could remember. There were many things that I didn't remember until they were brought up at the table. I had forgotten that Stann the man did receive the scout of the year award and was also a member of the Order of the Arrow. As kids we called Stann, Stann the man because he was tall and skinny with a shirt on he looked like the book warm that he was. However, once he removed his shirt he was a different person, he was then Stann the man. Stann was 100% mussel and not scared of anybody or thing. I told the story about my nose being broken three times, twice playing football and once by Stann at the cabin while we were having a free for all in the water. Stann, I remember thought that was the funniest thing. Carlos told the story of me breaking an ore on his butt in high school while he was pledging for Saxons. Carlos was really mad with me and didn't understand why I had done it at the time. I later explained I had done that so that the others wouldn't think I would be easy on him. Cat commented that I was hardest on the ones I loved. We all had stories of when we were kids. Cat also told the group that she was sure I would never grow up. He's still that 15-year old adventurous boy whom believes he is invincible.

Cat and Jacob excused themselves early, the rest of us visited one of the many bars and then a disco on board. We exited the ship just as it's departure was announced.

Carlos, Julie, Stann and Mary Ann got a taxi to the boarding house while the rest of us walked to the city dock. The girls took the "Salinas" and us boys the "Cat".

It was early Sunday morning; we all ate at the food carts parked at the wharf. The food was as good as usual everyone getting their full. We had scuba gear aboard for 5, and 4 would skin dive. Rusty said he would be the look out. We would be traveling still towing the new whaler. There would be three men aboard the whaler as one man would now stay at the wreck site as a custodian. The other two would return with us once we finished our dive. Martha would then once a day bring out one of the three men to change places. Once the other whaler arrived the turns would only be 8 hours them using one whaler on site and the other to transport supplies and the change of guard.

We shoved off at 8:30 a.m. as we would have to travel west and go through the channel and then come back east to the wreck. The Hatteras wouldn't make it over the banks of the reef like the "JOHNNY" could. Karen and Evette took turns at the wheel, the bridge would easily seat six.

Once at the sight the current was still going out but not so strong. We anchored not knowing if the spot was just right. I dove over with mask and fins to check the sight. Karen was at the wheel and Carlos working the anchor. I signaled to Karen to move the boat and anchor to the point where I was. With the assistance of the motor, Carlos got the anchor up and Karen brought the boat to where I wanted it. Carlos dropped anchor and we were sitting within twenty feet of the wreck.

We agreed that the scuba divers would dive first so that Ralph and I could accompany the skin divers when we got out. I would carry the bang stick just in case. Too many people in the water at once wouldn't enable was to get out of the water fast enough if a shark was on the prowl.

We went in as, Evette with Ralph as a pair and Karen, Martha and myself as a group. By now the current was gone and the water as clear as I had ever seen it. I warned everyone not to try and move and or even touch anything as just a small cut could bring in the sharks.

Ralph and Evette were right in there checking on several canons that I had already seen. I knew we would have to one day remove the canons just to get to what was under them. This wreck being right up against the reef and on its side would require a lot of work. A group of large rocks had broken the ship from its most forward mast section.

Only the top half of the port side of the ship was visible. The rest of the ship was mangled within wood planks and rocks under the port side and on the bottom.

I was mostly watching out for sharks as with this rocky bottom one or more could appear out of nowhere.

Karen had with her some kind of poker that Cat had given her to dive with. The poker she had resembled a long version of a rod that would be used to move logs around in a fireplace. Karen was poking and pulling with her rod. Karen waved at me like she had found something. I went closer and she pointed to an object that looked like a part of a rifle musket. I had on my gloves and dug enough sand and rock to permit me to lift it.

I looked at my watch and we had only been under 20 minutes. Not wanting to surface as yet, I carried what Karen had found with me.

Ralph also had something in his hand. My diving alarm soon sounded and I signaled to Ralph and Evette to head on up to the surface. The alarm wasn't for the air but the current.

Carlos and Stann the man were on the platform ready to assist us up. As my head came up I yelled to Carlos for him to put on a pair of gloves. Stann the Man helped board Evette, Karen and Martha. I handed Carlos my bang stick and then the thing which I thought was a rifle musket.

Ralph also handed something up to Carlos. Then Ralph and I came aboard. Ralph had picked some kind of small box. The box was jammed open and empty. I didn't pay much attention to either the musket or the box. I was in a hurry to get the next group in the water. Ralph and I shed our tank gear and were both back over, me with the bang stick. With Ralph and myself in the water the next group of four jumped in. They certainly didn't have to go far to see the wreck. This dive would be shorter than the first as now we were basically swimming on the top of the water. We did however swim from one end of the wreck to the other. We returned just as a bit of current started to come back in.

Once all of us were aboard we began to take a better look at the two items that Karen and Ralph found at the wreck.

Karen's was defiantly what was left of a long musket. Ralph's small box that was full of green overgrowth turned out to be a box of solid gold. Maybe when the ship hit the reef the owner of the box had grabbed it just before the ship sank. The box at one time had to have had in it something of great value. Ralph asked if he could stay and dive some more? Then he thought about it and said that he had a class tomorrow. By now the current was moving in. We pulled up anchor and headed west toward the channel.

It was now 12:30 p.m., we had just enough time to get back to the city docks and for the group to make it to their 3:30 p.m. flight back to Miami.

I was sure that Rusty would be sad leaving as he had grown very fond of Martha. I too would be sad to see Rusty go as him now living in Georgia and having family there would limit us seeing each other. I hoped to see him again soon. I gave Rusty a big hug and kissed his left cheek. Rusty looked at me and said that was something I must have picked over the years, then he laughed. All the rest of the gang lived and worked in Miami. When we arrived at the city dock Cat was there waiting. Cat said she would give Martha a ride home and then take Rusty to the airport. The two men that Cat had hired to work as custodians would help clean up the boat.

Stann the man, his wife Mary-Ann, Carlos and his girl would catch a taxi to the Boarding house and go to the airport from there. Karen, Evette and Ralph would go via taxi straight to the airport.

After saying my good-byes and they all had gone I headed to visit with Willy.

Well, Willy asked, how did it go? Well I said I was sad to see them all go. I wished Salinas could have joined us, she would have enjoyed the trip. She'll have plenty time in the near future Willy said. I told Willy that I hoped I'd be seeing him more often. I think I'll get a house here and do some diving on the wreck and a bunch of sailing. Willy asked if we were going to have the baby here in Nassau. I'd like that I said, as you know I consider this my home.

It's been rough to lose so much here but when I'm not here I miss it. Willy said that the last few years Michelle's charity had brought several good changes. Yes I said, but the slum is still there and we tore down one bar only to have another one open. Willy said what he was hearing was that the drugs were still coming from Columbia through Cuba. Willy said he heard that the fisherman on the south side of the Island would meet Cuban boats about two miles off shore and then bring the drugs in. The drugs Willy said, seem to be leaving on the cruise ships now that the shipping line has tighten up on inspections. Damn I said, I'd like to stay clear of all that but if I run across it I won't turn my head. Just be careful Willy said, they know who you are. I asked Willy if he knew the young man that was sitting on the park bench just across the street. Willy said he saw him there but didn't know him. Willy said maybe he's there to keep an eye on me. Well I said, if he's around tomorrow I'll be asking him a few questions.

Cat stopped by on her way home and asked how the trip went. I told her it couldn't have gone better. Cat said she had heard that Ralph had found a small gold box. Yes I said, him finding that sitting on the rocks gives me hope that there could be lots more. Cat said she'd be on her way and that she'd see me tomorrow at 9:00 a.m. in Jacob's law office. I told her to make sure that Janie was there too.

On the way out Cat again mentioned that I'd be taking her Sailing after the signing. That had me thinking so, I walked down to Martha's house to speak with Mary about getting Martha to go sailing with Cat and I tomorrow morning. Martha's mom said no but I talked her into it. I then asked Martha if she wanted to go along. Martha was thrilled.

The next morning, I was at Jacob's office at 9:00 a.m., and so were Cat, Janie and another man. The man was representing the property buyers. We signed all the paper work and I was given a check sealing the deal. The sale would be final once the check cleared the bank. Janie returned to work at the Tourist shop while Cat and I went to the bank to deposit the check. While at the bank I made it clear to Cat that all that was in my safety deposits boxes were to be moved at my death. While we were there we also set up safety deposit boxes that she could get into for storing any treasure that we may find. Cat new the government would receive a 25% share. I had the bank set it up that once the check cleared Cat and Janie would transferee $1,000,000.00 to the Michelle Charity and the remaining of the check would be transferred to the Caymans. I told Cat to find me a house over on Paradise Island on the bluff that overlooked the beach that we all enjoyed so much. That money was to come from the Cayman account.

Cat said she take care of it. I told Cat that Martha would be meeting us at the Hunter. Cat asked if I felt I needed Martha to be our chaperon. I told Cat that I wanted her and Martha to master the Hunter.

One day both of you will be taking tourist out sailing. My Friend Johnny had always dreamed of taking tourist sailing. Cat asked about the other Hatteras and if we were going to use it for tourist? I told Cat that I wanted both the "SALINAS" and the "CAT" on stand-by so that I could get Carson more interested in flying in and using either boat. We don't need the money I said. If the "Nassau Queen" was damaged or under maintenance, then to keep up with reservations she could use the "SALINAS".

It was almost 11:30 a.m. before we were backing the "CAT" out of the slip. We motored out the Harbor and then raised the sails and were on our way. Both Cat and Martha took turns at the wheel. I had them both tacking and coming about without jibing. The two of them worked well together. We were out there for a good two hours and then I had them start the engine and lower the sails to re-inter the Harbor. Pulling into the slip was tricky due to the current but with me standing by near the wheel, Cat at the wheel and Martha working the bow line, they brought her into the slip like pros. I told Cat and Martha both, that unlike the motor boats, I wanted them to wear a life jacket at all times while under way.

I also said that while they were under sail they should have a tow line in the water at all times in case someone fell over. Having a tow line in the water would make recovery much easier. In a big boat like this, I said it's not easy to spot and get back to a person that had fallen over. With a tow line already out, the person falling over has the chance to grab the line as it goes by or when the boat come back around. The girls said they understood.

As we walked over to Angee's for a bite I stopped at the park and told the girls I'd meet them at the restaurant. I turned and walked back where the young man that I thought might be watching me was sitting. I sat down next to him and said I was sure he knew but my name was Captain Jim, what's yours? At first he didn't answer then he said, Jonas. As in Jonas and the whale I asked? I guess so the young man said. Well Jonas what do you have on your mind, looking for a job I asked. The young man looking straight ahead shook his head and said he had a job. How much does watching me pay I asked? I get paid well the young man said. What do the people want that are paying you I asked? My uncle is in a wheel chair for life, what do you think he wants the young man asked? I think he was lucky to live through that night I said. Your uncle attacked me from behind, a cowardly act I said. My uncle says you're nothing without a gun, nothing the young man repeated.

You, the young man said have the guns and the money. My uncle has nothing but his wheel chair. The choices your uncle made were made long before he met me I said. Jonas said his uncle said that I had hired a man to come to the bar and kill his best friend. The truth I said, it was a Columbian that killed your uncle's friend in the bar. Your uncle's friend owed the Columbians money and they killed him for it. When I heard of the short fight that killed your uncle's friend I hired two investigators that followed the trail all the way to the Columbian drug cartel. If you want, I can bring a photo of the man that did the killing with a copy of the investigation.

Take the photo and ask your uncle and others in the bar if that man was the killer. You will get a yes from everyone that was there that night. The investigation will also have more than one photo. One photo is of the killer meeting with your uncle in Columbia just a week after the killing. I don't believe you the young man said, you are a liar! Come with me I said. I stood and we walked to Angee's restaurant. Cat and Martha were there and asked what had kept me. I said I had run into an old friend. Martha stood and asked Jonas if he remembered her from school? Jonas paused and then said yes. I then asked Cat for the keys to the Hurricane house. Cat disappeared into the kitchen and brought out the keys. I 'll have to take a rain check on lunch I said. Martha told Jonas it was good to see him, Jonas didn't reply. I took the keys and Jonas and I walked through the warehouse and out the back door. We crossed the street to the Hurricane house and I opened the door. I walked to the safe and asked Jonas to turn around. Jonas turned and I unlocked the safe. Ok Jonas I said, you can look now. I stepped in and pulled out a box of files. I picked out the one I wanted and asked Jonas to sit at the table. As Jonas sat I placed the file in front of him. Jonas was only interested in the photos. The first photo he pulled had marked in red letters the killer. Then as Jonas kept looking he stopped and pulled out the second photo. It was a photo with the man marked as the killer with his uncle.

You can have the photos I said, I have the negatives. Jonas just sat looking at the photos. I picked up the folder and placed it back in the box and the box back in the safe. I shut the safe and relocked it. Jonas was still sitting there looking at the photos. I reminded Jonas to be careful of who he showed the photos too. The photos could get you killed I said. I walked to the door and waved Jonas to the door. I have to catch my plane I said. That is unless you're going to stop me. Jonas stood and walked out. As I locked the door, I told Jonas if he wanted a good job that could provide a future that he should see Cat. Jonas asked, you'd give me a job? If you're willing to work, yes I said. I walked across the alley into the warehouse, when I turned Jonas had disappeared.

I handed the keys back to Cat and said to keep the keys in the safe at the beach house. I hugged and kissed Martha and told Cat I was ready to go to the airport. The trip to the airport was quiet. Tommy was there waiting. I kissed Cat good-buy and said I should see her next week. Cat said it would help if I brought Salinas along.

It was good to see Tommy again. The co-pilot gave me his seat after we took off. Tommy said he had gotten Lee and the ex-navy divers over to Andros without any problem.

Tommy asked what was next and I said that we were waiting the answer from the Navy. I mentioned that if Carson didn't contact us soon I would go to Grenada and look for him. I would also need to take a trip down to the Caymans in about a week. I mentioned to Tommy about Salinas not being able to travel, I hoped that the Doctor would lift that ban next week. We talked about him giving air support once the two barges were delivered to Nassau. I didn't know when, but we would have at least two more divers starting soon. Before I knew it we were landing at Opa-Locka airport.

I caught a taxi and went straight home to see Salinas. She was more than happy to see me. Betty said she had a hard time keeping Salinas in bed. Salinas said that she didn't have any spotting and she wanted to call Doctor James for his permission to leave the apartment. I said she could call but that the good Doctor wouldn't give his permission until he saw her again next week. I called Karen to let her know I was back and asked about Carson. Karen said there was still no answer at his house or the school.

Salinas and I had a quite evening at the apartment talking about her having the baby in Nassau and us living there.

Salinas asked about Haiti and I said that we could still visit now and then. She asked about her mom and I said if she wanted her mom was welcome to stay with us for a few weeks after the baby was born and that if her mom wanted, I'd find a nice place for her there on the Island. Salinas said she would like to have her horses moved to where ever we would live. I told her I'd see what we could do.

It was good to be with Salinas. I felt that just may-be I was on the right track with my life. I could see myself living in Nassau and enjoying life; I was looking forward to being a father too.

CHAPTER XXIII

THE CAVE

The very next morning, Lee called and said he thought I should come to Andros and see what the divers had brought to the house, I asked what it was, and Lee noted just come. Lee didn't sound worried, he sounded excited. I had Karen call Tommy and ask what time he could be ready. Tommy said to come on. Within an hour Tommy had me aboard and we were headed to Andros. Lee was waiting at the airport.

I asked as soon as I saw him what it was? Lee said I'd have to see it to believe it. As we pulled up to the Andros compound I noticed that we now had a guard at the gate. I didn't ask why. Lee pulled the truck up under the house and then went and opened what I called the garage. There on the floor was two skeleton structures. The first one was head of the largest Crocodile that I ever could have imagined. The head was about 5 feet long and almost 3 feet at its widest part. Look at this; Lee said as he pointed at the second structure. The second structure was a set of large vertebras that had been connected by a large spearhead. The spearhead that appeared to be made of stone had cut into the two vertebras joining the two. The bone had grown around the spear head making it seem that the spear head had been there quite some time while the crocodile lived. As I continued to look it seemed that the two vertebras had also grown together. I figured that this growth could have taken years making me sure that the spear wasn't the cause of death. I walked back to the scull and as I looked I noticed a hole the size of a quarter that started at the center of the scull between the Crock's eyes going back at a 45% angle all the way through. A few of the Crocks top and bottom teeth at the front left side looked to be sheared off. Lee saw me looking at the teeth and said he had something else upstairs. When Lee came back down he was carrying a box. Inside the box was something that looked like it was a steel tooth that would be used on some kind of large digging bucket.

The steel tooth was about 4" wide with the tooth part more curved inward than a normal tooth from say a caterpillar machine's bucket. The cutting tooth looked like it had been broken maybe from a bad molding material as the break wasn't a sharp break and the material at the break was kind of porous. Lee put on a pair of heavy gloves and with one hand picked up the steel tooth and with the other opened the crocodile's month. What Lee was showing me was distinctive. The Crock's top and bottom broken off teeth matched the steel tooth. This leading me to see what Lee was showing me, we both came to the conclusion that the crock had bitten off that steel tooth from some machine. Not only the crock's teeth were damaged but also the bones surrounding its teeth. Then looking at the quarter size hole in the crocks head it looked like it was burned there. Oddly it looked like the hole was formed by some kind of laser. If so, maybe whomever was operating the machine that the crock had attacked had shot the crock in the head with whatever. Lee said that the bones and the metal tooth had that same low level of radiation.

Lee said that the divers said that the metal tooth was about the same size as the groves in the side walls of the cave. Lee said the divers were sure that the cave was being made bigger for something to pass through. It looked like the digging was being performed by some kind of underwater machine.

The divers said that they believed the cave entrance was natural and had enough space for a car to fit through. The cutting was about 75 yards short of reaching the Blue hole.

The diver said they would attempt to recover the rest of the crock's bones, but that the remaining 30 feet or so were sitting in an area that was tight to get into.

I told Lee that I wanted to somehow box up what we had so that I could carry it with me back to Miami on the leer jet.

Lee jumped into the truck and would go to our construction site to get some of the men and material to box up the bones.

When I left Andros the leer was carrying the three boxes and we would fly back to Miami. I had left instructions for the divers not to concentrate on the other bones unless they thought there was something else in that same hole. I wanted them to keep going inward into the main cave just as far as they could.

On the flight back my mind was flying with imagination. I thought I had it all figured out. Someone or thing was cutting a hole big enough to get from the channel to the blue hole in some kind of vehicle. Why and when were just some of the questions. What if the Navy had spotted some kind of vessel and after trying to communicate with them, they failed and then nuked them with some kind of radiation that lasted for thirty years or so?

Maybe only in the last couple years the site's radiation levels have become low enough for the Navy to try and recover whatever is down there. What an imagination I thought.

The next thing I knew, we were landing in Miami's Opa-Locka's airport. I didn't bother going through customs, we landed and I hired a truck to take the boxes to my house. I followed the truck to make sure I didn't somehow lose the boxes.

Once at the apartment, I had the boxes taken upstairs and placed out on the balcony of my apartment. Salinas saw and was curious about the boxes. I told her that it was just some bones that the divers had brought up from the cave.

It was now almost 9:00 p.m. but I called Bob and asked if he knew any professors at the UM that might be able to help with some old crocodile bones. Bob laughed until I told him the size and circumstances in which I had the bones. I also mentioned that he wasn't to tell where the bones were found. Bob said he would make a call and call me back.

Ten minutes hadn't passed when Bob called back and said he and a professor friend were on the way. I told Salinas that I didn't want her to get even close to the bones. I got a pair of plastic kitchen gloves, a plastic table cover and some card board. I then opened the boxes and placed the bones and metal tooth on the card board that was now on the dining room table.

Betty had heard that Bob was coming over and started cooking.

Betty hadn't seen Bob for quite some years. I could smell the fritters cooking.

In 25 minutes there was Bob knocking on the door. Betty was right there to open the door for Bob. I thought she was going to suffocate him with her hug. Bob and his friend came in with Bob introducing the man as Professor Cunningham. The Professor spotted the bones on the table right away, I warned him not to touch them as they had a slight touch of radiation. The first thing out of the professor's mouth was that it was a prehistoric salt water crocodile. Maybe a thousand years or older he said. Then, what's this he asked in a queer voice? A spearhead lodged in between two vertebras he said. This is almost impossible he said looking at the stone with a magnified glass. This spearhead can't be much more than a hundred years old, at most he said two hundred. It looks American Indian maybe even Seminole. Yes he said, I believe it was made by a Seminole Indian. The professor kept right on looking and saw that the vertebras indeed had grown over some of the stone and that the two vertebras had definitely joined together. Then the professor looked back at the croc's teeth glancing at the chunk of metal which was as the professor put it, some kind of cutting tool. He looked at me and asked? You think that this croc bit this metal off don't you? I'm sure of it I said.

I put on another kitchen glove and lifted the top part of the scull and turned it over. It was clear that the top and bottom of the interior of the croc's mouth was damaged. I then lifted the metal piece and placed it into the damaged section. The fit was almost perfect. This isn't some kind of trick you have made, or is it. No professor it's exactly what you see. The professor soon found the quarter size hole and said it looked to be machined in. Or burned in I stated. Yes, burned in the professor said. Where did you find this beast the professor asked? It's a secret for now professor but you are the first to see it that might have more of an educated guess as to what happen here. And the radiation the professor asked? We just don't know I said. So I asked now that you've see what you've seen, you still think the croc is one thousand years old. No, the professor said, but by the size of that head, the croc must have been almost forty feet long and likely well over 100 years old. The other thing is that it would be hard to believe that this would be the only one living at the time it was killed. I would guess by the head this maybe a female and she could have been protecting her young. Oh, that's a nice thought I said. Whenever they fine one skeleton they always find another the professor added. What about the metal the professor asked? Have you had it analyzed as yet? No sir, you know almost as much as we do.

Oh no he said your hiding something very important you're not willing to give up. Just as the Professor said that Salinas open the door and asked if she could pass to the kitchen. I said yes of course my dear and as she walked into the kitchen both men stared. Bob made the comment that I'd been hiding that too, meaning Salinas. Bob then asked are you sure that's Papa Doc's daughter? Salinas was on her way back to our room when she heard Bob's comment. Salinas stopped and asked if Bob had known her Father. Bob answered that he had and said that she was too beautiful to be his daughter? Yes, Salinas said everyone says I look like my mother. Bob then said that I was a poor host and introduced himself and the professor. Salinas said she was glad to finally meet Bob as she had heard quite a bit about him from me. Bob asked how she put up with me and my gun. Salinas said the gun's not allowed in the shower or the bed. That's the rule Salinas said. Salinas noted that Betty had some fritters ready and to help themselves. Betty heard Salinas and yelled there coming right out. Salinas said it was nice meeting you both and returned to our room. Bob then headed into the kitchen, he then came out with a plate full of fritters and told the professor that Betty was only one of the women that I had stolen from him. Then Bob finally brought out that distinctive laugh of his. The professor kept right on looking and thinking.

The professor asked if the remaining skeleton could possibly be dug up. I believe it can I said. Please let me know when you have more. This thing needs to be in some Museum somewhere the professor said. It could even change the way we look at things, if you know what I mean. Yes Sir I said, I do agree.

As Bob and the professor were getting ready to leave, we heard a key in the door and it opened bringing Karen and Evette in through the door. Karen seeing Bob said, hello Bob what brings you to visit? Bob looked at Karen and asked the same. Karen replied that she and Evette lived here. Bob on his way out looked at me and said, "you're living a dangerous life, but you are certainly living it." Bob and the professor said their good-buys and they left.

Salinas came out of our room to greet Karen and Evette. All three looked at the bones and the metal tooth. I told them it was a salt water croc and Evette, right away asked if those were in the water where we were diving. I told the girls that I had never seen a crocodile in salt water and had only heard of one sighting of a salt water croc and that was in Sand's Key safe harbor's brackish water. Karen said but it had to come from somewhere? Yes I said, it most likely came from the everglades. Australia has some bad ones I've heard.

But here and in the Bahamas there has never been a confirmed saltwater croc attack on record. Evette said that looking at what we had on the table she didn't want to be the first. I re-boxed the bones and metal tooth and then placed the boxes on my safe's floor.

Later in bed Salinas asked what all the bones meant. I told her that if the croc was some kind of pre-historic beast that may-be there were more down there. The part about the hole in the croc's head meant that at some time in the past there was someone or thing that was much more advanced than we are. Like from outer space, she asked. Well could be I said, but I believe in the end we will find out exactly what happened. I told her that the Navy knew a lot more than what they were telling us. And the spear Salinas asked? Well I said during the Seminole Indian Wars it was said the at least one group of Seminoles retreated from Florida reaching Andros and even Cuba. I would have not liked to have been an Indian fighting with that croc I said. The owners of that spearhead were most likely eaten.

The next morning at work I asked Karen if she heard from Carson, she had not so I asked her to start calling again.

At noon the Admiral himself called Karen. He said he wanted for us to come on back up to sign contracts. Karen said that I would want to see the contracts first. The Admiral said that they were all the same. Karen asked him to please send them. He said he would just as long as she came to sign as a witness. Karen said she would. The Admiral said that we needed to bring a list of anyone that would be associated with or working on the project, this he said so that their security could provide the TOP SECRET clearance that was required. Karen said she would bring the list that was available at the present. The Admiral said he'd leave Friday afternoon open for our visit. Karen then informed me of the call saying that the Admiral didn't even ask for me. I knew just what she was getting at. Ok I said buy that new dress for the trip. I didn't have to give her my credit card as I now didn't have any credit. Karen had all the company credit cards! Karen started getting the new list adding the divers, Evette and Salinas to the list, Karen was already on it. Karen informed Cat and Janie that if nothing changed, Tommy would pick them up at 6:00 a.m. Friday morning. Cat and Janie were the signers on the Navy contract. At almost 4:00 p.m. Karen said she had again called the university where Carson was but couldn't get an answer. I said to keep trying.

Thursday morning, we had a visitor from the Navy that was hand delivering the contracts with new drawings. Karen signed for the packages. Evette took the contracts over to Roy's office where she was to wait until Roy signed the receipt. Roy called back that afternoon and said the contracts were identical to the first except for the plan ID numbers and amounts to be paid. The one contract said that it was based on cost plus 40%. Roy said he too wanted such a contract. Roy said we could sign without any changes. He also wanted me to come by the office sometime to talk strategy on my will and the IRS. I asked how long he would need me and he said one hour. I asked if I could come now and he said to meet me at his house at 6:00 p.m. Roy said he'd take the contracts home with him.

At Roy's home, Roy was quick to point out that the IRS bill was growing and would continue to do so. Roy had no idea how much I was worth and even I wasn't sure. All I knew that the monies in my foreign banks were growing by leaps and bounds. Our Bahamian construction company, Blue Ocean now had over $10,000,000.00 in its account. The signers here were Cat and Janie. Roy didn't know the amounts there, but did know what the casino property had sold for. Roy said that sale amount should be moved to a Swiss or Cayman account. Roy said he rather see it in a Swiss bank. He asked me about my will, my present will he said had people listed that were no longer living. We changed a few names and added a trust fund for any children I may have. Roy said that I needed someone to know how to find the money. I said I would think about it. Remember the IRS still has five more years to collect what they believe is theirs, if they find a much larger fund, Roy said they could try to take it all.

From Roy's house I went straight home, Salinas also had no idea where or how much was in banks. I had asked Salinas to open an account in her name in Haiti. No not a Haitian bank, she had done this and I was now ready to transfer funds. I was going to wait until the baby was born but decided to do it now, If Salinas didn't have a good since of security, she now would. I told Salinas all this plus that I was sending Jacob back to Haiti to start a trust that included money and the Chateau. Salinas started to cry as she thought this meant that I was leaving her, no my love it's to make you feel more secure. I told her that if anything did happen to me she would be fine. Salinas said she didn't want the money, she just wanted us to be together. The three of us. You, me and Karen I said jokingly. Salinas growled. I sent Jacob a telex bout going to Haiti and starting the trust. I would see Cat tomorrow on our DC trip and inform her to transfer money and make it possible for Salinas and Cat together to be able get into my safety deposits if I died. Sometime next week I would fly to the Caymans to check the accounts and move some money around. Karen and Evette got home after shopping, Karen showed off her new dress. You think the Admiral will like it she asked? He'll like whatever you're wearing I said. Evette asked if she could go? I said no. I asked about Carson and Karen said, still no luck. I made it clear that tomorrow Evette was to keep calling.

Friday morning found Karen and I heading to Opa-Locka. Tommy and the girls were there waiting. Tommy had picked them up as we planned. While flying I asked Tommy if some of the seats could be easily removed to transport the additional boxes of bones that could soon be ready from Andros. Tommy said that he could remove the last four rows and have room.

We arrived in Washington with plenty of time to spare. Karen had a limo waiting. Once at the Admiral's office the Admiral came out to meet us in the lobby. You could clearly see his main attention was on Karen. The poor man was almost drooling over Karen in her new red dress. That dress brought out every curve that Karen had. I always told her she was going to have back problems when she got old. Karen told me I was going to be old, fat, bald and single and that I would never grow up.

The Admiral walked us into his office where Cat and Janie signed both new contracts, Karen along with the Admiral's secretary signed as witness. The Admiral said he had heard that I was going to be a father for the first time. It's true I said, I'm really looking forward to it. The Admiral looked at Karen and asked when she was going to settle down and have some children. When I find the right man she said. The Admiral said she should find a good Navy officer. Karen asked if he knew any. Ouch! The Admiral said he had heard that we already had divers in the cave and asked what they were doing? I told him they were looking for Lusca. Lusca he repeated, that sea monster? Come on Captain Jim you don't believe any of those stories of sea monsters do you? Well I said if you had told me that there was Crocodiles down there more than 30 feet long I wouldn't have believed that either. In fact, there are many things down there that I wouldn't have believed. Rest assured

Admiral before we finish the job I'm sure we'll learn a lot of things that we don't know now. The Admiral asked if we could stay overnight, if so he'd invite us for dinner. I thanked him for his kind offer but said we needed to get back. Taking Karen's hand, he then walked us to his lobby. The Admiral then wished us all luck and we were on our way. On the limo ride back to the airport I asked Cat to sit with me on the flight back. Once on the leer I told Cat to transfer monies to Salinas's Haiti account from my Cayman account. I also told her of changes in my will and that I would go to Nassau and provide instructions to the bank about my deposit boxes. Cat understood and for the rest of the flight had her head on my shoulder.

Tommy would only make a quick stop in Miami letting Karen and I off then heading back to Nassau with the girls. Karen had our signed contracts and would return to the apartment with me to lock them up. While visiting Roy he had mentioned that the apartment was now in a corporate's name and me not owning that corporation the IRS had no way of interring the apartment. In other words, my safe was now safe. Roy had changed my official address to the third apartment on the floor which was empty. Roy said I should maybe have Karen move there but in any case I should have it furnished with some of my clothes being there.

It was late afternoon when Karen and I arrived at the apartment.

Salinas was still grounded but we had a doctors appointment for the next morning. Karen went back to the office but I stayed with Salinas. I would use the time to move things back from Jena's apartment safe to mine. It had been quite some time since I had heard from Jena, even though we paid all her bills, the amounts she was spending had slowed quite a bit. I wondered if she was getting tired of spending it or had become little more mature. No I thought maybe she found someone who had money. Anyway I would reach out to her and find out what she was up too. It took me almost two hours to move everything, Salinas watching where everything went. Salinas was amazed with some of the jewels and asked if that was what I expected to find at the new wreck sight? I told Salinas that whatever we found down there would be of interest. That ship I said had maybe been down there two hundred years. If it had a treasure aboard, maybe it was taken by the survivors at the time of the wreck or maybe the survivors had later come back for it. If it was the sister ship to the first ship, we had found then at one time it had quite a treasure aboard. I then told Salinas the story of Sir Frances Drake, his failed attack on Puerto Rico and his retreat to Panama where he died from his battle wounds. I told her about the broach that was given the Queen of England by the King of Spain and how the Queen had given that same broach to Drake. Drake, when he died he was one of the richest men in the world. Panama, ruled by Spain at the time was at war with England. Drake had paid a small fortune in treasure to Panama's Governor for safe haven in Panama. The Spanish King hearing of Drakes death in Panama sent ships and men to recover Drake's treasure. The Panama Governor was hanged in Spain but the treasure disappeared on the voyage back to Spain. The first treasures we found were part of Drakes treasure. Salinas was intrigued by the story, she seemed to understand my passion for the wreck.

Late Friday night, I got a call from Bob telling me of a coup in Grenada; thus far, Bob said it had been relatively peaceful, resulting in President Bishop being held under house arrest. The coup leader coming from within Bishop's own group. So far Bob said no violence. I thanked Bob and asked him to keep me informed. I then called Big Ted, but only received a recording. I left Ted a message to call me back no matter the time. Ted called back at about 3:00 a.m.. He apologized for the late call. I told him that he and his men needed to be on alert as the situation in Grenada could need a visit at any time. Ted said he would start getting things ready. It had been quite some time since the group had seen any kind of action. I wondered how ready they could be. I then put a call into Lee asking him to put a hold on any diving until we had a better idea of what was going on in Grenada and where Carson was, the four ex-Navy seals could be useful. I waited until I thought Ralph was up and also called him to see if he could be available just in case we were to fly down to Grenada. Ralph still having the hatred for the Castro regime, he said he'd be ready.

Salinas and I had a 9:00 a.m. appointment with Doctor James, Salinas was anxious to get an all clear to return to normal activities.

The good Doctor said that everything appeared normal however Salinas would need to limit her activities and get lots of rest. No horseback riding, he said. It wasn't what she wanted to hear but much better than being in bed all day. It was early but Salinas was ready to do something, anything. We went to Michelle's in the Gables and ate crapes. I said that was enough moving around until dinner when we would go to Joe's and then maybe the 1800 club.

There was absolutely no news on the TV about Grenada. I was worried that Carson would somehow get involved. Saturday afternoon I sent the leer to Andros to pick up the Divers. My call to Lee was no gear necessary but if there were any more bones ready to bring them. I called Ted and requested a planning meeting for Sunday afternoon at the apartment. Ted called back saying they'd be here at 4:00 p.m. I got that message to Lee and called Ralph to come if he could.

Salinas and I would enjoy a nice night out with dinner at Joe's and a movie that was playing at a beach theater. Even though she didn't admit it, I could see Salinas was tired. We had a good night as if we were just an old married couple. At least that's what I though.

Sunday Salinas wanted to go to the beach, so we went to Key Biscayne for about three hours; of course, we visited that old lighthouse. Salinas was aware that I needed to be back by 4:00 p.m.

By 4:00 p.m. we had a small group of 11 men. I had asked Karen to be home for the meeting as we were going to need a lot of logistics. The plan was simple, myself and someone else would fly down to Grenada tomorrow and each day after that two more of us would do the same. Friday's flight would have three men aboard. We would all travel as tourist staying at different hotels. All of us to meet at the university's chapel. Of course if or as any group made contact with Carson, they would notify Karen to stop the others. Moving in by twos or threes may not be so suspicious. We wouldn't take anything that would make us standout other than being tourist. If the rumors were true and there was some kind of military buildup, there should be plenty of guns down there to play with. Ralph said he wanted to go along with me tomorrow. Once we found Carson Tommy would come pick us all up. Dan one of the x-navy seals said that they had participated in a pock invasion of Grenada. He said he made a few calls this morning and said the Navy was watching the situation very closely. Dan said he wouldn't be surprised if The President didn't do something soon. Well I said what we want is to get in and get Carson out just as fast as possible. We closed the meeting having Karen being the focal point. I wished everyone good luck and we closed the meeting.

Salinas had overheard some of what was going on and asked how long I thought we'd be gone. If Carson is where he's supposed to be it should be just a day or two. I don't see it being much more than that. That night I called Bob to see if he had heard anything new. Bob said that there seemed to be a lot of chat going on. I told him I had headed down there again tomorrow morning, not telling him anything else.

CHAPTER XXIV

GRENADA

The next morning Ralph and I took off for Grenada. We hoped it was going to be like a vacation. Ralph had taken off work for just that. Ralph said he had someone else filling in for him for a few days. We didn't sit next to each other as was the plan we would go our separate ways and check into separate hotels. We would be telling the hotel we were going to hike the Island and leave the next morning. Once on the commercial plane I noticed something very odd. Half the plane was empty and of the other half were seats mostly filled with either media looking people or young men of military age. To strike up conversation I would ask the men sitting near me what they would be doing down there on the island. One said fishing, another skin diving, another hiking, and another said he was just going to relax and get a tan. I didn't believe any of them, to me they were all military with some kind of job to perform to get ready for an invasion. Well at least that would keep the locals busy following them and or us.

Once we landed I didn't see much of what I expected. Everything looked quite normal. Customs and immigration was smooth. I didn't see any Cubans, at least not in uniform. I checked into my hotel and decided not to wait until the next morning to leave. If things were so normal why didn't that SOB call us back?

What I did bring was a pair of walking boots, binoculars, a good Swiss army knife a small flash light and my boy scout compass. Oh yes and money lots of money. Looked like it wasn't going to take me any time to get to Carson, I'd just get in a cab and go so far and then get another until I got there. Sounded good until we came across our first road block. We were stopped not checked, we were just told to turn around. Here for the first time there was at least one uniformed Cuban with a radio. What they were doing was controlling movements. When the taxi turned around I asked him what was going on. The taxi driver said that more and more Cubans were coming in and that he didn't like what was going on. He said that he knew that Mr. Bishop wasn't in charge anymore since a few days ago. I hope this don't turn into another Cuba he said. Here we got a good life with Mr. Bishop running the show; I don't want change he said. I took out money and asked if he could get me around the stop. He looked at me and smiled. He headed up a hill side road and cut through a section that didn't have a road. At the top of the hill he stopped and asked where I wanted to go. He got out and walked to his trunk and brought out a map and his own binoculars. He put the map on the hood. I got out and he showed me the way. He said that he would take me to this point, pointing to a location on the map. He said, from there the school was a short distance. It looked like no more than 2 miles. He took his binoculars and started looking in a 360 -degree circle, and then he stopped. Then he said to get in quick. The driver said as he was looking and they too were watching us. He dropped me on the bottom of the hill and said that there was bar down the block, as I got out he handed me his map saying to stay until dark. I thanked him and he and his taxi were off.

I found the bar and had a seat, with only one other person besides the bar maid. It couldn't have been very popular. The bar tender asked if I had heard about the curfew? What curfew I asked? The curfew that was announced over the radio just moments ago the woman said. She said that there had been a problem with the students at the medical school. We heard two loud explosions last night she said. The curfew starts at 8:00 p.m. and ends at 6:00 a.m. in the morning. The curfew the radio said was for the public's protection. I asked about a nearby hotel and she said there was boarding house up the street about four blocks on the left. I finished my warm beer, paid and walked on out.

I walked to the boarding house and paid for a room and sat in the small lobby until dark. I then went to my room and climbed out the window. I stayed out of the street lights and really I didn't see any police or military vehicles.

Slowly but surely I reached the school. The neighborhood looked to have lights but the school did not. I then saw something that I was hoping I wouldn't. There in the field were two somethings that were still smoking. Looked like a helicopter and the other was for sure a tank. It was strange but I didn't see any military people on the outside. I decided to walk the perimeter and found three points with only two men at each. On my second round I saw what was my best chance to run across the field to the schools outside wall. I went running in a zigzag and made it to the wall. Almost at a craw I made it too a section that looked like the tank had hit with one of its rounds. At a whisper I said Carson you in there? Then a little louder. That you Jim a voice asked? It's not your grandmother I said. Come on in the voice said, but watch your step. As I walked through the rubble Ralph started me. What took you so long he asked? Where's Carson I asked. A woman's voice said they took him early this morning. They, who's they I asked? The military she said. Carson the woman said, Carson was badly wounded. He wouldn't have made it through the day here she said, he had lost too much blood. The woman said she had walked out with a white flag and asked them to take him to the hospital. They agreed if we promised to stay put. We agreed. Was he conscious I asked? No she said he was awake for about an hour then passed out. We did what we could and stopped the bleeding but there was just so much blood. Where were his wounds I asked? Well she said the most blood was coming from the large hole in his back. But he had several wounds. The helicopter was first, Carson shot it down. Then a tank appeared out of nowhere. As it pointed its gun toward us and Carson fired his weapon. The tank fired a round at almost the same time. The impact from the tank hit just above where Carson was, the wall came crashing down on him. The Tank was hit by Carson's shot causing it to catch fire.

Ralph said that we were well armed and he had two captives. Ralph said he had an argument with them on his way in. We also now have two H & Ks he said. We have plenty of ammo, water and food. How many are in here I asked? 27 students the young lady said. We have a gun at each side just like Carson showed us. What started all this, I asked? Well, she said the military came in and said the school was temporarily closed. We refused to leave, and they pointed their guns at us. Carson took their guns and pointed them on the way out. Later that helicopter came and sprayed the wall with gunfire.

I asked the young lady where she thought they might have taken Carson. She said that there was a small hospital about a half mile away. I pulled out my map and she pointed where it was. I asked by any chance if Carson had left her with a handgun. She brought me Carson's Walter 9 mm. Carson told her to point and pull the trigger. The gun had a bullet in the chamber and a clip of 7. I took the gun and told Ralph I was going to check on Carson. Debbie was a medical student and had told Ralph that she didn't see any way possible Carson was still alive. Ralph took me aside and passed along what Debbie had told him. Maybe so I said but I have to see him one way or the other.

It was still dark when I reached the Hospital. I did so without running into any police or troops. At the Hospitals front door there was one Grenada military person sleeping in a chair. I walked around to the back door, it was locked but I knocked on the door. A nurse came and opened the door and I said I was a friend of the American that was brought in during the morning. She told me she had a John Doe and yes he came in that morning. I also told her I didn't need any attention. I only wanted to see him. The nurse whispered that she understood. As we walked she said that there really wasn't anything they could do for him. His back is broken and his liver has irreversible damage. She said even the Doctors and Nurses had donated blood. When she pulled back the curtain there, he was. I went to him and in his ear I whispered, Carson. He at once opened one eye as the other was tapped over.

Hey friend he said, glad you could make it. Sorry I won't make the wedding. Jim he said, also whispering, try to reach Bishop. He's at his house under guard. I still have some gear in my right side fender. 20 pounds of C4 plus a few other things. I told him not to talk, he said he was only waiting to talk with me one more time. Did you see the helicopter and the tank he asked? I only wished I had seen the tank a few seconds before he said. We both traded shots at the same time. What a good feeling it was to see that copter come crashing down. You never called me by my first name, its Gary he said. Remember that name for one of your boys. I killed the bear that killed me.

Those were the last words that Carson spoke, the tears were rolling down my cheeks, Carson was gone.

The nurse still there said she was sorry. I handed her a bunch of cash which she said she didn't want. Do you have a working phone I asked? No she said there's been no phone service for several days now. Please I said, I'll be back just as soon as I can for the body. It might be a few days. I understand she said. From there I returned out the back door.

I had wanted to make the call to stop the others and maybe get Tommy in here to pick us up. With no phones maybe the flights in would soon be canceled. I got back to the school before day break. Debbie took the news badly. He was a good friend she said. Debbie said that the attack was brought on by the Cubans not the Grenadians. The prisoners that we had were Grenadians. I talked to Ralph and we decided to release them both.

When we untied them their hands were purple. I said I was sorry and hope they would be ok. They thanked us and as they got ready to leave, Ralph told him we had only come looking for our friend whom was killed by the Cubans. The two Grenadians said they too were sorry it had to end as it did, then they were on their way. Ralph and I decide to wait one day to see if the next group would make it in.

That same night we received the second two men. They also said that the plane had too many young men on it. Too many to be on vacation. Ralph and I thought about getting back to the hotels and airport, maybe there was a phone somewhere we could use. Instead we crawled out to the tank and took the 50 Caliber and what ammo was still good.

I had asked Debbie about where Mr. Bishops house arrest might be and she said somewhere in George Town. On the radio there was now a lot of pros and cons on what was taking place. One station said there were hundreds of people outside of Mr. Bishop's house. The announcer said there had been fighting between the crowds and the police. Shots had been heard and there were several fatalities. Then the radio went dead. Only one radio station was now broadcasting, it was of course pro Government, backing the new leaders and music lots of music. Now the only thing I thought we could do was to protect the students until help arrived if and when it would. Carson would have wanted us to stay with the students. We decided to stay.

With still not much military around the school I decided to go to Carson's house and look for that C4 that he was talking about. Having Debbie mark Carson's house on the map, I would sneak out at dark and go to his house. The C4 was where he said it was along with several hand grenades. Carson had stored food and when I left his house I had quite a back pack full. By Saturday we now had all 11 men at the school. The last men in said they had heard that Mr. Bishop had been killed while trying to escape. I thought that the US Government would have to know what was going on and would act soon.

That night the four x-navy seals along with, Ralph and I would attempt to make it to the airport. It was now dark and raining we all had dark green or black ponchos on.

We carried the one 30-06 with a scope, 12 of the twenty hand grenades and the two H and Ks that Ralph had borrowed from his two ex-guest. Ted and his men would stay with the students.

We walked out either not being seen or being seen and them not engaging us.

Within two hours we arrived on a hill overlooking the airport. Sitting on the hill using our night binoculars we spotted an antiaircraft gun set up just below. It wasn't our intention to take it out at this point, just to locate it. As we sat there on the hill we kept searching the panorama with our binoculars. We soon notice a small group of men moving slowly from the north heading south east toward the antiaircraft gun. Just by the way the group were moving we thought they must be friendlies. It looked as if they were heading right for the anti-aircraft gun.

Maybe they would get close and leave two men dug in until our planes came in. We had with us the radio that Ralph had taken from his two ex-guest, the two military men. We listen to the chatter mostly in English and Spanish. Ralph picked up a Cuban warning of a group moving on the antiaircraft gun. As we heard this I spotted what looked like a bunker to our left at about our same height. I sent two of the Navy Seals to circle back and come up behind them, they would hit them with two grenades, taking the spot and retreating with any weapons they could carry back to the school. Ralph started signaling what we believed to be friendlies with a small flash light in Morse code. With my body I blocked the light so that the antiaircraft personal wouldn't see the light.

We knew that the bunker at our left would see the friendlies response so Ralph first sent word "not to reply", then "you need to take cover and stay put". As I watched the friendlies, they disappeared into the brush. They had gotten the message. Ralph then flashed more Morse code that we were at the university. Then within ten minutes there was a loud bang and machine gun fire. Then quite. Now looking at the antiaircraft gun, it was turning toward the friendlies. We were too far from the antiaircraft guns to do any good so Ralph took his and my two grenades and started down the hill. Me, I sat there with the 30-06 pointed at the man sitting at the antiaircraft gun. If he moved toward Ralph or began shooting I would take him out.

On the radio, now it was pure Spanish and I didn't understand a word. I figured someone was asking for reinforcements. Within minutes the antiaircraft area was blown up by at least two blast. I then flashed the word go to the friendlies. We waited for Ralph and then swiftly headed back to the school. On our way to the school we did see more activity but not as much as what we thought. Most of Cuban's there were working on the other airport and at quite some distance away.

We got back to the school, again we believed not having our movements seen. It wasn't long before we spotted a small light doing Morse code requesting permission to come in. We sent back the ok for one unarmed person only. They flashed ok.

A moment later someone ran across the field and dropped against the wall. They then crawled to the door. We opened the door and with their hands up, they walked in. Ted was at the door with one of his men and checked for weapons. He was clean. The man said his name was AT and he was a pre-invasion scout. He said they had planned to take the gun and disable it. He thanked us for warning them. AT said there were several groups now on the ground. AT asked about the helicopter and the tank? I told him that one of our friends was just a little over protective of his students. I noted it cost him his life. American AT asked? Yes I said, he was a retired CIA that had been down here before warning his boss what was going on here but they didn't listen.

Well the man said we've been waiting on them to finish the airport for us, then he smiled. Sorry about your friend he will be the first American killed here. So AT asked, what was our group doing here? We came for my friend; he hadn't answered our phone calls in quite some time. When we heard about the coup we decided to come on down. We came kind of like you all, one by one. Well AT said they killed Bishop on Thursday. I expect the troops will be on the way. Most of our people are concentrated around the main airport and two schools this being one. The State department issued a no travel ban on Friday and has asked all Americans to evacuate. I would think our people should move in here and you all could evacuate. What about Carson's body I asked? I don't want to leave without it.

AT said with his people here protecting the school this area would not be a priority. What about arms I asked? The arms will be dropped in he said. I made the decision that Ted and his men along with Ralph would try to get out while the Navy Seals and I would stay. I told Ted to talk with Karen and to tell her about Carson and to send Tommy the first day he could land after the invasion. Please tell her that we are doing fine and for Salinas not to worry. Five of our group staying would give AT's men a bit more support and this way it should insure I would leave with Carson's body. Ralph, Ted and his men got away from the school before daylight. They would separate and make their way back to their hotels and get flights out. As Ted went out, AT's men came in.

AT's men were surprised that it was civilians that had brought down the helicopter and stopped the tank. They were even more surprised to find that civilians, had warned them that someone had eyes on them and done the jobs on the machine gun and the antiaircraft gun. Jack looked at the used Red Eye cartridges that Carson had used on the copter and tank, he and I knew they were apart of the items that he had donated to Carson. We had four M16s with plenty of ammo and four H and Ks with about 160 rounds, 13 grenades, the 50 Calabria and rounds from the tank, the damaged 50 Calabria plus ammo from the airport, a 30-06 with 25 rounds and Carson's Walter with 50 rounds. Food for all of us was another mater, With the 27 students there was 40 of us.

Eating one meal a day we would only have about four days of food. Someone, sometime would have to make a food run. That same morning a Grenadian Captain walked out with a white flag. The Captain stopped half way. With the Walter tucked in my belt behind my back, I walked out and met him. First he mentioned that last night there was an attack on the Cubans. He asked if I knew anything about that and I said no. He asked what I was doing here and I told him I had come only to find my friend which the Cubans had killed. Now I was worried about the students. I asked the Captain if he could bring the American Ambassador. Maybe he could arrange the safety of the students, call in a privet plane and I would leave with my four friends and Carson's body. The Captain said he would do his best to do just that.

Please remember I said, that the responsibility of the safety of the students was now on his shoulders. The Captain didn't like what I said but when I stuck out my hand, he returned his.

When I got back inside the school I told AT that it was really important that his men not be seen. At this time, I was quite sure that the Grenadians and maybe the Cubans thought that there were only 5 of us in the school. Of course if they had any good trackers and had followed the mud tracks they might have or certainly would have known we were a larger force and that it was us that had attacked the Cubans at the airport.

The very same day the Captain showed up with an assistant to the American Ambassador.

They again walked out half way and again I met them. The assistant introduced himself and showed his credentials as working for the state department. I intern showed him my passport. The state department man said that the Grenadians were willing to get me out just as long as I didn't have anything to do with the school shooting. I told him that I and my other four friends came into the country after the downing of the helicopter. The state department man checked my passport entrance date and showed the captain. The captain nodded his head yes. I gave the State department man Karen's phone number and said if he could contact her she would send a privet jet for the six of us. The state department man said he would arrange it at once. He said he would accompany us until we were all on the plane.

The Captain said he would guarantee the safety of the students. On the morning of the 23rd the State department's man showed with two trucks. They had already picked up Carson's body and were ready to take us to the airport. I said my good-byes to Debbie, I had already told her that once everything was finished here I would send someone for her so she could attend Carson's funeral. I had also promised her that I would pick up the tab for her education at the UM. I gave AT a hug and wished them luck. The five of us walked out to the truck. I took my pocket knife and cut open the wrapped up body to insure it was Carson. Once I was sure I too got in the truck. We arrived at the airport, it was good to see the leer sitting out there on the run way.

The trucks stopped at the jet and the men took Carson's body up the stairs. Once aboard I walked back down the steps to shake both the captain's and the state departments man's hand, I thanked them both. I walked back up the steps, it folded up behind me. Tommy asked for permission and when he got it we were off.

Once in the air and over open water Tommy said we had two visitors coming up very fast on the radar. I was now in the cockpit when Tommy said they were ours. The jets pulled up one on each side and asked if the Traveling Cat was aboard. I took the mic and said, yes Sir, read you loud and clear. The jets pilot said they were dispatched from the USS Independence to escort us pass Cuba. The Admiral sends his regards Sir.

The pilot went on to say that two MiGs had just taken off from Cuba heading in our direction. The Pilot also said that two F-15s had taken off from homestead two minutes behind the MiGs. The pilot said the MiGs were closing in and should fly by within 3 or 4 minutes. Just then, Tommy said the two MiGs were on his radar closing fast. Just as Tommy said that he confirmed that now appeared two more blips that should be the F-15s. Sure enough the MiGs bussed by and right behind them the Pair of F-15s. The pilot from the Independence said, don't worry the MiGs won't be back. I asked the Navy Pilot to pass the information that we had 8 of our own and 27 students at the University and that they need a drop off of supplies. I also mentioned that of the 27 students 9 were Americans. The Navy pilot said it was being done as we spoke. Rodger that I said.

I had told Tommy to drop the boys off at Dominica for some R&R but now changed up the order to go straight into Opa- locka, drop Carson and me off then take the boys to Dominica. As we moved in closer to Miami the pilot from the Independence said they were being replace by the two F-15s and that the Admiral asked that I fly directly to Washington for a debriefing. I replied that I would see Salinas first, then head up that way. Tommy heard the news and said if ok he would drop off the boys and then come back and get me. That was the plan. When we got close enough Tommy called ahead and asked to have an ambulance stand-by to move Carson's body to a funeral home.

Carson would be kept there until the arrangements were made for him to be buried in Arlington.

The burial would have to wait until Debbie could attend. Once I got back from Washington I would visit Carson's house to look for information on any living relatives to notify them on what had happen.

The F-15s followed us up to the end of Key Largo, they waved their wings, we also did the same and they disappeared into the sky.

We landed at Opa-locka, the men lowered Carson's body into the ambulance and returned aboard. I gave the men some of the cash I had left and thanked them for their help.

I hopped in a taxi and headed home to the apartment. I had been gone 8 days, with no keys I knocked on the door.

Salinas opened the door and pulled me in. She latched on to me and didn't let go. She said she was so sorry about Carson, she also said I was never leaving again, never she said! I picked her up saying hello to Betty on the way to my shower. Wow what a difference a week made in Salinas's belly! The shower was great and off to bed we went. In that 8 days I didn't sleep in a bed not once. I got up and then told Salinas that I was on the way to Washington. Betty knocked on the door and said I'd better come and see the news. I walked in and we were being informed that our barracks in Lebanon had been hit by a suicide bomber taking most of the building down. The casualties were high! I called Karen and asked her to find Tommy, Karen said that Tommy would be back by the time I could get back to Opa-locka.

I went and started dressing, Salinas was not happy. I tried to cheer her up by asking if Cat had found a house for us in Nassau. At first she didn't say a word then said with a smile that yes Cat had found a beautiful house on what Cat said was my favorite beach on Paradise Island. I asked if it was furnished and Salinas said it was not. Ok I said, call Karen and you Betty and Karen go shopping while I'm gone. I'll be back tonight or tomorrow morning. Salinas asked if we could take a few days and go to the Chateau. If the barge wasn't ready, then yes we could I said. I said the next thing I needed to do when I got back was to look for any relatives of Carson. I called Karen and gave some instructions. I was at the door before I knew it not taking anything but my brief case and of course my guns.

Salinas walked with me to the door and down the elevator to wait for my car. Salinas said to come back soon, kissed me and I was off for the airport.

Tommy was there gassed up and ready to go. Tommy mentioned how terrible the Lebanon information was. Tommy said the toll was now over 200 dead.

It was late when we arrived in DC. I grabbed a limo but when I got to the Admiral's office they told me to come back the next morning. I got a hotel, called Salinas and watched CNN. The news was bad; a French barracks was also bombed. I knew there would be a huge response but while I watched it didn't happen.

The next morning, I was at the Admiral's office at 7:00 a.m. His secretary, already there said he would see me at the pentagon. There was no helicopter waiting so I went back to the airport and Tommy flew me the short trip on over to Arlington. I felt it strange, but here at the small airport there were no limos, I caught a taxi. Once at the Pentagon I noticed the place was buzzing. There were people coming and going. I waited two hours before I was sent for. The Admiral was in one meeting but stepped out for a moment. I apologize the Admiral said, it's been a rough 24 hours. Tell me he said what's going on over there on the ground. Well I said my objective was to get Carson out. We were a bit too late for that. Sorry to hear about your friend he said but I did hear that he took down the only helicopter that the Cubans had over there and maybe their only tank. Yes Sir, he did do that I said.

He died with his boots on so to speak. Ok what else the Admiral asked? Well Sir we did take out one antiaircraft gun and a 50 Calabria bunker at the southern airport. I'm sure that's wasn't there only defense I said.

The Admiral said we're all going in tomorrow, would you like to go back? No Sir I'll sit this one out. I missed eight days at home and the misses just wouldn't understand me going back. I will go back once our boys have secured the place.

I said it was unfortunate about Lebanon and asked what we were going to do about it. The Admiral said that the Secretary of State wants to pound Iran's Revolutionary Guard but our brave Secretary of Defense won't give the ok.

The Navy will find some way to light them up just you wait and see. Yes Sir I said.

I thanked the Admiral for his fighter escort on our way home, the Admiral said it was the least they could do.

Ok Captain let's talk about our Andros project. I understand you've found what was what you and the Natives down there called Lusca. Well I said what we found has been dead for quite some time and could have very well been the beast that started some of the stories of Lusca, but my gut feeling is that some type of Lusca could be still down there. I've done a little research and I have a hunch that, not that anyone needed to know before now but I know you have a lot of information that you're not sharing with me. Information such as what the Admiral asked? Information like what was down there that scared us so much we decided to nuke it or them.

What gives you that idea the Admiral asked? If you're not going to tell me just say so I said, it's quite evident that there was some kind of disastrous amount of radiation contamination down there. It was probably about the time that we developed that salted bomb at the end of world war two I said. At the Crocodile site we also found a tooth form some kind of digging machine that was carving its way through the caves. That's where the croc attacked the digging machine and whom or whatever was using that machine killed the croc with some kind of high powered laser beam that left a quarter size burned hole through the croc's brain. We believe that croc was killed between 50 and 100 years ago. I don't think we had then nor now that kind of underwater digging machine or laser capability.

I think that during or right before the war the Navy found or picked up on something down there that worried them. It might have even been the Brits that discovered something down there and looked for our assistance. Whatever, I think we attempted to communicate with them or it and when we didn't get a response, we nuked them. Now that the radiation levels are low enough the search for their vessel and or technology is on. It's obvious that from the design of the center of the new construction that you plan on bringing something up from the bottom that you don't want the Russians or the world for that matter to know about. The Admiral paused and then said that I was pretty smart for someone that didn't graduate from the Naval Academy.

I'm not going to confirm or deny that your theory is or isn't correct, however I'm glad to have you on board and will expect any and all additional information as you get it.

My last thought was asking how to go about getting Carson buried in Arlington Cemetery? The Admiral said I should contact the Air Force. At the end of conversation, the Admiral handed me one of those envelopes that said for me to report to the CIA office before I left the compound. I went from the Admirals office to the exit without stopping at CIA's office. I got a taxi to the airport and flew home.

From the Airport I stopped by the apartment and visited with Salinas. Salinas said I was a day late but she was glad and happy to see me. I called Karen and received all the updates.

Lee had called along with Bob. Ralph had called and wanted to know what was next and if I, we were going back. I called Bob first and Bob wanted dinner, I told him that maybe we could do lunch tomorrow. Lee said that the divers had run across three large Crocs about 13 to 15 feet long, all were located in one cave another 50 yards east from the first one. Lee said the divers said the crocs seemed like they were not bothered by the divers. I also called Ralph and assured him that the Cubans would be dealt with soon enough.

Once I got off the phone I told Salinas that I would be going over to Carson's house to try to find a next of kin. I only knew that Carson had one daughter that taught school somewhere in the Midwest.

When I got to Carson's house someone had been there. They were looking for something. Things weren't thrown around but I could tell they were looking. Carson's safe combination dial had been moved. The last I saw it the number was set on 3 and now it was on 7. I didn't bother to open the safe as I knew what was in there. What I wanted to open was his safe in the floor of his garage. I went through the process of opening the safe and pulled out his water and fire proof box. As I expected there was his farewell letter letting me know where his daughter Sandy was. In the box there was almost $200,000.00 dollars that Carson wanted her to receive in her hand from mine. Jim he wrote I know you don't need the money so please get it to her. Enclosed is my will, everything except the sailboat is left to Sandy, the boat is yours. I wasn't such a great father. It will also be hard for you. I hope I got to see you one more time before I go, you've been a good friend. I've been kind of a loner leaving for here or there at a moment's notice. Please look through my things, if there's anything that you'd like please take it. Take my notes and photos on the JFK assignation. Please don't let them fall into the wrong hands. If you ever want to talk to anyone about the assignation find Howard Hunt, he was there for the show. Hate to cut this short but I got to go do this, thanks for the gear hope it doesn't leave you short. Keep having Fun. Your friend Carson.

I thought that SOB. He probably didn't even know he was my best friend. I would miss him.

I took the Sandy information and the will and using the same protocol relocked the safe.

It was funny but I thought I was being watched. I was sure that the garage light couldn't be seen from the outside. And I had walked through the kitchen without turning on any lights and did not turn on the exhaust fan. My car motion detector hadn't gone off but I started it from inside the house just in case. I walked out, got in the car and left for the sailing club. Paul would want to know about Carson.

Paul didn't take it well; he sobbed as he poured a shot for everyone in the bar. Here's to a good friend, an advent sailor and a man that died protecting our freedom. Here, here, we all said and then bottoms up. I asked Paul if Carson owed any bar tabs or club dues. Paul said on the bar part that Carson always paid as he went. Paul didn't know anything about the dues nor mooring fees. I reminded Paul of the first time that Rusty and I met Carson. All the bar laughed. I didn't stay long as Salinas would be waiting up for me.

The next morning, I was up and gone early. I was listening to the radio for any news of our men invading Grenada but heard nothing.

I gave Karen Sandy's address and phone and asked if she could somehow fine out Sandy's schedule and make arrangements for Tommy to fly me out here without her knowing I was coming. I wanted to break the news about her father's death in person.

Bob called me at noon saying that our forces had landed on the beaches of Grenada. The 6:00 p.m. TV national news was the first broadcast news that we heard. There wasn't much except that it was a coordinated invasion using our Navy, Air Force. Army, Marines and Coast Guard. Most of the news was still on the Lebanon bombings. I was still waiting to hear about what our response would be but nothing was said as yet.

The next day I did lunch with Bob. I had asked him if he could help with Carson's burial plans with someone from the Air Force. Bob said that he was sure that with things as they were, it would be weeks if not more before the Air Force would be putting a date to the services, besides Bob said the Grenada thing will drag out much longer than our military has planned. Seemed that after the first day of fighting, we had under estimated the opposition and have requested reinforcements. Just as Carson had told the CIA there were more Cubans down there than they figured and the Cubans weren't the only communist regimes on the island. Seems there were Soviet's, North Korean's, East German's and may be even Libyans down there fighting. We lost 6 helicopters within the first few hours, this even though we had over 80 pre-invasion people on the ground.

Speaking of the Cubans, I said, when are you going to stop helping the Castro's make themselves richer than they already are? What Bob asked, you're tired of making money while doing nothing? And it's not me Bob said it's we. You get that quarterly deposit just as I do Bob noted. Well I said those SOBs just killed my friend and I'm thinking about going after them. Well Bob said why not go after their expansion programs. Us stopping to move their oil surplus would only produce someone else getting involved. Bob said the Castro's bank accounts aren't being used to spread communism, it's just making two fat cats fatter. Grenada and Nicaragua have been buying Castro's surplus oil for no less than four years now.

Bob said that Carter dropped the ball on the fight of the communist expansion, the President, Bob said has his hands full. You haven't met the new CIA Director as yet Bob mentioned. The Director said he requested to meet you when you were in Langley last week. But you were a no show. They didn't listen to a word Carson had to say about what was going on in Grenada I said. It was the new man that didn't listen I said. They want your help Bob said, with your capabilities and expertise you can travel to any part of the word Bob said. Besides you have money and the balls to do what is necessary. The President is having to deal with the Soviets, North Korea, Libya, Iran, Angola and now the fronts on our side of the world, Grenada, Nicaragua, and El Salvador. All three of these trouble spots are sponsored by the Cubans and the Soviets. The helicopter that shot up the university and the tank that killed Carson were Soviet equipment. We will certainly kick their butts in Grenada, it might take a week or two but it's a done deal. The Soviets that were on the Island were the first to high tail it back home. Nicaragua and El Salvador won't be so easy but if we can stop the Soviets and Cubans in those two spots, we have a good chance of stopping them from spreading their wings throughout Central America. Think about it Bob said.

I told Bob that I would be moving to Nassau the first chance I got. I mentioned the house that Cat found on the bluff near the north east side of Paradise Island. Bob said I'd get bored there soon enough. He also said I would miss not having Karen and the other girl to look at. I laughed. Bob laughed harder than I did.

Bob asked about the wreck and Andros and I told him that they would be enough to keep me busy. Bob asked how long it would be before the Andros project was completed and I said to ask me in two years from now.

Bob noted that the shipping business was doing well and that his Purchasing Company was busier than ever. He said his love life sucked. We both agreed that we should see each other more often.

I called Karen and said we were ready to go with the Sandy visit. I asked if we had time to get to her house at a decent hour tonight and she said that we should make it for tomorrow. This because she would have to get the cash from the bank. Ok I said tomorrow it is.

When I told Salinas my plan she said she wanted to go with me to see Sandy. I agreed and we would leave the next day at about mid-day.

The next day Salinas and I were on our way to Lincoln, Nebraska. We would have a limo waiting at the airport and hopefully be arriving at Sandy's house as she was returning from work. As we pulled up outside of Sandy's house there were two cars in the driveway. Both Salinas and I got out and walked to the door. A boy of about 16 years old answered the door. I asked if his mother was at home and he turned and yelled "Mom there's someone at the door for you". Within a moment a young woman came to the door. I asked if she was Gary Carson's daughter Sandy and she said yes she was. Before I could say another word, she said, "he's dead, isn't he." I said, I deeply regretted to say he is. Sandy then asked if we like to come in and I said we would. Sandy then turned and yelled "John" please come into the living room. Sandy led us in and asked us to sit. Before I sat I introduced Salinas and myself. I mentioned that her dad Carson as I called him was my best friend. As I finished, Sandy's husband walked in and Sandy introduced us to him. Sandy looked at John and said Dad's dead. John asked us all to sit and we then did. John asked how it happened and I told him that Carson was killed by a Soviet tank on the Island of Grenada. John then asked when? I told him that he was killed on the 13th of this month. Grenada John asked, but the fighting just started two or three days ago? Yes Sir I said, put Carson was teaching at one of the University's and when the Cubans ordered to close the school. Carson refused to leave the school and the Cubans came back with a Soviet Helicopter and sprayed the school with machine gun fire. I bet that pissed off my Dad Sandy said. Well yes it did I said, on the next pass, your Dad downed the helicopter. Next they sent in a tank and your Dad traded shots with the tank. Your dad took out the tank but it managed to mortally wound your Dad. Your Dad died an American hero I said. My Dad deserted us long ago Sandy said. He didn't visit, write or even call, he only sent money. I looked at Salinas, her and I thinking the same thing. I had $200,000.00 in my jacket pockets. I came to invite you to the funeral, I said. Sorry Sandy said we won't be going. From around the corner a voice said I would like to go. Out stepped the young man that had answered the door. My name is Malcolm, and I'd like to go to my grand Fathers funeral. When is it, Malcolm asked? Well I said we don't have a date as yet as the fighting is still going on. But your Grand Father will be buried in Arlington cemetery. With your permission, mam, I'll keep young Malcolm informed, and when the time comes, I'd like to return and have young Malcolm accompany me to the funeral. Please, Dad can I go? Malcolm asked.

We'll talk about it, John said to Malcolm. Malcolm looked at me and said please, Sir, just come for me. I'll be ready. I said there was a will and most of everything was left to you Sandy. Sandy shook her head and said she didn't want anything from her Dad. I said that I understood and said it was much more than it would cost for a fine college education. Young Malcolm could attend any college he chose to. John said we will be happy to accept the money sir, and yes, we'll use it for Malcolm's education. Malcolm, do you like flying? I asked. I always have wanted to learn to fly he said. Well I said your Grandfather left you his plane. If your parents agree I can have his plane moved here and you could take lessons. I've looked into lessons, Malcolm said, and I'd have to get a job to pay the fees. Malcolm's father broke into the conversation and said he and Malcolm's mother would discuss it. I took the hint and took Salinas's hand and stood to leave. Well I said sorry for the circumstances but it was a pleasure to me you both. Malcolm walked us out seeing the limo, then asked how long I had known his grandfather. Since I was 16, I said, that's 15 years ago. Malcolm reached into his pocket and pulled out a coin. What my mother said about my grandfather never contacting us wasn't exactly true. When I was 10 he sent me this coin. Do you know anything about this coin he asked? Yes I do, I said. It's part of a treasure that was from the Sir Frances Drake fortune. Tell you what, the next time I see you I'll tell you all about. I'd like that very much, Malcolm said. Your grandfather was a good man I said. I shook his hand and then Salinas and I got in the limo and were off to the airport where Tommy was waiting to fly us home.

Salinas said that Sandy was bitter and that I was right not to have mention the money to them. Do you think she'll go to the funeral? I don't think so but only time will tell I said.

Salinas slept most of the trip home. I could see that Salinas was getting tired much easier week by week. This I thought would be Salinas's last trip except for us making the move to Nassau. We got home late and Salinas went right to bed and to sleep.

The next morning, I Called Karen and asked her to get me an appointment with the CIA Director. Karen called back and said that Friday would be my day. I told her to make the arrangements with Tommy and that I wanted to get Salinas and I down to Nassau within the next couple days. I reminded Karen that it wouldn't be long before Salinas wouldn't be able to travel. Karen said that the furniture and things that they had purchased should arrive in Nassau during the weekend and be delivered to the house on the Tuesday or Wednesday coming. I told her to get Betty and Salinas's mom over there right away.

Karen said she also had gotten the call that the barges were ready to be inspected on the river. Karen asked if she could make the trip to Langley and visit the barges with me. I said yes to both questions.

That same day I met Karen down on the Miami River where the barges were sitting in the water. Although the barges looked a bit weird, they were built just as I had requested. Now all that was needed was to have a tug boat tow them on over to Nassau. Karen said she would have the barges moved so that I could receive them in Nassau by next Thursday. I mentioned that before the barges left they were to be fully supplied to include about 20 more full diving tanks and to make sure the fuel tanks were also full. Get word to Lee so the divers can add a list of whatever they can think we may need and for them to plan on being in Nassau no later than Wednesday.

Karen said that we now hired two more divers that Ted had recommended. Both were as the others, ex-navy seals. One was already here in Miami and the other was living the keys. Both had their references and backgrounds well checked out. I said that they, too, should be in Nassau by Wednesday.

CHAPTER XXV

THE CIA DIRECTOR

Friday morning Karen and I flew into Langley. There was a limo waiting. When we arrived at CIA headquarters we were well received. We were both registered but when they called for me, Karen was politely asked to wait in the lobby.

I was walked straight into the Director's office. There waiting was the Director, he stood and walked around his desk to shake my hand. Well finally we meet he said. You have quite the reputation he said. I hope it's not too bad I said. Well, he said we've been dealing with Castro for some time and we still haven't killed as many as you did with 55 gallons of molasses. Yes, I've done my homework he said.

Sorry about your friend Carson he said. Carson tried to help us but we just couldn't help ourselves. Carson gave us this map, and we distributed it among the different military groups but they decide to each use their on surveillance. Most of the troops that landed were supplied with a tourist map of the Island he said. The coordination between our military branches has been terrible. We've lost too many men and too much equipment. Why didn't you listen to Carson and go in sooner I asked? It was Carson that didn't listen the Director said. I told him we were going to wait until they finished that airstrip. Carson always seemed to make his own rules. In Angola he was ordered out a month before he was captured. All but his group got out just fine, but no, Carson had to keep on fighting. I figure it cost you about one and a half million to get them back he said. Yes, and you still owe me a million

I said. If it was I that promised, it would be me paying he said. Well I said, I did appreciate the money exchange, it's kind of a shame that money didn't reach Cuba and get into the hands of Fidel. It could have been a game changer I said. The Director said that the tainted money was originally meant for Fidel, the case was prematurely opened by the person that was to deliver it to Castro. He only lived a few hours, and we recovered his plane that had crashed off the Florida Keys.

Again we're sorry about Carson. The Director said Carson's body had already been moved and just as soon as our small war was over Carson will be buried with honors in Arlington.

The Director said he had two items to speak about. One was our fight to run the communist out of Central America and the other the Andros project.

We could sure use your assistance down there the Director said. When we finish talking I'm going to bring in the Colonel who is heading up the resistance down there. The Colonel is the President's personal pick, the Director said.

Now for Andros, he said, I'll tell you a story that, you being a man that lives on the edge of adventure won't be able to sleep nights he said.

In early 1941 a British Destroyer was shadowing a German sub that once the sub reached the TOTO channel the sub started its dive to the bottom. The Destroyer then started picking a second vessel that was moving in on the sub with a underwater speed that was something that the Brits had never seen. There were two expositions then a third. With the third exposition the sub disappeared from the Destroyers sonar. The faster vessel then darted off at a speed that was calculated in excess of 60 knots. The Destroyer searched for the other vessel for the next twenty-four hours but found nothing but debris that had floated up from the sub. The British Captain was so sure of what they witnessed that once his ship returned to port he was sent to Washington to inform our Navy. Our Navy, still not at war at the time, sent a newly built 14 man specially equipped sub to the area to investigate. Once the sub entered the channel it was never heard from again.

One year later with the U.S. and British now being allies in the war the US Navy and the British decided to build a small base near the site where the German sub was sunk. To be able to get into shore, the Navy contracted Great Lakes Dredge to open a basin and channel at the sight. The Bahamian Government requested them to open two such channels adding one toward the north east end of the Island. The Navy of course agreed. The Dredging Company was supplied with several Navy personnel that were on board as spectators and a small cutter size vessel to record anything unusual.

The Dredging Company cut through at the north end first. There were no reports of any problems. The Dredging Company then moved to the south deciding to dredge the basin first. Here too there were no unusual reports. During those two months all the personal working and staying on the Island heard all kinds of stories about "Lusca" the monster from the locals. The Monster as they called it was named "Lusca". This monster was said to be as big as 75 feet in length, have the body of an octopus and the head of a shark. The monster they said could swallow an entire boat with ease. The other rumors were that there were large moving lights in the channel at night. The locals did not swim in the Blue holes nor use the beaches. This as they said that Lusca wouldn't have to get out of the water to pull you under, Lusca's tentacles would come up from the water and just grab whatever it wanted. These were only rumors from the locals as again during the Dredging thus far there were no sightings of anything that wasn't normal. All the material that the dredge cut and moved was piped up on shore. This material would be used in whatever facility that would be built.

All was going well and the dredging was within days of being completed. The dredge had cut all but the last two yards of within the reef. Thus far the channel was 50 feet deep and 60 feet wide. As the dredges ball of teeth cut thought the last part of the reef. The ball stopped cutting and fell down into the channel disappearing into the deep. The dredge operator was surprised by the loss of the cutting ball and lifted its shaft out of the water. The barge was then moved back into the basin to see just what had happened. The shaft was boxed in a sleeve of 1" thick steel. The Monel shaft itself was a solid 3" in Diameter.

All of this steel had been cut like butter. It wasn't broken, it was cut. What they were looking at was impossible! No one could believe what had just happened! With no believable explanation the dredge crew began to rebuild the cut off end and replace the cutting ball. This time the Navy placed a 40- foot cutter on the channel side of the cutting ball. As the cutting ball began to cut the navy cutter witnessed a large light beam come up from the deep again cutting the cutting ball off. There didn't seem to be any threat of life but whatever it was didn't want the man made channel to be completed. Needless to say the dredging was stopped.

The Director then took a break and asked if I wanted coffee to be brought in. I asked him to continue his story.

The Director said that then President Roosevelt ordered the construction to a halt. Instead the Navy set up sonar and tried to communicate with whatever was down there.

At the wars end and Truman as President, the President ordered that the Navy send out five torpedo bombers to destroy whatever was down in the channel. Those five and a rescue plane didn't come back. The President then ordered the use of a nuclear device known as a salted bomb. This bomb, an experimental device that would do very little physical damage but would produce a high amount of Radiation debris. Truman's fear was that if anyone could get ahold of the technology of that powerful type of laser it could very well disrupt the balance of world power.

The bomb was dropped from a B52 right on target. Afterward Sonar devices were deployed along with Radiation detectors that would send any movement information along with radiation levels to our Destroyers that would pass by the area.

Almost ten years would pass and with nothing being picked up on sonar and the ocean's radiation levels dropping the Navy began sending our subs back into the area.

In 1958 the U.S. and the British agreed that they would once again start and this time finish a base on the spot that was originally dredged. This time the dredging was completed without incident. Whatever was down there before seemed to have no say in the matter now. During all that time that passed there was not one movement detected. They decided that whatever had been down there was either gone or killed by the radiation.

We've been searching for something down there for more than thirty years. Your sonar balls picked up quite a lot of movement but the most interesting things down there don't move. We believe we have found a vessel of some kind and maybe even some kind of small out post.

I guess you heard the Presidents speech in March he said. His Star Wars defense is based on us bringing whatever is down there up and gaining it and putting into use the technology we find. The President believes that our present defense, that nuclear wars deterrent is that no one survives is un-acceptable.

So here we are, we are moving ahead with plans to build the Andros facility to house whatever we bring up and we will bring it up he said.

If I may bring in my assistant in, I have a few items that will catch your eye, I said. Karen was called in from the lobby carrying a briefcase that looked like she was one of those traveling medicine peddlers that were always waiting in Doctor's offices to show them the latest medicines. I introduced Karen then Karen walked over to the table that was there, and with her key, opened the case and pulled out a rolled up piece of cloth. Karen then started rolling out the material. As she did I explained to the Director that I had sent two groups of archaeologist to the Island, one group on the north end the other to the south.

On the northern tip they found a small buried settlement that could be dated back to the Columbus days, the late 1490s to the early 1500s.

At the southern end, they found several Indian burial mounds. There were many mounds, all circled around one larger one. They dug the large one and found this.

First the cloth that wrapped this man was, is like no other. It did not rot or even fade. After washing it, the cloth looked as if it were new. Wrapped with a man, presumably an Indian Chief, were several items. First a knife that appears to be made from one of those giant Crocodiles teeth. The knife looks to be cut and sharpened with some kind of hi-tech machine. It is still razor sharp. Second is a Black Panther skin that has drawings on the inter side. The drawings told some kind of story. The Director came closer and looked, I didn't have to say any more. The story showed several natives battling with what looked to be a giant crocodile. The Croc had its mouth shut with hands hanging out one side and feet the other. The croc was standing on its four legs being taller than the Natives by at least a foot. The Natives had these large spears that took two Natives to handle. The next drawing showed many dead Natives on the ground with someone bending over one of the injured Natives. The next drawing was the most distinct of all. It was a face that looked human. Maybe it was human but if it was, it was the smallest skinniest one I had ever seen, no it was not someone from the neighborhood. The next items that Karen pulled out of the case were wrapped up in deer skin. Karen rolled out the skin and inside were small surgeon like tools with an odd thing that reminded me of one of those new battery tooth brushes. It was smaller in diameter than a tooth brush with a glass or crystal tip on one end and a ball on the other. The ball could be rotated at its center and could be screwed open were the ball was attached to the shaft. Twisting it open there was a void that looked like maybe the power source may have once been. Go on I said to the Director, pick it up, it's harmless. Yes I said, it is what you're thinking. It's some kind of miniature laser I said. The last item that Karen pulled out was a mechanical arm and hand that was housed into an elastic skin like material that had a partial skeleton's left arm inside almost down to the elbow. A small cable like material that had led out of the skin like material and up to the skeleton's right back shoulder blade. The mechanical hand itself was a much smaller hand than the skeletons own hand. Apparently the Mechanical hand was built for a much smaller person. The Director looking at it in amazement and Karen mentioning that the glove was still attached to the person at burial. Yes someone had fit the man with a mechanical hand. The glove like hand had some kind of metal like material that looked like a bone skeleton but with motors to control movements. This all looked like something that we would see in a science fiction movie.

I looked at the Director and said that if someone hadn't come looking for them by now, we just may have destroyed an entire race.

The Director asked, if none of them are left down there what destroyed our last two-man sub? Lusca I said, Lusca. From what I heard the sub's attachment was broken or ripped off that sub I said. The sub's structure would have been breached causing it to have collapsed. You may need something bigger, something that's not attached, has good movability and can fire some kind of attached harpoon with a small war head.

The Director was impressed with our show and the way we handled the situation. Anyone seeing what we brought with us would have been impressed, anyone except my Dad. He wouldn't have liked the thought of us disturbing those burial grounds.

Just showing someone the Panther skin might have someone thinking that we forged it, but the other stuff, it was quite unquestionable.

The Director asked if he could borrow the case for a couple days to show some of the people on the Hill. I said that should he call I would make the items available for a privet inspection. The Director replied yes of course.

The Director said he heard I was pulling my divers to Nassau. I told him that we had built two barges that we were going to place over a wreck that we had located. I told him that just as soon as we got set up over the wreck I'd have three of the divers back at Andros.

Just as we were getting ready to exit, the Colonel was called in and introduced us. The Colonel said he was sorry to hear about Carson. The Colonel said he had been briefed on some of my work and liked what he had heard. The Colonel said that he could use all the help he could get to fight the advance of the communist. I informed the Colonel that I would be moving on down to the Bahamas but that if he got into a bind to give me a call. I could tell the Colonel didn't like my response and he said he'd keep me in mind. We all shook hands and Karen and I were off. Karen said she didn't get a good feeling from either man.

Karen and I jumped into the limo and headed directly to the airport. When we got to the airport Karen had to make a bathroom run. We then made our way to the privet strip where Tommy would be waiting. As we stepped onto the tarmac there were two men that had that Fed look. One had papers in his hand and as we got closer he held out the paper work and said our black case was being confiscated in the name of national security. Karen then grabbed the case with two hands. I took the papers and they were signed by the Director himself. I nodded to Karen to release the case and she did so begrudgingly. The man that took the case looked at Karen and apologized. The other man asked Karen for the key and she pulled it out and threw it just as far as she could. We then continued to walk to the jet. As the door closed behind us Karen smiled from ear to ear. Karen said that I had called that one correctly. Karen's bathroom trip produced a briefcase exchange with Evette. Evette had taken out the goods and put into a suit case. Big Ted and Steve would now accompany Evette to take a limo to Baltimore where a helicopter would fly them to Newark Airport where they would catch a commercial flight to Miami. Big Ted and Steve would see her home.

The trip back was fast with Karen and me getting in a lot of talking. Karen said that Evette was doing great at the office work and inter works with Sea Containers.

Evette's hots for men had now slowed down where she could keep her mind off men and could concentrate on work. Karen also said that Tim was now just about running Omni by himself. Karen said that the Sea Container office had mentioned that they were having lots of trouble in their New Orleans facility. I told Karen that I wanted to slow down not speed up. I told her that maybe after the baby was born we could go and take a look at New Orleans if she was still interested. I told her that with the three new projects we had going on we'd all be keeping very busy.

When we arrived home Betty had packed up and returned to Nassau. Salinas was excited, she had talked to her mom and said that Tommy was to pick her up tomorrow morning. When can we go Salinas asked? I want to be there when all the things we brought showed up. I said we had a few days but Salinas wanted to go now.

We weren't home 10 minutes when there was a knock on the door. It was too early to be Evette and she has a key I thought. Who comes visiting on a Friday night? I looked up at the monitor and saw it was our long lost neighbor. I opened the door and Jena jumped in my arms.

Jena must have kissed me 5 times before she noticed Salinas standing there. Well Jena said, if it isn't the little horse girl. Pointing at Salinas's stomach, Jena ask, and what have we got here? Salinas said it's our little girl, Jena now advancing toward Salinas said it better be a boy. Jena came at Salinas and said give me a hug little sister. The two hugged as I shut the door. Then Jena turned again and came and hugged me again. Jena then turned and said that she had searched the entire planet and couldn't keep still with one man. My curse Jena said was that next to Jim all the men were boring. Jena looked better than I remembered, I also remembered that she was a bitch. Salinas, maybe feeling just a little insecure said that we were moving to Nassau in a few days. Jena said, well it's not the Rivera but I could use some of the quite life. At that point Karen came walking out of her room ready for a Friday night out. Jena was also excited to see Karen. Jena asked, you live here too? Karen said that Evette also lived here. Oh boy Jena said if I knew I had such neighbors I would have come home much sooner!

And Betty Jena asked? She's already in Nassau, Salinas said. When did you get in I asked Jena? Jena said about 10 minutes ago. I didn't unpack because I wasn't sure I was going to stay Jena said, but now that I see my families is here, looks like I shouldn't move to Star Island. My grandmother died two weeks ago Jena said. Sorry I said I didn't hear the news. Well Jena said she died in her sleep. I didn't make the funeral Jena said, where I was at the time doesn't have much contact with the outside world. So Jena asked Karen, where's the party tonight? Karen said she was going to the club and depending on what time Evette got home, go dancing in the grove. Well Jena said if Evette doesn't make it I'd love to keep you company. Karen looked at Jena and said you'll do me that favor will you. Sure Jena said. Salinas said she'd like to go to the club too. I said that I would stay and wait for Evette. I asked Karen to drop off Salinas on her way to the grove if I hadn't arrived as yet. Karen said she would.

Evette made it home just after 11:00 p.m. She said they didn't run into any problems except delays at Newark Airport. I took the suit case in my room and opened it to check the contents and then locked it up in the safe. I was still dressed, Evette had called the club and Karen and the girls were still there so I took Evette to the club and brought Salinas home with me. Salinas said she really enjoyed going out with Karen but that Jena was really full of herself. I said yes, Jena is a certified bitch. Salinas said she really wanted to go to Nassau and see the house and her mom. I mentioned that I still had some unfinished business and that I couldn't go to Nassau until Tuesday night or Wednesday morning. If Salinas was to go ahead of me, we would have to visit Doctor James tomorrow morning and she could leave either Saturday afternoon or Sunday morning.

As it was Salinas and I did get in to see Doctor James the next morning. Doctor James said the baby was doing fine but that Salinas needed to eat more. The Doctor Ok'd the trip and wished us luck with the delivery in late March or early April.

With that news we called Tommy and he flew the both of us to Nassau. Salina's mother and Betty were already there staying at the Boarding house. Salinas was happy to see them both. As it was, Salinas would be celebrating her 17th birthday Sunday. Yes 17 years old. I could still see her in my mind the first time brushing her horses and riding with them down the beach. Sunday morning, we both saw the house for the first time. Cat took us out there when she returned from her Saturday night fishing trip.

The House was incredible, the ocean could be seen from the master bed room as well as the living room and kitchen. The pool and deck were on the east side of the house with an unbelievable view of the morning sun. Cat had also purchased the property on the west of the house. A small barn was being built to house no more than six horses. No, no grass, once we did have a horse or two their the food would need to be brought in. Salinas loved the house and said she couldn't wait to receive the furniture and begin actually living there. I reminded Salinas that her mom would only be there to help with the baby and that I would be more than willing to find a house for her mom somewhere close by. I told both Salinas's mom and Betty what the Doctor had said about Salinas needing to eat better. Betty didn't take that too well but said she understood.

That afternoon we had a small celebration at which time we visited the Nassau city stables that housed the carriage horses. Salinas's birthday gift was that her favorite two horses were already here. She couldn't ride them but they were there. Salinas appeared to be completely surprised and happy. She jumped into my arms and didn't let go.

With that Cat and Salinas would deliver me to the airport where Tommy was waiting. Salinas hugged and kissed me and wished me luck. Salinas was the only one besides Karen that knew where and what I would be doing the next morning. If everything went well, my tomorrow's trip would bear fruit for many years to come.

On the flight home to Miami not only did I copilot I actually flew the jet, well kind of. Tommy knew where we were headed tomorrow morning and at what time our appointment was. We would need to leave Opa-Locka by 5:00 AM. Roy whom was also making the trip had already gripped about what time he would have to get up to be at the airport before 5:00 a.m. in the morning. Jim, Roy said that's two hours before the sun comes up!

The next morning Roy and I were on our way to an appointment in Fairchild's Connecticut. Roy had pulled more than a few strings to get us an appointment with the head of GD's Futuristic Development Division. You got it, we were taking them that electric tooth brush and mechanical hand to have them take a look. Our Idea was to get a paten and share it with GD with an agreement that it would never be used in a weapon.

In setting up the appointment Roy had told them that we would need an unusual power source. Once the GD team saw what we had they came up with what they could and you guessed it the hand actually moved. It didn't just move it crushed a full coke can like it was warm butter. The Tooth brush was another story. When supplying the same power to move the mechanical hand the lasers beam that was pin size, could cut a piece of 1/8 inch thick steel. The round ball when twisting increased the power of the beam. As the GD people raised the power to the small laser we all were astonished! The small hand held tooth brush suddenly became very powerful. The beam increased to about 5/32 of an inch and cut thought steel plate of 1/4" thick. The engineers weren't impress with the cutting power they were shocked at the distance that the beam kept its power. The source of power that the engineers were using was from a machine the size of an average car. They would have a long way to go to reduce their power source to the size of an tripple "A" battery. Such a battery wasn't made as yet and although what we had was unbelievable and could be used in some limited way, the full potential would need a power source break though that would take years. So I asked what if we had the batteries that had operated this equipment. The engineers said if they had the batteries they should be able to duplicate them. The entire time we were in the lab, there were two men watching us all through a window. At the apparent end of the show one of the men in the window asked if they could speak with me in privet. They buzzed me in and asked Roy to wait in the lobby. I gathered up my toys and walked thru the door. I was introduced, and the man that did the talking said he was impressed with the mechanical hand and that they would be willing to have their legal team meet with mine to work up some agreement. The man said the laser wasn't anything new, it would be the power source that would be remarkable if we had it.

They were interested if I was in possession of any of the remains of whom or what was carrying the laser. The man said that my particular laser was they believed to be a part of a medical kit not a weapon. I agreed. The man said they appreciated the fact that I was looking for an agreement that the find wouldn't be used as a weapon. They mentioned that they believed that the government was in possession of such a weapon that was confiscated from a being that was killed several years back. I was asked to look at a drawing of which they believed was similar to the being that was carrying a small medical kit plus a larger weapon. The drawing they said was from an eye witness. The being in the drawing was much larger than the being that I had on the panther skin. I told them that I too had a drawing of a being as they called it but that there was no resemblance of the two. The man asked if I was at the site where the objects were found and if there was any possibility that someone, anyone could have taken by mistake the power source. It had crossed my mind but I hadn't had the chance to investigate as yet. The man said that the source should be relatively easy to track. If not encased in a lead container the person or persons in contact with the power source would be at a high risk of Radiation poisoning that over a period of time, would cause death. The men gave me a phone number and a code that I would be required to enter into the phone that they would receive the call. They said there was not to be any information over any phone lines. Big brother as they call them would be listening. The man then called in a woman that they said would accompany me to Roy and then to their legal department. Should we come to an agreement we would need you to leave the mechanical hand here with us.

The agreement which was reached was signed and sealed. The mechanical hand was left with GD. Roy and I had arrived just before 10:00 a.m. and were leaving just after 6:00 p.m.

Once in the leer I called Karen to get word to Lee that I would be at the Andros airport 7:00 a.m. the next morning and we would be traveling directly to the Southern digging sight and everyone involved in the dig must be there at the sight. Please repeat that everyone must be there without exception. Karen said that Bob had called more than once. He wanted to know where you were and I told him you were out fishing. I told Karen I knew it was short notice but that I needed a sealable lead container about the size of a briefcase. Karen said she do her best.

I also called Lee but couldn't get an answer. I wanted to find those missing power sources but most importantly insure that no one had taken the power sources and was being effected by the radiation. In the Limo and in the jet I had plenty time to speak with Roy. This was really our first time talking that I wasn't in some kind of hurry or trouble. Roy said if he didn't know me and hadn't seen it with his own eyes that he'd never would have believed a word of it. Giant Crocodiles, Space men and Laser weapons. I told him that I wasn't going to tell him more because he hearing any more would most likely have him rethinking the whole thing and even though he saw what he saw he just might change his mind and start doubting the entire thing.

Roy asked what we'd do if we find the power sources. Then I said you'll go back alone and make the best deal to can. How long do you think it will take the CIA Director to find out about your trip to GD Roy asked? I told him that Karen said that Bob had already called looking for me. That means that Director called Bob for him to talk to me. Roy said that the paper work that the two men gave me at the airport in Washington to give up the briefcase wasn't even legal and he wondered to what end those two men would have gone to get it from us. Roy said he'd liked to have seen the Director's face when he opened the case and found those dentist tools and specialty that electric tooth brush!

Just for a moment on the trip back to Miami, I closed my eyes, I smiled and though about it all. I thought about the time in high school when I sewed Roy's son ear back on after he was in a fight with Alex Math. I did the sewing in a phone booth using the light when the door was closed. My Dad taught me to always carry in my car and boat, a blanket, change of clothes, a first aid kit, sewing needles an thread. When I got through sewing his ear back on, I took Roy's son home, sat him on their porch knocked on their door real hard and ran back to my car. Roy came to the door and helped his son to bed. Rick's mother woke him up for breakfast the next morning and when she saw him she started screaming for Roy. Roy took his son to the ER, but there they told him they couldn't do anything and said the stitch job didn't look to bad. Roy's son got cleaned up and a shot of antibiotics. The hospital asked Roy's son who did the stitches and he had said he didn't remember. Still with my eyes closed, I was now laughing but didn't tell Roy why because I still didn't know if Roy knew it was me that stitched up his son that night.

I soon fell asleep thinking of the good old days. I awoke when the wheels hit the ground in Miami. As I walked off the jet Tommy said he'd see me again tomorrow at 5:30 a.m. As Roy got up and headed out I heard him say that there must be a better way to make money and not have to get up so early, both Tommy and I laughed.

I drove right to the 1800 club, it had been a while since I'd been there alone and it was already 11:00 p.m. I sat at the front bar in my old seat where I could see both doors. Wow I thought it had been a while. I kept thinking how ugly their being drawing was compared to ours. In my wild thoughts I imagined the smaller being in our drawing could have been running or hiding from the bigger ugly ones. Well I said we took care of that. I imagine how it could have been different if the German's sub hadn't fired on them, if that was what happened. As I day dreamed the front door opened and in walked Karen and Evette. Ok Karen said, we got another big day ahead of us tomorrow let's go. Nop, I said I'm waiting for my breakfast. Karen and Evette sat down and their usual was placed on the bar in front of them. Karen said she brought Evette to drive my car home. Evette said it was her idea. It wasn't long we had steak and eggs sitting in front of the three of us. Billy came up behind the bar and said the food us on him. Billy said that if I kept getting married that it could ruin his business. We all got a kick out of that.

The next morning, I was again on the jet heading to Andros. Karen had located some lead foil that could be sealed not to leak any radiation, at least that what the man that sold it to her said. We landed and Lee was there waiting. It was just over an hour ride to the sight. I gathered the men and was straight forward with what I had to say. I didn't care, and wasn't mad, but if anyone had the power sources for the two devices that we had found. If these power sources were with them or even in their tents they could have received an unwanted dose of radiation. One of the Doctors stood and said that the power sources were in his tent and yes he and Johnathon had been feeling poorly for almost two weeks now. We went and secured the two power sources that did look somewhat like normal batteries. We packed the material up in the lead foil and with the two sick men headed back to Miami.

Thus far we had dug up 16 mounds. Everything was photo'd, tagged and most replaced back in the mounds. We were searching for the possibility that one of their little friends may have gotten buried with the Natives. So far the only things that were found buried beside Indian bones and artifacts were some gold coins used as neck wear. Again the coins were photo'd tagged and reburied back in the same mounds. Each mound had a stainless steel rod with a welded tag plate that was stamped with a number. I would do my best to also buy the property at the sight.

Back in Miami the two men were taken to Mercy Hospital and I tried to explain what had made them sick. The hospital of course asked to inspect the source but I declined. The hospital said that they would have to report any such exposures to the proper authority. I said that I understood. I doubted that they even knew whom to report to. Both men ended up being admitted into the hospital with the Doctors saying their treatment would last several days. I was relieved that it appeared that the men would be ok at least for the short term. Both men expressed that they didn't think that the batteries were important.

I called Roy and told him that I had the power sources and he said he thought I was kidding about him taking them back up to Fairbanks. Yes, I was but he needed to either go back with me or set things up so he didn't have to go. Roy asked if I had tested the battery as he call it in the laser. I said I had. Roy said that they would for sure want the battery for the mechanical hand but since they already had what they said was a similar laser that maybe GD wouldn't want the laser battery.

Karen had set up dinner with Bob at Joe's on the beach, Karen of course wanted to go and Bob said it was ok.

That night at dinner Bob said that CIA Director was quite upset and was adamant about getting that laser into their lab. I informed them that it was a done thing with GD. Bob said he figured I would do something like that. Besides I said GD said that our government already has a similar device. Bob said that Director had inform the President about the switch I had made. If need be Jim, the President said he would need to speak with you. Sorry I said, like I mentioned, it's a done deal. Bob said that they might be searching my apartment as we are speaking. I told Karen to call Evette and make sure she wasn't at home. Bob asked why and I told him that my safe was bobbed trapped and that if opened the explosion could take out the apartment. Your bluffing Bob said. Bob I asked have you ever known me to bluff. Bob removed his bib and headed for the phone. Karen then asked if she really needed to call Evette? Karen didn't carry her purse, that black bag she had was her cellular phone. Call her I said. Karen called and didn't get an answer. You don't really have the safe bobby trapped with explosives Karen asked? Hell no I said but that fog horn is set to blow and I'm sure that will cause some wet pants, that's if they can open it. Besides the laser isn't in there. We waited until Bob came back and said that the Director's people hadn't gotten their search warrant as yet. Bob said that Director had been in contact with GD and that they said they did not have the laser as yet. I reached in my pocket and pulled out the laser and put it on the table in front of Bob. Here it is Bob, tell the Director that I was so scared of them that I gave it up to you. Its only on loan I said and I want it back. It's a $5,000,000.00 favor to you Bob. Favor Bob asked? Yea and if the favor's not returned you owe me the $5,000,000.00. Bob looked at it and asked if it was safe to touch? Well I said, it just came out of my pocket didn't it. Bob took the laser and again left the table two make the call. Karen asked why all the theatrics? I laughed. Bob came right back and said that the Director asked if I could deliver it tomorrow? I said no. Bob said then he'd have to go and asked if I could lend him Tommy. I told him that Tommy was delivering me to Nassau. Well then Bob said you'll have to pay for dinner. Bob was now in a much better mood. He now had the Cuban cigar in his hand and was letting out that loud obnoxious laugh of his. Some things never change.

When we got home I had a pleasant surprise, Salinas was in my bed waiting for me. Salinas said she just couldn't wait another day. I was pissed that she had made the trip but happy to see her. I hadn't had one of those showers in a few days and it sure felt great!

The next morning, I was off flying back to Fairbanks. Karen was to call Roy at 9:00 a.m. to have him change the paperwork for me to deliver the power source for the mechanical hand and the one from the small laser. Yes I had given the Director the laser without the power source. By the time I arrived everything was ready. GD took and connected the power source and went through the hands movement. GD was happy and we signed all the new paper work. This time I was out of there by 12:00 p.m. We flew back home I went and got Salinas and just as soon as we got aboard the leer we were off to Nassau. Salinas had taken some of my clothes the week before and this trip even more, almost everything. Salinas suggested that I sell the apartment and I told her that I didn't own it, the construction company did. I could see where her thinking was going and tried to comfort her telling her that I would do my best to stay close to home. Salinas said she came to Miami because she remembered Cat's advice to keep as close by you as possible. Salinas said that Cat was working at the house every day making improvements. The furniture should have been delivered today and she asked everyone to wait until we returned to start placing it. Salinas said she loved the house and was sure we would be happy there.

I told Salinas that my barges should be in Nassau by now or tomorrow at the latest. I would be spending every day except Sunday with the divers. Salinas asked that once the house was settled if she could come out to the wreck with me and I said I would love to have her there. It made me happy to see that she was interested. Salinas said that Karen and Evette would be visiting to help with the house over the weekend.

I asked Tommy to fly over the Harbor and as we did I could see the barges at the dock. I was itching to get down there with the divers and start working.

Cat met us at the Airport and drove us to the Hurricane house where I preferred to stay. Cat said the furniture trucks were parked at the house, and we could get to the unpacking whenever Salinas was ready. Salinas said we would start tomorrow morning.

From the house I walked over to the dock where the barges were, there aboard were all six divers. The Divers were checking all the goodies and had already put their gear aboard. Nassau probably had something that could pull the barges but Peter had the Tug boat standing by to make the move. The men were ready to get started. We agreed that we would leave just before day break tomorrow morning. It was now about 7:00 p.m. with another hour or so of day light. I went to the house and got Salinas, we walked over to the City dock and watched the sun go down. It was a beautiful sunset. Red sky at night sailors delight. From there we walked back and stopped into see Willy. Welcome home Willy said as he walked around to our side of the bar. Willy hugged me and kissed Salinas. Willy said he was happy to hear that after all these years that I was finally going to be a full time resident of Nassau.

The next morning the barge was on its way to the south west cannel. Peter was aboard the tug giving directions, it would take the tug a good three hours to get to the channel and another hour to arrive at the sight. Myself, I had a good conch salad breakfast at Angee's and then would meet the divers at the Chris Craft where Captain Mike would take us to meet the barge. The divers had ordered and we had made to their specifications several post that would be placed in the water around the wreck that the drivers would use to tether themselves too.

The barge had posts located at each corner that would be released to reach the bottom anchoring the barges. The barges could easily be moved by lifting the post and pushing or pulling the barges with the Boston Whalers. Each barge post was operated by an electric motor that would lower or raise the posts, the electric coming from the generator that each barge had on board.

Today the barge would be placed alongside the wrecks position while the divers figured where they would start. The barge was in place and the tug boat and its crew headed off back to Miami.

The divers started placing the tethering poles. As they worked the inbound tide started to go slack. The divers and I took advantage of the approaching slack tide to do some looking around. It seemed that we all agreed that we should first move the cannons from the wreck. So far we had located seven cannons. With the help of the barges wenches we would be moving and stacking the cannons. Moving the cannons should take about a full day. Once the cannons were out of the way we would then start removing some of the larger wooden beams. By 5:00 p.m. I was exhausted! I hadn't worked so hard in many a year. I did my best not to show the men how tired I was. At 7:00 p.m. the men called it a day. They were all ready to stay on the barges but I was headed back to Nassau with Captain Mike. Once at the city dock I walked to the Hurricane house but no one was home and our things were gone. I jumped into a taxi and went to the new house. It was now almost 9:30 p.m. and the house smelled like cooked crawfish. I was wowed when I opened one of the double doors. The place was beautiful. I walked into the kitchen and there was Betty and Salinas's mom cooking. Then Salinas came from behind and put her hands over my eyes and pushed me through the house into our bed room. Open your eyes she said. I open them up and couldn't believe the furniture and the view were so nice. I turned and Salinas jumped into my smelly arms. I need a shower I said. Yes, you do she agreed and I got my first shower in the new house and I didn't get to eat any crawfish.

Things were good, Salinas and I were happy. Looked like I would be out on or in the water almost every day, something that I had dearly missed.

Miami shouldn't need me; Lee was on track to get our new construction project started. That Grenada thing was over and we were just waiting for a date to put Carson to rest.

Diane was getting married in April or June, Cat seemed to have settled into being a mom and our top tourist guide along with managing the Charity operation.

Martha now just about owned the harbor and city docks with her launch service. Otis and Maggie were now living in their new house on the spot where Angee's original shack had been, they too would be getting married at any time. And Angee says she's just waiting for that first grandchild.

I had ordered to stop the digging at the northern site of Andros and moved that crew to the southern site, this so we could maybe wrap that up by year end. I wasn't expecting to find anything new but we were going to turn over each and every stone over there. The Nassau fishing and tourist business was as good as we wanted it to be. Once we finished looking for treasure at the wreck my idea was to put things back as they were when I found it and offer once a day diving trip for the tourist to see a real ship wreck.

Of course I was counting on Salinas having that baby boy that I could raise on the water sailing and fishing until he could take over if I ever got old. Ok even if the baby turned out to be a girl, I'd still be happy and still do all the stuff with her and her mom. Things were good and going to just get better. Oh yes, even though Salinas hadn't mentioned it lately, Salinas and I would also be soon be getting married. Life looked and felt good.

www.ingramcontent.com/pod-product-compliance
Lightning Source LLC
Chambersburg PA
CBHW030359200726
48286CB00015B/1674